GRAVE DANGER

RACHEL GRANT

JANUS PUBLISHING

BOOKS BY RACHEL GRANT

Flashpoint Series

Tinderbox (#1)

Catalyst (#2)

Firestorm (#3)

Evidence Series

Concrete Evidence (#1)

Body of Evidence (#2)

Withholding Evidence (#3)

Incriminating Evidence (#4)

Covert Evidence (#5)

Cold Evidence (#6)

Poison Evidence (#7)

Evidence Series Box Set Volume 1: Books 1-3

Evidence Series Box Set Volume 2: Books 4-6

Romantic Mystery

Grave Danger

Paranormal Romance

Midnight Sun

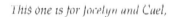
This one is for Jocelyn and Cael,

This is the only page of this book you are allowed to read. You will thank me for this rule when you are older.

You both make me so proud every day.

1

July 2002
Coho, Washington

Libby Maitland's truck was gone. She stood in the tiny, eight-space parking lot, gripping her keys until they dug into her palm, and wondered where the hell her truck was. The Suburban couldn't have been towed. The lot was too small and her truck too large. Towing would have caused a commotion. It must have been stolen. A lousy end to a rotten day.

She couldn't care less about the truck. Old, beat-up, and rusted, the beast drank fuel like a dehydrated camel, and a tank was more maneuverable. But it was the only vehicle she had, and, even worse, the excavation notes from the archaeological dig were inside. She mentally listed everything she'd loaded in the back when she left the site an hour ago: the stratigraphic drawings, the photologs, the burial notes, and the field catalog. If she didn't get her truck back, her career as an archaeologist could take another major nosedive.

She turned around to go back inside the restaurant, planning to call the police, but she must have been their last customer for the night because the door was locked and the shades lowered. The windows vibrated with a loud bass beat she could hear through the glass. The cleaning crew had turned up the stereo. They would never hear her knock.

She fished around in her purse for her cell phone, and then remembered the phone was in the damn truck. She looked up and down the street. Who would have thought her truck would be stolen in Coho, Washington, a quaint little historic sawmill town where everyone knows everyone? Maybe this was a game the locals played: mess with the city girl who moved here only two weeks ago.

At ten p.m. on a summer night, the lengthy Pacific Northwest twilight was just starting to lose the battle with darkness, but there was enough light for her to see the police station, only a few blocks down Main Street. She headed in that direction, disconcerted to see the street was empty. Coho, a town at the edge of Discovery Bay on the lush green Olympic Peninsula, did not seem to offer an exciting nightlife.

The police station was a prime example of 1970s civic architecture: low, long, and brown. She went in the visitor's entrance and was greeted by a series of windows reminiscent of ticket booths. Behind the first window sat a woman in uniform. Her name badge said *Eversall*. "May I help you?" she asked with the smile of someone relieved to have something to do.

"My truck was stolen."

The officer looked surprised. "Wow. It's been a while since we had a GTA in Coho."

"GTA?"

"Grand Theft Auto. Give me the make, model, and plate so I can radio the patrol officers, then I'll buzz you into the interview room, and an officer will take your full statement."

Libby gave her the information and then went through the inner door.

"First door on the left," Officer Eversall said.

The first door to the left was open. She flipped on the lights but thought the room held more promise when dark. The décor was bland industrial with a hint of municipal barren. Everything was clean, functional, made of metal, and at least twenty years old. She pulled out a chair and sat down facing the open door.

A man in plain clothes entered the room. Tall with broad shoulders, he was masculine in a way that would have flustered her if she were still seventeen. He walked with confidence and purpose that also would have befuddled her at a younger age. Thank goodness she'd said goodbye to seventeen half a lifetime ago.

"I'm Chief Mark Colby, ma'am. I can take your statement. I'm sorry to hear your vehicle was stolen." His deep, warm voice held genuine concern.

Surprised to be greeted by the police chief at this late hour, she stood and shook his hand across the table. "Thank you. I'm Libby Maitland." His handshake was firm and solid, and, like the rest of him, contained an air of authority. He was no backwoods hick in a small sawmill town. "I can't think of why anyone would steal a beat-up old truck like mine."

"What kind of vehicle is it?"

"A 1987 Chevy Suburban Silverado four by four. Black, gray, and rusty, it's as big as it is ugly. And it's really big." She noticed his slight smile and felt entirely too pleased with herself. She wanted to flirt with him as if she were in a bar with her friend Simone and they were betting to see who could collect the most phone numbers. Of course, Simone always won because she had bigger breasts and wasn't afraid to use them.

You are not in a bar. This is a cop.

"I don't care about the truck so much as what's inside it. All my field notes are there, and—" A wave of horror rippled through her and she gripped the edge of the table. "The GPS mapping unit is in the back. It costs two thousand dollars a week just to rent it."

"If your truck was taken by kids on a joy ride, it'll turn up quickly."

Even in her worried haze, she felt the irony and scoffed, "Believe me, driving that truck is no joy."

His eyes crinkled with a faint smile. "Then maybe it'll turn up even sooner." He grabbed a clipboard loaded with forms from the tabletop. "You had GPS mapping equipment. You're a surveyor?"

"I'm an archaeologist."

"The big dig out on the reservation road? You must be working for Jack Caruthers."

"Yes. He hired my company, Evergreen Archaeological Consultants, to excavate the site on the proposed Cultural Center property."

"Ever since hearing about your dig, I've wondered why you have to excavate before they can build the Center."

She smiled. This, at least, was familiar territory, a question she was frequently asked about her job. "Archaeological sites are protected by law, just like endangered species. Construction, road building—these things destroy archaeological sites, and information about past human culture is lost forever unless we can recover it first. Jack Caruthers applied for a permit from the US Army Corps of Engineers to begin construction on the Cultural Center. The Corps won't give him that permit until after I've done my job, which is to recover as much archaeological data as possible. No excavation, no permit. No permit, no Cultural Center." What she didn't say was: no Cultural Center, no new jobs for Coho, something the town desperately needed considering Coho's primary employer, Thorpe Log & Lumber, had closed its doors two years ago.

"That makes sense." He returned to his clipboard. "Is your vehicle company owned?"

"No, but I use it for project work a lot."

"Are you the registered owner?"

"Yes."

"Do you have a local address?"

"We've moved here permanently. As part of my contract, I'm living in one of the Thorpe Log & Lumber houses in the historic district, the Shelby house," she said, aware that most of the townspeople knew the mill houses by name rather than address.

The police chief wrote on the form, and then looked up. "You said 'we.' Are you married?"

"No. I was referring to my business and employees." She wondered whether she should be flattered until he checked a box on his form. Oh, yeah, marital status would indicate joint ownership of the stolen property. Apparently her brain had been stolen along with her vehicle. She shook her head and cast about for something to say. "What an end to a stressful day." She rubbed her temples. "You know, I lived in Seattle for more than ten years and never had anything stolen. I've been in sweet, idyllic Coho all of two weeks."

"Coho's appearance can be deceiving—perfect on the outside but we have problems like any other place." He flashed her a full smile, which brought out the wrinkles around his deep blue eyes and a dimple in his left cheek. "That said, car theft is unusual."

He probably gets whatever he wants with that smile. Combine his smile with his easy good looks, the smooth, deep voice, and his air of assurance, and he was one dangerous male. She glanced at his left hand. No ring. Perhaps Coho wouldn't be a bad place to live after all. And because her project had just gone to hell, she couldn't afford to move again anyway.

He slid the clipboard across the table. "Here's an inventory sheet. Please list the equipment that was inside the vehicle."

She began to write. She was almost done when Officer Eversall stepped in the doorway. "I've got good news, Chief. Ms. Maitland's vehicle has been found—it's on the street—near the restaurant."

"You're kidding," Libby said. "Is everything in it?"

"The officer on patrol said it looks fine."

The police chief rose. "Let's go check it out. You can tell me if anything's missing."

Together, they walked at a brisk pace down the street. The Suburban was parked in the shadows a block past the restaurant where she'd had dinner. She walked straight to the rear and looked inside. The field equipment was there. She rested her hand on the back window to steady herself and took several deep, calming breaths.

The police chief conferred with an officer inside a patrol car. She was eager to open the back and check the equipment, but worried she would ruin fingerprint evidence if she touched the door handle. After a moment, the chief stepped back, and the police car drove away.

Darkness had descended and the only sound to break the stillness of the night was the distant hum of the moving vehicle. Libby stood alone with the police chief. He studied her, and she wondered what he and the other officer had spoken about. Had his friendly manner really disappeared? Or was it just the effect of the dim streetlight and deep night shadows, which reduced his handsome face to only the sharpest angles: prominent squared jaw, forbidding brow. His deep blue eyes, warm cobalt in the fluorescent light of the police station, were now black.

She had the feeling he was waiting for her to speak. "Did I do something wrong?"

"Is this where you parked?"

"No. I parked in front of the restaurant."

His shoulders dropped, giving her the impression she'd disappointed him. "Let's see if everything's here." He opened the back of the Suburban. "Was this locked?"

"Yes. I always lock it when there's field equipment inside."

"Any chance you forgot tonight?"

She paused for a moment to consider her answer. "No," she said firmly and scanned the contents of the back of the truck. "It looks like everything is here. The burial notes." She flipped through a binder. "The field catalog, the photologs, the excavation notes." She pulled out a bucket, revealing a bright orange case. "That's the GPS mapping unit."

He pulled out the case and opened it. The expensive survey equipment was nestled in gray foam padding. Relief rushed through her. She'd live to dig another day.

Leaving the equipment, the police chief walked a complete circle around the SUV, scanning each surface. He opened the driver's door. Curious, she walked to the passenger side and peered through the window. He used his flashlight to inspect the interior, and then pulled the latch to release the hood. His gaze met hers briefly across the seat, and she felt a strange foreboding. He left the cab to raise the hood. She followed.

He rested a hand on the radiator and then touched the spark plugs, followed by the engine block. He straightened and studied her. He wasn't happy. "Ms. Maitland, I'll ask again. Is this where you parked your truck?"

"And again, no. I parked in front of the restaurant."

"What time did you enter the restaurant?"

"A little before nine. I think they were just getting ready to close the kitchen."

"What time did you leave?"

"Just after ten. When I realized my truck was stolen, I walked straight to the police station."

"Ms. Maitland, have you been drinking?"

She felt blood drain from her face as his meaning sunk in. He thought she was so drunk she hadn't seen her beast of a truck on an empty street. "I had a glass of wine with dinner, yes. One glass." She reached into her purse. "Here's the receipt." The contempt in her voice adequately conveyed her outrage at his question, but inside, she could teach Jell-O to quiver.

"It doesn't look like your vehicle's been stolen. There's no forced entry on any of the doors and no sign of how the engine was started. Is there any chance you parked here, then forgot, and didn't see it when you left the restaurant?"

"How on earth is that possible? I'd have to be blind or crazy!"

His look was pointed. "You don't appear to be blind."

She took a startled step backward and then gathered herself enough to say, "I'm not crazy."

"The engine is barely warm. It isn't hot enough to have been driven on a joyride. It couldn't have been driven more than a block, if at all. Don't waste my time here. If you forgot where you parked, say so now. We'll have a good laugh and you can go home."

"When I left the restaurant, my truck wasn't here." She touched the engine herself, desperately seeking something hot, something to prove him wrong, but she couldn't.

He studied her intently, evaluating and judging her.

"My truck was stolen," she said with a firmness she no longer felt.

"Is there anyone you know who could be playing a joke on you? Or anyone who might have borrowed it?"

"If one of my employees wanted to borrow it, they would have come into the restaurant and asked. Besides, I'm the only one with keys."

"Do you have a key hidden in the undercarriage?"

"My only spare is in my desk at the Shelby house."

"Look for it when you get home. Maybe you gave it to an employee and forgot."

"I wouldn't forget something like that."

"Do you know how much gas you had in the tank?"

Hope blossomed. She could prove she wasn't crazy. "The tank was full. I filled it this morning." She could show him the receipt.

With her key, he started the engine. She watched anxiously. Hope fled when the needle rose to the full line.

Chief Colby cut the engine. "Okay. You're free to go."

"Aren't you going to dust for prints?" she asked. He could at least *pretend* to investigate.

"No reason to. Be grateful you won't have black powder every-where. This isn't a GTA—the vehicle's here, undamaged, and no gas burned. No crime."

"So this was a total waste of your time."

"Pretty much," he said, heading toward the police station.

"Is there anything else you need from me?"

"Believe me, I'm done," he said as he walked away. "Goodnight, Ms. Maitland."

Libby stood next to her vehicle. The hood was up, the driver's door and the rear doors open. Strewn on the ground was the field equipment she'd removed to check on the mapping equipment.

What had just happened?

Unsure of herself, she stared at the parking lot in front of the restaurant, and tried to remember how her truck had looked when she'd parked it there, but now she began to question her own memory.

She collected the equipment and closed the doors. The police chief's reaction shook her. As she slammed down the hood, she glanced in the direction of the police station. He was gone. He must have run the last blocks to the station. She looked up and down the empty street. The only movement came from insects flying in the dim cones of light cast by streetlamps some distance away. Standing in front of her truck, centered in the long stretch of darkness between two streetlamps, a chill ran through her.

Her truck had been left in the darkest stretch of Main Street on a nearly moonless night. She hadn't made a mistake. She didn't imagine this. She pressed her palms flat against the cold hood of the Suburban and took a long, slow breath. Her heart began to race. Cold sweat broke out on her face and neck. Someone was out there, watching.

Oh, God. It was happening again.

Mark Colby stood in the shadows, watching the archaeologist as she gathered her equipment and reloaded her truck. He wanted to see her reaction. She slammed the hood and glanced up and down the empty street. She looked afraid and the cop in him felt a trace of guilt for letting her believe she was alone in the darkness.

He waited until she was safely in her vehicle and driving away before he headed toward the station. As far as he could tell, she really did believe her truck had been stolen. But still, she could be just another flake who'd forgotten where she parked and refused to admit it.

He stopped and glanced back at the empty street. Coho was quiet as usual, the fire station the only other Main Street building with lights on. He considered stopping in to have a cup of coffee with whoever was on duty. Short-staffed all week, he still had eight hours to go on this double shift, and the ten minutes he'd just spent on the street with Libby Maitland were likely to be the most interesting of the night.

He should be grateful the paperwork on this was minimal and file his report and be done, but her insistence her truck had been stolen troubled him. He wanted to believe the only reason he listened to her was because he was a sucker for tall women with deep green eyes, and he was tired from working doubles since Monday, but the truth was, something about her story bothered him.

Her name was familiar. She'd mentioned living in Seattle, and he had a feeling he'd heard her name when he was on the Seattle police force. He dropped the idea of coffee at the firehouse and hurried to the police station. He wanted to run a background check on Libby Maitland.

2

Libby cursed as her keys slipped from her fingers, bounced off the edge of the flowerpot, slid under the banister, and landed somewhere in the shrubs that bordered the back porch of the Shelby house. After a sleepless night, she should have known better than to handle keys before her morning coffee had kicked in.

She was on her knees in the damp grass searching for her keys when she heard the insistent chirping of her cell phone. She toyed with the idea of ignoring it, but that ringtone meant it was a business call. Caller ID said it was Dan Parker, the Corps of Engineers archaeologist who had the power of God over Jack's permit, and therefore over her excavation.

"Hi, Dan, what's up?" She tried to put some enthusiasm in her voice, but calls from Dan were rarely good.

"Well, Libby, I'm pretty much reeling from a series of phone calls I've had this morning, starting with the one I received at six a.m. from the colonel. Do you know who he is?"

"You're not talking about the Kentucky Fried Chicken guy, are you?"

"No. He doesn't have my number. The colonel I'm referring to is the head of the Seattle District US Army Corps of Engineers. He called me at home. Care to guess how many times that's happened in my twenty years at the Corps?"

"I'd guess never, Dan." Libby sat with a thump on the bottom step of the back porch staircase. Dan did not have a flair for the dramatic, making her certain something with huge fangs was about to bite her on the ass.

"I always knew you were smart. The colonel called me at six, because the Kalahwamish tribal chairman called him at five to initiate some nation-to-nation consultation, and it was all about you. There's a problem with the background section of your survey report."

Acid formed in her stomach. The report ran through her mind. She could think of nothing that would trigger a high-level, early-morning nation-to-nation confab. "The background was only preliminary. The scope of work states plainly a more detailed background section will be included in the final report, after we finish data recovery."

"I know, and I explained that to the colonel. The chairman was acting at Rosalie Warren's bidding. She is requesting—insisting, really —that the background section state exactly the way the tribe was treated by Thorpe Log & Lumber for the nearly one hundred fifty years they were in operation. Specifically, she wants Lyle Montgomery's abuses to be documented."

"Why?"

"She wants his actions to be part of the public record."

Rosalie Warren was an elder of the Kalahwamish tribe, and considered a living treasure by all the Northwest tribes. Her favor or disfavor could shape an archaeologist's career. Libby needed the Kalahwamish's cooperation to remove the burial on her site, or her project was in the toilet. "Why now? Why my project?" she asked.

"The burial you found yesterday gave the chairman leverage, but more important, Rosalie was admitted to the hospital earlier this week. She's dying. I spoke to her this morning. She'd like to read your history before she goes."

Stunned, she groped for words. "I'm sorry."

"Look, Libby, I know this is highly unusual, but we've got no choice. You'll get full cooperation from the tribe."

"It's not the tribe I'm worried about. What does she want in the history?"

"Everything. How mill development affected the tribe. The way the Kalahwamish were treated by the white settlers. The difference in pay and treatment between white and Indian mill workers. She wants everyone to know what a bastard Lyle Montgomery was. She doesn't want anyone to ever consider naming a street or an elementary school after him."

"You need an historian to research and write that type of background history. I can recommend several."

"We don't have time. You can give her what she wants." Dan paused, and then said, "And I can force you to do this. I've got a permit application from your client, Jack Caruthers, sitting on my desk right now."

"But I'll have to interview Lyle's children. They'll never cooperate, especially if they know I'm researching at Rosalie Warren's request. Plus, I don't have the budget for this kind of research."

"You'll have to work that out with your client. Usually I'd call him first, but I wanted to give you the heads-up as soon as possible. I'm calling Jack next. I'm going to tell him that if you don't do the work, we're pulling the permit. I mean it."

She resisted the urge to bash her head against the banister.

"And Libby, because of Rosalie's health, I need a draft in two weeks."

"Two weeks? But, Dan, I've got the burial to deal with. I can't possibly—"

"Two weeks is pushing it for Rosalie. She wants to talk to you. She can give you names of people to interview to speed things along. You need to meet with her today. She's at the community hospital in Coho."

"I'm on my way to the site now. I can go there afterward." She glanced at her watch: seven a.m. "I'll be there by nine."

"Good. You need to come through on this one. I get calls from permit applicants all the time asking for the names of reputable consultants. Now, *I* can't recommend anyone, but I can direct requests to the tribes who aren't afraid to name their favorite archaeologists."

How like Dan Parker to offer her veiled references for lucrative contracts as he ruined her current one. She hung up and dialed Jack, wondering if he would pay for this additional work, or if he'd hold her to their original contract and she'd end up working for nothing.

S imone Atherton sat at a table in the small RV used as a field office by Evergreen Archaeological Consultants. Libby Maitland, her boss and closest friend since college, sat across from her. Together they gulped coffee while Libby gave her a hurried update on what happened last night. "So the cops aren't doing anything about your truck?" Simone asked.

"I think as far as the police chief is concerned, I'm a nutcase."

"But you think Aaron is stalking you again."

"It makes sense. The Anti-Harassment Order expired a month ago, and the new judge refused to issue a new one." Libby stared into her coffee mug. "I'd almost prefer to be a nutcase. I can't deal with Aaron again."

"Maybe the cops in Coho will be different," Simone said, trying to find a hopeful note. Four years ago, Aaron Brady's stalking had changed Libby. She had lived in fear for nearly a year, until a judge finally granted a restraining order. Only recently had Libby begun to return to her old confident self.

"We really should be talking about Rosalie Warren's report."

"I think the fact that Aaron may be stalking you again is more important. One is your job, the other your life."

"Listen, we're screwed if I can't do what Rosalie wants. If Jack can't get his permit, we'll never get another contract. From anyone."

"You need to tell the police about Aaron."

"After last night, I don't think they're going to believe me. Right now we need to work on the project. I've got another problem. I need to work on the background report, but, according to our agreement with the tribe, I'm the only person who can excavate burials. Neat trick, huh?" Libby began to chew on a thumbnail.

Simone knew that was the first sign stress was getting the better of her friend. She pulled Libby's hand away from her mouth and gave her fingers a squeeze. "I could work on the background."

Libby's shoulders relaxed slightly. "I need you to oversee the excavation while I set up interviews with locals. Jack suggested his son might act as an intermediary so I can get the history from Lyle's children. Being their grandnephew and an equal share owner of Thorpe Log & Lumber, Jason's pretty much the only person in Coho they trust. Jack's one concern was that Jason might not have time—he's juggling law offices in both Seattle and Coho—and is swamped."

"I bet he'll make time," Simone said. "He likes you. When he came out to the site last week, he hung on your every word."

"God, I hope he's not interested in me."

"Are you crazy? He's the sexiest millionaire playboy since Batman."

"He's our client's son. I'm not getting involved with the relative of a client again."

"Jason Caruthers is nothing like Aaron Brady. Stop comparing everyone you meet with Aaron. I'm sick of watching you go through the motions of living, Lib. You've taken what happened with Aaron and used that as a reason to stay away from men altogether. The contest of collecting phone numbers in bars was to try to force you out of your shell. Now you've got a drawer full of phone numbers, but you've never made a single call. You need to date again. Jason is available. That's all."

"Maybe I'm not interested in dating right now. Lord knows I don't have time. Did you talk to your previous bosses this way?"

"Don't try that boss bullshit with me. In college, I held your hair while you puked."

In spite of Libby's obvious efforts to stifle it, a smile and a laugh broke through. "I knew it was a mistake to hire you. Just don't pass your attitude on to the crew, okay?"

Simone was relieved to see that Libby could still laugh. But the possibility that Aaron had fixated on her friend again had her very worried. She'd already planned to spend the weekend in Seattle, leaving right after work tonight. While in the city, she would check up on Aaron's whereabouts.

Libby pushed open the door and entered Rosalie Warren's hospital room. Rosalie lay sleeping in the bed. A male tribal member Libby didn't recognize sat dozing in a nearby chair. The soft click of the door closing woke him. He looked up and signaled for Libby to stay, but held his finger to his lips.

"No need for silence, Lou," Rosalie said, her voice weak. "I'm awake. Just resting my eyes. Tell me, who is our visitor?"

"Some white woman," Lou answered, before Libby could speak.

Libby stepped closer to the bed. "I'm Libby Maitland, Ms. Warren. I believe you were expecting me."

"Ahh, yes. The archaeologist."

Lou looked disgusted, not an unusual Indian reaction to her profession.

Rosalie's eyes remained closed. "Don't mind him. Lou doesn't believe archaeologists can tell us Indians anything we don't already know about ourselves. But he'll come around when he understands that you are going to be our voice." Her lids lifted, revealing clear, sharp brown eyes in stark contrast to the woman's emaciated body and frail voice. "You're younger than I expected."

"I have a master's degree in archaeology, and Simone Atherton, my senior staff archaeologist, has a PhD."

Rosalie raised a boney hand and waved Libby's words away. "No matter. I was just surprised, is all So, Libby Maitland, this is my grandnephew, Lou Warren. He is going to help you as much as he can. I understand you have found one of our ancestors during your excavation. Lou, here, will monitor the removal of the remains and perform a cleansing ceremony for the site."

Lou Warren studied her with glittering eyes. So far, nothing about the Cultural Center project had gone smoothly. The tribal monitor's glare assured her that wasn't about to change anytime soon.

"I read your report. The one you wrote after your survey for the Cultural Center. Not bad for a two-page summary of my people's existence since the beginning of time," Rosalie said.

Libby hadn't been aware a whisper could convey sarcasm so well. "It wasn't intended to be complete," she defended herself. "I'm working on a bigger history for the data recovery report."

Rosalie hit the button on her bed and brought herself up to a sitting position. "No matter. After reading your report, I realized you can serve a purpose for me. A quarter century ago, my mother, Frances Warren, encouraged an anthropologist, a woman she trusted, to study the Kalahwamish. She was granted interviews with the elders. The council gave her access to tribal papers, and even allowed her to observe some of our sacred ceremonies." Rosalie caught her breath, and her frail fingers adjusted the oxygen tube beneath her nose.

"My mother told me that the study was really for a greater purpose: to document Lyle Montgomery's mistreatment of us—the Kalahwamish Indians. Lyle was still alive then. My mother wanted the study published, so the world would know of his treachery. The anthropologist was reliable; her work would not have been questioned."

"But any anthropologist's work would be questioned, especially if the report appeared biased."

"Not in this instance. The anthropologist was Lyle's own granddaughter."

"Lyle's granddaughter?" Libby repeated. She'd studied the Thorpe/Montgomery family tree for the historical background section. As far as she could remember, Lyle Montgomery only had one granddaughter. "You mean Angela Caruthers? My client, Jack Caruthers' wife?"

Rosalie nodded. "She was Angela Montgomery longer than she was Angela Caruthers. But she disappeared before her work was finished, and my mother died not long after. Some say Angela just left one day and never came back. But that never rang true to me. She was a good woman who was devoted to her son. She would never have left him behind." Rosalie began to cough. Violent spasms racked her body.

Panic filled Libby as the most revered living elder in the Pacific Northwest gasped for breath. Should she get a doctor?

"You should rest," Lou said, adding a phrase Libby suspected was a form of "grandmother" in Salish. The word trailed off in a sound she couldn't reproduce. "You can talk to the archaeologist later."

Rosalie took a sip of water and shook her head at her grandnephew. "No. I will talk now." She turned to Libby. "I was disappointed Angela's work wasn't included in your report. Didn't her husband provide you with her research?"

"I didn't even know she was an anthropologist."

"Get her husband to give you her research notes. Use them to write your report. Before I leave this earth, I want you to finish Angela's work. Close the circle for my mother, myself, and my people."

So Libby remained by Rosalie's bedside for another hour, interviewing the elder until she fell into an exhausted slumber. Before she left, Lou agreed to be at the site on Monday morning for the burial removal.

She returned to the site and spent most of the day in the RV, developing new research questions for the more detailed background history, finalizing the protocol for burial removal, and arranging interviews with retired mill workers and tribal members. She talked to Jack, and he promised to search his Seattle house for Angela's papers.

At four o'clock, Libby's cell phone rang; caller ID said it was Jason Caruthers. Hotshot lawyer, potential Bruce Wayne, and her client's son, all rolled into one enticing and conflicted package. Simone believed he was interested in her, and now Libby desperately needed his help.

"Good news," Jason said. "It took some work, but I've gotten my aunt and uncles to agree to meet with you."

"You're a lifesaver. When?"

"Sunday, two o'clock."

"Do they know Rosalie Warren is behind this?"

"No way. I just told them you're doing an expanded background section."

"Every time I've requested an interview, they've refused. I'm impressed you managed to coerce them."

"We've got some plans in the works for the mill properties, and I used that as leverage. They will meet with you, and they've promised to talk. I'm going with you to make sure they follow through."

"I don't care if you blackmailed them, Jason. I'm just grateful."

He laughed. "I didn't have to go that far."

"Has your dad had any luck finding your mother's papers?"

"No, but I've got some ideas about that—I think they're in Coho. I had to return to Seattle this morning, but I'm on the ferry right now, heading back to Coho. I'll be there all weekend and should be able to locate the boxes."

"You're a peach. I can't thank you enough."

"I'm glad my mom's work will be useful. It was important to her. Listen, Libby, before you delve into her papers, you should probably know more about her. I'll be back in Coho in two hours. Would you like to have dinner tonight?"

Was it a business dinner he was suggesting, or something else? This project was more important to her than anything she'd worked on before. She'd given up her home and office in Seattle for this job. If it went south, she was completely screwed. The silence stretched out as Libby floundered for a response.

"I know it's short notice, and on a Friday."

Simone's words ran through her head. Jason wasn't Aaron. Libby was being an idiot, and besides, it was only dinner. "Dinner would be...lovely."

"Great. I'll pick you up at seven."

She hung up and breathed deeply. Whether he intended it as a date or not didn't matter. What mattered was that she'd taken a step away from the past. She wasn't going to let what happened before control her anymore.

The crew finished digging for the day and dispersed, many, including Simone, heading to their apartments in Seattle for the weekend. The field technicians were largely temporary hires, and would leave Evergreen Archaeological Consultants as soon as the field phase of the project ended. Simone and three others had made the commitment to see the Coho project through to the end of the reporting phase and were in the process of moving to Coho for the duration, but only Libby had completed her move before the project began.

She didn't know anyone in town yet, and the weekly exodus of the crew made for some lonely weekends. Company for dinner tonight would be enjoyable, if only Jason weren't related to her client.

At six o'clock, she locked up the RV. The dig was located on the edge of a light industrial area, with the road seeing very little traffic. The area was quiet, serene. Coho through and through.

Out of habit, she inspected the site, looking for tools to lock up or bags out of place. One portion of the site had been filled in and paved in 1984. Prior to excavation, the asphalt had been removed and the fill dirt scraped away by backhoe. A crescent-shaped mound of yellow fill dirt ringed that part of the site, giving a volcanic appearance. In the center of the crater lay the burial, now covered with a cedar bark blanket provided by the tribe.

Blue and green tarps sheltered other open units. Bright orange string sectioned off the grid in areas where entire blocks were being excavated. Part of the site sloped down along a dried riverbed and continued more than a hundred meters to the shore of Discovery Bay. Waist-high sea grasses tilted gently in the breeze.

Standing close to the cedar bark blanket, she wondered about the person, buried here five hundred years before Columbus set sail on a voyage that would forever change the Americas and the people who lived and died here. What had made this person laugh? Cry? Despair?

She always wondered about the unknowable. Through archaeology, she could understand what a person ate, how they worked, lived, and sometimes, even died. But she could never understand the similarities of their human existence to her own. What had this person dreamed about? What had he or she feared?

During the excavation, her crew would unearth tools that hadn't been touched by human hands in four thousand years, tools made by people who were different from her in culture, sustenance, and survival. But perhaps not so different in thoughts and feelings?

In her mind, she could see the landscape as it once was, with the now-dry river flowing swift and fierce down to the bay. During spawning season, its banks would have overflowed with salmon. She imagined a longhouse at the heart of the village. White clamshells covered the ground. The shells had crushed smaller and smaller underfoot, defining the well-traveled pathways. Hundreds of people lived together, worked together, loved, laughed, cried, and died together. Now, all that remained were piles of broken shell, charcoal, fire-cracked rock, discarded animal bones, and the occasional tool. Artifacts that were once a matter of survival.

What had Angela Caruthers wanted to know about the Kalah-wamish people? Were she and Libby at all alike in what drew them to their chosen professions? Perhaps Jason could shed some light on that.

She grabbed a blue tarp and carefully draped it over the burial, covering the cedar bark blanket. Only a handful of people knew they'd discovered human remains, and she wanted to keep it that way. Sometimes looters were drawn to open burials.

She turned toward the parking area and approached her truck, the crunch of gravel underfoot a distant echo of the sound the shell walkways would have made a thousand years ago.

She stopped suddenly. The Suburban looked lopsided. She walked around the vehicle. Dammit, one of the rear tires was flat.

Movement in the thick blackberry bushes along the road caught her peripheral vision. Probably a squirrel or raccoon. She ignored it and studied her truck.

A loud, gravelly cough came from the blackberries.

She whipped around. "Who's there?"

A choking, gurgling noise followed. The sound was human, but with a menacing tone. Someone being strangled?

Instinctively, her hand touched her own neck as adrenaline-laced fear spread through her. She glanced at her flat tire, and then back at the shaking blackberry bushes. Someone was watching her from less than ten feet away. Had they slashed her tire?

Her busy workday had allowed her to ignore what happened last night. But now she knew with certainty. Someone was threatening her.

She grabbed the best weapon she had, a shovel, and then pulled out her cell phone and called 9-1-1.

3

"Two-Lincoln-One respond to archaeological site at 6200 Discovery Bay Road. Possible suspect still in the area. Reporting party states person or persons unknown have tampered with her vehicle. She believes suspect might be hiding in bushes nearby."

Mark was in his woodshop making furniture for his four-year-old niece's playhouse when he heard the call. He grabbed the radio, "Three-Oh-One to Two-L-One, what's your location?"

"I'm at the intersection of Highway 119 and Olympic, Chief."

The officer was a good ten minutes away from the site. Mark was closer. "HQ, I will respond to that call too. I'm nearby." He ran to his work vehicle.

A half-mile from the site, he hit the siren. As he approached, he recognized Libby Maitland standing by her truck, holding a shovel in front of her like a weapon. He pulled into the gravel lot and cut the siren.

She lowered the shovel and ran toward him. "I'm so glad you're here." Terror showed in her wide eyes. "There was a man in the black-berries."

"I'll check it out." He pulled his gun and approached the thick, tangled blackberries that bordered the road.

The bushes appeared to be empty. He circled the vines, searching for evidence that someone had been there. No footprints, no trampled vines. No gaps wide enough for a person to pass through. In the distance, he heard his backup's siren. He radioed to disregard the call and the siren stopped.

He glanced at Libby Maitland. She stood with her back against his SUV as though she wanted to absorb the safety the police vehicle represented. Was she repeating an old pattern? The image fit with what he'd learned in the background check. Was she just another cop groupie, looking for attention in a new town?

He approached her. "If there was someone there, they're gone now."

Her face flushed. "*If?* There was someone there." Her voice was flat, angry.

"Tell me what happened."

She told him about finding the flat and then hearing a cough. "After I called out, he—"

"He? Why do you assume the suspect is male?"

She shrugged. "I don't know. I guess the cough was deep. Loud. Masculine. After I called out, he made another sound, which sounded like someone being choked—strangled."

"What does someone being strangled sound like?"

"Gasping for breath, wheezing, a struggle." A convincing shudder passed through her. "Look, I know what choking sounds like, and the point is: someone was in the bushes making sounds meant to threaten me."

"Why do you think it was a threat?"

"All I could think was that he was trying to scare the hell out of me. Maybe that was the point of taking my truck last night, too. To scare me. It makes sense."

"And who would do this to you?"

She looked away. "I don't know."

A lie. Was her whole story one big lie? If so, she was a fine actress.

The late afternoon sun shone on her medium-length, dark hair, revealing warm red highlights he'd missed the night before. Her simple beauty caught him off-guard, but it shouldn't have. He'd noticed last night, before he discovered her complaint was bogus.

It was time to find out if she had a thing for cops. He took a step closer and reached out, lifting her chin in a reassuring gesture and flashing a warm smile. He could act, too.

Her eyes conveyed tension and suspicion, but still, an electrical current of attraction arced between them, disturbing him with the way it went both directions. He didn't do groupies. "Why would someone try to scare you like this?"

"I have no idea." She stepped back, breaking contact, but the unsettling electrical undercurrent remained. Her gaze turned to the blackberries. "I think he wanted me to know he was there. That he'd been waiting for me."

"He who?"

She faced him again. "I don't know."

Her denial squelched his foolish reaction. "He staged all this just to threaten you?"

"Either that or he didn't expect me to have a cell phone—which would be stupid."

"He may not have expected you to be so quick to grab a shovel."

"He had plenty of time to come after me before I got the shovel. Why cough and draw my attention to him? Until that point, I thought the flat tire was an accident."

"Let's talk about the tire," he said, moving to examine the flat. He glanced over his shoulder to gauge her reaction. "This looks like a normal flat. Here's the nail."

She stared at the silver nailhead, her frustration evident in her pinched lips. Finally she said, "It could have been set up to look like a normal flat."

"Which do you think is more likely?"

"Well, since there was someone in the blackberries making horrid sounds, I'd say I think someone put a nail in my tire while I was working in the RV."

"Are you familiar with the theory of Occam's razor?"

"When given two possible explanations for a phenomenon, the less complicated one is the most likely. I know what you're implying, but you're wrong."

"You don't think you could have picked up a nail in this gravel lot? Or that an animal rattled the bushes and then made sounds you mistook for something else?"

"Listen, if you're not going to bother investigating this, I'm going to change my tire and go home. I've got things to do." She pulled a jack out of the Suburban.

"I'll follow you home and check out your house." He grabbed the tire iron. He didn't know whether he believed her or not, but he wouldn't ignore the possibility that she could actually be in danger.

With her back to him, she positioned the jack. He knelt next to her with the tire iron. She stared at him for a moment and then said, "Thank you."

Ten minutes later, they were both on the road to the Shelby house. He turned in to the alley that ran behind the historic houses on her street and parked next to her in the two-car driveway. He took her keys and climbed the back porch stairs. "I'll go in first."

He searched the house from the basement to the attic while she waited in the kitchen. He'd been in the Shelby house once before, after a prowler complaint, but the house had been vacant at the time. Until now, Jason Caruthers had kept this house for his personal use. The same antique furniture filled the rooms then and now, telling Mark nothing about Libby Maitland. He returned to the kitchen. "House is clear."

She opened the back door, ready to dismiss him.

"We're not done yet."

She looked at him warily. "I wouldn't want to waste any more of your time."

He smiled. "I can decide for myself what wastes my time."

"Look, you've already told me you think I drove over a nail and heard an animal in the bushes."

"It's my job to consider every possibility."

Her expression softened, and she closed the back door. "But what do you believe?"

"I saw nothing to indicate there was anyone in the bushes. The vines didn't look trampled or crushed. There were no footprints." He paused. "You believe your truck was stolen last night. That could have put you in a mind-frame to misjudge what you heard today."

"My truck was stolen." Her voice shook with frustration. "It was *gone* then returned to a different spot."

"But it makes more sense that you parked your truck on the street and forgot. You could have parked in that lot sometime in the recent past, then been confused last night. You were tired and indicated you'd had a stressful day. It happens."

"No. I parked in the lot in front of the restaurant." She took another step closer and planted her hands on her hips. "You've spent more time trying to convince me I'm crazy than investigating my call. What kind of cop are you?"

He'd given her an easy out, and she'd not only refused it, she'd gone on the attack. He leaned toward her. "I'm the kind of cop who questions a victim's story about a stolen vehicle when that vehicle is found fifty yards from where it was allegedly taken." He held up a hand and ticked off his reasons one by one. "A vehicle with a cold engine, a full tank of gas, not hot-wired, and with no sign of forced entry. The kind of cop who answers a suspicious circumstances call when the victim has a flat tire with a nail and assumes it's a set-up because she hears rustling and gasping from bushes that show no evidence of anyone being there. I'm the kind of cop who follows that victim home and checks out her house for her. This is the same victim who *refuses* to tell me who she suspects is threatening her."

The distance between them could be measured in inches. The heat between them could boil water. "So, you want to tell me about Aaron Brady now, or do we just call it a day?"

4

Libby felt the blood drain from her face. She should have known it would come to this. "You're just like all the other cops, aren't you? You've already made up your mind."

"What have you given me to work with other than two bogus calls? You want me to change my mind, Libby? Start by answering my questions. Start by telling me the whole truth."

She'd be damned if she let him address her informally while she called him Chief Colby. "I'm sure you don't need me to tell you about it, Mark. I'll bet you've already formed an opinion."

"Humor me. I want to hear your version."

She wished she could call what she was feeling déjà vu, but she knew exactly when she'd lived this moment before. She began to pace the wide aisle between the two counters that ran the length of the one-hundred-twenty-year-old kitchen. "As I'm sure you know, Aaron Brady is a Seattle cop. He was also the brother of a client. He came out to visit a project I ran for his brother. I gave him a tour, and afterward he asked me out.

"He seemed nice enough, so I was a fool and said yes." She stared out the window above the sink. Four years ago, when she first met Aaron, she had been twenty-nine years old and had just started her own company. The world was wide open, and Aaron Brady had been another new opportunity.

"We went out a few times. There was nothing wrong with him, per se. There was just…no spark. I wasn't interested. The ending didn't go well." That was an understatement. "I worried how my client would react to my dumping his little brother, so when Aaron continued calling me, I put up with it and pretended I wanted to remain friends. But then he started to say things to let me know he was keeping tabs on me. He knew what time I got home at night, where I'd been, and what I'd been doing. He seriously creeped me out, so I told him to stop calling me."

"But that didn't stop him."

"No." She allowed a bitter smile. "That was only the beginning. Aaron started to show up wherever I went—in his police uniform. As a cop, you must know how unnerving that is. No one wants trouble with the police."

"What else did he do?"

"He followed me to business meetings in his patrol car. He drove by the excavation several times a day and sometimes parked nearby for long periods. I couldn't ask him to stop because he only bothered me in public places. And the site was his brother's project.

"I began to avoid leaving my house, knowing he would follow wherever I went. If I wanted to see an art house movie, one only seven other people would make the trek on a rainy night to see, I didn't go. Seven wasn't a big enough crowd. And forget dating. He'd made that impossible. Finally, I confronted him in a crowded coffee shop. I told him if he didn't stop following me, I would call his supervisor."

"What did he say?"

"He said *I* needed to stop following *him*." She returned to that moment in her mind, feeling again the sickening dread that infused her as the light glinted off Aaron's badge, reminding her that among cops, his word would be more valuable than hers. "That night, I heard someone trying to break in my back door. I called 9-1-1."

"And Aaron responded to the call."

She nodded, leaned back against the counter, and met the police chief's gaze. "Imagine you live alone, and someone tries to break into your house. You can hear the screen being ripped off the hinges. You call the police, and soon after, hear sirens. You open the front door to your savior, only to see the person you know damn well was at the back side of the house minutes before terrifying the hell out of you."

"So you reported your suspicion to his supervisor," Mark prompted, his voice flat, but there was something like sympathy in his eyes.

"And I found out he'd been documenting my 'stalking' of him. He accused me of faking the attempted break-in and calling the cops that night just so he would answer my call. He said I was a cop groupie who wouldn't leave him alone." Libby shuddered. She'd learned a cop groupie was a whack job who hung out at cop bars and gave officers blowjobs in the parking lot.

"What did his supervisor say?"

"He wanted solid evidence against Aaron. At that point, it was just my word against his. And my word wasn't worth a damn thing." By the time Aaron's captain was done questioning her, she was hysterical, her credibility shattered. This was where her sense of déjà vu came from. She wouldn't make that mistake here.

"How did the other officers in the precinct respond to your charges?"

One look at his face and she knew. "C'mon, Mark, you know that. I bet you even spoke with some of them today."

His head dropped in a slight nod.

"His partner backed him up, claimed he couldn't have been at my back door at the time of the attempted break-in. And his buddies vouched for him at other times, or said they'd witnessed me following him." She took a step toward him. "What about you? Do you always side with the one with the badge, even if he's a *Goddamn loon*?"

"My job isn't to side with or against other cops. It's to find the truth." He crossed his arms over his chest and leaned back against the counter. "Tell me how you finally got the Anti-Harassment Order."

"After Internal Affairs investigated, with inconclusive results, Aaron became even worse. In addition to being followed, I started getting crank calls at all times of the day and night. Of course, I got a trace on my line. One call came from a pay phone located in front of a convenience store. I had read the police blotter in the newspaper and knew that a convenience store had been robbed that night. I checked with the manager. He confirmed that Aaron Brady had been one of the officers to respond to his call. Aaron did that two more times—called me from a phone that was near a call he'd answered while on duty.

"I documented everything. My neighbors helped. They were sick of being spied on by a cop. We got pictures of Aaron parked in his car in various places in my neighborhood. With a date and time stamp. I took pictures of him when he followed me, and friends got shots of him at my destination, all with date and time stamped on them. I had witnesses. Then I got lucky. The judge at the hearing was sympathetic. She said the evidence showed adequately that he'd engaged in a 'course of conduct that alarmed, annoyed, and harassed me which served no lawful purpose and was likely to cause me substantial emotional distress.'" Knowing they described the threshold she needed to meet to get her life back, she'd memorized those words long before the final hearing. "In King County, the Anti-Harassment Order allows some leeway—meaning I didn't have to show bruises, thank God."

"Then Aaron left you alone?"

"Yeah, but there were other repercussions. Aaron's brother said I was a psycho bitch who harassed his little brother, and when Aaron wouldn't have anything to do with me, I tried to ruin his career. He pulled his project. This was nearly a year after the first time Aaron and I went out, and we were done with the fieldwork by them. The report was nearly complete. He turned all the lab and field notes over to a competitor—one I can't stand, by the way—and had them write a lousy report that in no way resembled our findings. He refused to honor our contract and I spent two years in court trying to get him to pay the thirty thousand he owed me."

"Did you get it?"

"No. Why do you think I drive such a crappy old truck?"

His eyes softened and his lips twitched, but his cop face returned before a second passed. "Have you seen Brady since?"

"No. It's been three years."

"Four months ago, you requested a new Anti-Harassment Order. Why?"

"Same reason I did twice before. It's only a yearlong order, and the third one was due to expire in June. I wanted to make sure he stays away."

"Why wasn't the order reinstated?"

"The complaint was old; the new judge didn't believe Aaron was still a threat to me."

"How did you feel when it was denied?"

"Disappointed."

"Disappointed enough to stage a few incidents, so the order would be reinstated?"

It took a moment for his words to register. Her face heated as acid filled her belly. "I see the blue brotherhood is alive and well."

"This is called investigating, Libby. You may not like every path my investigation takes, but I've got to examine them all." He stepped toward her.

She instinctively retreated, her back brushing up against the counter. "You should be investigating Aaron Brady, not me."

"Funny. He said the same thing about you."

Her throat seized. He'd talked to Aaron. He'd sided with the cop before he even arrived at the site with sirens blaring. She finally managed to speak. "Get out!" She pointed to the back door.

"We're not done yet. There are differences between your story and Brady's. I can think of one major detail you've left out."

Her blood simmered as she stared at him. She knew exactly what he waited for. She had no choice but to say the words. "Aaron told you some of the photos—my evidence against him—had been doctored."

"Did you doctor them yourself?"

"A friend who was trying to protect me edited some of the date and time stamps. I didn't know anything about it."

"You admit the photos were altered."

"I didn't find out about it until a few months ago—when I read Aaron's statement demanding the renewal of the order be denied. I questioned my friend and she admitted it. But those photos weren't the only evidence. There were several that hadn't been altered. Plus I had the calls and witnesses."

"He had witnesses, too. Witnesses ready to testify that you were stalking him."

"His buddies who didn't care about what was really going on." She swallowed a frustrated groan. How could she ever have thought Mark Colby handsome? She'd known he wouldn't be any different from the cops in Seattle, but his pretense of investigating had triggered a smidgen of hope. "Someone put a nail in my tire and hid in the bushes to scare me, and instead of getting help, I'm being treated like a criminal because a jerk cop harassed me four years ago."

"I have to ask these questions, Libby."

The doorbell rang and she realized it must be seven already. "Jason. Crap. I forgot about dinner." She wasn't ready for a business dinner. Could this day get any worse?

"Jason Caruthers?"

Of course he knew Jason. You couldn't live in Coho without knowing about the four owners of Thorpe Log & Lumber. "Yes," she said, heading toward the front door.

"Your client's son."

She stopped dead. *Oh shit*. The day had just gotten worse. She whipped around and faced him. "It's not what you think."

He took a slow step toward her. "You almost had me. I was starting to believe your story about being afraid, losing your client and a lot of money. Then who do you have dinner plans with on a Friday night? Jason Caruthers. First a client's brother, now a client's son. We're done here." He walked to the front of the house where Jason waited, which had to be deliberate, because he'd parked in the back.

Jason was clearly visible through the long windowpane inset in the antique door. Mark reached for the doorknob and then turned and faced her again. "Don't think you're going to screw over my department or my officers with your games. I will find out what's going on." He brushed past Jason as he left the house. "Caruthers," he said in acknowledgement and kept walking.

"Colby," Jason said and then looked at her questioningly.

She swallowed hard and battled mortification. "Come in," she said.

Jason stepped into the living room. "Is this a bad time?"

"No. No. I just need a few minutes." She glanced around the room, trying to figure out what to do, still reeling from the police chief's reaction. Her brain wasn't working properly.

"Do you need help, Libby? Legal help, I mean?"

"No. No. It's nothing like that." She had to get herself together, or Jason was going to think she was a bigger fruit loop than the police chief did. "I'll be right back," she said and then headed to the bathroom.

She splashed cold water on her face and stared into the mirror. Seconds became minutes. She didn't know what to say to Jason, or how to deal with the mess she was in with the Coho police. All she knew was that at some point, she had to leave the bathroom and face Jason Caruthers. How could she possibly sit through dinner with him tonight?

Quite simply, she couldn't.

She blotted her face on the towel and opened the bathroom door, and then squared her shoulders as she marched into the living room.

He stood by the fireplace, cool, composed, and handsome, staring at a wooden mask carved in a Coast Salish motif, which was mounted in a place of honor above the mantel. "If I remember correctly," he said, "my mom bought this mask while we traveled in British

Columbia. The carver gave us a tour of his workshop and showed me how he mixed the pigments in the old style. No modern paints or tools were used to make this mask."

He wanted to talk about his mother, and she needed his assistance with the background research, but at the moment, she didn't care. "Jason. Tonight isn't good for me. Can we do this another time?"

He paused. "Sure," he said finally. "I'll call you tomorrow." He turned, started for the door, and then stopped. "Libby, do you want to talk about what's going on?"

"No, it's nothing," she lied.

"Call me if you change your mind."

She closed the door behind him and flopped down on the couch. A surge of anger and frustration ran through her. She twisted a silk throw pillow and then stared in horror at the creases she'd created in the fabric. Nothing in this room belonged to her. The furnishings belonged to Jack and Jason, who'd given her the use of this house for the duration of the project.

She smoothed the wrinkled cloth in a pathetic attempt to undo the damage. She wanted to blame Aaron. He was the psycho. He was the one who'd victimized her. But deep down she knew that if she'd handled things differently almost four years ago, then Aaron wouldn't be a problem for her now. Like the crumpled pillow, the police chief's suspicion was all her fault.

She couldn't count on the police for protection. From here on out, she could only depend on herself. She couldn't make any more foolish mistakes. Only one thing would make her feel safe. Tomorrow she'd buy a gun.

5

T he bell above the door jingled as Mark stepped into the Coho Diner, the only restaurant in town that served breakfast. He scanned the room, seeing the usual Saturday morning crowd. He ate breakfast at the diner several times a week and more often than not ended up dining with a resident who was anxious over something. The meals provided a casual forum for people to talk about their concerns with the police chief. He was never truly off the job in this small town.

He nodded to Chuck Nalley, the mayor of Coho, and then realized Chuck was having breakfast with none other than Libby Maitland, who sat with her back to the door. The woman had a history of filing charges against cops. If she was dining with the mayor to complain about him, she was in for disappointment. Mark had good reason for the way he'd handled her and the mayor wasn't one to second-guess police matters. He strode to the table and stood directly behind Libby. "Morning, Chuck."

Her posture shifted subtly, a slight stiffening of her spine. On the table, the pen in her hand stopped moving and the word she'd been writing became an indecipherable blot of ink on the page. Still, she didn't turn around, and he had to admire her poise. A small audio recorder sat on the table; the power light glowed bright red. Why was she recording her conversation with Chuck?

"Mornin', Mark. Have you met Libby Maitland? She's the archaeologist who's excavating that site for Jack." Chuck's introduction answered one question; they weren't discussing yesterday's incident —or lack thereof.

She turned to acknowledge him, offering a wry smile that held an unexpected appeal. "Good morning, Mark."

"Libby." He nodded to her. "Looks like you two are busy. I'll chat with you later, Chuck." He sat at a table that faced Libby and ordered coffee.

He could tell from her posture she was aware he watched her, but slowly she relaxed. He picked up snippets of their conversation, and Chuck did most of the talking. She laughed at something he said, releasing a warm, natural peal that didn't mesh with Aaron Brady's characterization of her. Mark didn't know Aaron Brady, but he knew and trusted Chuck Nalley.

In a relaxed moment, she glanced his way. He took a sip of coffee and held her gaze, caught by the confusion in her wide green eyes. She stiffened and reached for her water but her hand hit the glass, knocking it over. She snatched up her notebook and recorder. Mark was by her side instantly, throwing his napkin over the spreading water.

"You seem rattled, Libby. Is something wrong?"

Her lips tightened. "Everything's just peachy. Nothing I can't handle myself."

He couldn't resist needling her. "I've seen no evidence of that."

"That's because you don't see evidence, period."

He smiled. She was quick. "It's hard to see something that isn't there." Mark ignored Chuck's curious gaze and resumed his seat. He continued to stare at her. She avoided him, turning her seat a few degrees so his view was of her back more than her profile. Interview completed, she packed up her recorder and notebook, thanked Chuck, and left the restaurant without another glance Mark's way.

He moved to her vacated chair. "Looked like Libby was interviewing you. What about?"

"She's working on a history of Coho. She needs to interview a lot of locals—especially lifetime residents, like me—so don't feel bad if she doesn't interview you. I take it you've met her already?"

"We've crossed paths."

A speculative gleam entered Chuck's eyes. "You know, she's single. I can tell she's whip-smart. Attractive, too, I think."

"You sound like your wife. I can find my own dates, thank you."

"You wouldn't believe what she's working on—instead of a boring history of the town, she's trying to find out all of Lyle Montgomery's nasty little secrets."

"That sounds more tabloid than professional archaeologist. Why is she doing it?"

"A government agency is playing politics with Jack's construction permit. They won't give it to him if she doesn't write a history that a tribal elder has demanded. Jack is in a panic. He must have called me six times yesterday. He's invested too much money in the Cultural Center to lose it all over one small permit. He's pulling all sorts of strings to help Libby set up interviews. Jason, too."

A slow burn began in Mark's stomach. Was it possible he'd misjudged her? "Jason is helping her?"

Chuck nodded. "She needs to interview Lyle's family, point of it up. Listen, I gotta run. We're babysitting my grandson today. The missus or I will call you about dinner, okay?"

"That's not necessary."

Chuck waved off his protests and left the restaurant. Mark paid his bill. He'd planned to go home, but nagging doubt sent him to the police station. There, he nodded to the desk sergeant on duty. "Anything I need to know about?"

"Just a barking dog and stolen trash can."

"Sounds like you have things under control." He continued through the security door and down the drab hallway to the squad room. The station was quiet, a typical Saturday.

At his desk, he flipped through the stack of messages that waited on his blotter until he found one from his ex-partner on the Seattle police force. He picked up the phone and dialed. "What'd you find out for me, Bobby?"

"Not much on Libby Maitland. Far as I can tell, she's no groupie. No one but Brady claims to have seen her at any cop hangouts. She doesn't have a history of staking out police stations at shift change. Haven't met anyone who's tapped her. If she's into cops, then she might be looking for a Mrs., not a quickie."

"I'll consider that fair warning."

"I'd consider you lucky. I've seen photos."

"She could be a whack job, Bobby."

"I've dated whack jobs who weren't half so good-looking."

"You've married whack jobs who weren't half so good-looking," Mark said.

"Ouch."

"How's the divorce going, anyway?"

"Same old. She's getting everything but my dick."

"Well, considering that's what's caused the divorce, I'd say you're lucky to keep that."

"You ever consider taking my side?" Bobby asked.

"No."

He laughed. "You want me to look into Brady some more?"

"I'd like to know if he's in Seattle right now, and where he was Thursday night and yesterday evening."

"You thinkin' she might be on the level?"

"Just covering the bases."

"Okay. I'll go to Brady's favorite bar tonight and see what I can find out. You're buying, by the way."

"I owe you." He hung up. Last night the evidence seemed to support Brady's claim Libby was a nutjob groupie, but today Mark wasn't so sure.

His first impression of her had been positive. Hell, more than positive, if the slight rush he'd felt when she told him she was single were any indication. And he couldn't deny the spark that flared when he'd questioned her at the site yesterday.

Right now, there was no proof a crime had been committed. He could write a report, file it away, and be done. But he'd never been one to take the easy out with a case. It was possible—even probable— Aaron Brady had stalked her in the past. And now that the restraining order had expired, Mark had to consider the possibility Brady had picked up where he'd left off.

Libby sat in her home office going over the notes she'd made during the three interviews she'd conducted over the course of the day. The doorbell rang. Hallelujah, the pizza had arrived, a welcome and very late lunch. She looked at her watch. Make that early dinner. She grabbed her purse and headed down the stairs.

She paused when she saw Mark Colby at the door. The main drawback to living in a gorgeous old Queen Anne house with antique doors inset with long panels of cut glass had to be that the police chief could see her just as clearly as she could see him. She sighed and opened the door. "This is a surprise," she said without warmth.

He glanced at her purse. "You on your way somewhere?"

"No. I thought you were the pizza guy."

"I need to ask you a few questions."

She stepped outside and shut the door, and then crossed her arms over her chest and leaned against the doorframe.

"I jumped to the wrong conclusion last night," he said.

That was not what she expected him to say. She cocked her head to the side and uncrossed her arms, studying him. Finally she said, "Yes, you did. Jason asked me to dinner so he could tell me about his mother's research."

His brow furrowed. "You've lost me. Why would he want to tell you about his mother's research?"

"In order for Jack to get his permit from the Corps of Engineers, I need to follow up on research Jason's mother started in the 1970s. It's a long story."

A Volkswagen Beetle pulled up in front of the house and a moment later, the driver walked up the front sidewalk, carrying her pizza.

"Hey, Chief," the pizza boy said.

Libby dug around in her purse, looking for her wallet. Her fingers brushed against the unfamiliar shape of the Taser she'd purchased earlier in the day. The gun dealer had convinced her to buy a Taser to avoid the five-day waiting period required for handgun purchases. She found her wallet and looked up to see the police chief handing the delivery boy cash.

"You decide between Wazzu or U-Dub yet, Tommy?"

Tommy handed Mark the pizza. "I'm going to the University of Washington."

"Good pick," Mark said. "That's where I earned my master's degree." He waved off the change Tommy offered him. "Keep it. You'll need it."

"Thanks, Chief." The boy returned to his car.

They stood on the porch in silence.

Mark took a deep breath. "Smells like pepperoni. My favorite." He slowly smiled.

The warmth in his eyes and cocksure smile triggered a flutter in her belly, proving her body was a complete traitor. "You wouldn't like it. There's pineapple on it, too."

His grin deepened. "I love pineapple."

The silence lengthened as she held his gaze and battled her body's betrayal. She finally accepted defeat. "Would you like some pizza?"

His eyes lit with humor. "Thought you'd never ask."

She shook her head, laughed and then led him inside. He followed her into the dining room, carrying the pizza. She went to the kitchen to fetch plates, napkins, and drinks. They sat opposite each other at one end of the long, formal table.

"So why does Jason Caruthers need to talk to you about his mother?"

Due to his suspicions, she wanted to make one thing clear from the start. "When Jason invited me to dinner, I wasn't sure if he was looking for a date, but I'm not in a position to say no to a source of information." Between bites, she brought him up to date on the project. He asked questions but his demeanor had changed. He seemed to have come over to make amends.

"Tell me why you didn't mention Aaron Brady the night your truck was stolen."

"I didn't think of him at first." She could see his skepticism. "Really. When my truck turned up missing, I just thought it'd been stolen. When it was returned, I figured that whoever took it decided it was a pain in the ass to drive—which it is—it wasn't until you pointed out the cold engine that it started to seem like something else. But stealing my truck wasn't Aaron's modus operandi, so I didn't think of him until after you walked away."

He sipped his lemonade and studied her, but without the open distrust, his gaze was no longer unnerving. "Why didn't you tell me about Aaron yesterday when I asked who you suspected?"

She frowned. That had been her one mistake. "The truth? You're a cop. I was afraid to tell you about Aaron. I didn't think you'd listen." She paused and then added, "And I'm an idiot."

He nodded.

She suppressed a smile and gave him an amused glare. "You don't have to agree so quickly."

His lips curved in a diminished version of his devastating smile. "Okay, how 'bout we downgrade to 'foolish?'"

"Fair enough." She leaned back and studied him. What would Simone think of him? She could guess easily enough—he's hot, but more than that, focused. Confident. Appealing.

Mark took another slice of pizza. "Do you have any colleagues who are incompetent? Or even negligent?"

His question was a jarring contrast to the adjectives she'd been thinking. "What?"

"Are all archaeologists perfect at their job?"

"Hardly. We have our share of incompetence."

"Who should I base my opinion of your entire profession on? You, or the incompetent ones?"

His meaning was more than clear. "I didn't give you a chance, did I?"

"No, you didn't."

"I'm sorry."

He smiled. "And I'm sorry for jumping to conclusions yesterday."

Warmth spread through her. After the way he'd questioned her last night, she would never have guessed the initial attraction could return with such force, but here she was in the full throes of fluttery anticipation, something she hadn't experienced in a long time.

She may as well ask the question that had nagged her since she noticed the paint stains on his jeans when he helped change her tire. "Why did you answer my 9-1-1 call yesterday? The way you were dressed—you weren't on duty."

"I was closer than the patrol car and didn't want you to be out there alone."

She stared at him in silence, the air thickening as it entered her lungs. She knew her weaknesses all too well. She was a sucker for men with a protective streak, probably because her father hadn't been around much during her adolescence. Simple attraction ballooned into full-blown desire.

Talk about foolish.

Mark Colby sat across from her wearing an expression that hinted at a similar interest, reminding her that on her second date with Aaron she'd made a stupid self-conscious joke about her lack of father figure making cops appealing. Her words had been a feeble attempt to convince herself to be attracted to him, but it had backfired, and later Aaron used those words against her.

Now she had to wonder, did Mark know about that? He could be testing her, to determine if she were a groupie.

The doorbell rang, an excuse to escape the moment, the attraction, and the suspicion. She jumped up, seizing the opportunity. After rounding the bend from the dining room to the living room, she saw Jason Caruthers through the door and came to a dead stop.

Mark walked into her. He placed his hands on her hips to steady them both, triggering yet another foolish flutter. His fingers clenched as he said, "Jason," and then he released her.

What had she done to deserve this karma? Couldn't things go smoothly for ten minutes? She faced him. "We didn't have plans."

His eyes were intent but unreadable. "Then you should find out why he's here."

She opened the door. Jason glanced at Mark and then leaned toward her. She stiffened as he kissed her cheek. They barely knew each other and he kisses her hello in front of the suspicious police chief?

"You okay?" he whispered.

"Just dandy," she said, barely succeeding at keeping sarcasm from her voice.

He stepped into the room and stood protectively close to her. "Sorry to drop in unannounced, but I found the boxes containing my mother's research materials. I hope I haven't come at a bad time?" He studied Mark warily.

Jason's protective manner made sense; he was, after all, a defense attorney, and yesterday the police chief had rattled her to the degree she'd cancelled their dinner plans.

On her other side stood Mark, equally wary, gauging every nuance of her interaction with Jason. "Mark came by to ask me some questions about what happened yesterday."

"What did happen yesterday?" Jason asked.

"I had a scare at the site, that's all."

Mark placed a hand on her shoulder in a gesture that wasn't the least bit comforting.

Jason's gaze fixed on Mark's hand. "A scare? Is this something Jack should know about?"

Mark squeezed her shoulder in an intimate manner. "We're handling the situation. If we need your assistance, we'll let you and your father know."

Tension arced between the two men. She stepped away, disengaging her shoulder and trying to remove herself from the crossfire.

"Are you done questioning her?" Jason asked Mark, as if she wasn't part of the conversation.

Mark walked to the sofa. "Have a seat. We shouldn't be too much longer."

Annoyed, Libby said, "I think we're done."

"Great." Jason ignored Mark's offer to sit on what was, in fact, his own couch. "I've got a dozen boxes in my car. You can help unload them, unless you need to leave because you're on duty?"

"No. Today's my day off." Mark crossed back to Libby's side.

Jason took his turn placing a protective hand on her shoulder, but did Mark one better and went for the opposite shoulder, so his arm draped behind her back. "Then your dedication to Libby's case is commendable."

Christ. She was coveted territory in a pissing contest.

Mark shrugged. "Just another public servant doing my job."

"I knew we could count on you to get the job done. That's why I recommended you to the hiring committee."

Mark grinned. "You have uncommonly good judgment—for a defense lawyer."

"Someone needs to keep the police honest."

The testosterone level in the room had reached choking levels. "Why don't you two start unloading those boxes?" Libby said.

"Sure. After that, we can talk about my mother's research."

She was done with both men. All men. Perhaps even the human species in general. "We can talk before we meet with your aunt and uncles tomorrow."

"Great," he said, with the satisfaction of a ballplayer who knows he's about to score. "It's a date. I'll pick you up at noon and take you to lunch."

There was no way out. "That would be lovely," she said and turned to Mark. "Are we done?"

"With everything but the pizza." He turned to Jason. "Let's unload those boxes, so Libby and I can finish our dinner."

She shouldn't have underestimated Mark's ability to get the last word. But both men had underestimated her. The two full staircases between the ground floor and the attic would put all that extra testosterone to work. "The boxes need to go up to the attic. I'll make sure there's room, while you two start unloading." She walked toward the long, steep staircase and hoped the boxes were very, very heavy.

The cop bar hadn't changed in three years. The pool tables in the back still had a long line of people waiting their turn, and the dart boards on the side were still a focal point where patrons played Cricket for pitchers of beer and bragging rights. The jukebox played an old Jimmy Buffet tune, and a group of young men, arms linked around each other's shoulders, sang along, loud and off-key.

Simone had seen the same scene a hundred times before; the singers just kept getting younger. She smoothed her skintight dress as she walked by and headed to the bar. The quartet paid their regards to her breasts as she passed.

She'd get this over with so she could go home and finish packing up the study. Her days as a resident of Seattle were almost over. But first, she had to find out where Aaron was and if he could be stalking Libby again.

During the early days before the restraining order was in place, to help Libby's case Simone had made a point of finding out what Aaron's favorite hangouts were. Unknown to Libby, Simone had spent many nights in this bar asking questions and trying to find other women who might have suffered from Aaron's obsessive attentions.

It wasn't easy. Petite with long blonde hair and endowed with a pair of double-Ds, some women hated her on sight. But false modesty wasn't her style. She dressed to please herself, and if that got her more than her fair share of male attention, so be it. Over time, information on Aaron trickled in, including third-hand knowledge of a woman Aaron had harassed before he fixated on Libby. Simone had been trying to convince the woman to come forward when Libby's restraining order was granted.

Now that the order had expired, Simone feared that Aaron had turned his attention back to the one woman who'd stood up to him and refused to tolerate his stalking.

She worked her way toward the bar, passing a woman too drunk to be holding a sharp implement as she threw a dart. It hit the Budweiser lamp above the board. The woman laughed uproariously and then flopped down in a nearby chair and took a swig of a beer too pale to have flavor.

Simone sat on an empty barstool and waved to the bartender, surprised to see a familiar face from three years ago.

"Hello, gorgeous. Haven't seen you here in ages," he said.

"Redhook ESB, please," she said, waving a bill. "I'm looking for someone. Perhaps you can tell me if he's here."

The man next to her leaned close. "I'm right here, baby. Look no further."

Simone rolled her eyes. Why didn't the lines ever change? She shook her head. "Sorry, but it's not you. I'm looking for a cop. Aaron Brady."

"I'm a cop, too. A better cop than he is."

She didn't doubt that for a moment. But then, Aaron set the bar low. The bartender gave her the beer, but the cop next to her paid for it. She would miss the city. The few times she'd gone out in Coho, she'd had to buy her own drinks. "Thanks," she said. "Simone Atherton." She held out her hand.

He shook it and said, "Mike Ford."

She addressed both Mike and the bartender. "Is Aaron here tonight?"

"Haven't seen him," Mike said.

"Me neither. He usually comes by if he's off-duty," the bartender said.

She looked at Mike. "Has Aaron been around much lately?"

"Why are you so interested in Aaron?"

"You friends with him?" she asked.

His shrug was indifferent. "Not particularly."

She guessed this was the truth. "Neither am I. I just need to know where he is."

"So you won't be there?"

"Something like that."

"I can tell you where he's not." He paused. "At my place."

"Nice try."

"Won't work?"

"'Fraid not."

Two men joined them; one of them slapped Mike on the back and begged for an introduction. She opened her mouth to give her name.

"Simone Atherton. What the fuck are you doing here?"

There he was, surly and in the flesh, Aaron Brady. The noise decreased as nearby patrons paused to listen. "I can be wherever I want. There's no court order restricting *my* activities."

The look on his face made her happy she'd dressed to flirt tonight because it had already gained her at least one friendly cop, and she'd need someone to escort her to her car later.

"Last I checked, there wasn't one on me, either. You can tell your bitch-friend that, too."

"Is that a threat?"

"Just a fact."

"Have you been in Seattle the last few days, Aaron?"

"None of your damn business."

"Why are you afraid to answer? Been somewhere you shouldn't be?"

"There is no *shouldn't* about it. The restraining order is history. Now I'll tell you the same thing I told the hick cop in Coho. Your friend is a fucking psycho." He turned and left.

Simone faced Mike. "Well, I think that went well, don't you?"

Another man approached. "Ms. Atherton." He flashed a badge. "Bobby Johnson, detective with the Seattle PD. I'd like to ask you a few questions."

6

A t noon on Sunday, Libby watched from the bay window of the Shelby house as Jason Caruthers parked his gold Lexus in a no-parking zone. Last night the chief of police hadn't said a word as he helped Jason unload boxes from that very same illegal parking spot. But then, you can do almost anything when you own the town.

She stepped out on the front porch to greet Jason, who looked like a girlhood fantasy come true. His mocha eyes were set off by dark brows and thick unruly brown hair that captured and held the mid-day sun. He was good-looking in a *GQ* sort of way that Libby had never been fond of—too pretty, too smart, too privileged. She expected him to have a healthy ego and was wary of him for that, among other reasons. He dressed professionally, including a tailored suit that probably cost more than her entire wardrobe. She'd opted for a fitted skirt and jacket with low-heeled shoes—nothing low-cut or remotely alluring, caution being her rule for dealing with Jason.

He once again kissed her hello. She wished she could accept it as a simple gesture of friendship but the kiss put her on edge. "I made reservations for us at the restaurant in the Thorpe Hotel," he said.

"Great. I love that old building."

"Let's walk," he said.

The entire historic district of Coho was still owned by Thorpe Long & Lumber—and therefore, Jason himself. First occupied by white settlers in the early 1850s, by the mid-1870s Coho was a thriving mill town. Now Coho was a pristine example of a late-nineteenth century community. Developed before mass-production of the automobile, one of the things Libby loved about the place was in the historic district, everyone walked everywhere, rain or shine.

Today the weather was shine—a perfect Pacific Northwest summer day. They neared the general store, where people stepped out onto the wide front porch, bags of groceries in hand. Residents going about their normal, everyday lives, the only difference from a hundred years ago being that back then, the store would have been closed on Sunday. Shoppers waved to Jason, who waved back.

Farther up the road, they passed the Masonic Hall, followed by the mill-owned church, where children raced through the arched doorway as services let out. These families were counting on Jack to build the Cultural Center to provide jobs and tourists for the depressed economy, a reminder of what was riding on that permit.

At the end of a beautifully maintained driveway lined with madrona trees stood the waterfront hotel. A stately old building, it was the jewel in the crown of TL&L's holdings. The bustle of activity inside surprised her after the tranquil walk through town. A group of tourists gathered for a walking tour of the historic district, their guide an elderly mill worker Libby was scheduled to interview later in the week.

The hostess fawned over Jason as she led them to a booth in the back of the restaurant. A half-dozen stunning Tiffany-style chandeliers decorated the room with warm, colorful light. Ceiling-to-floor wooden partitions elaborately carved more than a hundred years before by a master of the craft separated the booths. The hotel and restaurant were the most upscale establishment in town. That the gorgeously maintained building was in tiny Coho remained a marvel to Libby.

The hostess gave Libby a menu, but not Jason, and immediately poured him a sample from a bottle of red wine that was waiting on the table. As a show of status, it was a bit heavy handed, and she wondered if it was done at Jason's request or if the hostess was trying to curry favor.

Jason took a sip and nodded to the hostess, who then filled his glass. "Wine, Libby, or would you prefer something else?" he asked.

She agreed to wine, simply to speed the hostess' departure. When they were alone, she took a deep breath and said, "I have a question for you about the scare I had at the site on Friday and related legal issues."

"Good. I was hoping you'd tell me what's going on."

She told him about her Suburban being stolen, and then her suspicion that someone threatened her from the blackberries. She sipped her wine and then broached the first topic she wanted his opinion on. "I called the police for help, but my report wasn't taken seriously. Then I became the focus of the investigation."

"Not taking the victim seriously happens all the time for minor offenses, and from what you've described, I hate to say it, but Mark's reaction is understandable. He came on pretty strong on Friday, though."

She frowned and reluctantly told him what happened with Aaron Drudy three years ago. Her only solace was his expression, which remained sympathetic.

Jason remained quiet for several seconds after she finished, but methodically buttered a slice of bread and then set it on his plate without taking a bite. "I would look at Mark's investigation in a few different ways, Libby. First of all, after your truck was found, it would have been reasonable, given the circumstances, for him to drop the whole thing. The fact that he continued investigating and found out about the Anti-Harassment Order is promising. It means he took you seriously that night. And yesterday, based on what I saw, he seemed to be coming around to your point of view. Not so much the day before...but in light of the story you just told me, my showing up at the door probably didn't help your case."

She smiled wryly. "That's an understatement."

"I wouldn't worry too much," Jason continued. "He does have to investigate all possibilities—including you."

"He said as much to me."

"As far as any implied threat goes, outside of protective custody, there's not much the police can do, except add you to the patrol route. Tell you what, if the focus of the investigation remains on you, I want to know. I have influence with the review board."

"I don't want you to intercede on my behalf. I just want to salvage my credibility."

"Don't stress about that. Some cops would investigate Mother Theresa."

She laughed. "I'm in good company, then."

The waiter arrived and took their orders. After he left, Jason said, "So, have you found anything interesting in my mother's research?"

"I found some of your old report cards and school papers. You really should have studied your spelling lists."

"Hard to believe I became a lawyer." He smiled. "But I was only nine when I packed those boxes. You can't judge me by the contents too much. I found my focus in school later."

His words brought her up short. "*You* packed the boxes?"

"It was a few months after my mother disappeared. I had waited in the front window every day—before school, after school, weekends—certain she'd come back. When she didn't, I got mad and gathered up all her things and dumped them in those boxes."

"I'm so sorry, Jason."

"Someone had to do it and Jack was...busy."

Her own father was no model parent, repeatedly abandoning her brother and sister and her to their increasingly bitter mother. She understood all too well what it was like for a child to be left with one negligent parent.

"When my mom's car was found, all fingerprints, even her own, had been wiped clean. The police found it suspicious, but that information wasn't shared with me until I was old enough to ask the right questions. Even now I find myself believing she'll come back. It's difficult not knowing what happened." He sipped his wine and was quiet for a few seconds and then his look changed and he said, "So, now you'll be finishing her work."

"I can't do that. Your mother was an ethnographer, I'm an archaeologist."

"What's the difference?"

"Your mother studied living culture. I dig up the remains of past cultures. We're both anthropologists, but we collect information in different ways. There's some overlap in our areas of expertise, but another ethnographer would be more suited to write the report Rosalie wants."

Jason looked at her speculatively. "Interesting." He paused. "I have a confession to make. I didn't really ask you to lunch to talk about my mother." He reached out and covered her hand with his, his fingers trapping hers in the intimate hold.

Crap. Her entire body stiffened. She fought the instinct to snatch her hand away.

"I invited you here so we could talk about the report."

His words, so incongruous to his actions and so unexpected, made her blank on a response.

"I'm very concerned about the historic background you're writing. Frankly, I don't want you to write it at all, but if you do, then you must only include sustainable facts." His grip on her hand tightened, but his expression remained friendly.

"What do you mean you don't want me to write it? You've been helping me."

"I read the new research questions you submitted to Jack on Friday. I want you to drop most, if not all of them, but without killing Jack's permit application."

"I can't. I consulted both Rosalie and Jack on the research questions. The Corps approved them and have made them part of the scope of work."

"Then I need you to stall producing the report for as long as possible."

"My deadline is firm. Believe me, I want more time."

"Damn. I'd hoped this wouldn't be necessary, but it looks like I don't have a choice. I'm giving you fair warning, Libby, you need to be very careful of what you put in writing." He looked at her steadily, leaving her no doubt he was serious. "Destroying the reputation of my great-grandfather will get you sued for libel."

She pulled her hand away. He'd said it was a warning, but it felt more like a threat. Hysterical laugher threatened. And Simone thought Jason was attracted to her. "Lyle Montgomery's reputation is already pond scum."

"But my grandfather's bigotry and misconduct have never been documented in a public report. TL&L has an important business deal in the works. Whatever you put in print, you'd better be able to back up. No conjecture. No suppositions."

She knew from his firm voice and clear gaze that the full power of his Seattle law firm stood behind his words. "I understand." Libby sipped her wine without tasting it. She'd been given a very fine line in which to draft her report. If she pleased Rosalie, she ran the risk of a lawsuit, because most of Lyle's worst deeds were based on hearsay. The beating death of the union man in 1939 was out, as were several other crimes attributed to him. "Your restrictions could limit the report to the extent that the Corps won't issue the permit. Is that what you want?"

"Absolutely not. Listen, Libby, I'm in the same bind you are." His voice and eyes softened. "I want the Center built. But your report can't compromise my family and the business. I convinced my great-aunt and uncles to let you interview them. I've given you the boxes that contain my mother's research. Now I expect you to help me."

7

A tap on Mark's office door interrupted his concentration. Officer Luke Roth entered the room and sat. "Thanks for taking the suspicious circumstances call for me Friday night, Chief. Isn't Libby Maitland the same nutjob who reported her car stolen Thursday?"

"She reported her car stolen."

"So, what did she want on Friday? Did she think the people on TV were watching her?"

"She's not one of those. I've made some calls to Seattle, and I don't think she's a crank." Mark sat up and riffled through his papers to find the list he'd made earlier. He found it and said, "I want you to check alibis on a few people." He handed Luke the paper. "If someone's messing with her, they might be doing it because of the Cultural Center. They could have targeted Libby as a way to stop the project."

Luke scanned the list of names. He looked up. "What's Jason Caruthers doing on this list?"

"A hunch," Mark said.

"Everyone in Coho likes him. They think he's some sort of golden boy, but if you ask me, he's just a throwback to the old man. Jason's the new Lyle in town."

"Why do you think that?"

Luke shrugged. "Lyle bullied people. Jason out-smarts them. Different methods, same result. Jason closed the mill and fired more people than Lyle ever did, yet he convinced everyone that shutting down was in their best interests. Half the old mill employees thank him for 'looking out for them.' What a load of bull. Jason Caruthers only knows how to look out for himself."

"Don't bring anything personal into this investigation, Luke. It's just a simple inquiry as to where people were at the times in question." He'd cautioned himself in the same way when he added Jason's name to the list.

Luckily, his phone rang and he waved Luke out of the room and took the call.

"I owe you a beer. Make that a case of beer," Bobby said, "I'm sitting in the bar last night, bored as hell and waiting to see if Brady will show up when this tiny little blonde with the most amazing rack walks in. Next thing, I know, she's arguing with our boy, giving me the perfect excuse to talk to her."

"Please tell me you questioned her before you hit on her."

"Hey, man, I'm a professional."

Mark laughed. "Yeah. Right. What'd you find out?"

"She's friends with Maitland. She was checking up on Brady, because for some reason she didn't think you would. I got an earful on the evils of Officer Brady, but more important, the woman seemed credible."

"Which part of your anatomy finds her credible?"

"My gut says she's telling the truth."

"You sure? Because your dick doesn't have the best track record."

"And yours is so much smarter."

"I just don't let mine make decisions for me."

"Yeah, right. Listen, after I walked Simone to her car, I went back in and observed Brady. My take—he's an asshole who uses his badge to wield power over anyone he perceives as weaker. Probably stunned the hell out of him when Maitland reported him. Didn't you say he had her trapped financially?"

"His brother was her client."

"Sounds like his style. I don't know if Brady is stalking Maitland again or not but it wouldn't be out of character from what I saw."

They talked for a minute more and then Mark ended the conversation. He sat in his quiet office, thinking about Libby Maitland. She wasn't paranoid, a groupie, or a flake. It sounded as if she'd had real reason to fear Aaron Brady in the past. Her belief someone put a nail in her tire and hid in the blackberries to scare her seemed plausible now.

The beautiful old Victorian mansion sat high on the hill on the edge of the historic district and loomed over the town and mill properties. The residence had been known as Thorpe House until 1940, when Lyle Montgomery fired two mill workers for using that name in front of him. Forever afterward, the house was called Montgomery Mansion.

Back then, the company provided nearly all employee housing. TL&L owned the company store, the gas station, the hotel, the church; even the United States Postal Service paid rent to TL&L to have an office within the town. The only building in the area not owned by the company was the Masonic Hall, and the fired workers and their families had to stay in the Hall until they could find a way to leave Coho forever.

The mansion sat in a park-like setting, with huge old oak trees and a manicured lawn. The Queen Anne-style house had a complicated, asymmetrical shape, which included a wide porch next to a rounded tower on the east-facing front of the house. Decorative shingles adorned the upper floors and stained glass sparkled in the smaller side windows. Carved moldings adorned every window frame and most joints. The ornamental balusters that supported the porch railing were a work of art in their own right.

From the first time Libby had driven through Coho, she'd wanted to enter this house. Architecturally, it was superb. Built in 1885 after the first Thorpe House burned down, it wasn't the oldest structure in Coho, but it was the most gorgeous. As Libby and Jason stepped onto the porch, she was saddened such a beautiful old structure had a long history of needless cruelty.

Jason opened the front door and she entered a tiny vestibule with a second door inlaid with stained glass. He opened the interior door and she stepped into the entrance hall. A central fireplace with an elaborate mantel sat cold and empty. Arched doorways flanked the fireplace on either side. To the right of the door was the staircase, decorated with ornate railings, which zigzagged to the upper floors. Above the first landing were the round stained-glass windows with a flowery design that glowed with warm shades of red, orange, blue, and purple in the afternoon sun. In spite of the vibrant hues, the entire entry hall seemed cold, forlorn. A letdown.

The front room was stark. No knickknacks on the mantel, no

coatrack, no umbrella stand. Not even a comfy bench to sit on while removing muddy shoes. The room—larger than her bedroom—was a space one passed through on the way to more important things.

"It doesn't look like anyone lives here," she said to Jason.

"Aunt Laura says this is the way their father liked it." He shrugged. "Lyle's only been dead for twelve years, and Aunt Laura is seventy-eight." He smiled as though that explained it, and she supposed it did.

He led her to the sitting room to the left of the foyer. "Wait here, I'll round them up." He disappeared through a different doorway leading to the back of the house.

She wandered around the room, which at least held furniture and a few items that gave her clues to the occupants of the house. One shelf held an array of artifacts, including arrowheads and other projectile points in identifiable styles. Someone had traveled throughout the Pacific Northwest and into the Great Basin to collect artifacts from different archaeological sites. There were several point styles from Eastern Washington and beyond.

The artifacts reminded her of her purpose in being here. Rosalie Warren and the Kalahwamish tribe were counting on her to be their voice. She had to give Rosalie the report she wanted without opening herself up to a lawsuit. She'd decided on a course of action. She couldn't publish conjecture or supposition, but she could publish verbatim transcripts of her interviews with the living members of the Montgomery family. She had to get them to say what she needed.

She sat on the couch and pulled out her annotated Montgomery family tree, which would help clarify the familial relationships while she conducted the interviews.

Jason returned with Laura Montgomery in tow. Laura was a whisky-voiced chain-smoker with stooped shoulders and more wrinkles than rayon at the bottom of a laundry basket. She was also the one Libby had pinned most of her hopes on. As the eldest living child of Lyle and Millie, she'd be most likely to have the information needed. The transcript of this interview could become a vital piece of Libby's report. Laura sat in a silk-covered chair with a tiny dog in her arms. The dog glared at Libby for several seconds before settling in its owner's lap and going to sleep. Libby placed her tape recorder on the coffee table and hit the record button before asking Laura whether she agreed to the taping of the interview.

Thorpe/Montgomery Family Tree

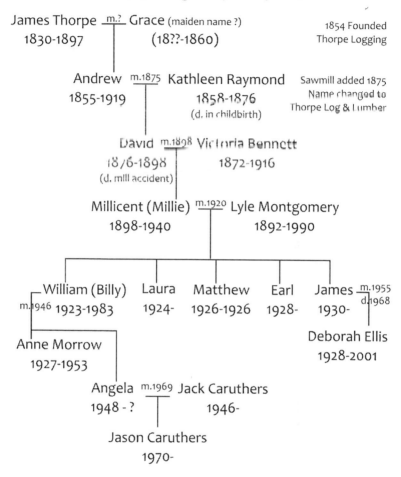

James Thorpe — m.? Grace (maiden name ?)
1830-1897   (18??-1860)

1854 Founded
Thorpe Logging

Andrew   m.1875   Kathleen Raymond
1855-1919   1858-1876
(d. in childbirth)

Sawmill added 1875
Name changed to
Thorpe Log & Lumber

David   m.1898   Victoria Bennett
1876-1898   1872-1916
(d. mill accident)

Millicent (Millie)   m.1920   Lyle Montgomery
1898-1940   1892-1990

William (Billy)   Laura   Matthew   Earl   James — m.1955
m.1946 1923-1983   1924-   1926-1926   1928-   1930-   d.1968

Anne Morrow
1927-1953

Deborah Ellis
1928-2001

Angela   m.1969   Jack Caruthers
1948 - ?   1946-

Jason Caruthers
1970-

"Fine," Laura said.

Libby's eyes flicked to Jason, who sat in a chair behind Laura, facing Libby. His expression remained passive. "And, Ms. Montgomery, will you grant me permission to publish a transcript of this interview as an appendix to my report?"

Jason looked as if he wanted to object.

Libby tried to look ingenuous.

"Whatever," Laura said. "I don't care. I know why you're here. We know more about what's going on in this town than Jason gives us credit for. That awful Indian woman, Rosalie Warren, wants you to write a history of Coho that only includes the Indian side of the story. I don't give a damn about Jack's permit or his Cultural Center. Why would we want to celebrate the Indians and their backwards practices? Waste of money if you ask me."

"I'm here to document the history of Coho, Ms. Montgomery," Libby said with restrained calm. "And if I only wanted to publish the tribe's version, I wouldn't interview you. I understand you managed the hotel for more than fifty years, starting during World War II. Can you tell me about that time?"

Libby could see the struggle on Laura's face. Plainly visible was her yearning to share stories of her proudest moments. From her research, Libby already knew about the time the hotel served as a hospital and shelter for passengers of a ship that sank in the Strait of Juan de Fuca in 1949. But her pride warred with her need to snub Rosalie Warren, and therefore, Libby.

"Girls like me who worked after the war instead of having children were resented for stealing jobs from the men," Laura began. "I had no choice. Daddy needed me to run the hotel." The desire to speak had won out. But based on Laura's expression and tone, she had chosen to make the interview as unpleasant as possible.

"When your mother died, her children—you—inherited Thorpe Log & Lumber. It was your hotel. Not your father's. Why did Lyle continue to run the company?" From Laura's expression, Libby knew she'd made a mistake.

"It's so easy for you to sit in judgment of us. You've heard some bad things, untrue things, about my daddy, and you want to know why we continued to let him run our company. You don't know anything about me, about us." As she spoke, she continued to pet her dog. But she'd become agitated and the dog must have sensed this because it looked again at Libby with belligerent eyes.

"I was only sixteen when my mother died," Laura continued. "My brothers Earl and James were even younger. Billy was eighteen, but he went off to fight the war in '42. Daddy'd been running the company since 1920, so it made sense for him to stay in charge. As we got older, we each took on jobs and responsibility for the company. Yes, I managed the hotel and restaurant. I worked there from my eighteenth birthday until I retired in 1995. Earl took over property management, which he still does, and James ran the logging operation, which closed down in 1999."

"What about Billy?"

"When he got back from the war, he tried to take over management of the sawmill, but Daddy didn't think he was ready for such a big job. Earl and James agreed." She paused, and then added quietly, "Eventually, so did I. Billy worked alongside Daddy to learn the ins and outs of sawmill management. He was preparing to take over. But that never happened because Daddy outlived him by seven years."

The Montgomery family operated on a business structure that resembled a monarchy. No new king until the old one died. Libby searched for a way to introduce a subject closer to her research questions. "Did the hotel employ any Indians under your management?"

"Oh Lord no! You can't trust an Indian to do an honest day's work."

"Aunt Laura," Jason said. "You can't say things like that."

"Let her speak, Jason," Libby said, knowing she wasn't defending the elderly woman so much as trapping her. "What about logging?" she said quickly to keep the interview momentum going. "Did any of the Kalahwamish do any logging for TL&L?"

"Yes. They were cheap labor."

"So they were paid less than their white counterparts?"

Laura's eyes hardened. "I wouldn't know about that."

"It was dangerous work," Libby added.

Laura said nothing more.

Libby made a note to check the mill's personnel records to see what the standard compensation for Indians had been. Jason couldn't sue her for including information documented in TL&L's ledgers.

The more she learned about the discrimination the Kalahwamish people had suffered at TL&L, the more she understood why Rosalie wanted this part of the history of Coho documented. But, if it was any comfort to the local tribe, Lyle hadn't treated his white employees much better.

"I do remember one time when an Indian worked in the mill management office. In the early fifties, I think. Billy hired him. Daddy caught the man stealing and beat him, then threw him out. No Indian was hired to work in mill management after that."

Billy was Jason's grandfather. Emotion flickered in Jason's eyes, but it passed before she could discern his reaction to Laura's words.

The interview continued for another forty-five minutes. For Libby's report, the conversation went splendidly. Laura continued to say things to paint the management of TL&L in the worst possible light with her racist comments. Sickened by Laura's words, she couldn't help but feel sorry for this woman who was raised with the anger and hate of a bigot like Lyle Montgomery. Who could Laura have been if she'd been born into a different family?

When Laura and her dog left the room, she looked satisfied that she'd vented some of her hostility, but Libby suspected she'd end up regretting their conversation.

Jason went in search of his Uncle Earl and returned with a wary-looking Earl in tow. She changed the cassette and hit record. She asked for permission to tape the interview and include the transcription in the report. His softly voiced "Yes" would protect her legally, but once again she wondered whether she'd pay a family price.

Yesterday she had conducted oral interviews with different mill workers, gathering as much information as she could about the settlement and management of TL&L. She had heard stories that Millie Thorpe Montgomery unwillingly gave up control of her company to her husband. Kicking and screaming, they'd said. One man commented that Lyle did the kicking, Millie the screaming. Some of those kicks broke Millie's ribs. Libby wanted to hear the official Montgomery version of events. "Your mother, Millie Thorpe Montgomery, ran the mill from the time of her grandfather's death in 1919 until she married your father in 1920. Then Lyle took over at TL&L. I'm wondering what you, Earl, and Laura were told about how that came about. Was the transition smooth?"

"My mother had no business running a sawmill," Earl said.

"My understanding is that her grandfather," Libby glanced at the family tree, "Andrew Thorpe, practically raised her in the mill management office. I would think she'd have known quite a bit about running the mill."

"That was before I was born. But the woman I knew could never have held such an important job."

Sadly, Libby suspected this statement was true. By the time Millie had Earl, she'd been married to Lyle for eight years. In that time, she'd had two late-term miscarriages and given birth to four babies, three of which survived. Libby couldn't help but wonder whether the miscarriages had been caused by Lyle's beatings. Earl's memories would only be of the grieving mother and defeated wife who'd lived in fear.

Jason sat in the same seat as before. His face remained impassive, and Libby wondered what he knew about his great-grandfather's abuse of his wife. Given their lunchtime conversation, she didn't think he'd volunteer the information.

"Laura told me her job at TL&L was running the hotel. I understand you took over property management when you turned eighteen."

"Yes."

Libby reminded herself not to be vague. To get him to talk, she'd need to ask pointed questions. "So your job was to manage the employee housing. There were many Indians who worked for the logging operation, and some who worked for the mill, but I've found no records to indicate any tribal members lived in company housing. Why is that?"

"The loggers lived in tents in logging camps," Earl said.

"And the mill workers?"

"The Indians preferred to live with their own kind on the reservation."

"But wasn't it company policy to exclude them from housing?"

"No, they didn't want to live in the TL&L houses."

"That seems odd. The mill houses were, and are, constructed better than the reservation homes. On the reservation, you might find two or three families living in one small house. I would think they might prefer a mill home."

"Libby," Jason said, casting her a warning look.

She knew she traversed a fine line. She'd managed to get her opinion into the transcript. It wasn't exactly what Rosalie wanted, but it would suffice.

Earl looked at Libby with unflinching coldness. "If you aren't going to listen to my answers, Ms. Maitland, then I hardly see the point of this interview." He stood and left the room.

Jason leaned forward and picked up her tape recorder. She fought the urge to grab it back. He wouldn't erase her words, would he? With Earl's last statement, she would look worse in the transcript than he would.

To her relief, Jason only hit the stop button. "I know what you're doing," he said.

"I'm doing my job."

"You could try your best, but fail. Rosalie can't fault you for that."

"Maybe I don't want to fail. Maybe I want to accomplish what Rosalie asked for." And for the first time, she realized she did. Millie's nightmare spoke to her on a very personal level.

"I'm watching your face as you ask these questions, and I can see that you're bothered. You don't like putting them on the spot."

"No. I don't. I feel sorry for Laura and Earl."

"But you're going to publish the transcripts. That's going to make them look bad."

"Yes," she said softly. Guilt stabbed at her. "Jason, I'm not doing this for myself. I'm doing it to get your father his permit. I'm doing it for Coho, which will benefit from the jobs the Cultural Center will bring. It's business I'd expect you to understand."

He stood and handed her the tape recorder. "I'll get James." He left the room.

She pulled out the cassette and broke off the tab that allowed the tape to be recorded over, and then labeled the tape with the date and Earl's name and tucked it away in her bag.

James entered the room behind Jason. James was the first of the Montgomerys to greet her with a handshake and a smile. "Let me guess," he said, "Laura was belligerent and Earl didn't say anything?"

Libby smiled with genuine relief. This interview looked promising. "Before we start, I need your permission to tape this and publish the transcript in the report."

"Sure. So, what do you want to know?"

"What I really want to know is: was your father the bastard everyone says?"

"He was worse."

Jason gave her a hand signal she interpreted as him taking his hat off to her. He leaned back, but she still felt his sharp scrutiny.

James sat at the edge of his chair and looked eager to speak. "What I really want to talk about is Billy."

"Why Billy?"

"He was the best of us. Jason here, his grandson, takes after him. You can write whatever you want about my father, but you need to balance the bad with the good that my brother did."

"What did Billy do?"

"Billy arranged the secret meetings that launched the first union strike in 1946. He knew Momma would have wanted him to. Momma hated the way our father ran the company. Billy was smarter than the three of us put together. My biggest regret is being browbeaten into voting with Earl and Laura to give our father his way. If I'd voted with Billy, it would have been a tie. We would have had to compromise."

"Billy didn't agree with Lyle?"

"Never. The two were always at odds. At first, Billy fought him in the open, challenging his decisions and demanding that things be run differently. But Lyle was relentless and would convince Earl, Laura, and me to oppose Billy. So Billy found other ways to get around Lyle. Everyone suspects it was Billy who got the union going. He didn't just arrange the secret meetings. He also must be the one who selected the strike date that would best serve the union. At least our mother had one kid to be proud of."

Millie Thorpe Montgomery was at the center of all that interested Libby in this heartbreaking family saga. The bright, vibrant girl who'd married badly. "Tell me about your mother."

"I was only ten when she died, but I know her grandfather raised her to run the mill. She cared about Coho and the mill and all the people who worked there. I understand she was a different woman, vivacious and warm, before she married my father and let him take over."

"I've asked your sister and brother this, it's important. Did she give up control willingly?"

"No," James said. "He used his fists to convince Momma to give up control. People here played dumb and acted like she betrayed them each time she signed another legal document that my father needed from her. But they all knew he beat her into it. We all knew. My earliest memories are of my father backhanding her across the room, grabbing her by the hair. Even threatening us, if she didn't do what he wanted.

"People blamed Momma. But no one stood up for her. No one protected her. And us." He looked down. "I hope some of them will begin to understand if they know the truth. Your report can do that for her."

According to Rosalie, Libby's job was to give the tribe a voice. Now James wanted her to speak for Millie. Yesterday a mill worker eagerly told her the story of how Lyle fired people for the absurd cause of calling his home "Thorpe House." Everywhere she turned, she found people begging for vindication because Lyle Montgomery had mistreated them. She feared the list of grievances was endless.

She interviewed James for over an hour, changing the tape several times. Unlike the interview with Laura, it was a pleasant conversation and would give her plenty to work with. Finally, James stood and reached out a hand to her. "It's been a pleasure, Ms. Maitland. I look forward to reading your report."

She quickly packed up her things and then stepped out the front door onto the wide front porch to wait for Jason as he shared a private conversation with James. She stared out over the town that unfolded below them. More than a hundred homes owned by TL&L were laid out in an even grid pattern, with the largest houses positioned closest to the seat of power.

It was here, on this porch, that Lyle had stood and viewed his domain. He probably felt as if he ruled the world. Behind him, inside the house, lived the wife and children he controlled through palm and fear. In front of him were the homes of his employees, people he controlled with low pay, poor working conditions, and the ever-present threat of firing and eviction.

Libby took a deep breath of sea air, hoping to cleanse her lungs and her mind from the oppressive thoughts. She looked down on the Shelby house across the road from Discovery Bay, pleased her borrowed home was as far from the Montgomery mansion as possible.

Jason joined her on the porch. "Well, I think you got what you were looking for," he said with mild sarcasm.

"Are you going to cause legal trouble for me?"

"At this point, my actions will all depend on the presentation. You're smart, Libby. Legally, I can't stop you from publishing the transcripts." He sighed. "Aunt Laura was a real piece of work. Nice job getting her to vent. Usually opinions like hers are only shared in the safety and comfort of a Klan meeting."

She smiled. "Now tell me what you really think."

He laughed and stepped off the porch.

She followed. "You're just angry with her because she spoke so frankly. I'm appalled by her views, but I realize where they came from. Personally, I feel sorry for her. For all of them. Everyone I talk to has a grievance with Lyle."

"Be grateful you never met him."

"I am. What was your relationship with him?"

Jason looked sideways at her as they strolled across the lawn to the front gate. "Is this for your report?"

"Personal curiosity. Off the record question."

"He was the meanest sonofabitch I've ever met. And that includes some of the scumbags I've defended in my law practice." He stopped in front of a rose bush. "And no, I won't elaborate, even off the record." He reached out and plucked a perfect flower just on the cusp of opening. He offered the rose to her.

Pleasure mixed with dread. Maybe Simone was right about Jason. Maybe he wanted to be something more than a legal advisor. She reached for the flower, noticing for the first time that he'd rolled up his sleeves, exposing his skin. On his forearms were several long scratches. Scrapes he could have gotten from blackberry vines.

8

Hours later, after interviewing a few Kalahwamish tribal members, Libby returned to the Shelby house. The disturbing encounter with Jason weighed heavily on her mind. She considered calling Mark and telling him about the scratches she'd seen on Jason's arms, but wondered how that would be perceived. And if Jason got wind of it, what would it mean for her relationship with her client?

But if Jason had been hiding in the bushes, he wouldn't want her to see the scratches, she reasoned. And scratches weren't conclusive evidence. Telling Mark would probably cause her trouble, make her seem as if she were overreacting again. She would, however, remain guarded in her interactions with Jason.

Tired, she headed for the staircase, looking forward to a long, hot soak in the claw-foot bathtub. She came to a surprised halt on the upstairs landing. Bright light spilled into the hallway from under the door of her office. She approached the room slowly, wondering whether she was being foolish—foolish for being afraid, or foolish for entering the room, she didn't know which.

She turned the knob, and pulled the door toward her, glad that this door opened outward, and therefore couldn't serve as a hiding place for anyone inside the room. She scanned the room, and then slowly stepped inside. She circled her desk, opening drawers. Everything looked normal. She sat in her comfy desk chair, noticed the flashing light on the answering machine, and hit the play button. The voice message was short and sweet: "Back off, bitch."

She dropped her head to the desk. Caller ID had said "Blocked" but she recognized the voice: Aaron. *Dammit.*

With a deep breath, she stood from her desk and looked around the room one more time but didn't see anything out of place, so she flipped the switch and left the room. She must have left the light on this morning.

She started to head to her bedroom, when another dim light under the door of the adjacent office caught her eye. Simone had a key to the house, and she used this office. Maybe she came by today?

She pushed open the door and glanced inside. The light table glowed eerily in the otherwise dark room. She slowly approached the table.

A piece of paper rested on the bright surface, a photocopy of an October 1940 newspaper article, which she'd made at the library just that morning. The headline read: MILLICENT MONTGOMERY DIES IN FIERY CAR ACCIDENT.

There was no doubt in her mind. She had left that page in her office on her desk this morning with the rest of the copies she'd made at the library. A tremor began at the back of her neck and spread the length of her body. Was this a warning? A threat?

She should call the police, but feared that once again, no one would believe her.

A loud bang sounded and she jumped.

Ohmygod. The door to her office had slammed shut. Someone else was here. She raced down the stairs and out the front door as she dialed 9-1-1 on her cell phone.

"Ms. Montgomery, I realize you're upset, but I can't arrest Ms. Maitland for stealing an arrowhead based on nothing more than your belief that she took it." Mark stood in the stark foyer of the Montgomery mansion with Luke Roth and Laura Montgomery. He'd been called there on his night off because Laura felt her charges deserved none other than the police chief's attention. He wouldn't have given in to her demands, except Libby was involved and somewhere along the line, he'd begun to feel protective of her.

Laura's drama had started when Luke showed up at the door to ask Jason his whereabouts on Thursday and Friday. According to

Luke, Laura Montgomery had immediately gone into hysterics, insisting Libby had stolen an artifact she'd just noticed was missing.

"But she was here today, in that room," Laura argued. "Who else would take it?"

"I'm afraid that's not enough for an arrest," Mark said patiently.

The front door opened and Jason Caruthers entered the house. His face showed surprise at finding two police officers in the foyer. "What's going on?"

"That woman you brought here stole from us. She took one of Earl's artifacts."

"What are you talking about, Aunt Laura?"

"Follow me," Laura said and marched into the room just off the foyer, where she pointed to a shelf on which several artifacts were carefully arranged in an arch. There was an obvious gap at the apex.

"Right there. That's where it was. Libby Maitland took it."

"Aunt Laura, that's ridiculous. Just because it's missing doesn't mean Libby took it."

"I know she did," Laura insisted.

"Why would she take it?"

"She's an archaeologist. Of course she'd take it. They all want the best artifacts for their collections."

"I'd like to speak with Earl," Mark said. "It would help to have a description of the missing artifact."

"He's not home, but I found this." She handed him a photograph of a shiny black arrowhead. "That's the one. You get a search warrant for Libby Maitland's house."

He swallowed his laughter. "I'll look into it."

Jason turned to him. "Can I talk to you in private?"

"Finish taking Ms. Montgomery's statement, Luke," Mark said and followed Jason into the foyer.

Jason glanced back at his aunt, who stood poised to eavesdrop on their conversation. "Let's go outside," he said. On the front porch, he turned to Mark. "You can ignore everything Aunt Laura said. There's no way Libby took anything. Aunt Laura probably hid it upstairs."

"What does she have against Libby?"

Jason sighed. "Libby interviewed her today. Laura said some things she shouldn't have while a tape recorder was running. She's probably trying to figure out the best way to discredit Libby. Maybe she's hoping to blackmail her into handing over the tape. Keep in mind, she's Lyle's daughter through and through."

Luke stepped outside. "Chief, a call just came over the radio. Libby Maitland has reported a B and E at the Shelby house. She doesn't know if the suspect is still there."

Mark was down the front steps before Luke finished speaking. "Radio HQ. I'm taking the call."

Jason followed him.

"Stay here. I don't need a civilian in the way." Mark hurried to his vehicle. When he pulled up in front of the Shelby house a minute later, Libby stood by the road under the old gaslight, clutching her cell phone in a tight fist.

"What happened?" he asked.

"I think there was someone inside the house. In my office."

"Wait here."

He cautiously entered the house. The back door was locked from the inside. If someone was there, they didn't leave that way. He searched the basement and ground floor for intruders and then headed upstairs to search the offices, bedrooms, and attic.

Search completed, he returned to the office where she believed the intruder had been and scanned the organized space, when he heard the sound of a car door. He glanced out the front window. Libby leaned against his vehicle, her arms crossed over her chest. Jason was with her.

"Crap," he muttered as he headed down the stairs, hoping Jason hadn't told Libby about Laura Montgomery's accusations. Mark wanted to see Libby's initial reaction firsthand. He hurried down the stairs and out the front door. "I thought I told you to stay out of the way."

Jason shrugged and placed an arm around Libby's shoulder. "I just wanted to make sure she was okay." Mark knew the motion was calculated, as it had been last night. But still, Jason's action irked him. Mark was dangerously close to feeling jealous. Surely it was only because of his and Jason's history.

"Thanks," Libby said. "I'm fine. Just a little freaked out." She looked uncomfortable, and shifted her shoulders.

The collar of her pumpkin-orange shirt caught under Jason's arm, exposing a bra strap in the exact same shade, making Mark curious—did she wear pumpkin-orange panties too? Damn, that was a tangent he didn't need but suddenly couldn't stop thinking about.

"Call me if you need anything." Jason caught Mark's gaze and smiled knowingly and then let go of her. "I'm heading to Seattle tonight. I'll be back Wednesday for the lecture at the library." Jason nodded to them both and then climbed into his Lexus and drove away.

Last night Jason had reacted to Mark's baiting with baiting of his own. Tonight he defended Libby from his aunt's charges and showed up to comfort her when he heard she was in trouble. Mark suspected Jason's actions were more complicated than simply helping out his father's consultant.

"There's no one in the house. Now I want you to do a walk-through with me, to tell me if anything's out of place."

They started with the basement, where a load of clean laundry lay on a counter. Several bras in vibrant colors were draped over a drying rack. He hadn't focused on this when he'd been down here before, but with the titillating glimpse of her bra strap, he now found he couldn't look away. Yesterday, she'd worn navy blue. A navy blue bra sat in the unwashed pile. Did she always match her bra to her blouse? The scientific method and ways of further testing this hypothesis came to mind.

He caught her flush as she noticed his gaze and smiled.

"Everything looks the same," she said and started for the stairs.

He touched her arm, stopping her. "I enter every room first."

"Fine," she said and stepped behind him, close enough for him to smell her perfume as they climbed the stairs. On the ground floor, there was nothing out of place. Same in the bedrooms on the upper floor. Outside her closed office door, she touched his shoulder to stop him. "This is the first room I entered," she said. "The light was on. I could see it under the door. I turned it off after I didn't find anything wrong. I figured I'd left it on myself."

"But now you don't think so."

"No, I think the intruder left it on."

Inside, she played the message on her answering machine. No proof Brady was the caller, but the voice sounded right. He collected the tape to send to Bobby, who would be a better judge of the voice.

He glanced at her desk. "Something I've been meaning to ask you. Did you ever check to see if you still have the spare key to your truck?"

"As soon as I got home on Thursday." She opened her desk and dangled a key from her fingers. He could read the word "Suburban" on the white tag.

As they were leaving the room, he noticed twelve familiar boxes stacked against the wall. "Aren't those the boxes we hauled up to the attic yesterday?"

"Uh, turns out they were handier to have in here."

"But if we'd carried them straight here, then we wouldn't have been walking up so many stairs."

She smiled. "Not nearly enough stairs considering the way you and Jason were acting."

He and Jason had been no better than two dogs fighting over a bone. He laughed, liking the fact that she was willing to call him on his behavior.

The second office was dim, lit only by the eerie glow of the light table. He read the headline on the page.

"You said this was your photocopy, right?"

"Of all the copies I made this morning at the library, this is the only one that mentions death. I know I left it on my desk with the other copies."

Mark switched on the overhead lights. "And you called 9-1-1 because you feel this is a threat."

"That and because I heard a door slam. It scared the hell out of me."

"Do you know which door you heard?"

"It sounded like my office door."

He stepped back into the hallway. Her office door swung outward into the hall and remained wide open, just as they'd left it. Mark remembered opening the door when he'd searched the house before Jason arrived. "Did you close this door earlier, before you went into the other office and found the light table on?"

"I don't think so."

A breeze flowed through the hallway. The office door slammed shut.

He turned to look at her. Libby's face turned white, and then she flushed and hid her face in her hands. "Oh, God. I'm sorry. I panicked. The window at the end of the hall is open, isn't it?"

"Yes."

She looked vulnerable, regretful. "I forgot I opened the window this morning to let air flow through. The hallway gets pretty stifling."

"You did the right thing by calling 9-1-1."

"No. I'm an idiot."

"You didn't know it was the wind," he said.

She dropped her hands. "I'm not doing much for my credibility, am I?"

"You're doing fine." The door slam had done more for her credibility than she realized. For one, it confirmed her story. Plus, seeing her fright and mortification told him more about her than any interview could. He led her back into the office with the light table. "Is anything else out of place in this room?"

She glanced around the room. "Nothing that I can see, but I'm not in here often. This is Simone's office."

"Who?"

"Simone Atherton. She's my field director. She runs the dig."

So, the woman Bobby met at the bar last night worked for Libby. Interesting. "I thought running the dig was your job."

"I can't be on site all the time. Especially with all these interviews I need to complete."

"Does Simone or anyone on your crew have a beef with you?"

"Simone's my best friend, and I haven't heard any complaints from the crew."

Mark jotted this information down, and then pulled out the picture Laura had given him of the artifact and handed it to Libby. "Do you recognize this?"

"It's a point. Looks like an Elko-Eared."

"If that Elko-Eared point was for sale, what would it be worth?"

She made a face. "Archaeologists don't buy or sell artifacts. I have no clue what that, or any point, would sell for."

"I thought the point of digging was to find artifacts."

"We only want to find artifacts if they can tell us about the culture of the people who made and used them. A point like the one in the photo is useless without context—I don't know where it was found, what soil level it was found in, what other artifacts or features were associated with it. I can't estimate its age beyond a two thousand year range—which is too broad to be useful—or even interesting. Without context, that point is nothing but a pretty chunk of obsidian."

"Do you keep the artifacts you find?"

"No. They go to the landowner, the government agency, or a tribe. We generally try to convince private landowners to donate artifacts to the local tribe."

"Do you own any artifacts?"

"No. Definitely not. This isn't a gray area. Owning artifacts could ruin me professionally."

"Laura Montgomery accused you of stealing that point from their house today."

She looked startled and flopped into a chair. "Oh, God. That poor woman," she murmured. "I knew she'd regret what she said." She looked him in the eye. "Just the implication that I stole an artifact could destroy my career. What are you going to do?"

"We're not going to expend manpower on an unsubstantiated claim of petty theft."

"I didn't steal anything from her, certainly not a point." She dropped her head into her hands and rubbed her forehead, and then looked at him, her clear green eyes questioning. "So what happens next?"

"I write up two reports: one for your B and E, one for Laura's missing Elko-Eared point. I investigate your complaint and file Laura Montgomery's."

"What if she doesn't let it go?"

"Without proof you took it, she can't do anything." He held out a hand to her. "C'mon. We're done in here."

She took his hand and he pulled her to her feet. She paused and looked at him questioningly. He liked the way her hand felt in his, so he tightened his grip and led her out of the room. He didn't let go until they reached the staircase.

Downstairs, she headed for the kitchen. She opened the refrigerator and took out a bottle of wine. "I've had a long day and I'm going to have a glass of wine. I'd offer you some, but you're on duty."

"I'm not on duty. This call was a freebie."

She began twisting a T-shaped corkscrew into the bottle. She glanced at him over her shoulder. "I'm getting a lot of special attention from you." She gave him the barest hint of a smile. "Should I be concerned?"

"Only if Laura Montgomery is right."

She rolled her eyes and turned back to the bottle on the counter, but struggled to remove the cork. He stepped behind her, took the bottle, and easily plucked out the cork.

She stood completely still, trapped in the circle of his arms. She turned and faced him. Her body remained stiff. "I'm not a groupie," she said softly. "If—if you're testing me, you can stop. I'm not a groupie."

"I stopped testing you yesterday."

"Then what is this?"

He grinned. "Extra credit." Her eyes flashed with heat and he could swear he saw her pulse jump. "Let's make a deal." He reached into his pocket, pulled out his badge, and placed it on the counter. "While we enjoy a glass of wine together, I'm not a cop. You're not a victim." He stepped back, immediately missing the rush of standing close to her.

"Deal," she said. She poured the wine and he joined her at the kitchen table. She took a sip and sat back in her chair, her tension visibly draining away. "So tell me something. Are you for or against the Cultural Center?"

"Mostly I'm for it. Jack's plan to build it could be a huge boon for Coho, a tourist attraction to provide jobs. The museum will be a big draw and Coho has needed a new library for a long time. The plan to include space for major retail chains has the Main Street vendors worried, and I know the tribe doesn't want corporations to sponsor their potlatch ceremony. But when you get right down to it, unemployment means crime. The more people employed in Coho, the easier my job will be."

"Do you think what's happening to me could be related to the project? Someone who thinks they can intimidate me to stop the project and therefore the Center?"

"It's an angle I've considered."

"Good."

"Why?"

"Because I thought I was your only suspect."

He smiled. "We've been checking up on a few people. Has anyone treated you oddly?"

"Laura Montgomery comes to mind."

He laughed.

"Do you think that artifact was really stolen?" Libby asked.

"No."

"Pothunters usually respect, or at least are interested in the native cultures they loot. Yet she said the most awful things about Indians during her interview today. But she collects Indian artifacts? I don't think so."

"She said the artifact was Earl's."

"That makes more sense, I guess. Most likely that artifact was stolen, but not today—it was stolen when Earl collected it." Her voice held a note of annoyance. "He probably took it from public land, which is illegal."

Libby played with her wine glass, and then took a sip, before continuing. "People tell me all the time about arrowheads they've collected from national parks and other federal lands. It's a difficult situation. I don't blame people who keep artifacts they find on the ground surface. It's really exciting to find a tool, even for me, after all my years in the field. But taking artifacts is looting. It destroys the context, all the information tied to the artifact is lost."

"Like when people move things at a crime scene. It can ruin the investigation."

She smiled. "Exactly, but the consequences for us aren't that crucial." She paused. "We use the Latin term *'in situ'* to describe an item that's been found in its natural or original place. Archeologists want to find everything *in situ*. I know the term is also used by other scientific disciplines with variations on the meaning. Do you use *in situ* to describe the position of items in a crime scene?"

"We don't, but it's not a bad idea." He sipped his wine and studied her, hoping for another glimpse of her orange bra strap.

The conversation flowed to other things. They talked easily, done with awkward silences and suspicion, and Libby's free laugh triggered a rush every time he heard it.

He was certain she was far too sane, far too intelligent, and had far too much going for her to be the groupie type. And she wasn't paranoid, which meant Aaron Brady or someone new was harassing her.

Mark's job was to find out who and why, and unfortunately, he should avoid her on a personal level until her case was solved. He glanced at his watch and was surprised to realize they'd been talking for over an hour. He needed to leave, now, before he acted on impulse and explored her creamy skin in a very thorough but un-police-like search. Regretfully, he collected his badge from the counter. She walked with him to the front door.

"Lock up behind me. If you hear anything that worries you, anything at all, even a door slamming, call 9-1-1."

She tucked her head in embarrassment.

He reached out and lifted her chin and then brushed his thumb across her bottom lip. "I want you safe. I'm glad you called tonight. I don't care that it was the wind. Promise me you won't second-guess yourself in the future."

"I promise," she said, her voice husky.

Her sexy voice went straight to his core. Want conquered restraint. He slipped an arm around her, pulled her to him, and then lowered his lips to hers. Her soft mouth pressed to his, welcoming but hesitant, while her hands rested on his chest. Cradling her face with one hand, he explored her lips with gentle, coaxing kisses. Her lips parted. A ripple of satisfaction coursed through him as he pressed closer to slide inside and taste her.

Her arms stiffened and she gently pushed him back. "I—I can't. I can't do this again." She looked down at the floor as she flushed. "I'm sorry," she murmured.

Her words brought their situation back into focus. The last time she'd gotten involved with a cop, she'd ended up with a stalker. Again he reached out and touched her chin, urging her to look him in the eye. Her eyes showed desire and confusion. He could be satisfied with that. For now. "I'm the one who should be sorry. But I'm not."

She laughed softly. He traced her bottom lip with his thumb one last time and then said, "Goodnight, Libby." He heard the slide of the deadbolt as he descended the porch steps.

He could get past her fears. She just needed time. He climbed into his vehicle, hearing Bobby in his head, calling him on the carpet for getting involved with a victim. But still, he planned to convince Libby that Aaron was the exception, not the rule.

He watched from across the street, in the shadows by the bay. His arms ached from holding the binoculars to his eyes for so long, but he didn't dare look away. He watched each of the front windows for an interval of five seconds and then moved to the next. He wished he knew where they were inside the house. He had to know what was going on. The police chief had been with her for over an hour. No one should have answered this call. No one should believe her at this point. What had gone wrong?

A muscle spasm in his shoulder caused him to drop the binoculars. He kept his gaze focused on her door and stretched his arms, feeling the pins and needles sensation in his fingertips and palms as circulation returned. The ache reached the excruciating peak, when there was movement by the front door. His hands felt like clubs as he raised the binoculars again. Pain shot through him as the weight of the glasses pressed against the raw nerve endings on his palms. But that was nothing compared to the frustration that flared when the police chief pulled her against his body and kissed her. *Shit.*

He dropped the binoculars and rubbed his eyes. Instead of putting them at odds, his plan had brought Libby Maitland and Mark Colby together.

The chief left the house. The tingling in his hands eased. He kept the binoculars focused on Libby. He used the zoom on the binoculars until he could count the faint freckles on her nose. Clearly visible was her dazed expression, the warmth in her eyes as her gaze followed Mark Colby.

He shifted the binoculars to the chief's face. The man looked pleased with himself.

He rubbed at the healing scratches on his arm, which he'd gotten when he scoped out the site, planning his strategy. He'd been so careful. He'd laid out the evidence to make her look paranoid. Insane.

The police chief should have written her off as a lunatic, a nuisance.

Time was running out. He needed a new approach. He had to scare the hell out of her.

9

L ou Warren, the tribal monitor personally selected by Rosalie, once again tried to put Libby in her place. "The Burial Treatment Plan clearly states that you are not to analyze the remains," he said.

"I'm not analyzing, Lou. Merely looking at the skull to decide how best to remove her." She instantly recognized her mistake and wanted to bite her tongue.

"Her?" he asked, drawing out the single word, making it an accusation.

"I'd have to be blind not to notice she's female. Even with that crack in her forehead, you can see how straight it is, and her jaw isn't even slightly squared. There's nothing remotely male about her."

"I suppose next you're going to say she's white," he said, full of self-righteous hostility.

"Not a chance."

Lou referred to a nine-thousand-year-old skeleton that had been recovered in 1996 near Kennewick, Washington. Kennewick Man became controversial when the examining archaeologist determined that the features of the skull were "caucasoidal." Archaeologists and other scientists wanted to study the remains further, as it was one of the oldest, most complete skeletons ever recovered in the Americas. Several tribes still fought in court to keep the analysis from happening. The Kennewick Man controversy was why she had to jump through so many hoops to please the tribe now.

"Don't write down the gender in your notes either," he said.

She tried to keep her voice cheerful. "I wasn't planning on it. My notes will be minimal." The post-Kennewick Man Burial Treatment Plan forbade scientific analysis and required that the soil around the body be collected and given to the tribe. She could not screen the dirt. She was allowed to write the location, type, and style of artifacts found in association with the remains, but couldn't photograph or even draw them. The artifacts would be reburied with the remains. That was about as minimal as you could get.

She scraped away another layer of dirt and her trowel snagged on a rock. Brushing it off, she expected to see another chunk of fire-cracked basalt, but was surprised to see a caramel-colored chunk of cryptocrystalline silicate. She quickly uncovered it. She had found a tool. After marking the location on her map, she picked it up.

"Here's the top half of a projectile point," she said and handed it to Lou, bracing herself for his next complaint.

He didn't disappoint her. "The break looks fresh," he said, clearly implying she had broken it. "Where's the base?"

"I couldn't have broken a rock that thick with just my trowel. It must've broken last week when we were using shovels—before we found the remains. We'll look in the soils we collected on Thursday to find the other half."

Lou placed the broken artifact in the bentwood box made by a tribal member to hold the remains and associated artifacts.

Libby wrote as much as she could about the point tip and then resumed digging. Her thoughts returned to the life of this woman, who'd lived and died around the time of the Battle of Hastings. Her teeth didn't show the usual wear patterns associated with prehistoric burials, especially for women, who tended toward more dental wear than men because they used their teeth to soften hide. Perhaps this was an indication of status, that she didn't do the same work as the other women in her tribe, or it could be a simple indication that there was natural fluoridation in the water supply. Regardless, that was the type of detail Libby wasn't allowed to record.

When the surrounding soil had been removed, she lifted the skull and handed it to Lou. He placed the cranium in the bentwood box, closed his eyes, dropped his head, and murmured softly.

She waited in silence, dropping her own eyes respectfully. She would give him as much time as he needed. She knew that most tribal members loathed working with remains of the ancestors. It went against their deepest held beliefs. But the spread of urbanization made

it increasingly necessary. Most tribes had to find one or two willing
individuals to consult with archaeologists during the removal process.
But being willing didn't mean it was easy or pleasant to oversee burial
removal. This was a spiritual issue, which explained Lou's hostile attitude. It must be difficult for him. Libby's annoyance evaporated as she
witnessed the toll it took on him to go against his belief in the name of
progress.

Lou's face was grim when he nodded for her to continue. Back
down in the excavation unit, she looked for the first time at the
smoothly indented soil where the base of the skull had rested. And
she had a problem.

The dirt was the wrong color.

She reached down and touched the yellow sandy-silt, sifting a tiny
amount between her gloved fingers. The soil should be the same rich,
dark brown floodplain silt she'd been digging through, but this looked
more like the fill dirt that had been imported to the site in 1984.

No. Not just more like. *Exactly* like the modern fill.

A few weeks ago, before the excavation began, the imported
yellow dirt had been scraped off the top of the site with a backhoe,
and was now piled in a large mound that cradled that part of the site.
She felt Lou's scrutiny as she climbed out of the excavation unit to
examine the yellow dirt. With her trowel, she scooped a sample from
the mound into a small zipper-top artifact bag, and then stepped back
into the pit.

"What are you doing?" Lou asked.

"There's something strange here. Soil where it shouldn't be. I
needed a comparative sample." She placed the bagged dirt next to the
indentation where the skull had been. The colors matched and the
sand and silt content looked the same. "Lou, we've got a problem. I
know you're not going to like this, but I need to look at the skull."

"Why?"

"The soil under the skull is modern. It's the fill that was brought in
before they paved over this area for the school bus lot."

Lou stared at her for a long moment before finally giving a slight
nod. He stepped away from the bentwood box, as though he wanted
nothing to do with this new desecration she was about to commit. But
at least he allowed it.

She climbed out of the pit and examined the skull. *Damn.* She
knew she was right, but she needed a second opinion. "Lou, I need
Simone to look at this too."

"Why?"

"There's something odd about this skull. I don't think she's part of the site."

He gave her a curt nod. "For your sake, Libby, you'd better be right." One phone call was all it would take for him to shut down the dig—permanently. In an obvious power play, he pulled out his cell phone.

Libby turned and called out for Simone.

"What's going on?" Simone asked, looking warily at the skull in Libby's hands.

"I need you to look at this."

Simone glanced at Lou, whose gaze was hard, meaning to intimidate. "Do it," he said.

She took the skull in her gloved hands, holding the mandible against the maxilla, preventing the loose jaw bone from opening. "What should I look at?"

"Her teeth."

Simone moved the mandible so she could see the teeth from all angles. She looked up at Libby, her shock clearly visible. "She's not prehistoric. She's not even Indian."

10

Mark stepped into the doorway of the squad room in time to hear Luke say to Sara, "I heard on the radio a minute ago the Maitland nutjob thinks she found a murder victim in the archaeological site. Ten'll get you twenty she's crying wolf 'cause she wants to get into the chief's pants."

"No way am I taking that bet," Sara said.

"But I will," Mark said, leaning against the doorjamb.

Luke's cheeks reddened as he faced Mark.

"Stepped in it again, didn't you, Luke?" Sara snickered.

Mark entered the room, pulling a ten-dollar bill from his wallet. He handed the money to Sara. "Give her ten, Luke. Sara'll be the judge."

"You can't be serious, Chief," Luke said.

"I'm completely serious. Care to make it twenty?"

Luke shook his head. His mouth moved, forming words, but no sound came out. He grudgingly handed Sara ten dollars.

"Okay, Sara, if Libby's found a murder victim that money's mine. If she hasn't, it's Luke's."

Luke recovered his voice. "Dispatch ordered a patrol car to the scene, but you called them off. If you believe her, why did you do that?"

Ordinarily, Mark wouldn't explain his actions, but he had been mentoring both officers so he gave Luke some leeway. "Because I'm going to check this one out myself." He turned to Sara. "You're assisting," he said.

"Yes, sir."

He faced Luke. He was pissed at the young officer but he needed another investigator at the scene and Luke needed the experience. "I'll meet you both at the site."

He left the room and headed to his vehicle. Several minutes later, he pulled into the gravel parking area that bordered the archaeological site, Luke and Sara driving right behind him.

"Stop being a pussy and get over it," Mark overheard her say as she climbed out of the squad car. "You only stand to lose ten dollars, not your job." Mark knew she hated whiners and treated them with the maximum contempt allowed by law. Luke must have had one hellish car ride.

Libby approached them from across the site. She was different today. Gone was the sleek professional who'd dressed in business attire to interview locals all weekend long. Today she wore a ragged pair of jeans with holes in the knees, an old stained T-shirt, and dirt on much of her exposed skin. He found this grubby, rugged change sexy as hell.

The last time he'd seen her, she'd pushed him away. Since then he'd spent more time than he cared to admit considering ways to change her mind and hadn't factored in seeing her in these circumstances.

A hint of nervousness flashed across her face before her features settled in what he'd come to regard as her cool work demeanor. Mark introduced her to Sara and Luke, and then said, "So, what's going on, Libby? I understand you think you've found a murder victim."

"I *know* I've found a murder victim," she said.

"That's for me to decide. You and others can speculate, but the homicide detective makes the call," Mark said, as much for Luke's benefit as Libby's.

"Okay then," Libby said with a slight smile. "I *know* we found the bones of a woman who was buried here on April ninth or tenth, 1984 —just before the area was paved. I'm speculating someone was hiding a body."

"How do you know the date?" Sara asked.

Libby's smile became a confident grin. "Like most archaeology, the information is in the strats."

"Strats?" Luke asked.

"Stratigraphy—the different layers of dirt. Come on, I'll show you what I found after I removed the skull."

Libby's employees were gathered next to a large rectangular area sectioned off with orange flagging tape. Within the rectangle, yellow string divided the area into a grid. Each square looked to be about a yard on each side. The rectangle was seven squares long by three squares wide. Several of the twenty-one squares had been dug. Three in the middle row were excavated consecutively, one several inches deeper than the other two. A skull lay at the base of the deepest one. In the other squares, long bones protruded from the dark soil.

Libby handed Mark a stack of papers. "Jack gave me these. They are part of the site history. Back in 1984, he had this area graded, filled, and paved into a lot for City of Coho vehicles and equipment. These are copies of the ." She then explained the difference between the types of soil, how she'd found the yellow fill dirt under the skull, and why that was significant.

"So," Mark said, "the fresh fill spilled into the hole someone dug to hide the body." He glanced through the papers in his hands and found the invoice for the fill. "It says here the dirt was delivered on April ninth."

"Exactly," Libby said. "If you look through the papers, you'll see paving began on April eleventh."

"So there was a two-day window when someone could have buried the body," Sara said.

Mark scanned the site. He could see tracks and teeth marks from the backhoe, which gave him a rough idea of the size of the area that had been paved. "She was buried right in the center of the paved area."

Libby nodded.

"So the person who buried her knew where and when the paving would happen," Sara said. "We can contact the construction company and see if they can give us a list of employees."

"Your first task," Mark said, knowing it was doubtful they'd learn anything useful, but they had to start somewhere.

"What else can you tell us about the skeleton?" Sara asked Libby.

Libby pulled on a pair of surgical gloves. "I'll show you what we found. When you walk around the open excavation units, please walk on the boards we've laid out. If you step too close to the edge, the sidewalls could collapse. And please use buckets as steps to climb in and out of the pits." She stepped onto an upturned bucket to descend into the pit and then picked up the skull, revealing the yellow fill underneath.

"See, here on the jawbone, she doesn't have wisdom teeth, but you can see by these bumps that they were removed. Probably surgically, because the wound healed cleanly. These other holes are where the molars should be. There is no healing; this is outside my expertise, but I'm guessing they were removed post-mortem."

"Which would make it harder to identify her in 1984—before DNA," Mark said.

"Someone pulled her teeth after she was dead to hide her identity," Luke said.

Libby shrugged. "I guess."

"Can you tell if she's Caucasian, Indian, Asian?" Sara asked.

"She lacks shovel-shaped incisors, which can be indicative of Native American ancestry, and none of her remaining teeth have wear patterns you'd expect on an adult prehistoric female. But I wouldn't dare try to guess her race without extensive study of the entire skeleton. What I *can* say with confidence—and my field director agrees—is this is a modern female skeleton, between the ages of twenty-five and fifty years old at the time of her death." She held out the skull. "She's not part of the site. Except for the skull, her bones are *in situ*—in their original, natural position. When we initially discovered the burial, we began saving the soil without screening. Those bags over there contain the soil that came from these three pits."

Mark glanced in the direction Libby pointed. Several dozen bags were lined up in the mid-morning sun. Condensation from the damp soil had built up inside the bags, making the plastic more opaque than clear. He turned to her. "Go ahead and put the skull back in the pit. The coroner will want to see where you found it."

A Native American stepped forward and picked up a wooden box that rested near the pit. He pulled out something from the box and handed it to Libby. "I'm leaving now, Libby. The tribe doesn't need to be involved with this. I'll take the box. You don't need it."

She smiled and nodded to the man. "Thanks, Lou."

Mark caught Sara's eye and inclined his head toward the man. Sara chased after him. Mark heard her say, "I need to ask you a few questions before you can leave."

"I need copies of all your excavation notes and everything you can give us that came out of this pit. As of now, we're considering this site a crime scene."

Libby turned to her crew, who had been watching their exchange with interest. "Let's get out of their way. Finish up your excavation notes under the canopy." To Mark she said, "I'll be in the RV if you need me."

"No one leaves the site until after we've gotten their statement," Mark said as Libby headed to the RV and her crew crossed to worktables covered by a large tent.

A few minutes later, Sara returned. "What did you find out?" Mark asked.

"His name is Lou Warren. He was here to monitor the burial removal," Sara said. "If he believed the bones were Indian, he wouldn't have left. He's no fan of Maitland, but he admitted she followed the tribe's protocol to the letter—at least until she found the dirt under the skull. He said he could've had the whole company fired from the project when she allowed her field director to examine the skull, but he permitted it because he knew she must've had a damn good reason for breaking protocol."

"If he knew about her three bogus police reports, he wouldn't be so quick to trust her judgment," Luke said.

"I handled all three of those reports," Mark said. "She's credible."

Luke's face showed his disbelief.

"You'll need to develop a better poker face if you want to make detective," Mark said.

"Am I allowed to speak freely?" Luke asked, a slight edge to his voice.

"Go for it."

"This is a load of crap. It's just a little yellow dirt. As far as Maitland goes, it's three up, three down, end of an inning, time for a psych exam."

"Good thing I'm in charge, not you," Mark said.

"Luke," Sara said, "none of us knows about skulls and shovel-shaped incisors."

"Okay, say she's right about the teeth," Luke said. "Those bones could have been buried here in the '40s or '50s and the headstone removed when the area was paved. Then all she would have to do to create suspicion is dump a little yellow dirt under the skull."

"Yes, and finding out the truth is our job. It's time we got started. You both grew up in Coho. Did anyone disappear from around here in 1984?"

"Not that I can remember," Luke said.

"Jack Caruthers' wife disappeared a long time ago," Sara said. "She was never found."

"Angela Caruthers disappeared in the late seventies. This can't be her," Luke said.

Mark considered Sara's statement. Angela Caruthers. Jason's mom. He hadn't heard of Angela or her disappearance until two days ago, when Libby explained why she needed Angela's research for the historical background report. He looked at the bones lying at the base of the pit and wondered what Libby could tell him about Jack. This was Caruthers' property. Had he balked at funding the excavation, knowing his wife's remains might be found? Did he have reason to believe the bones might be missed, or, as almost happened, been mistaken for a prehistoric burial and turned over to the tribe?

"Luke, call the coroner then start taking photos. No one goes in the pit until the coroner gets here. Sara, I want you to begin questioning the crew. I'm going to question Libby."

The door to the RV was open, so he stepped inside. The space was crowded with plastic bags, papers, and office equipment. Everywhere he looked were more archive boxes, including a tower of them that reached the ceiling just inside the door.

Libby sat across from a blonde woman, who was looking at a map that covered the booth table. Libby glanced up.

"I have a few questions I need to ask you," Mark said.

"Sure. Mark, this is Simone Atherton, my field director and right arm."

The blonde stood. "That would be a compliment if she weren't left-handed." Simone shook his hand.

He laughed. So this was Bobby's Simone. "Glad to meet you."

She held his gaze for a moment and Mark knew she was assessing him. He knew from both Bobby and Libby the two women were close, and Simone was extremely protective of Libby. He must have passed because Simone gave him a knowing smile and said, "I'll leave you two alone."

The door clicked shut behind her. He was alone with Libby for the first time since last night. She stood and looked flustered. "Coffee?" she said, brushing past him to reach the coffee pot on the counter.

"Thanks," he said. It took her a moment to recover her composure and resume her professional demeanor. He, too, needed to be professional and slid into the booth seat instead of doing what he really wanted and press close to her in the confined space.

She handed him a mug of coffee and sat opposite him.

"You've told me why you're digging here—Jack won't get his

Corps permit unless you excavate and get all the information from the site before it's destroyed. Do I have that right?"

"Essentially, yes."

"Could Jack have changed the plans for the Cultural Center so he wouldn't need that Corps permit and wouldn't need your excavation?"

"No. The issue here is a wetland smack dab in the middle of the construction site. He'd have to avoid the wetland and that isn't possible. Besides, Jack could hardly call it a Cultural Center and not fund excavation of a site that's important to the local tribe."

"Did Jack ever consider dumping the project altogether?"

"No way. He'd already spent hundreds of thousands on the project before he learned he'd need to fund this data recovery excavation."

Jack would be a fool to build on the property where he'd buried his wife. Mark knew Jack wasn't stupid, unless he assumed the body wouldn't be found. "Let's say you missed the burial during excavation. The site will be dug up during construction, right? The bones would have been found then."

"Not necessarily. It's easy to miss a few bones in a large construction project, especially if the equipment operator looks the other way —which happens, even with an archaeologist monitoring construction." She smiled. "It could be a honest mistake or incompetence."

He smiled at her reference to their conversation Saturday. So it was possible Jack had played the odds, but lost. "I want a copy of your proposal."

She paused longer than he expected for the simple request. "I can give you the scope of work."

He recognized evasion when he heard it and wondered why. "What is the difference between the proposal and the scope of work?"

"The proposal includes my overhead and budget."

"I might need that information."

"Then I would give it to you, but frankly, I'd rather not."

He wanted to follow that line of questioning but her reason for being protective of her finances wasn't pertinent to this investigation. "Tell me how you choose where to dig."

"Before we began excavating, I had a geomorphologist come out to the site with a ground penetrating radar. The radar shows anomalies, like how loose or compact the soil is, which can indicate a pit, or something structural like longhouse remains, all without the destructive process of digging." She pointed to the map on the table. "This is the map my geomorphologist made with the GPR readings. This star is the symbol he used to label anomalies that could be archaeologically significant. So we've placed at least one excavation unit wherever there's a star. This cluster of stars is where the burial is located."

Mark studied the map. Several places on the map were marked with one star; a few were marked with two stars. There was only one cluster. "Did Jack know you'd be using ground penetrating radar?"

"Yes. GPR is expensive. I explained how it would save money in the long run—with more focused excavation, we'd have less fruitless digging. He agreed."

"Has he seen this map?"

"He has." She met his gaze. "You think we found Angela Caruthers."

"I have to look at all possibilities."

"The dates don't match. Angela disappeared in '79."

"That's when she disappeared. We don't know when she died or even if she's dead."

"Good point."

He stood. He had one last question for her. The fact he hadn't asked this question first was a sign he wasn't treating her like a regular witness, a mistake on his part. "Libby." He paused. "Is there any chance this is just a normal grave?"

She stiffened. From the set of her shoulders and the tightness of her mouth, he could see she was angry, more than he would have expected from the implication she could have made a mistake.

"So we're back to that again. You don't believe me. You think I'm making this up for attention."

Caught off-guard by her interpretation, he threw up his hands and stepped backward. "No. No way. I'm just asking if you're certain, if there's any chance you could be wrong."

She stood; her movements were sharp, angry. "So you think I'm crazy, not calculating."

Damn, she was touchy. "Not that either. I have to ask this question. It's my job. You've convinced me, but I'm no expert on teeth and soil. I need to know if it is possible this could be a burial from, say, the 1930s or '40s, and not a murder victim at all."

She crossed her arms. "I don't know how the fill could have gotten beneath the skull if she was buried there before April 9, 1984. It would defy one of the most basic geological principles. Listen, if you don't believe me, there are tests you can do. Strontium-90 is a radioactive marker found in anyone who was alive during the age of above-ground nuclear testing. If she was alive after 1945, there will be Strontium-90 in her bones."

He reached out and pulled her to him, determined to break through her hard shell. She remained stiff in his arms but didn't push him away. "I believe you. But it's my job to ask for the test."

"I can give you the number of a lab that does Strontium-90 testing."

She smelled of earth and rain. Before he realized what he was doing, he'd reached up and traced her lip with his thumb, just like last night. "You're awfully prickly about this."

She relaxed by slow degrees. "I'm sick of having my credibility questioned."

"I wasn't questioning your credibility. Perhaps I should have asked this way: on a scale of one to a hundred, how certain are you you're right?"

"One hund—" She stopped abruptly and sighed. She leaned her forehead against his chest. "Ninety-two," she murmured.

He smiled. "So you're not infallible."

She looked up at him, her eyes no longer angry. "I make my share of mistakes. But this isn't one of them."

He smiled at that and then reluctantly let her go. He studied the map again. "Can I keep this?"

"It's yours. I have more."

He began to roll up the map, looking at the telltale cluster of stars. "That star cluster practically shouts 'dig here.'"

"Which is why we placed an entire twenty-one unit block there. I was hoping we'd find a longhouse." She shook her head. "Thursday was a bad day all around."

"You found the burial on Thursday?"

"Yes."

"The night your truck was stolen."

"Yes. Because of the burial I was here late, trying to get everything approved by the tribe so we could continue excavating the next day. I was starving and barely made it to the restaurant before they closed the kitchen. You know the rest."

"Yeah, I was an ass that night." His own words surprised him. He never apologized for doing his job.

She smiled. "You've grown on me since then."

At last, an opening. "You didn't act that way last night."

She raised her chin in a forthright manner. "That was instinct. Self-preservation. You're a cop. That alone scares me. But I'm also afraid you think I'm attracted to you *because* you're a cop, not in spite of it."

He allowed a small victorious smile at her admission. "You pushed me away because you were afraid it was another test."

"Yes."

"I'm done testing you. It wasn't fair."

"How so?"

"Because I'm attracted to you, too." He stepped closer to her. "You're attracted to me but you still pushed me away when I kissed you. I must not have done it right. I should try again."

She laughed. "And people think I'm crazy."

"I suppose now isn't the time. We'll just have to go out on a date."

"Is that really a good idea? I mean, with everything that's going on?"

"Probably not. Let's have dinner tomorrow."

"I can't believe I'm even considering going out with you."

He smiled. She was on the verge of capitulating.

"It's that damn dimple. I'm a sucker for them."

He deliberately widened his smile, knowing it brought out a rarely seen dimple in his other cheek. "Any other weaknesses I should know about?"

"You'll have to find them on your own." Her eyes held a challenge.

"I intend to," he said. He liked challenges. "So you'll have dinner with me?"

"I've got an interview scheduled tomorrow. Sometimes they go on for hours. On Wednesday I'm giving a lecture at the library, but I should be done by eight thirty."

"Okay. Wednesday. Eight thirty."

The crunch of gravel signaled the arrival of the Jefferson County coroner's dark gray panel van.

"Crap, it's Kreegen," Libby said. "The misogynistic, racist pig."

Mark laughed and said, "You know the county coroner."

"Whenever bones turn up that are more than a hundred years old, the coroner will call in an archaeologist to deal with it. His reputation precedes him. Have fun without me."

"Speaking of, I need you and your crew to vacate the site."

"Can we stay long enough to cover the pits and organize our equipment?"

"Of course," he said.

"Do you have any idea when we can dig again?"

"You should be able to resume on Thursday or Friday."

"Okay."

"I'll see you Wednesday night," Mark said, heading for the door and feeling pretty good. By Libby's own estimation, he had a ninety-two percent chance of winning the bet with Luke. But Mark had an ace in the hole, one that put him closer to one hundred percent: Libby could get into his pants without having to cry wolf. And she knew it

11

A t seven o'clock that evening, Libby served Simone dinner at the Shelby house. "I went to the site before coming here," Simone said as she filled her plate with spaghetti. "The cops were still there. The police chief said they weren't going to get the bones out of the ground today."

Feeling like a foolish schoolgirl, Libby wanted to press Simone for every detail of her conversation with Mark. "What's the delay?"

"Kreegen screwed up and the chief pulled some strings to arrange for a Seattle medical examiner to come out. The ME will be here tomorrow. They're leaving a cop to guard the site overnight." Simone twirled her spaghetti around her fork and looked Libby in the eye. "While I was there, the police chief questioned me about Aaron."

"And?" Libby asked, wondering why Simone seemed nervous.

"He told me to tell you what I did this weekend."

Alarm spread through Libby. "And what did you do this weekend?"

"It's no big deal. I decided to check up on Aaron and went to his favorite cop bar."

"Are you nuts? The guy's a lunatic. You shouldn't go near him."

"I was in a bar surrounded by cops. I was safer than a lamb in a vegan restaurant."

A small laugh escaped before Libby could stifle it, but the idea of Aaron fixating on Simone sobered her. "First, you shouldn't have gone there. Second, you should have told me."

"Listen, Lib, Aaron took a hefty chunk out of you, and the damage still hasn't healed. I'm not about to let him hurt you again." She paused. "I didn't tell you because I knew you'd get upset."

"Promise me you'll stay away from him."

"I'm just looking out for you."

"You can't, Simone. You'll only make things worse." Libby fixed her friend with a suspicious stare. "How did Mark know what you did?"

"Well, I had a little, teeny-tiny disagreement with Aaron in the bar…"

Libby didn't know whether to laugh or groan. "What did you do?"

"Nothing really, but another cop witnessed our argument. He questioned me about Aaron. Turns out the cop, Detective Johnson, was checking up on Aaron as a favor to Chief Colby."

"You're kidding."

"I wouldn't kid about this."

"When was this?" Libby asked.

"Saturday night."

"You mean you knew Mark had another cop checking Aaron out last Saturday night and didn't tell me?"

"I didn't know or I would have told you. The detective didn't tell me *why* he wanted to know about Aaron."

"When did you find out?"

"Twenty minutes ago when I talked to the chief at the site." Simone sipped her wine. "The good news is the police chief here is investigating Aaron. He's looking out for you." She smiled slyly. "You never mentioned that compared to him, George Clooney looks like a gorilla."

"He asked me out."

"George Clooney?"

"That ape? No."

"And you didn't tell me? You complain that I'm holding out on you!"

"He asked me out this morning. After you left us alone in the RV."

"I knew it! I could tell by the way his eyes followed you that he's interested. You did say yes, right?"

"I'm not a complete idiot." Libby chose to leave out the fact that she'd almost refused. Simone would harangue her for that alone.

Simone laughed. "It's about time you realized that."

"We're going out Wednesday. After the lecture."

"Perfect! Okay, for the lecture I want you to wear red, it's a power color…"

Libby knew her enthusiasm was genuine but suspected Simone had a reason to seize the change in subject. She didn't want Libby to ask her anything more about why she was checking up on Aaron herself.

S imone awoke to the ring of her cell phone. She found her glasses on the nightstand and stared at the lighted clock face. It was two a.m. She checked the display on her cell phone. The call was from Libby. Simone flipped open the phone. "Libby, what's going on?"

There was no sound.

"Libby?"

She heard an odd noise and then a loud shrill scream. The scream cut off abruptly, replaced by a gasp and a choking, gagging sound.

"Libby? Is that you? I'll get help!"

The caller hung up.

She dialed 9-1-1 and told the operator what happened as she threw on clothes. With the phone clutched to her ear, she locked her apartment and hurried to her car, trying to remain calm. The scream hadn't really sounded like Libby. She repeated that to herself and the 9-1-1 operator over and over.

She immediately heard the wail of a siren. She sped across the historic district and turned onto Libby's street in time to see a patrol car pull up in front of the Shelby house. The officer ran up the front walkway as Simone parked behind the police vehicle. The operator insisted she remain in her vehicle while the officer secured the premises.

The lights on the patrol car spun in circles, flashing an ice-blue glow on the house at regular intervals. Each ice-blue second felt endless as a thousand awful scenarios flashed through her mind.

The officer pounded on the door. When no one answered, he pulled back a large baton, looking as if he intended to smash the adjacent window. But the porch light came on and he checked his swing. The door opened. Libby stood in the circle of light.

Simone told the operator Libby had answered the door and hung up. She jumped out of her car and ran up the walkway.

"Simone?" Libby said. "What the hell is going on?"

"He was in the house. With you. Just minutes ago."

"What are you talking about?" Libby looked from Simone to the police officer.

Simone held up her cell phone. "I got a call a few minutes ago. Caller ID said it was from you. The Shelby house number, not your cell phone."

Libby's eyes widened with fear. "He was in the house?" She took a step forward, away from the open front door.

"I heard a scream. Then a choking sound—like what you described coming from the blackberry bushes."

"I need to see your cell phone, ma'am," the officer said.

She read the nameplate—Edelson—as she handed him her phone.

Officer Edelson checked the call log. "I'll need you two to wait here while I search the house."

They sat on the porch railing. "That was the scariest five minutes of my life," Simone said, feeling rotten—infused with adrenaline and stomach knots. Relief that Libby was okay mixed with anxiety. She'd stirred up Aaron, and he'd made her pay. He'd scared the hell out of her.

Libby had wrapped her arms around herself as she stared at the front door. Simone hadn't seen Libby this frightened since the last days of Aaron's stalking. And it was her fault. "You were right," she said finally. "Aaron is getting back at us because I went to that bar on Saturday."

"It's not your fault he's psycho."

"I shouldn't have let him know I was checking up on him. I should have been more careful."

They sat in silence, Simone stunned by the speed with which the situation had spiraled out of her control. Right now it didn't matter that her intentions had been good. Her intentions had been good when she altered the photos to help Libby too, but now those photos would prevent her from ever getting another restraining order.

Officer Edelson stepped onto the porch. "The house is empty. The windows are all locked and the back door is bolted. Ms. Maitland, was the front door also bolted before you opened it for me?"

"Yes. And the chain was on."

"You answered the door quickly. Were you awake?"

"The siren woke me. When it stopped right in front of the house, I got out of bed. I was almost downstairs when you pounded on the door."

"You were asleep before you heard the siren?"

"Yes."

"There's something I need you to see. I've already radioed for a crime scene investigation unit."

Curious, and more than a little worried, Simone slid off the porch rail. She followed Libby and the officer into the house. Upstairs, they stopped in the hallway between the two bedrooms. "Ms. Maitland, is this the room you were sleeping in?"

"Yes."

He turned to the second bedroom across the hall from hers. "When was the last time you entered this room?"

"I was in there Sunday when the police chief searched the house."

The officer pushed open the guest bedroom door.

Above the bed hung a carved Native American mask in a Northwest motif. A pickaxe had been hurled into the mask with enough force to embed the axe in the wall. Streaks of red spread from the wounded mask and dripped down the wall onto the white bedspread and pillows. The strong metallic scent told Simone that the streaks were blood.

Revulsion spread through her. *This is my fault.*

Libby staggered backward, as if hit in the gut. A noxious cocktail of guilt, anger, and dread mixed in Simone's belly.

She ushered Libby to the kitchen. The crime scene unit arrived and set to work. Simone sat and stared into a mug of coffee she had no intention of drinking. "As soon as they're done upstairs, you're coming home with me."

Officer Edelson entered the kitchen from the basement stairs. "I just found an unlocked basement window. The suspect could have climbed in and out through the window."

"That's a relief," Libby said. "I was beginning to think whoever it was had keys to the house."

"Who does have keys to this house?" Edelson asked.

"Simone. Myself. Jason. Probably Jack. You should ask them."

The officer looked at Simone. "I need you to tell me exactly what you heard on the phone."

"I think I heard a click before the scream. It could have been a recording."

Libby set her coffee cup down. "I wonder if the choking sound I heard from the blackberry bushes was also a recording."

"You're referring to the report you made Friday evening?" the officer asked.

"Yes. I heard choking sounds then, too."

"Using tape recordings is…different," Simone said. "He wasn't that methodical before."

"Maybe Aaron's not the one doing this," Libby said.

"Of course it's Aaron. Who else would it be?" Simone was surprised by Libby's doubt.

"At this stage of the investigation, it's unwise to make assumptions," Officer Edelson said. "We will investigate every possibility, including Officer Brady, but we won't limit the investigation to him."

So, he knew exactly who Aaron was. Simone studied him, trying to decide from his tone and facial expression whether he'd already taken Aaron's side. It was difficult to believe the investigation would be thorough. Cops had provided false alibis for Aaron before.

By car and ferry, Seattle was more than two hours from Coho. Aaron would need large gaps in his schedule to harass Libby during his off hours. Ferry workers would see him, perhaps remember him. She would find a way to prove he was the stalker. The first step would be to get a copy of his work schedule. That would be easy enough. She'd done it before.

Libby awoke to the sound of knocking on the bedroom door. Disoriented, it took her a moment to remember that she slept in Simone's guest bedroom.

Simone opened the door. "The police chief just called. He's coming over."

Libby glanced in the mirror. Tired eyes framed by hair that stuck out in all directions greeted her. A girlish shriek escaped as she fled to the bathroom, followed by the sound of Simone's laughter.

Simone lived in a small apartment building built by Thorpe Log & Lumber in the early twentieth century to accommodate the growing workforce. Five apartments had been provided to Evergreen Archaeological Consultants to house the crew.

While Libby showered, thoughts of what happened the night before ran through her mind. What did it mean that both she and Simone heard choking sounds? She rubbed her neck, remembering the feel of Aaron's hand closing around her throat. He'd been about to rape her, but with luck, she'd managed to get away. Physically, all she'd suffered was a few bruises.

Now someone used the sound of strangulation to terrify both her and Simone. She doubted she'd ever feel safe in the Shelby house again. But wasn't that the point?

She shut off the water and stood dripping in the tub for a long moment, gathering her composure. She didn't want Simone—or Mark —to know how rattled she was.

Dressed and in control of her emotions, she joined Simone in the small kitchen. "How long until Mark gets here?"

Simone glanced at the clock. "Any minute. There's coffee."

Libby poured herself a cup, sat and took a sip. She sighed. "I love you."

"Me or the coffee?"

"I'm not really sure. Both, I guess."

"You feeling okay?"

"Tired. Four hours' sleep isn't enough."

"At least we're not digging today," Simone said. "You can sleep after the chief leaves."

"I can't. I've got interviews scheduled from noon on."

"Are you going back to the Shelby house?"

She considered lying and saying she wasn't afraid of the house but decided she could show Simone some reasonable fear. "Not today. My interviews are at people's homes. I don't need anything from the office today and frankly, I don't want to go near the place right now."

"You can stay with me as long as you want."

"Thanks."

"Of course, you'd be better off moving in with the hunky police chief."

"Let me get through the first date before you start planning the wedding, okay?"

"For the bridesmaids, I was thinking of something froofy in a God-awful shade of purple," Simone said.

"I'm thinking fuchsia, with lots of bows. Especially in your hair."

"That's beyond cruel." Simone paused. "I like him, Libby. Don't let the fact that he's a cop scare you away. He's nothing like Aaron."

"I know. I'd be lying if I said his being a cop didn't worry me. Then there's the fact that it's been too long since I've dated. I've been ignoring my libido for so long I forgot I had one. Now it's awakened with a vengeance, and I'm worried the whole attraction thing is just resurrected libido."

"You're overanalyzing again. Enjoy it."

"Easy for you to say. I'm no good at casual sex."

"I had casual sex once," Simone said. "It was great."

"I'm pretty sure it was more than once."

Simone smiled. "Yeah. So am I." She poured another cup of coffee and leaned against the counter. "I received a voicemail from Dan Parker. He heard that we turned the burial over to the police. He sounded worried, like he believed there was still a chance the remains were prehistoric."

"He's probably hoping otherwise—this will turn into another Kennewick Man controversy. I'll call him."

The doorbell rang. Simone slipped into her bedroom, leaving Libby alone as she opened the door.

Mark's clear blue eyes scanned her from head to toe. "You should have called me last night."

"I figured you should sleep."

"If there's a next time, let *me* make that choice."

She moved closer, and his arms slid around her. She leaned her head on his solid chest. How odd that this embrace should feel as natural as breathing. She barely knew him. After several seconds she stepped back, feeling calm for the first time since seeing the blood-drenched mask. "Thanks. I needed that."

He smiled. "So did I." He took out his notebook. "The blood on the mask and wall was bovine. It could've come from supermarket meat."

"The pickaxe came from the site," she said. She began to pace. "We noticed it was missing yesterday when we took inventory after you shut us down. I figured it was buried in a backdirt pile, which happens all the time." She paused and then decided share her main concern. "My pickaxe, a mask in my home, and blood I could have gotten at the supermarket."

"Yes."

She stopped and faced him. "Mark, am I a suspect?"

"I can't rule anyone out without corroborating evidence."

Disappointment filled her. "So you think it was me."

"I didn't say that."

"But what do you believe? And I don't want an answer worthy of a politician."

"I don't date suspects."

She stopped pacing. Was he going to cancel? Maybe it was for the best.

"And I'm still looking forward to tomorrow."

She let out a breath she hadn't realized she'd held. "So am I," she admitted. "Does anyone else in the Coho Police Department believe me?"

"I haven't asked."

She resumed pacing.

He caught her hand and stopped her. "We're checking Aaron's alibi for last night."

"What about the other incidents? Could he have been here on Thursday, Friday, or Sunday?"

"He could have been here on Thursday and Sunday, but he has an alibi on Friday."

"Was his alibi one of the officers who vouched for him three years ago?"

He nodded, his face giving none of his thoughts away.

"You can't trust the alibi. They all lied three years ago."

"I need more to prove Brady is your stalker. If it comes down to your word against his, you'll lose. You've admitted the photos were doctored last time. I'd have to tell the judge that under oath."

"Great, I tell the truth and it's just another nail in my coffin. I didn't know the photos had been altered until after the fact."

"It doesn't matter. Your credibility is shot as far as building a case against Aaron." His look was apologetic. "If he's doing this, I need to catch him in the act."

Again she remembered Aaron's hand on her neck, cutting off her air as he worked his belt buckle with his other hand. She'd been alone, but she'd gotten away from him. She could face Aaron again if she knew someone would be there to protect her. "Then use me as bait."

"Like hell I will. We'll catch whoever is doing this with good old-fashioned police work."

12

O ver the last twenty-four hours, Mark had gathered information on the disappearance of Angela Caruthers. On August 21, 1979, she told fellow graduate student and officemate, Dan Parker, she was going to Coho to gather research for her dissertation. She climbed into her Volkswagen Rabbit, drove away, and was never seen again.

Weeks later, hikers found her car on an old logging road in the North Cascades National Park. The car had been completely cleaned. No fingerprints were found anywhere—not even Angela's. Jack had always been the prime suspect, but at the time of his wife's disappearance he'd been in Spokane with Jason, visiting his parents. The only way Jack could have killed her was if she lied to her officemate about her destination and drove to Spokane.

The Seattle Police Department, the US Park Police, and the Coho Police Department had investigated her disappearance, and Mark had leveraged Seattle's past involvement in the case to get them to provide a medical examiner in Coho. He had no proof the remains in the pit were Angela, but finding remains on Jack's property was enough for ME Rita Leavenworth, who now knelt in the excavation pit and used a small vacuum device to collect dirt from the abdominal area of the skeleton, while Mark made phone call after phone call, contacting the officers who'd investigated the 1979 disappearance.

After Kreegen's bumbling yesterday, it was a relief to work with a professional crime scene investigator, and Rita was the best Seattle had to offer. Mark turned away, satisfied she had her task in hand, and dialed the next officer on his list, when Rita suddenly swore loudly.

"This is a waste of time," she said. "For all of us. Come and look at this. You aren't going to like it."

Mark looked into the burial pit. The carefully cleaned skeletal fingers clutched an arrowhead.

"This isn't a murder victim," Rita said. "It's an Indian grave, just like it's supposed to be."

L ibby drove to the site immediately after receiving Mark's urgent call. The two officers she'd met the day before stood by the excavation area with Mark, and she was relieved to see Doc Kreegen wasn't present. Instead, she was introduced to a Seattle medical examiner, a petite dark-haired woman who greeted Libby coldly.

More disturbing was Mark's manner, which reminded her of Friday night, when she answered questions about Aaron. The exciting sizzle that usually emanated from him was absent. "I'm hoping you can explain something," he said.

She glanced into the excavation units. A bowl-shaped chunk was missing from the once vertical wall and the pit was a half-meter wider. "What happened?" she asked.

Mark answered. "The wall collapsed. Kreegen stepped too close to the edge, which is why he's not here. But that's not why you're here. Look at her hands."

The skeleton was completely exposed now. The yellow-tan bones lay in sharp relief against the dark soil. Interwoven between phalanges and carpal bones was an artifact, a large pale-green lanceolate blade. Libby looked at the ME. "May I look closer?"

"Pick it up if you want. She's not a murder vic, so I don't care," Dr. Leavenworth said.

Libby climbed into the pit and studied the tool. The size and shape seemed to be the most perfect example of Clovis she'd ever seen. But that just wasn't possible. A Clovis point would make this the oldest skeleton ever found in the Americas, and no human remains had ever been found in association with a Clovis point. Clovis artifacts were the oldest universally accepted evidence of the existence of humans in the New World.

"If she's not Indian, how do you explain the arrowhead?" asked Officer Roth, the young cop who'd been cold to her the day before.

"Give me a second," she murmured. "This can't be right." Baffled, she leaned closer. The sunlight caught an edge of the stone, making the glossy surface shine. The pale-green stone wasn't a cryptocrystalline silicate, as she'd first thought. The projectile point was made out of obsidian. It took her a moment to recognize the material, but when she did, the tension knot in her belly unraveled and she laughed. What a beautiful fake.

"What's so funny?" Officer Roth asked.

"Sorry," she said, "It's just that I nearly fell for it."

"Fell for what?" Officer Eversall asked.

"It's a perfect fake."

"You know that from a ten-second look?" The younger officer sounded incredulous.

"Yes. To start with, this is supposed to be a Clovis point—a spearhead for hunting big game. Clovis is the oldest of the Paleolithic blades, and pre-dates this site by eight to ten thousand years."

"That doesn't make the arrowhead a fake," Officer Roth said.

"Spearhead," Libby corrected automatically. "The implied age alone isn't what makes this spearhead a fake, but I can say that no Clovis tool could be associated with these bones. There is no way a ten- to fourteen-thousand-year-old skeleton would be as well-preserved as this one is. Bones would be broken, missing.

"You've probably heard of Kennewick Man. He's young compared to Clovis. Only about nine thousand years old. Scientists are eager to study him because he's the oldest, most complete skeleton ever found in the Americas. He was nearly complete but his bones were in pieces and fragments missing." Libby looked at the ME. "That's not the case here, is it?"

"No," she said. "This skeleton appears to be complete."

"But that doesn't mean this isn't a one-thousand-year-old skeleton buried with a twelve-thousand-year-old point," Roth persisted.

"You are correct. Archaeologists always have to consider such a possibility. Later cultures could have easily found and reused spearheads from earlier time periods and even buried them with their dead. But not in this case, because that spearhead is younger than you are, Officer Roth."

"What?" Mark said.

"How do you know that?" Officer Eversall asked.

Libby directed her answer to Mark, the person she most wanted to believe her. "The obsidian rock it's made of was manufactured after 1980."

"The rock was manufactured?" Mark asked.

"Yes. I've seen that type of obsidian many times. My master's degree is in lithic analysis. I studied stone tools and the way they were made. I worked with a professor who flint knaps—"

"Flint knaps? What is that?" Eversall asked.

"Flint knapping is part of experimental archaeology—a branch of archaeological research where we try to duplicate the tools made by prehistoric cultures."

"Why would you do that?" Roth asked.

"To help us better understand the culture and their technology. Anyway, I had a professor in graduate school who is known for his skill at flint knapping. He's known among archaeologists as the Lithic Master. I can say with one hundred percent certainty he made that point."

"I didn't see a signature on the rock," the ME said.

"His signature *is* the rock. Obsidian that shade of pale-green isn't natural. Not in the Pacific Northwest. That color obsidian is manufactured. It's been dubbed Helenite, because it's made from rock dust from Mount St. Helens. The professor I worked with uses Helenite to replicate stone tools. He uses it because of the distinctive color. It's his way of maintaining the integrity of the archaeological record. Every archaeologist in the Pacific Northwest knows that if you find a Helenite point, it's not an artifact. The Lithic Master made it."

"And how did your professor's arrowhead end up here?" Luke asked.

"Over the years, he's sold hundreds to tourist shops. Anyone could have bought it. Someone tried to make this grave look prehistoric, and it's not. Fortunately, obsidian hydration-dating will prove the stone is only about twenty years old."

Dr. Leavenworth held out her hand to Libby. "I'm sorry for doubting you."

"I understand. I was worried at first myself."

The woman climbed back into the pit and resumed cleaning the hand bones. Libby wished she had a vacuum like that for excavating.

"I'd like the number of a lab that does the obsidian-dating test," Mark said.

"I have the number in my Rolodex."

"And your flint-knapping professor?"

"I have his number, too."

"Of course you do." Mark smiled. "So my suspect knew this was an archaeological site. We're back to square one. This body had to be buried here on April ninth or tenth, 1984. In 1984, who knew this was an archaeological site?"

"In 1984, officially, no one. But the tribe has references to this area in their oral history so any number of pothunters could have known it was here."

"So the suspect knows enough about archaeology to recognize a site when he or she digs through one," Eversall said.

"Yes," Libby answered.

"Why didn't he or she just use an artifact from the site?" Roth asked.

"They might not have found one." Libby shrugged. "This part of the site isn't artifact-rich. The only tool I found while excavating the burial was broken. But your suspect placed a fake with the body, so doesn't that mean he—or she—knew this was a site and came prepared?"

"It looks that way," Mark said. "Keep that in mind as you inter-view people for your report. I want the name of anyone who had prior knowledge this was an archaeological site."

"Sure," she said.

Eversall hit Roth on the shoulder and waved a twenty-dollar bill under his nose. "You lost the bet. This goes to the chief." She handed the money to Mark.

"Told you we needed to wait until Libby got here before you decided the winner." Mark winked at Libby and then handed the twenty back to the officer. "Donate it to the fallen officer's fund, Sara." To Libby he said, "Let's get those phone numbers."

Inside the RV, Libby copied the numbers for the lab and her former professor. "I don't know what your bet was about, but if you knew I'd be able to explain the Clovis point, why were you so distant when I first got here?"

"I'm walking a fine line here. I called you in as an expert. I needed your professional opinion and our personal relationship couldn't influence your evaluation of the spearhead."

He called the tool a spearhead instead of using the terms artifact or arrowhead, both of which would have come more naturally to him. She liked his way of letting her know he was paying attention. "If I hadn't been able to explain away the spearhead, what would you have done?"

"Work here would have stopped pending the Strontium-90 test results."

"You still would have done the test." Warmth rushed through her. He respected her professional judgment enough that in the face of contradictory evidence, he still would have believed her.

"I'd have done the test because I would want to be sure one way or the other."

The warm rush left her in a flash. She'd read too much into his statement. She stepped away and turned her back to him. She began shuffling papers, anything to distract her from the sharp edge of disappointment.

A moment passed, and then his hands slid around her waist, and he turned her to face him. "If it were up to Rita, she'd have packed up and left right after she uncovered the artifact. I called you because I hoped you would have a reasonable explanation. You hit it out of the park." His lips touched hers in a brief kiss. "And I'm deeply impressed."

"And my sister said specializing in lithic analysis was a waste of time."

He laughed and brushed her hair off her cheek. "You sure you're not free tonight?"

The air thickened between them as warmth spread from her belly outward. "I wish." She chuckled at the longing in her voice and then sighed and stepped away. "I'd like to take pictures of the pit. To document the damage to the site."

"You got it."

She grabbed her digital camera and they both left the RV. Mark's phone rang and he stepped away to take the call. She snapped photos and chatted with the ME—Rita—about her methods for cleaning and analyzing bones.

"Why is there so much shell in the soil?" Rita asked.

"The shell deposits are from thousands of years' worth of shellfish harvesting. Shell neutralizes the soil's acid content, which preserves some wood and most bone. It's great for archaeological sites because it means we find plenty of charcoal for carbon-14 dating, animal bones to determine the type of game they hunted, and we sometimes find structural remains of dwellings."

"I'd heard that shell could deacidify soil, but haven't ever worked a body buried in shell until today." Rita went on to share with Libby details of some of the more bizarre cases she'd worked. While she talked, she worked her way up the spinal column for a final cleaning of the bones.

Rita stopped suddenly and turned off her vacuum. "Do you know bones?" she asked.

Libby nodded.

"Look at this." Rita pointed to a clavicle.

"That doesn't look right." Libby studied both of the exposed clavicles. After a moment, she understood. "They're reversed. And upside down."

"Exactly," Rita said. "Hey, Mark. You need to see this."

Mark pocketed his notebook and walked to the pit. "What is it?"

"She was buried here after the soft tissue decomposed," Rita said. "Whoever laid her out switched the collarbones. They're on the wrong sides, flipped backward, and upside down. Clavicles are tricky because they have an S-shaped curve that can look the same when flipped."

"If she was a skeleton by the time she was buried here, then we might be able to get some fingerprints from the bones." He paused. "Someone worked very hard to make this look like an old Indian grave."

"They nearly succeeded," Rita added.

"Libby, I have to ask this," Mark said.

That was how he started every question she didn't like. She braced herself but made a mental promise not to take offense this time.

"Is it possible this is a prehistoric burial that was uncovered when they graded the site, but they didn't want the hassle of dealing with the tribe, so they reburied her?"

"In 1984, they would just turn the remains over to the Kalahwamish or an anthropologist. Remember her teeth? No shovel-shaped incisors, no wear patterns, surgically removed wisdom teeth. And you have the fake Clovis point thrown into the mix—which no one would add if they were trying to *hide* this was an Indian burial. She's not prehistoric. But to prove it, you need to do a Strontium-90 test."

Mark looked at Rita. "Could a body decompose down to just skeletal remains in less than five years?"

"In the right conditions, decomposition can happen in less than six months," Rita said.

Libby had been thinking the same thing. If Angela Caruthers died at the time of her disappearance in 1979, she could have decomposed elsewhere, and then in 1984 she could have been hidden here.

13

On Wednesday morning, Libby returned to the Shelby house. She needed to go through Angela's boxes. With the dig shut down, Simone offered to come with her but Libby declined. She didn't want to be babysat. She promised Simone she'd keep her Taser and cell phone with her at all times. First she checked all the windows in the house. Each one was securely locked.

She believed focusing on work would keep her from getting spooked, so she went straight to her office and opened one of the boxes stacked next to the door. Angela and Jack must have saved every piece of paper that crossed their path. Angela's work was inter-mixed with old phone bills and receipts for everything from ice cream cones to automobiles. She had trouble finding transcripts of interviews with tribal members in the mishmash of papers, because none of the boxes was conveniently labeled "Dissertation."

Thrust into the role of voyeur, it was immediately apparent she was about to learn far more about her client and his missing wife than she wanted. She'd done a fair amount of archival research in the past, but this was the first time she'd ever searched a relatively recent collection of papers. The first time she personally knew the people involved.

Their phone bill consistently ran in the three to four hundred dollar range, with frequent calls to Japan. In the days before credit cards had become ubiquitous, Angela carried three in her name. They were probably the first on their block to have cable TV in 1977, and they chose Betamax over VHS.

Angela frequently wrote checks to the Warrens, the largest family on the Kalahwamish reservation. Libby wondered if the checks were payments for interviews and, not being her specialty, whether that was a breach of ethnographer ethics. Paying for interviews would have gotten expensive if word got around.

The Caruthers spent money extravagantly, with lots of cash moving in and out of their various bank accounts. No account ever held a large balance for long. Libby found stacks of collection and past-due notices, which were presumably offset by Jack making a big sale in his real estate business.

Jack and Angela had lived a wealthy lifestyle on sporadic income. Libby assumed that Jack's net worth took a permanent turn for the better during the late eighties and early nineties, because now Jack was a very wealthy man.

Jason had been a good student and his teachers included comments like "student is a pleasure to have in class" on his report cards. Curiosity drove her to look up his birth date on a report card to compare with a bicycle receipt. The BMX dirt bike was purchased two days before Jason's birthday in 1979. A copy of a police report was packed in the box as well—Angela had disappeared five days after Jason's birthday. The dirt bike was the last gift his mother had ever given him.

By the end of the workday, Libby had gone through and sorted eight of the twelve boxes. Papers were organized in piles within and around each box, with Angela's dissertation research on top, ready to be photocopied. She glanced at the clock. No time to make copies today. Simone would pick her up soon to take her to the library for the lecture. After that, the moment she'd been anticipating all day would finally happen: she and Mark would go out to dinner. She had just enough time to shower and dress.

Libby stood with Simone to the side of the Coho library lecture hall, watching as locals filed in and grabbed the last remaining seats. More than sixty people had gathered in the small room. A dozen would have been a good turnout. Already the room felt hot, over-loaded. "Apparently, all you have to do to generate interest in local history is find a murder victim," she muttered to Simone under her breath.

"I'm sure they're all here for *The Archaeology of Coho, Washington and Neighboring Environs from Prehistory to Present*. It's such a sexy title," Simone said.

"You would prefer *Temple of Doom*?"

"Now there's a name."

"I'm more of the Lara Croft-type."

Simone snorted.

Libby's entire crew was seated in the front row. She almost didn't recognize them. She rarely saw her employees without a coating of dirt.

Jack Caruthers was in a corner, conversing with a group of Cultural Center investors, who stood in a pack, all wearing the requisite dark suits and tasteful ties. Jack's distinguished graying head nodded in time to the enthralling conversation of the suits. A consummate professional, Jack knew how to work a room and make each individual feel as though they were the most important person there. He caught Libby's eye and winked at her. She wondered if he could read minds, too.

Most of the investors had strong ties to the community. Libby had interviewed a few of them for the project, including the mayor, Chuck Nalley, and James Montgomery, both of whom stood with Jack now.

Jason entered the room, looking like a cover shot from a men's fashion magazine, right down to the slightly mussed hair and evening stubble. Simone came to attention. Libby knew Simone better than anyone, and for the first time realized her best friend was infatuated with Jason Caruthers. Somehow she'd missed this completely. Even more odd, Simone wasn't the type to sit back and wait for a guy to notice her. So why hadn't she been her usual brazen self and gone after Jason?

The answer came to Libby in a rush. Her friend had worried about Libby's reluctance to date after Aaron, and so Simone had urged her to pursue the one man she wanted for herself.

Jason approached them, his gaze on Libby, ignoring Simone. This was a first. Blonde, buxom, and built, Simone had a loud voice, a louder laugh, and no shyness that Libby had ever been able to discern. Simone was usually at the center of any gathering. Some readily dismissed her as a bimbo, but she had an IQ in the genius range and a PhD to prove she was willing to use it.

When greeted by Jason, Simone coolly shook his hand and remained uncharacteristically quiet. With a polite nod, Jason joined his father and the Cultural Center investors. While Libby had been focused on Jason and Simone, Mark had arrived. He stood in the back next to Officer Roth. She caught his eye and smiled. His answering grin triggered a shiver of anticipation.

"Did you know Dan Parker was coming?" Simone whispered, nabbing her attention.

"What?"

Simone poked her in the ribs and subtly flicked her head toward the doorway where the Corps archaeologist stood.

"No," Libby said. "I had no idea he'd be here."

"Do you think he's here because he's still worried about the burial?"

"I hope not. I told him the medical examiner found conclusive proof that the burial was less than thirty years old."

"Knowing Dan, he won't relax unless he reads the medical examiner's report himself."

Dan made a beeline to Jack and his cronies. Jack patted him on the back and introduced him to the group. Libby supposed they'd met face to face while working out the details of the project, but still, the greeting was friendlier than she would have expected.

Lou Warren pushed Rosalie Warren's wheelchair into the lecture room. Libby hadn't been aware the elder had left the hospital. Now she was nervous. Bad enough that everyone in Coho was here. She hadn't expected the representative from the Corps of Engineers or the elder. These people had the power to make or break her project.

Libby stepped up to the podium. "Good evening," she said into the microphone. "It's almost time to begin, but I see that we have a crowd that will test the limits set by the fire marshal—unless he's the only person in Coho who isn't here?"

"Nope, I'm here," a middle-aged man called out, garnering chuckles from the crowd.

"I just want to make sure you're all in the right place. Tonight I'll be lecturing on the archaeology of Coho. Are you all sure this is where you want to be?"

More laughter followed, especially from her crew. Alex stood, pretending to leave.

"Sit down, Alex, or you're fired," she said.

Her crew laughed the loudest, and Alex winked at her and dropped into his seat.

"You should all be aware," she said, "that I will only talk and take questions about *archaeological* findings. For something to be archaeological, it must be at least one hundred years old. If it happened after 1902, then neither I nor my staff will discuss it."

A man in the back row said, "What about the body you found? Will you talk about that?"

"No. That's not part of the site." She waited a moment. No one left the room.

M ark stood against the back wall next to Luke and watched Libby. She looked stunning in a red blouse that was a striking contrast to her pale skin and dark hair. He remembered the red bra he'd seen in her basement a few nights ago, and the first few minutes of the lecture was lost as he pondered her underwear.

A good lecturer, she was calm, poised, and smooth. He had to admit that while he found archaeology interesting, he wouldn't usually attend this type of lecture. But she made a point of including interesting little-known facts and joking asides about the trials of fieldwork that kept the audience amused and listening. She played to the local crowd and stayed focused on Olympic Peninsula prehistory. Much of the information came from the earlier testing phase of the excavation, and he looked forward to a follow-up lecture when the current dig was completed.

His cell phone vibrated on his hip. He checked the caller ID display and then quietly slipped out of the room. "What've you got, Sara?"

"I'm still with Rita. We finally located the dental records. Because of the missing teeth, the ID is only preliminary but we're ninety percent certain it's Angela Caruthers. Angela had fillings in the missing teeth. If we had those teeth, we'd be certain."

Relief spread through him. He hadn't wanted to admit he feared Libby would end up being wrong. "We've now got a starting point for our investigation. Any prints?"

"No. She focused on the long bones and skull, and of course, the clavicles. Could be that the suspect wore gloves, could be time and erosion."

"Keep a lid on the ID until DNA comes back on Friday. As soon as the press gets wind of the fact that we found Angela, we'll have a circus. I'd like to do some investigating before that happens."

"You're not going to tell Jack?"

"He's waited this long. He can wait for the definitive ID."

"I'd like to stay another day and watch Rita at work. I'm learning a lot."

"Sure. Come back when she's finished processing the remains." Sara had good instincts; in a bigger police department she would go far but in Coho there wasn't much room for her to advance. He hoped her roots in Coho were strong enough to keep her here, but the day might come when she'd leave for the thrill of working in a larger city.

He'd done the same thing himself once upon a time. But after several years as a homicide detective in Seattle, he found he missed small towns and community policing. Unless Angela Lansbury lived in the neighborhood, small towns didn't have a need for full-time homicide detectives. The only way back to Mayberry was either to move up or down. So he earned a master's degree, which gave him the qualification he needed to be police chief, and the job opening in Coho had come at the perfect time. He had the life he wanted. All that was missing was someone to share it with.

Mark quietly returned to the lecture room and resumed his place in the back next to Luke. His mind raced, planning avenues of investigation. Jack would have been a fool to hide her body and then embark on a development project that would result in digging her up. But as he'd told Libby so often, he had to investigate every possibility.

He watched Libby, his mind focused not on the lecture but on the past two days. She could have ignored the subtle clues and blithely handed over the remains to the tribe. No one would have been the wiser. But she hadn't. She'd struggled with his skepticism about her stalking complaints yet she'd had the guts to step forward and say what she believed, knowing she would face more skepticism. He respected that.

He'd been attracted to her from the first moment he saw her, amused by the jokes she made about her truck, but the more he got to know her, the more impressed he was with her sharp mind. He trusted Bobby's judgment about Aaron, and he trusted his own instincts about Libby.

Finished with the lecture, Libby offered to answer questions from the audience. A man who identified himself as a reporter for the *Seattle*

Times said, "You've claimed a prehistoric burial you found in the site is a twentieth-century murder victim. You've also reported several spurious crimes to the police in the last several days. Ms. Maitland, are you trying to generate publicity for your company?"

"Perhaps you missed my earlier announcement. If so, I will reiterate. I will only answer questions about the archaeological findings at the site." She looked away from the reporter. "Any other questions?"

"The public has the right to know if a publicity hound is wasting taxpayer money on a ridiculous investigation," the reporter said

Simone Atherton and Jason Caruthers had both turned in their seats and glared at the reporter, who sat several rows behind them. A man Mark recognized from Libby's field crew stood, hands fisted. Mark stepped forward to prevent the young archaeologist from taking action that could land him in jail. "Questions about the investigation should be directed to the Coho Police Department, not Ms. Maitland."

"Does anyone have questions about archaeology in Coho?" Libby asked.

"My son is interested in archaeology," a woman in the third row called out. "He'd like to volunteer to dig on your project."

Libby's shoulders relaxed as she faced the woman. "I'm sorry, but supervision, training, and insurance all make it cost prohibitive to work with volunteers. He should sign up for a field school through a university."

The reporter headed for the door. Mark followed him out of the room and flashed his badge. "Mark Colby, Coho Police Chief. You seemed more interested in causing trouble than asking unbiased questions."

The man was unfazed. "My questions were legit."

"Your interview technique sucks. Either you're completely green or you've got a different agenda."

The reporter shrugged. "I blew it. I guess I must be green."

"Who told you Libby's been reporting spurious crimes?"

"I don't have to tell you that."

"I have an open investigation. The woman is in danger. Your source could be her stalker."

"I don't have to reveal my source. And I don't think she *has* a stalker. She's paranoid or she wants attention. Frankly, I think she's after attention. I'm gonna make sure she gets it."

Anger pulsed through Mark. The selfish bastard would ruin Libby's reputation by writing a lurid article for his own gain. "You go to press without including a statement the Coho Police Department has no reason to doubt her claims and you'll find yourself in a libel lawsuit."

"What's your beef, Chief? You sleeping with her?" The man's smug smile made Mark want to deck him.

"She's the victim of several crimes and you intend to victimize her again in print. I don't have to be sleeping with her to have a problem with that."

"The difference between you and me is I don't think she's the victim. I think you and the citizens of Coho are." The reporter left the library.

Mark stepped back into the lecture room to see that the question-and-answer period had ended. He quietly told Luke about Sara's phone call.

"Damn," Luke said. "I can't believe it. Around here, Caruthers' disappearance has the same mystique as Jimmy Hoffa's."

"Which is why we're keeping it quiet until the DNA comes back on Friday. I don't want any mistakes on this one."

Luke nodded and left.

Libby stood in conversation with Jason and another man Mark didn't recognize. She caught his gaze over the man's shoulder. He made a show of looking at his watch. It was exactly eight thirty. Her lips curved in a sexy smile.

Jason reached out and touched Libby's arm. He laughed at something the other man said. Mark couldn't help but notice Jason's hand lingered longer than necessary for a casual touch.

Mark had spent much of the lecture scanning the room for potential stalkers, wondering if the suspect was present. Could Jason Caruthers be the one, or was it their shared history that made Mark want to investigate him?

The reporter did his job well. His question was thinly veiled insinuation, designed to make the residents of Coho look at Libby Maitland with suspicion. Manipulating the reporter had been even easier than slipping the Suburban key back in the desk drawer at the Shelby house. The guy was a Bob Woodward wannabe, hungry for a salacious story, the kind of cub who believed his own lies. He'd told the cub he was a cop on the Coho police force and was frustrated to be working bogus cases reported by the chief's new girlfriend. The ruse was inspired, a guarantee the reporter wouldn't look too hard to find his source. Who would give up a cop as an informant?

Half the town heard the reporter say she was a publicity hound. Maybe the police chief would even have second thoughts about her.

Time was running out for him to deliver the final blow to Libby Maitland's credibility. He'd be waiting for her when she got home tonight. By the time he was through, she wouldn't be a threat to him anymore.

14

Libby stood with Dan and Jason, waiting for the endless post-lecture chit-chat to be over with so she could join Mark. She'd lost her focus on the conversation as soon as Mark stepped back into the room. She was certain the Corps archaeologist and her client's son were going to leave thinking she was a blithering idiot.

"Libby," Dan said, "I think I have a box or two of Angela's research papers to give to you, too."

Dan gained her full attention. "What? Why would you have Angela's papers?"

"I went to grad school with her. We were officemates at U-Dub. I've known Jason here since he was a pup, but hadn't seen him or Jack in decades."

A lightning-fast shiver ran through her. Dan could easily have gotten the spearhead from the Lithic Master. Had Dan known about the Warren site before they'd found it in their survey last fall? "Why didn't you tell me you had boxes of Angela's Kalahwamish research notes when you told me about the detailed background section Rosalie wants?" she asked.

"I'd forgotten which Olympic Peninsula tribe Angela was study-ing," Dan said. "It was nearly twenty-five years ago. You know how cultural anthropologists and archaeologists get along." He smiled at the inside joke. Libby knew well the friendly rivalry that existed between the two anthropological disciplines. "She didn't talk about her work much," Dan continued. "It was later that Jack reminded me she was studying the Kalahwamish."

Libby wondered why Angela's research had left such a void in everyone's memory.

"I packed up her remaining papers when I finished my PhD and moved out of the office in '81. Never got around to giving her papers to Jack. They're in storage somewhere. I'll see if I can find them this weekend." Dan paused. "How's the draft coming?"

"I'm nearly done with the interviews. Today I went through several of Angela's boxes. The police are allowing us to resume digging tomorrow, so I'll be at the site in the morning but by the afternoon Angela's papers will be my primary focus."

"I'd like to see a draft as soon as possible," Dan said.

Libby continued to smile, not wanting to show what she really thought. She was dealing with a stalker and finding dead bodies, and he wanted to see a draft.

Laura Montgomery tapped Jason on the shoulder. "I'm leaving," she said, casting a glare at Libby. Earl stood next to Laura, his look equally menacing.

It was too much. The stalker, a murder victim, this hostile elderly woman who'd accused her of stealing an artifact, and, she reminded herself, the nasty reporter who would probably be more than happy to ruin Libby's reputation. She wanted this part of her day to end. She had better plans.

At last, the room cleared, and she was alone with Mark. He smiled at her, and all worries slipped from her mind.

"I enjoyed your talk," he said.

She smiled. "Oh, is that why you left the room?"

"That was unavoidable. Work."

Something was different. She wasn't sure what. His curly light brown hair and blue eyes were as knee-weakeningly handsome as ever. The she realized the change: he was off-duty. Not like Sunday night, when he was off-duty but answered her 9-1-1 call. Tonight, he was completely off-duty. He always wore plain clothes, but tonight he was without the shoulder holster. Wearing a gun altered his stance; he emanated heightened awareness, reminding everyone he was top cop in town. But now he looked…relaxed. Ready for a night off. And yet she knew he would still answer his phone, during a lecture, in a restaurant, in a movie theater. For him to be truly off-duty, he'd have to leave town.

Could she really get involved with someone whose work was so much a part of him, so important, he had to answer the phone no matter what, even while making love?

"I don't pass inspection?" he asked.

She'd been staring at him, and now she realized she'd frowned. "You more than pass. You set a new standard."

"Then why the frown?"

"I was just wondering what the odds are we'd have a whole evening without any interruptions from your cell phone."

He flinched. Obviously, this had been a problem in the past. He put an arm around her waist, pulling her against him. "We have many issues to navigate, and that's probably one of the biggest. For now, just know I'm not waiting for the phone to ring. I'm not thinking about work. I intend to enjoy every moment we have together. The rest is out of my control. But I won't apologize for doing my job."

She rose up on tiptoes and pressed her lips against his. "I wouldn't expect you to. I'm sorry. I feel stupid for complaining. I want to bite my tongue."

His smile came like a breaking wave, pulling her into a dangerous undertow. "Thank you, but don't bite your tongue. I'm hoping that will be my job."

A fluttery, giddy feeling infused her as his mouth lowered to hers.

"Sorry to interrupt, but I need to lock up the library."

She flushed as she faced the head librarian. Caught making out in the library. She felt like a teenager, except they hadn't gotten to the good part yet. "We were just leaving."

Mark took her hand and led her through the doorway past the librarian, who, Libby could see, was having trouble maintaining a stern face.

"Couldn't you have waited thirty seconds, Wanda?" he asked, laughter in his voice.

"Honey, that was no quick kiss you were getting ready to plant on Libby."

Mark threaded his fingers through hers as they walked down Main Street. The Coho library was in the same part of town as the police station. After unionization came to Thorpe Log & Lumber in the late 1940s, a separate Coho developed outside the historic district. This secondary hub of shops, restaurants, and municipal buildings had been outside Lyle Montgomery's control.

Residential areas radiated outward from this part of town. The majority of Coho's three thousand residents lived and worked here, and more than geography separated the two town centers. While the historic district represented a community before electricity, telephones, and automobiles, Main Street was pure 1950s Americana. Neon progress.

Mark had made reservations at a small restaurant three blocks down. They sat in a private booth in the corner. All five restaurant employees found an excuse to come by their table to check Libby out. Everyone treated Mark with deference, and from the proprietor there was banter filled with genuine fondness.

She knew Mark was an outsider, like her. He'd only lived in Coho for two years. Yet they'd accepted him as one of their own. She couldn't help but compare Mark's interactions with the locals to the obsequiousness given Jason. More important, when she was with Jason, her body didn't hum like a tuning fork in perfect pitch.

Mark's gaze met hers and the pleasant hum changed octaves. She actually might sleep with him tonight. She'd caught Simone shoving condoms into her purse and scoffed at the gesture because Simone knew Libby never, ever, slept with someone so early in a relationship. She usually took weeks to decide if she was willing to get naked and vulnerable. She came close to breaking that rule with Aaron. The mistake had cost her.

But now, tonight, a terrifying but exhilarating recklessness swept through her. She sipped her wine and enjoyed the heat her companion elicited.

After dinner, they walked to the police station to get Mark's car. With an apology, he left her alone in the parking lot while he went inside. He returned moments later carrying a brown paper bag.

They drove to the historic district and parked next to the sawmill. He grabbed the bag and took her hand as they walked down a long dock that extended out over Discovery Bay. Full darkness had descended, and a canopy of stars glittered above them, the only sounds their footsteps on the wooden dock and the small waves lapping against the pilings.

They sat on a bench at the end of the dock. The water shimmered as ripples caught the starlight. Mark pulled from the bag a bottle of wine and two glasses, followed by two spoons and a pint of Ben & Jerry's Chunky Monkey ice cream.

Libby loved Chunky Monkey with a passion that bordered on mania. This was no lucky guess. "How did you know?"

"I asked Simone." He grinned. "I told you I'd find your weaknesses."

"No fair. If I want to know about you, who do I get to ask?"

"Me," he said.

"You'll answer any question I ask you?"

"We can even use the polygraph machine if you want."

"That sounds like fun."

She scooped a bite of ice cream, making sure she got the perfect ratio of banana cream, chocolate chunk, and walnut. The cold ice cream slid down her throat. She wanted to purr with pleasure, not because of the treat, but because of him.

How had she gotten so lucky that this incredibly sexy, amazing man was interested in her? Her life didn't work that way. Perhaps her luck had changed, but her pessimistic side worried he was too good to be true. If she had him strapped to a lie detector, she'd ask him if he was really as perfect as he seemed. She searched for a less neurotic question. "Baseball or basketball?"

"Football."

"Liberal or conservative?"

"Depends on the issue. Moderate."

"*Star Wars* or *Star Trek*?"

"*Lord of the Rings*."

She laughed. "Chocolate or vanilla?"

"Mint."

"Boxers or briefs?"

He flashed a sexy grin. "You'll have to find out for yourself."

She smiled. "I intend to."

He waited for her in the living room of the Shelby house. Crouching low, he looked out the front window. She would come home tonight. Her car was here. The chain locked the back door from the inside. She would enter through the front.

He'd unscrewed the light bulb above the entryway and shook it until the element broke and then put it back. He would attack her in the darkened living room before she got to another light switch.

He heard a car pull up in front. At last. He glanced outside.

Fuck. The car was driven by the police chief.

Maybe the cop was just dropping her off. His heart beat frantically when the chief climbed out of the vehicle. He held Libby Maitland's hand as they walked up the front path.

He had a split second to decide. Hide upstairs, in the basement, or in the entryway closet. The basement would be safest. If the chief was here to get laid, they'd go upstairs.

They reached the porch. He'd hesitated too long and dove for the closet, and then concealed himself as best he could behind the hanging coats. He stood absolutely still, his finger on the trigger of his gun.

He could hear the click as the deadbolt disengaged, "I don't like the idea of leaving you here alone," the police chief said as he entered the house.

"I just want to get the Columbun. I need it tomorrow. I'm staying with Simone tonight."

"There goes my excuse to invite you to stay at my house."

"You don't need an excuse." Even through the closet door and layers of coats, he could hear the blatant invitation in her tone.

"I know," Colby said in a low voice.

Christ, listening to their verbal foreplay made his finger itch on the trigger. He'd shoot them for sure if they started screwing in the living room.

"Was this light burned out before?" Colby asked, his tone changing to alert. He'd gone into cop mode.

"I don't think so."

"I want to do another walk-through, make sure nothing has been disturbed."

Fuck. Any other cop would have written off her complaints by now. This guy was taking her too seriously. If Colby searched the closet, he'd have to kill them both. He'd shoot the chief first.

He could hear only one pair of footsteps head toward the back of the house. Had they both gone, or just Colby? He couldn't hear breathing or other movement in the room. If she was waiting in the living room, he could shoot her and run out the front before Colby saw him. He'd have to aim for her head, kill her instantly, so she couldn't identify him before bleeding out.

He opened the door. The room was empty. He stumbled over her shoes in the dark as he silently slipped through the front door. No wonder he hadn't heard her footsteps. No shoes. He ran down the front steps, around to the side of the house, and into the backyard. Inside the shed, he threw a tarp over the stuff he'd stashed there. He'd get it later.

Right now Colby trusted her. If the cop was smart enough to follow the trail of evidence, his opinion would change. But tonight wasn't the night.

Tomorrow he'd try again. If she didn't return to the Shelby house, he'd get her at the apartment building. He'd burn the whole damn building down if he had to.

15

The first thing Mark noticed when he searched Libby's office again was Angela Caruthers' boxes. Libby had sorted the contents into neat piles, showing the boxes contained more than dissertation research. The stacks of phone bills, Master Charge statements, and receipts would aid his investigation. Given the room for error on the dental ID, he would wait for the DNA results before requesting a warrant for the boxes. "Have you gone through all these boxes yet?" he asked Libby.

She pointed to four taped-up boxes stacked at the end. "Those four are all I have left. I should finish tomorrow." She paused. "We found Angela, didn't we?"

"We're still looking into that possibility. I should have told you yesterday to stop going through the boxes." The fact that he didn't think of that until now was a sign of how distracted he'd become by Libby. She was affecting his job.

"But I need Angela's papers. I've got a deadline."

"They may hold important clues to what happened to her. I have a better chance of being able to use any evidence in court if they remain sealed."

She opened her mouth to speak, and then stopped.

"This is important, Libby. If the remains are Angela, then I need these boxes." He didn't want this to spoil what had otherwise been a spectacular first date. "Let's finish going through the house." He led her down the hall and stopped outside the door to the guest room. She remained in the hall while he searched the room.

Streaks of blood still trailed down the wall. She'd been sleeping across the hall while some bastard sprayed this wall with blood. Back in the hall he said, "Tomorrow I'll arrange for a cleaning service and hire someone to repair the damage to the sheetrock."

She stood with her arms crossed over her chest. "Thank you, but Jason has already done that."

He stiffened and reminded himself Jason was her landlord.

She shivered. "I can't go in there."

Jason may be her landlord, but Mark could comfort her. He pulled her into his arms and she relaxed against him.

"Do you hold every victim when you search their house?"

"First time," he said. "And I'm not on duty, remember?" The top of her head just reached his chin. He touched her hair; the soft curls looped around his fingers. He only aimed to comfort her, but something shifted. He wasn't sure what. The tension in her body changed and merely holding her was no longer enough.

He slid his hands down her back to cup her butt, while she looped her arms around his neck. She raised her head and stared at him for a long silent moment.

He traced her hairline, her ear, and then cradled her head in both hands. Finally he lowered his mouth and brushed his lips lightly over hers. He began to pull away but her arms tightened. She rose on tiptoes, demanding more than a fleeting kiss. He was more than happy to comply and pressed his lips firmly against hers.

She opened her mouth and his tongue slipped inside to stroke hers. She let out a soft purr. The sexy sound was sparks on dry tinder, the kiss a conflagration. He devoted himself to exploring her mouth, coaxing more sounds of pleasure from her.

His lips slid across her cheek to her ear and down along her throat. Her fingernails trailed along his scalp, causing a ripple of heat to run through him. He pressed her back against the wall and returned his mouth to hers.

Pinned, she let out a soft moan when he slipped his knee between her thighs and pressed against her center. The sound alone could bring him to orgasm.

He pulled back. Her green eyes stared into his. He saw the same raw need he felt. He could make love to her here, now. But she deserved better than a quickie in the hall.

"Do you need to be up early tomorrow?" his voice rasped with arousal.

"Yes."

"So do I." He held her face in his hands. "The first time I make love to you I want to explore every inch of you. Make you come so many times we lose count. Then I want to wake up with you the next morning and start all over again." He brushed his lips lightly over hers, "I'll pick you up Friday at six."

She rose on her toes and slipped her tongue into his mouth. She pressed her hips against his, "You sure?"

No. But he nodded.

"Friday, then."

He released her before he could change his mind. "I'm going to finish searching the attic. Then we'll leave."

Several minutes later, the house locked up behind them, he stood with her next to the Suburban. "Have I given you my home number?" he asked.

"No."

He wrote his number on the back of his card and gave it to her. "Call me if you see or hear anything that worries you, whether you're at Simone's or here. I don't care if the noise turns out to be a branch brushing against the house or a breeze slamming a door. I don't want to worry that you're going to second-guess yourself into a dangerous situation. If you don't think it's an emergency, call me; otherwise, call 9-1-1 first, then me."

"What if I'm positive it's a false alarm?"

"You call anyway."

"Are you planning to protect me from things that go bump in the night?"

He caught her against him for another deep kiss. Afterward he whispered, "I want to *be* the thing that goes bump in the night." He traced the outline of her bra. "One more question."

She tilted her head to the side and waited.

"Is your bra red?" he asked, gently tugging on a strap.

"It was your choice to stop before you could find out." She gave him a frisky grin. "I have no idea how I'm supposed to sleep tonight."

He pressed against her, his erection demonstrating his own frustrated state. "If you figure it out, let me know."

L ibby awoke with a start. The digital clock on the nightstand told her she'd kissed Mark goodnight hours before. She'd gone to sleep with the memory of his touch. Now sweat drenched her neck and pillow, and her heart beat with unfamiliar speed. The adrenaline that laced her system had nothing to do with Mark and anticipation. No, the feeling of fight or flight that had her shaking was the result of a dream.

The dream remained crystal clear in her mind. It began with the night she'd broken up with Aaron, and he'd attacked her. But then the dream moved forward in time, and she'd been at the library giving her lecture. In her dream, as she had in reality, her eyes drifted above the crowd, not wanting to catch Laura or Earl Montgomery's hostile glares. The crowd had been large, the faces an unfocused blur.

He'd sat near the back, slouched low in his seat. His hat was tilted low over his eyes. He'd put on weight. His hand had covered the bottom half of his face.

As much as she might wish otherwise, the first part of the dream— the night Aaron attacked her—was real. And Libby knew the second part of her dream was just as real. She hadn't consciously noticed him last night when she was giving her lecture, but he was there. Aaron Brady had attended her talk at the library.

16

Thursday morning dawned chilly but clear, a perfect day for digging. Simone took a shower. She would be covered with dirt by eight o'clock, but at least she would start the day clean. She dressed in freshly laundered field clothes. Wearing clothes that were Monday clean on a Thursday was a rare treat.

She wasn't surprised to see Libby at the breakfast table; she'd heard her come in last night. What did surprise her was Libby's clothing. "You're dressed for dirt. You digging today?"

"Just for the morning. I want to do the cleanup around the burial and finish excavating the adjacent unit. We're behind on volume. I'd like you to dig, too, until we're caught up. Are you up to a day without a screener?"

"Screeners just slow me down."

"I want to clone you."

"My dear, I am one of a kind." She poured herself a cup of coffee. "So how'd it go last night?"

"So you like froofy and purple?"

Simone let out a squeal and flopped into a chair. "Details. I want details."

Libby smiled. "He's dreamy. I'm seeing him again on Friday."

"Another date? No waiting by the phone wondering if he'll call? Ohhh, he really likes you. You're on the fast track."

"I need to ask you something. Did you see Aaron at the library last night?"

"No."

"He sat in the second row from the back. He wore a Mariner's cap, which hid his eyes."

"He couldn't have been there. I'd have noticed."

"I think he was."

There was no way Aaron could have been at the library. She had purposely scanned every face in the room. During the talk, she sat toward the front, so it might have been possible for him to slip in then, but she'd glanced around periodically and didn't see any new faces. Besides, Mark had stood by the door during the lecture. He must have seen photos of Aaron at some point. He would have recognized him.

She considered calling Mark and asking him whether it was possible Aaron was there, but discarded the idea. His relationship with Libby was too new, and the constant rehashing of her history with Aaron could only cause problems.

No, Libby's reaction just confirmed Simone needed to do what she could to prove Aaron was the stalker and get him out of her life forever. Libby was finally putting the past behind her. Simone wouldn't let Aaron drag her back under.

By noon Libby had finished excavating the burial units. She conferred with Simone on the progress of the dig and then headed to the Suburban. She had to get back to Angela's research, even though it meant working alone at the Shelby house.

"Hey, Lib," Alex called out as she was climbing into the truck. "We're all headed to the Coho Tavern tonight for dinner. Seven o'clock. Join us?"

She wanted to decline, but she hadn't spent much after-hours time with this crew. The team had been together for nearly three weeks, and they had more than two months to go until the field phase ended. They all would go through the full cycle of crew dynamics.

First came wary friendliness, and then a honeymoon phase as new and exciting friendships formed. Next, they would get sick of one another, which led to deep loathing and division into factions. Then the factions would shift and a second honeymoon would emerge. In the end, they'd all be relieved it was over, but there would be tears as they said goodbye. Libby'd been through it all so many times during her years as a dig bum, she could set her watch by the cycle.

They had now reached the end of the first honeymoon and little irritations were creeping up. If she didn't join them for dinner now, then it might be another month before the entire group was willing to have dinner together again. "Sure, I'd like that."

At the Shelby house, she took a quick shower to get off the top layer of dirt, and then she cleaned out the tub and filled it with steaming hot water. She soaked for a long time, letting her screaming muscles steep. Her previous excavation of the burial had been minor. She'd only used a trowel and hadn't screened her buckets. This morning's work, however, had been the intense physical kind that she rarely did anymore. Exhausting but invigorating, a reminder that she was one of the lucky people who got to work outside and get a workout no gym could provide. At least, she felt that way today because it hadn't rained and she'd had an amazing date the night before.

Clean and relaxed, she entered her office. Angela's work was still neatly arranged, awaiting her attention. She hadn't promised Mark she wouldn't make copies of the papers she'd already gone through. She'd avoided the question altogether because she feared he would tell her not to make the copies.

The pages were old and dog-eared, and some were within bound notebooks, so each page had to be hand-placed. It would take her several hours to copy everything she'd found in the eight boxes she'd already opened. She skimmed the notes as she copied them, considering the intersections between Angela's research and her own. She kept a notepad next to the copier and jotted down ideas as she worked.

There'd been no order to the boxes, no numbering. The only label was the word "mom" written in a child's messy scrawl. Anger at Jack surged. How could he have left it to Jason to pack his mother's belongings? He might be an excellent businessman but as a father he was as bad as her own. Jason had lost his mother. He'd been an only child, with no one to turn to but his father. She wondered whether Jack was too lost in his own grief to care about his son's.

At least Libby had had her younger brother and sister. After their father abandoned them the first time, their mother had been so devastated she could do nothing but stare at the empty chair at the head of the kitchen table. Days and weeks and months went by, and no one, not even the cat, was allowed to sit in their father's chair. During that time, her mother slowly disappeared. It was as if every time she looked at her children she saw the reason their father left.

Libby had been eleven years old, Maggie seven, Graham five. Their mother provided them with a home, food, and clothing. Libby did the rest. In third grade, Maggie begged for ballet classes. It took Libby two months to steal enough money from their mother's wallet to pay for the class. She bought Maggie shoes and a leotard from a thrift store, and once a week for four months, she loaded Graham onto the handlebars of her bicycle while Maggie rode alongside on her own bike to her sister's dance class. She had waited in the back of the room with a restless Graham and the other kid's mothers. If Libby hadn't had Graham and Maggie to take care of, she probably would have ended up as lost as her mother.

But Jason had no brothers or sisters. He often called his father by his first name. He treated him with the respect of a colleague, not a parent. Had anyone been there for Jason in the first months and years after his mother disappeared? She couldn't imagine Laura or Earl Montgomery stepping up to the task, but perhaps James, the most sensitive and reasonable Montgomery, had taken on a paternal role. He seemed to have a different relationship with Jason.

Finally, Libby came to a stack of transcripts of oral interviews with Kalahwamish tribal members. These were arguably the most valuable pieces of Angela's research, because several of the elders she'd interviewed were now deceased.

Libby carefully placed the first page of the transcript of the interview with Frances Warren on the glass. Rosalie's mother had been a revered elder in her time, and from Rosalie's own words she was the major supporter of Angela's research. She would have been a vital source of information. Libby was surprised to see that the transcript was only five pages long. She flipped to the last page, seeing that it cut off mid-sentence at the bottom, clearly in the middle of a story. The rest was missing.

She looked through the stacks of pages but didn't find the rest of Frances Warren's interview. Frances might have told Angela exactly what she wanted the world to know about Lyle Montgomery, which was exactly what Libby needed.

She sat on the floor and stared at the remaining four boxes that Mark had told her not to open. She only had until next Friday to finish the report. One week and one day, and she was still compiling information. She hadn't even begun writing yet.

Frances' interview could be the key.

Jason had placed limits on what she could publish—no supposition, no conjecture—and authentication of Frances' transcript might be necessary. That would be nearly impossible if the transcript was incomplete. What she really needed was the tape of the actual interview.

She hadn't come across any tapes in Angela's boxes, but she was certain Angela would've kept the tapes. She picked up one of the sealed boxes. It was heavy, and when she shook it, the contents barely shifted inside the cardboard box. Probably books and papers packed tightly. The second box weighed slightly less, but felt like it was full of the same mishmash of papers that had been in the other boxes.

The third box was lighter than the other two and made a distinctive rattling sound as she shook it. It sounded like plastic cassette tapes.

If she failed to get Jack his permit she'd never recover, not financially, not professionally. If she failed to get him the permit before the fieldwork phase was even complete, then the project would have no reason to continue. She'd invested too much in this project up front. She'd have to lay off the crew and wouldn't be able to recoup most of the upfront costs. Worse, no one would hire someone who couldn't even get a simple Section 404 wetland permit from the Corps of Engineers.

The Cultural Center wouldn't be built and, while controversial, it would still provide jobs for Coho and the tribe and prevent Coho from becoming another dead logging town.

Angela's husband and son had given her the boxes expressly for the purpose of looking through them and using the information she found. But Mark had asked her to leave them sealed. If she opened the box, would she be breaking the law? No court had issued an injunction, or whatever type of ruling that would prohibit her from cutting the tape that sealed the box.

Mark believed any evidence they *might* contain was more likely to be admissible in court if they remained sealed. But presumably the cops had gone through Angela's stuff years ago, when they investigated her disappearance. If they didn't find anything then, then why would these boxes be so important now? What were the odds this one particular box would be key to Mark's investigation?

If she'd just opened this damn box yesterday it wouldn't be an issue. And she needed the cassettes.

She quickly sliced through the tape, lifted the flaps, and looked inside. An open shoebox of cassettes sat on top of a stack of notebooks and papers. They were here. She sat back for a moment, relieved. She counted the tapes. There were twenty-two, three of which were labeled "Frances Warren." She needed to copy them.

She grabbed her purse and headed to the general store, which was just a quick walk up the road. She bought out the store's limited supply of blank cassettes and returned to the Shelby house. She opened the first package, wondering what sort of catastrophe the manufacturers expected the tapes to undergo to have wrapped them so securely, and then put the blank tape in one side of the dual cassette deck in the living room stereo, and dropped the first Frances tape in the other. Thank goodness Angela hadn't used eight-track tapes, which would have been common in the seventies. Libby hit the record and play buttons simultaneously.

Angela's voice filled the room. Libby had gone through this woman's research. She lived in one of her houses, knew her husband and son, and had, in fact, probably even handled her skull, yet she'd never seen a photo of Angela Caruthers. And now she heard her voice.

Frances Warren spoke, giving Angela permission to tape the conversation. The cadence of Frances Warren's voice told Libby as loud as her words that she was a Northwest Indian. A linguistics expert would easily be able to authenticate this tape, if necessary.

As eager as Libby was to listen, she still had hours of photocopying to do, so she went upstairs and resumed making copies, returning downstairs every half hour to turn over or switch tapes.

At six thirty, she stopped making copies so she could get ready for dinner with the crew. She'd almost finished copying the papers, but only managed to copy four tapes. She changed into her favorite casual dress and wondered whether she should move all her clothes to Simone's. Instead, she packed an overnight bag. She'd be back tomorrow anyway. She locked up the Shelby house and then headed to Simone's so they could drive together to the tavern.

He watched her leave the house a few minutes before seven. Would she return here or spend the night at the apartment? Or worse, go home with the cop?

It didn't matter, he told himself. He was prepared. He had his plan. Mark Colby was expendable. If need be, he could make the blonde's death look like an accidental victim of Libby Maitland's psychosis. A friend who had gotten in the way.

Yesterday he'd taken her spare Taser cartridge and gotten the gas cans, the duct tape, her belt, the pillowcase, and the wine bottle he'd stashed in the backyard shed. He had lighter fluid, which would work like ether to knock out the cop or the bimbo, if necessary. No matter where she went tonight, he'd attack.

If she lived, she would be arrested. If she died, all the better. She'd be out of the way and the evidence would still lead back to her.

17

When Libby and Simone arrived at Coho Tavern, they found the crew settled in for the evening with Luke Roth, Sara Eversall, and two other men, both Coho police officers.

Libby took a seat next to an officer name Roger. Simone took a seat on her other side.

Roger said, "I get to meet the Wolf Lady at last."

"Excuse me?" Libby said, feeling as if she must have missed the first part of the conversation.

"Just a little joke. You've called the station so many times in the last week with no real evidence to back up your calls. It looks like you're crying wolf. But don't worry, we'll always respond to a pretty thing like you." Roger winked at her.

"Roger, don't be an idiot," Sara Eversall said. "Tuesday morning someone sprayed cow's blood all over a wall in her house and smashed artwork with a pickaxe. If you think that's crying wolf, go back to the academy."

The officer turned red. "I guess the name doesn't really apply anymore," he mumbled and the conversation around the table resumed.

Libby smiled a thank-you to Sara and studied the menu to hide her anxiety. After the waitress took her drink order, she tentatively entered the conversation, fully aware of the chill that had settled over the table the moment she sat down. The male officers exhibited barely cloaked suspicion, making her wish the two groups hadn't combined.

Her gaze met Mark's across the artificially darkened bar, and her mood lightened. Maybe there was hope for this evening after all. He walked up behind her, placed his hands on her shoulders, leaned down, and spoke softly into her ear, sending shivers down her spine. "Purple." He pinched her eggplant-colored linen dress just above her bra strap, rolling the fabric between his fingers. "I didn't see this color on the drying rack in your basement."

She smiled at him over her shoulder.

"This calls for further investigation."

Simone jumped up. "Sit here, Chief, I need to make a phone call." She winked at Mark as she walked away. Mark took her vacated seat and draped his arm along the back of her chair. Libby's tension evaporated.

The waitress returned with a tray of beers. "Evenin', Mark. You want a black and tan or a ginger ale tonight?"

"Better make it ginger ale, Heather."

"You got it." She turned to Libby. "You ready to order, ma'am?"

"Simone, the blonde who stepped outside, wants the salmon burger and fries. I'd like the fish and chips."

"I'll have the same," Mark said. He took a sip of Libby's beer uninvited, an intimate action that caused warmth to invade her belly.

The waitress's gaze went to his arm draped on her chair. Mark had an admirer.

Simone returned and several seats shifted, but Mark stayed by her side. He leaned back and held her gaze. "I wasn't planning to be here tonight, but Sara called. I'm thinking a promotion may be in order."

She glanced at the lone woman officer of the group, who smiled when Libby caught her eye. Well, at least there was one cop besides Mark who didn't think she'd been crying wolf.

For the next hour, conversation flowed across the table as the cops and archaeologists traded stories. The novelty of having a new crowd to hang out with might save Libby's crew from the coming factionalism. The fact that the new friends were cops meant Libby wouldn't spend her nights worrying the crew was out drinking with no plan to get home. It would be a refreshing change as most field crews consumed enormous amounts of alcohol. The only way to ensure that no one drank and drove was when the project took place in a remote area that required camping. Then the trick was to get from the campfire to the tent without breaking a leg.

After they finished their meal, Mark took her hand. "Let's get out of here."

Pleasure mixed with a small amount of dread. She'd have to tell him about the box she'd opened today. She looked to Simone, who'd driven her to the bar. Simone waved her off. "Just remember socks don't count."

Libby laughed. In college they had shared a rule: when dating someone new, one had to keep two items of clothing on at all times. Of course, it was just one of many rules Libby adhered to and Simone circumvented with ingenuity. Good thing for Libby she'd been paying attention and knew exactly how to get around the old rule.

"Where are we going?" she asked as she climbed into Mark's car.

"For a drive."

She leaned back in her seat, not willing to tell him about the box yet. She wanted time alone with him. As he drove, she told him stories about the history of Coho and about the Thorpe and Warren families. Nearly one-third of Kalahwamish tribal members had the last name Warren and the rest were related to a Warren. Family history was tribal history.

"I've noticed you generally say 'Indian,' not 'Native American.' Isn't Native American the correct term?" Mark asked.

"In my reports, I use the term Native American. It's clearer than 'indigenous peoples' or 'hunter-fisher-gatherers' or whatever is currently being promoted. But in speech I tend to use the word Indian, because that's what the people I've worked with in this area tend to call themselves. They don't refer to themselves as 'hunter-fisher-gatherers.' Many prefer the term Indian, although more and more they're using the term 'native' so I'm working to retrain myself in that direction too. It takes time to make the shift."

"Why did you become an archaeologist?"

"I've always loved history and archaeology. When I was a sophomore in college, I suddenly realized that I wanted to study what interested me the most—not necessarily what could get me the best job or even *a* job."

"Your parents must have been thrilled," he laughed.

"I put myself through school. My dad wasn't around much, but he was a history buff. Whenever he showed up—and I'm talking about after at least a two- or three-year absence—he would bring lots of gifts to try to buy us off. Not normal children's gifts, but biographies, history books, things like that. I devoured them. I don't know if I was trying to please him—hoping he'd stick around if we appreciated what he'd brought us—or if I read them because I was genuinely interested in the subject matter. Somewhere along the way I got hooked." She left unsaid Simone's theory that she went into archaeology to win her father's approval.

"I had a harder time convincing my brother and sister that archaeology was a good major—we've always taken care of one another. And I've always been able to support myself. My sister the journalism major can't say that." She paused, realizing she didn't know anything about his family. "I'm the oldest of three. What about you?"

"I have two sisters. I'm the oldest."

"Were you the bossy older brother type or the protective kind?"

"They're five and seven years younger than me, so I was protective —I still am. But I was pretty bossy, too. I was in Seattle by the time they were in high school, so I wasn't able to be as protective as I wanted to be."

"Did you use your police uniform to intimidate their dates?"

"As often as I could."

"And cleaned your gun in front of them?"

"Only once. I *really* didn't like the guy my sister was dating."

He turned off the main roadway and onto a narrow state park access road. He parked near the beach and shut off the engine. "Let's walk."

As she walked toward the rocky beach, she was glad she'd chosen to wear the linen dress. Straight and slender with buttons down the front, the dress made her feel feminine every time the soft fabric brushed against her legs. The sensation intensified in his presence, proving her theory that things you liked were even better in the company of someone you were attracted to.

They crossed the beach to the water's edge. The tide was high and still coming in. Tiny waves lapped the shore. They strolled along the water's edge in silence. At the far end of the beach, she picked up a stick and stirred the water to see the bioluminescence. Glowing tendrils flashed in the swirling liquid.

Mark's hands slid over her hips. She dropped the stick and turned in his arms. The late July Pacific Northwest twilight cast him in sepia colors. His intent look made her belly flutter. She found it difficult to breathe.

He slowly smiled.

"That smile should be made illegal."

His dimple deepened and he kissed her with a confidence that turned her on as much as his lips did. She twisted her fingers in his hair in matching rhythm to the hot strokes of his tongue.

He broke the kiss and leaned his forehead against hers. "I've got a problem. I'm working on an extremely important murder investigation, yet you're all I want to think about. You're hell on my work schedule."

Her lips trailed along his cheek. She nipped his earlobe. "I'm having the same problem."

"I want you to know, I don't play around. I'm not seeing anyone else."

"I don't, and I'm not, either."

"Good. Now, I need to know something almost as important..." He deftly unbuttoned the top three buttons of her dress. The cool evening air hit bare skin, causing her nipples to harden even more underneath her purple satin bra.

"Purple. Just as I suspected."

She grinned. "You should be a detective."

"Smart ass." He reached out and cupped a breast in each hand, rubbing his thumbs over the satin bra that hid her aching nipples from view. He kissed the rounded flesh above the cups. His hands slipped down her sides to hold her steady as his mouth moved ever closer to the satin of her bra. She pulled his face back to hers and kissed him hot and hard on the mouth.

She ended the kiss and glanced around the deserted beach. "Isn't this the sort of thing you ticket people for?"

"This is a state park—not city. None of my people patrol here." He buttoned up her dress. "Now I'm tormented by a new question. Does your underwear match?"

She smiled and gathered the skirt of her dress with her fingertips, pulling the fabric up inch by slow inch. Before the hem reached the top of her thighs, he took her hands and placed them on his chest. She could feel the steady thud of his heartbeat. "I have to get up early tomorrow, and I still don't want to rush our first time together."

"Okay. Tomorrow night. Six o'clock."

"Wear red." He kissed her again, softly this time, and then entwined his fingers with hers and resumed walking the beach.

A euphoric mood enveloped her. This was the feeling people sought when experimenting with drugs, the highest of natural highs.

"How is your report coming?" Mark asked.

Libby came crashing back to earth. She'd forgotten about the box. She had to tell him. "I got a lot done today. Angela's research is vital. My report will be based entirely on her work." His hand tightened around hers.

"I told you to leave Angela's boxes alone."

"You didn't tell me I couldn't photocopy the pages of research I'd already found."

"I didn't say that, but I should have. There could be fingerprints on those pages." He dropped her hand.

"As I was making copies of the transcripts of her oral interviews, I realized that I hadn't found any of the tapes. Those tapes could become the cornerstone of my report—publishable accounts of Lyle Montgomery's treatment of the tribe. They could give Rosalie what she wants so the Corps won't block Jack's permit." She paused. "I needed those tapes."

He took a step away from her. "You opened the boxes."

"Only one box. I could hear the tapes inside when I shook it."

"Dammit, Libby!" He turned away and walked faster toward his car. "Don't you know what this means? You were tampering with potential evidence. You could have destroyed a clue that would have led me to the killer."

She ran to keep up with him. "The stuff in those boxes would have been gone through by the police in 1979. What makes you think there could be a clue in them now?"

He swung around and faced her. His eyes were cold. "Are your archaeological methods the same now as they were in 1979? Did you use ground penetrating radar back then?"

"No." Her heart sank.

"There have been changes in police work, too. We can lift fingerprints from surfaces that we couldn't before—including better technology for lifting from paper. And the technology for breaking apart audio recordings is worlds ahead of what it was then. Those tapes could be vital."

"All I've done is copy them. How does that hurt your evidence?"

"You opened the box and played the tape. It could be argued you tampered with it, altered the contents."

"All I did was copy it. I was given those boxes by Jack and Jason for the purpose of going through them to find what I need to write my report."

"You opened a box after I asked you not to."

"The boxes were mine to go through. If you think they're so important, why didn't you take them yesterday?"

"Because I trusted you. That was a mistake."

She felt his words as the slap he'd intended. "For all I know, the bones we found could be someone else. If she isn't Angela, then this whole thing isn't an issue. You yourself said we only know when she disappeared; we don't know if she's even dead."

"Don't split hairs, Libby. We both know you guessed the identity of the victim. I don't have DNA yet, but the dental records indicate a match. Don't you want Angela's killer to be found?"

"Of course I do. But Rosalie Warren specifically asked me to use Angela's research for my report. She wants closure, or maybe vindication for the tribe. I can't give that to her without Angela's notes. Many of the people Angela interviewed are dead now."

"So what Rosalie wants trumps justice for Angela?"

"I didn't say that, and I don't think the two are mutually exclusive. I'm not doing this just for Rosalie. It's for Coho."

"You can tell yourself that, but really you're doing it for your own business and reputation."

"Of course the business comes into it, but that's not my only reason. I wouldn't sacrifice justice for Angela for the sake of my job, and I don't believe I have." Tears of frustration threatened her composure. This was going so much worse than she'd imagined. "If I'd opened that box yesterday, you would have no right to question my actions."

"But you didn't open it yesterday, did you?"

"No."

"How many boxes are left unopened, three?"

She nodded.

"I'm taking them." He opened his car door and climbed inside.

She opened the passenger door. "Can you do that without a warrant?"

"If I have reason to believe evidence will be lost or destroyed, I can seize it now and get a warrant later. It's called exigent circumstances. I should have taken them yesterday. I won't make that mistake again. Get in."

"Maybe my research will help your investigation." She knew she was grasping but wanted to find common ground.

"Get in the car, Libby."

She continued to stand in the open door. "I know her subject, and I know the history of the property where she was found."

"The property belongs to Jack. That tells me plenty."

"Listen. How Jack came to own that particular parcel of land could be important."

"Then get in the car and tell me."

She climbed in.

Twilight had ended and it was now fully dark. The car's headlights illuminated only the narrow dirt road that cut through the forest. The world felt small, enclosed. Anger radiated from Mark in waves.

"In 1857, the Kalahwamish signed a treaty with the US government, which set up the current reservation," she began. "One Indian family refused to move to the reservation and remained on a parcel of land just outside the boundaries—land that the ancestors had occupied for thousands of years. White settlers harassed them, but they didn't give up. Eventually the land was granted to them. Other provisions in the treaty weren't enforced, so the tribe essentially got nothing. The Kalahwamish were forced to give up their language, the potlatch, their religion. In return, they got a small reservation and a promise that the whites would stop trying to kill them. They were granted fishing rights that they are still—one hundred fifty years later—having to fight to retain."

"Get to the point."

"The land that one Kalahwamish family fought to keep was passed on, eventually going to George Warren. In 1976, George sold five hundred acres to Jack and Angela Caruthers. But there's no explanation why George sold a white couple that land, when there weren't plans for the property at the time of the sale. When I asked Jack why he bought the land, he said Angela wanted it. She never told him why."

She had his attention now. "Even more curious is that George Warren absolutely hated the Montgomery family. The mill store had a sign in the windows until 1970 that said 'No Credit for Indians—Do Not Even Ask.' Lyle would follow Indians around his store as if they were thieves. Why on earth would George Warren sell his sacred land to Lyle's granddaughter?"

"The answer isn't so George could bury Angela in it several years later. Don't waste my time. I'm taking those boxes."

"Dammit, Mark! You can have the boxes, but listen. Last week, I found out Angela was an anthropologist. Jack never mentioned her studies. Whenever someone finds out what I do for a living, they *immediately* tell me about anyone they know in the same or similar profession. If their cousin's friend's brother's godson is a paleontologist, I'm expected to be his drinking buddy. But Jack forgets to tell me that his *wife* was an anthropologist? And, even more strange, she was working on a dissertation on the Kalahwamish—the very tribe associated with the site. So Jack doesn't know why Angela wanted the land and he didn't see the significance of what she was studying to the Cultural Center dig? That seems odd to me.

"Even more strange is the fact that Angela was granted unprecedented access to the Kalahwamish and now Rosalie Warren is granting *me* forcing upon me, really—the same privilege and I'm not even a cultural anthropologist—who Indians at least tolerate. I'm an archaeologist—from an Indian point of view I'm the worst sort of anthropologist—a grave desecrater. In fact, I was in the process of doing just that—at least that's what everyone thought at the time— when Rosalie demanded that I write this report for her. I'm not a cop, but I find all this curious. Why did Angela want that land? Why didn't she tell Jack? Is Jack lying? Why did she choose to study the Kalahwamish? And why did the Kalahwamish trust her?"

"You could have told me all this before."

"I've just been piecing it together. Today I made a list of questions while I was copying her research. You have to admit that my perspective is different than yours would be."

"Which is the only reason I'm listening to your attempts to justify this."

"If I don't do my job, there won't be a Cultural Center."

"I'm not fool enough to believe that the Corps of Engineers will hold you to your deadline. If they have problems with your report, explain the hang-up and give them a copy of the warrant."

"You have no idea how important Rosalie is. She's the most revered living elder in the Pacific Northwest. There's no telling what they'll do if Rosalie Warren dies before she reads my report."

"Well, I suggest you call your contact at the Corps ASAP and brace him because I'm taking the three unopened boxes tonight, then I'm coming back with a warrant for the rest."

"I'd like to finish making my copies first."

"Hell no! It's now evidence. If there was a signed confession in one of those boxes your actions have tainted it, and it would now be inadmissible."

"I hardly think you're going to find a smoking gun in one of those boxes. I've been through eight of them. They aren't that interesting."

"You need to understand you're a part of this case. You excavated the body. Your client is the victim's husband. You're staying in a house that belonged to her. You're even following up on her research. You are *not* an unbiased investigator. My job is to collect evidence to find out who killed her. That evidence will then be used in a court of law with the goal of sending her killer to prison. If there's anything in those boxes that exonerates or implicates Jack, then a judge will have a serious problem with the fact that you had access to them first."

"I'd like to remind you that you yourself helped carry those damn boxes into the house. You didn't have a problem with me having access to them then."

"That was before we had her body and an investigation. After that point, the fact that her papers had been saved in sealed boxes became important."

"If Jack did kill Angela, he'd be the idiot of the millennium to bury her on his own property then hire me to dig her up. And I hardly think he would store incriminating evidence all these years."

"People have done stupider things. I see it all the time."

They neared the Shelby house. They were no closer to bridging the chasm that separated them. She leaned back in her seat and closed her eyes. She knew he'd be upset, but had never considered his reaction would be this extreme. She'd been clueless to the consequences of her actions. "I'm sorry," she said softly.

He didn't even look at her.

"Mark, will you ever be able to understand my actions from my perspective?"

"I don't know." He pulled up in front of the house and turned to face her. "Are you sorry because I'm angry, or do you regret what you did?"

She didn't want to answer that.

"Tell me. If you'd known exactly what my reaction would be, would you still have opened that box?"

"I needed the tapes."

"It never occurred to you that I could give you copies of her research?"

"No."

"You should have asked."

"I've always found it easier to ask for forgiveness than for permission."

"Not this time."

Tense silence filled the space between them. Finally, Mark opened his door and climbed out. She followed. At the front door, she didn't look at him as she handed him her keys.

He took the stairs two at a time. She waited in the living room while he made three trips to his car. Boxes loaded, he returned to the living room. "I'll be back in an hour or so. I'm going to wake up a judge and get a warrant for the rest. Do you want to give me the keys now, or will you be here when I come back?"

"I'll be here."

"Good."

The door closed behind him and she locked it. She went to the stereo system and flipped through the shoe box full of cassettes. She had copies of the four most important tapes: the Frances and George Warren interviews. A bitter laugh welled inside her. She'd sacrificed a relationship with Mark, but at least she had four tapes to show for it.

She ejected the last cassette from the tape deck and replaced it in the shoebox. She went upstairs. At her desk, she pulled out a clean notepad and copied the names and dates written on each cassette. Then she flipped through the stacks of papers she hadn't photocopied and added that information to her list before she repacked Angela's boxes.

She didn't cry, but she had to fight the urge. Her pride wouldn't let Mark see her as a swollen-eyed blubbering mess.

Mark was the most interesting, exciting, attractive man she'd ever met. And he'd wanted *her*. But she'd screwed up royally. Simone would say she'd sabotaged their relationship on purpose, and Libby wondered whether that was exactly what she'd done.

When he arrived with the warrant, she'd hold her head high.

She finished packing the boxes and carried the first one to the living room. She'd hand them over to him through the front door and then head to Simone's. She no longer wanted to talk to him. Her hurt had changed to anger. Nothing like leaving a woman alone for an hour in mid-argument to let righteous indignation set in. She carried the rest of the boxes down one by one and lined them up by the front door.

Mark had been gone for forty-five minutes and could return at any time. She'd kill time with a glass of wine. She passed through the dining room on the way to the darkened kitchen and then groped along the wall of the pitch-black room for the switch. Panic shot through her as her fingers touched another hand, holding the switch in the off position.

Something pricked her on the back, just below her shoulder. A jolt passed through her body that had nothing to do with fear. A thousand tiny needles ripped her apart from the inside. Her legs buckled. She dropped to the floor.

She lost all sense of time and place. Pain from the needles continued. An endless agony.

Abruptly, the pain ceased. The sensation of being stabbed internally disappeared. Her ability to think returned. A cloth bag covered her head and tape covered her mouth. She tried to regain her bearings. Where was she? She rolled to her side and bumped into a cabinet. She reached out and touched the familiar wood. She was in her kitchen.

Someone grabbed her and pulled her arms together. From the iron grip on her wrists, she suspected her attacker was a man. He wrapped tape around her wrists. She kicked blindly, but her ankles were bound, and her thrashing was ineffective.

Mark, please come back.

The searing pain returned. She couldn't think. She couldn't move. All she could do was feel the agony of being shredded from the inside. He must be using a Taser on her.

Again, after seconds, minutes, or hours, the pain stopped. She tried to hit her attacker, but he moved out of reach. She could hear him. He was still in the room. Footsteps mixed with the sound of liquid splashing against the floor. She smelled gasoline. *Oh, God...*

Pounding—the noise sounded as though it came from the front of the house. Mark?

"Libby, open up. I've got the warrant. I'm here to collect the boxes."

Thank God.

She moaned in the back of her throat and rolled toward the cabinet. She kicked the cabinet repeatedly with her bare feet. Another Taser jolt tore through her. Tape over her mouth blocked her screams as the burning pain speared her again and again.

18

M ark stood next to Officer Lance Edelson as he pounded on Libby's front door. Lights were on upstairs, but the ground floor was dark. She said she'd be here. She was too smart to play games. The warrant gave him the right to enter the premises. Mark tried the door, but the deadbolt was set. He pounded again. "Libby, open up."

Nothing.

Lance shined his flashlight into the windows. The living room was empty. Mark could see the boxes lined up by the door, ready for him to take possession. In his gut, he knew she would answer the door if she could. The anger he'd harbored for the last hour evaporated and was replaced by fear.

"Police!" Mark yelled. "Open up!" He nodded to Lance, and they both pulled their weapons. Lance smashed the glass pane in the door with his flashlight. Mark reached in, unlocked the deadbolt and opened the door.

He heard a sound coming from the back of the house and ran to the kitchen. Lance's flashlight revealed Libby on the floor, a pillowcase over her head, secured with a belt around her neck. Her hands were bound with the roll of duct tape still attached at her wrists. She was kicking a cabinet with taped-together legs.

Mark knelt beside her. "I'm here, Libby."

She stopped kicking and turned toward his voice.

Lance turned on the lights. The back door was open. Mark nodded to Lance and the officer stepped out into the darkness, weapon drawn.

"Whoever did this to you is gone." Mark began to loosen the belt around Libby's neck, relieved to be able to place two fingers between the belt and her throat. The belt wasn't what prevented her from speaking.

He caught a whiff of propane, let go of the buckle and stood. The distinctive scent was nearly overpowered by the intense odor of gasoline, which he could see had been dumped all over the kitchen. At the cook-top, he found every burner set on high, filling the room with gas. He hesitated. Turning off the burners could cause a spark as the knobs passed through the light section of the dial. Between the propane and the gasoline poured everywhere, one spark was all it would take for the kitchen to explode. He located the emergency shut off valve and twisted it closed.

Lance climbed the back steps as Mark lifted Libby. "Stay out," he ordered. "The kitchen is full of propane."

"The back is clear," Lance said.

Outside, Mark set Libby down on the lawn, as far from the kitchen as possible. She still smelled of gasoline. He could see dark patches on her dress, places where the fuel had been poured over her. He finished unhooking the belt and pulled the pillowcase from her head. Her eyes were wide and scared. He gently worked at the duct tape that covered her mouth.

"I radioed for backup and an ambulance," Lance said. "I think the suspect is long gone. At least two minutes elapsed between the time we arrived and when we entered. The suspect had plenty of time to clear the alley."

Mark nodded. "No one is to enter the house until the gas dissipates. Radio for a fire truck, then check out the alley again. I don't like having her out here like this, exposed." He managed to work the tape off her mouth. He set the silver strip aside to be checked for fingerprints. She took a large gasping breath and then brought her bound hands to her face and rolled to her side. Her body shook as she let out a sob.

He reached out to comfort her, his fingers running through her hair. He didn't feel any bumps or other signs of head trauma. "I need to know what happened," he said softly.

"Jeez, Chief, is this how you entertain women?"

Mark glanced up to see Luke Roth approaching through the side yard. Mark's response was something of a low growl. The usual irreverent humor used to break tension at crime scenes didn't apply here. He was crazy about this woman. "What are you doing here? You're off-duty."

"I heard the call as I was driving by. Figured I'd come help out."

Luke knelt beside Libby, across from Mark. Libby put her hands beneath her and pushed off the grass. Mark helped her into a sitting position. She wiped at her eyes.

"Have you been drinking?" Mark said, looking away from Libby and studying his officer. The last thing he needed was a drunk off-duty cop messing with the crime scene.

"I was the designated driver. I was dropping Roger off when the call came."

Mark nodded, knowing Roger rented a house in the historic district, a block away. Luke's timing was suspicious and right now Mark wasn't in the frame of mind to trust anyone. Later he'd check with Roger and the others who'd been at the tavern to confirm what time Luke had left the bar.

He turned back to Libby and focused on her eyes. Her pupils were evenly dilated. "What happened?" he asked.

"I think I was Tasered," she rasped. She licked her lips and shook her head. "There was lots of pain. A big jolt, like needles were inside me, ripping me apart."

"Did you feel a prick anywhere, before the jolt?"

She nodded. "Below my shoulder."

Luke handed him a flashlight and he examined her back. Her dress had two small tears just below her shoulder blade. He pulled the fabric aside and found two puncture wounds. "You were Tasered all right."

"It was awful. I couldn't do anything. I couldn't stand." Her speech became clearer. "I don't even remember him putting the bag on my head and binding me. All I could feel was excruciating pain."

Luke cut the duct tape that held her legs together and then freed her hands.

"You said 'him.' Did you see who assaulted you?"

She shook her head. "It was dark. I was searching for the kitchen light switch. I touched a hand blocking the switch and he shot me in the same moment. I couldn't see or think or anything while I was being Tasered. Then the bag was over my head. I didn't see the person at all, but I thought the hands that held my wrists together felt like a man's."

"Did you hear anything that would help you identify your attacker?"

"No." She touched the damp spots on her dress. "I heard splashing. I think I smelled gasoline."

"There was a five-gallon jug in the room and it looked like it had been poured over everything, including you."

She began to shake again, so he placed a hand on hers. "We need to get back inside that kitchen," he said. "Libby, is there a fan anywhere in the house?"

"Upstairs, in my office."

"I'll get it," he said.

Luke stood. "I'll do it, Chief." He left them before Mark could stop him.

Two more police cars pulled up. Mark assigned those officers to help Lance patrol the yard, alley, and neighborhood.

An ambulance drove down the back alley and parked in the rear driveway. For the first time, Mark realized the Suburban wasn't parked there. "Where's your truck?" he asked.

"I left it at Simone's. She drove me to the bar."

He'd been so angry that he'd left her stranded and alone without giving a thought to the stalker who'd entered her house twice already. "I shouldn't have left you here."

"I'm just glad you came back."

He couldn't think about what might have happened if he hadn't returned with the warrant. What she'd gone through was bad enough: she was pale, her hands shook as she rubbed her eyes, and she smelled of gasoline. He wanted to hunt down the sonofabitch who'd attacked her and exact his own justice.

A gurney was unloaded from the back of the ambulance and two male emergency medical technicians rolled it to where they sat in the grass.

Libby stood. "I'm okay," she said. "Just a little shaky."

"We need to check your vital signs," the first EMT said.

"I don't want to go to the hospital." She sat on the gurney, remaining stiff, ready to bolt. Mark couldn't blame her. After what she'd just been through, the thought of being under someone else's control, even if it was a medical technician, was probably unbearable.

Mark told the EMTs that she was probably suffering from several jolts from a Taser.

"How many bursts?" the EMT asked.

Libby closed her eyes. After a moment, she said, "Three."

"How long did they last?"

"Forever. The first one lasted long enough for him to tape my mouth, put the bag on my head, and tape my legs."

All of Mark's officers were trained with Tasers. The jolt wasn't supposed to last more than five seconds but could be increased up to thirty, which wasn't long enough to bind and gag her. Had the suspect modified the non-lethal weapon to sustain longer bursts? "They're supposed to be quick," he said.

"That's what the guy at the gun store told me when I bought one Saturday," Libby said.

"You have a Taser?" Mark asked.

"It's in my purse."

The EMT interrupted. "Three extended blasts from a Taser is outside our training. You should go to the hospital for observation."

"No," she said. "I'm tired. Sore. But a hospital isn't going to help with that. If I start to feel worse, I promise I'll go."

"Then we'll stay and monitor your vitals for a while longer," the technician said.

"We need to call Jack," she said to Mark. "Let him know that the house was nearly torched. Jack's mobile number is programmed into my cell. I don't know if he's in Coho or at his Seattle home tonight."

He touched her hand; her fingers closed around his. Over an hour ago they'd argued, but he didn't care. Right now nothing mattered except the fact that she'd survived what seemed to be an attempt on her life.

Reluctantly, he let go. "I'll get your phone," he said. He had his own questions for Jack. He left her with the EMTs and walked around the house to the front where a fire truck blocked half of the road. Mark entered the house and found the fire chief standing in the dining room, just outside the kitchen.

The chief looked up. "The gas has cleared, but I want to give it another ten minutes with the fan blowing."

Mark nodded. "The suspect probably turned on the propane just before leaving. He wouldn't want the gas flowing while he was in the room, especially considering he used a Taser on the victim, which could ignite the gas. I'd guess the propane was on for two or three minutes, tops."

The fire chief pointed to a wine bottle stuffed with a scorched rag on the kitchen floor. "The suspect probably lit that as he left. The room hadn't had time to fill with gas yet or the kitchen would have exploded. Your victim is lucky that Molotov cocktail didn't shatter."

In his rush to pull Libby out to safety, he'd missed the bottle. It lay next to where her legs had been and probably didn't shatter and ignite the room because the bastard threw it directly at her. Maybe her legs broke its fall. She might have knocked the bottle and doused the flame when she kicked the cabinets.

He went cold. He'd been investigating her stalking complaints for a week and come up with nothing. He'd failed her and then left her stranded in her home with a person who intended to kill her. "We're looking at attempted arson and attempted murder," he said.

"I've already called my arson investigator. He should be here soon."

"I'll be outside with the victim until then."

They both headed for the front door. Mark took a throw blanket from the couch and grabbed Libby's purse, which sat on the floor next to Angela's boxes. His eyes lingered on the damn boxes, his reason for leaving her alone in the house. All signs indicated Libby was the target. But he couldn't help but wonder if someone hoped the fire would destroy the boxes as well as kill Libby.

He stepped out into the yard and called Jack from her cell phone. Jack answered on the second ring. "Libby? Is everything okay?"

Mark glanced at his watch; it was nearly midnight. "Hi, Jack, this is Mark Colby. There's been a break-in at the Shelby house. Libby is okay, but she was assaulted."

"What?"

"She was incapacitated with a Taser and someone tried to burn the place down with her inside."

"My God."

"She's being checked out by paramedics right now. Are you in Coho?"

"Yeah. I'm coming over." Jack hung up.

Back in the yard, Libby was up and walking around, trying to convince the EMTs that they could leave. She looked brave, strong, and very much as if she was trying to hide just how hurt she was. He wanted to pull her into his arms and hold her, but instead he sat her down and wrapped the blanket around her.

Minutes later, Jack and Jason walked up the back driveway. Mark studied Jason, looking for signs that the lawyer was hiding something. He checked his watch. Five minutes since his call. The assailant had left on foot and disappeared without a trace. "You got here fast."

"We're staying in the Dawes house, up the hill," Jason said. "Cut through a few yards and it's a quick walk." He approached Libby and knelt next to the gurney. "Are you okay?" He wrapped his hands around hers as though he was trying to warm her.

I'm fine, just sore, she said.

"What happened?"

Mark watched the two of them and made a decision he hadn't even realized he'd been considering. "Before you talk to Libby, I need to speak with you both," Mark said.

Jason reluctantly dropped her hands and stood. He didn't take his eyes off Libby.

She waved him away. "I'm fine. Talk to Mark."

He led Jason and Jack to the front of the house, where they could speak alone. He wouldn't wait for the DNA results. Fifteen years ago the dental records would have been enough for a positive identification and he had Jack and Jason's attention here, now. It was time to tell them Angela had been found.

19

The EMTs checked Libby's heart rate once again while Mark talked to Jack and Jason on the other side of the house. She knew he must be telling them about Angela. After several minutes, Jack and Jason walked back around the house. There was sadness in Jason's eyes, but determination, too. She stood and reached out to him, responding to his pain on a primal level. He hugged her fiercely. All her fears and reservations about him disappeared. She offered only comfort and that was all he took.

She pulled away and held both of his hands in hers. "I'm very sorry about what happened to your mother, but I'm glad we found her. I hope you'll find out what happened to her now."

"Maybe we will," Jason said, "if they don't waste all their time investigating Jack. I was with him when my mom disappeared. At nine years old, I may not have been considered a reliable alibi, but I'm not nine anymore."

She wondered if his career choice of defense lawyer stemmed from the need to prepare for the day when his father would need his counsel. His father hadn't been there for him when his mother disappeared, but Jason would support his father now.

The arson investigator arrived. He questioned Mark and Officer Edelson and then interviewed her. He then examined the kitchen and finally released the scene to the Coho Police Department, who swarmed into the house.

Libby moved with Jack and Jason to the relative comfort of the living room. The house was a strange hive of activity for one in the morning. An officer removed the boxes from the living room, loading them into the trunks of several patrol cars while Jason read through the warrant.

Libby told Jack and Jason what she'd found in the boxes and about the copies she'd made. She confessed that she'd opened one box after Mark had told her not to, knowing if she didn't tell them now then the omission could come back to haunt her.

Jack paced the living room while officers passed through, busy with the dual investigations. He glanced briefly at the broken window in the front door. "Is that how he got in?" he asked.

Mark walked into the living room and answered for her. "That's how Lance and I entered. We don't know how the attacker got in. Who has keys to this house?"

"Jason and I. Libby has two copies."

"Simone has one," Libby said.

"Do you have a cleaning service?" Mark asked.

"No one I use regularly enough to give a key," Jason said. He turned to Libby. "I'll call a locksmith and have the locks changed. You will have the only keys. I'll also have an alarm system installed by Monday."

Jack turned to Mark. "Do you need anything else from us tonight?"

"No. I'd like to talk to you at the station tomorrow, after we have the DNA confirmation."

Jack's spine stiffened. "I will do anything to catch Angela's killer."

An hour later, Mark closed the boarded-up door behind the last officer to leave the scene. It was time for the talk that had seemed so vital hours ago. Libby decided to begin with the biggest issue that stood between them. "Jason told me you could be fired because you didn't take control of the unopened boxes as soon as you had the preliminary ID."

"That would only be a threat if I were on shaky ground with the city council, then something like that could be leverage to force a resignation. But I'm good at what I do and haven't made enemies here."

"I had no idea those boxes could be so important that my actions could get you fired."

"No one is going to fire me over boxes that are probably inadmissible. Any good lawyer could get them excluded. They were out of police control for years. My best hope is they'll lead me to evidence that *is* admissible."

"I wish I could go back to yesterday."

He pulled her into his arms and kissed her lightly on the lips. "Right now all that matters is you're okay. I never should have left you here tonight."

A tingling sensation in her nose warned of tears. She fought crying the only way she could. She rose up on her toes and kissed him, but the tears came anyway.

Both his hands cupped her face. He brushed her tears away and kissed her tenderly.

"You make me feel things that scare me," she whispered against his lips. Mortification spread through her. She couldn't believe she'd said the words aloud. In her experience, nothing drove away a man faster than admitting feeling more than lust. In horror, she tried to pull away.

He locked his arms around her waist, preventing escape. "I'm scared, too."

Never in a million years did she expect him to say that. "What are we going to do?"

"I've gone skydiving. Scared the hell out of me, but it was an amazing flight. This feels the same."

"Do I have a parachute?"

He grinned. "Don't need it. We can fly."

Her stomach dropped, taking her heart along for the ride. She couldn't believe she was getting a second chance after so thoroughly screwing things up. She laughed and kissed him again, this time without tears.

She dropped down on her heels and leaned her forehead against his chest. He made her feel safe. As if she could forget what happened in the kitchen. There was one detail she wanted to tell him. "Mark, I think Aaron was at the library yesterday."

"He couldn't have been there. I watched the crowd, looking specifically for him."

"Have you met him?"

"I've seen photos."

"I think he sat in the second to last row. He wore a Mariners baseball cap."

"No. I'd have recognized him."

"Simone didn't believe me either. But I know he was there. I even dreamt last night I saw him there. Couldn't my subconscious remember what my conscious mind didn't?"

"It was probably just a dream."

"But it was so real."

"What matters is tonight. My ex-partner is checking his alibi as we speak. We'll know tomorrow morning if he could have been here."

"Ask about last night, too."

"You're exhausted and under a lot of stress. I understand why you think you saw him but he wasn't there. Listen, it's two in the morning and we both need to get some sleep. I'm taking you to my place."

"Is this a ploy to get me into your bed?"

"I'm not above capitalizing on what happened." He nipped her ear.

She chuckled.

"Seriously, I have a guest bedroom. But if you'd be more comfortable here, I can sleep on the couch."

"Your place is fine. Let me get some things for tomorrow." She was halfway to the staircase when she stopped. "I need to take a shower. I still smell like gasoline. I have to get this smell off."

"Go ahead."

She washed as quickly as possible. She wanted to get away from the house. Her anxiety to leave increased with every moment. Frustration filled her when she couldn't find her hairbrush. It was probably in the downstairs bathroom, which was next to the kitchen. She used a comb instead and dressed quickly in a T-shirt and jeans. At least now she smelled like soap, not gasoline.

They arrived at Mark's house at two thirty in the morning. He lived near Main Street, a small two-story house in a neighborhood of matching homes. The stillness of the night led to the fanciful notion that they were the only people for miles. She followed him up the front walkway, momentarily distracted by the beauty of the clear, cool, silent night.

How close had she come to not having this moment?

A shooting star streaked across the sky, stopping her in her tracks. "Did you see that? We should make a wish."

"You're fine. Alive, uninjured. What more could I possibly want?"

His words caused something in Libby to break. She reached out, pulled him to her, and kissed him. A hot, hard, open-mouthed kiss that held nothing back. She needed to feel something, anything, everything.

He pulled her to the porch and somehow unlocked the front door without breaking the kiss. They stumbled into the entryway. He closed the door and dropped his keychain and her overnight bag on the floor. She dropped her purse and began pulling apart the buttons on his shirt. Her mouth followed her hands and explored his muscular chest. She tugged his shirt out of his pants, and then traced the straps of the shoulder holster that made removing the garment impossible.

"I've never had sex with a man wearing a gun before."

"Does it excite you?"

In the strangest way. But how do we get it off? I want to feel your skin against mine."

He removed the weapon and shirt, dropping them to the floor next to her overnight bag, and then he pulled her T-shirt over her head and tossed it over his shoulder. He reached out and cupped her bra. "Green. You're messing up my theory. Your shirt was gray."

She glanced at her satin bra. "I don't bother matching T-shirts—"

His fingers covered her lips. "Don't tell me. I'm going to figure out your system on my own." His lips trailed along the exposed skin of her breasts. He looked up. "I like green. The color matches your eyes."

His thumbs traced her nipples under the satin bra, causing them to stiffen. He followed the edge of the fabric with his mouth, but went no further. Her nipples begged for his attention. She let out a soft plea.

He looked up at her. His clear blue eyes touched something deep inside her. Making her aware that her intense arousal matched his. They'd only just begun foreplay, and yet she was ready for him. But then, she'd been ready since Tuesday.

She reached down and traced the outline of his erection. Her eyes closed as she imagined the feel of his hard length inside her. His tongue swept across her bare nipple and she grabbed his biceps for support as her knees buckled.

Without taking his mouth from her breast, he guided her to the entryway bench. He moved the fabric aside from her other breast and sucked on her aching nipple while she grasped his hair.

His hands slid over her, cupping her butt and pulling her against him. His erection pressed against the inside of her thigh. She shifted so he pressed against her center and pulled him to her for a scorching kiss.

She found his fly and undid the buttons and then reached inside and slid her hand down his hard length, smiling with satisfaction as he growled low in his throat.

"I have condoms in my purse." She reached for her bag. Without moving from her position, she fished out the foil packet and set it on the bench. "Simone loaded me up before our date."

He laughed. "Bless her." He reached for the button on her jeans and deftly removed her pants, smiling at the sight of her green panties. "Do all of your bras have matching underwear?"

"Most do."

He groaned. "And the red one?"

"You'll find out."

She slid his pants over his butt and down his legs. He kicked them aside. She pulled down on the elastic waistband of his boxer shorts. In moments, he stood naked before her.

She paused to stare at him. She'd had a pretty good idea of his build from the several times she'd been in his arms, but now she could see for herself he was perfect. His skin was smooth and taut over muscular shoulders and arms. His chest had a light covering of dark hair. His flat belly boasted well-defined abdominal muscles. She mentally compared him to Michelangelo's David, for the first time in her life thinking Michelangelo had a few things to learn about the male form. Her throat was dry as she rasped, "You're beautiful."

"Not nearly as beautiful as you are. And as sexy as your underwear is, it's in my way." He dispensed with her bra and then knelt on the floor in front of the bench and gave her nipples the attention she craved while his hands worked her underwear down her thighs and tossed them aside.

His touch made her ravenous. She tugged at his shoulders until he stood, and then she slid her tongue down his abdomen, following the line of hair from his navel. She looked up and made eye contact with him as she took him in her mouth. His eyes smoldered, a dark, hot blue. He groaned as she sucked and took him deeper, and then repeated the strokes, reveling in his taste, the feel of him against her tongue.

He threaded his fingers in her hair and gently slid from her mouth. "Later I want to come that way, but not this time."

He nudged her onto the bench. She barely noticed the cold wood against her bare butt as he spread her legs, dropped down between her thighs, and tasted her. The stroke of his tongue brought forth electrical surges of pleasure. Intense. Hot. She panted as he pushed her closer and closer to an explosive orgasm. She pulled back, dizzy with pleasure and wanting to feel him inside her.

He kissed along her torso as he shifted his position, his lips joining hers as his hips settled between her thighs. With a groping hand, she managed to find the condom. She ripped open the package and slid the circle of latex over him.

With one thrust he filled her, completed her. She was so aroused, she felt sparks of orgasm with the first intense stroke. She kissed him as she wrapped her legs around him, taking him deep.

He groaned and trailed his lips along her throat to her breast, where his tongue teased her nipple and then his teeth gently tugged at the taut peak. She made a noise in the back of her throat, the sensation of his hot length inside her and his mouth on her breast a potent combination that brought her to the edge.

She felt absolutely wild. He kissed her again, his tongue sliding along hers in time to his thrusts. His movements slowed.

"Don't stop," she panted the words. "We can go slower later."

He laughed, "Later? Woman, how old do you think I am? Eighteen?"

She orgasmed before she could answer. A powerful, shattering sensation that lasted and lasted. He dropped over the same edge, and he pulled her tightly to him as he came.

Spent, he dropped soft kisses along her throat. She enjoyed the weight and feel of him as their heartbeats gradually slowed and speech became possible again. "I'm not sure how old you are Mark, but I'm thirty-three. I'm at my sexual peak. You'll have to try to keep up with me."

"I'm thirty-eight. My peak occurred about twenty years ago— when I was way too young to appreciate it. If you don't kill me, keeping up with you will be my pleasure."

"I'll try to be gentle with you."

He laughed. "You know, I don't think I've ever had a wish granted so quickly."

"But you didn't make a wish."

"Well, there was one thing I wanted."

"Then we both wished for the same thing." She glanced around. "Nice house."

"Believe it or not, there's more to it than a foyer."

"Please tell me that somewhere beyond this entryway there's a bedroom."

He stood and lifted her off the bench. "With a king-sized bed."

He carried her upstairs, impressing her to no end. Once in his bedroom, he tossed her onto his bed, and climbed up after her, his naked body sliding against hers, his lips trailing along her skin until his mouth reached hers. "You look even better in my bed than I imagined."

"Everything about you is better than I imagined."

"Does that make me exceptional or were your expectations low?"

She reached between them and wrapped her fingers around his cock and slid her hand up and down the shaft. "You are, without a doubt, exceptional."

She explored him, with hands and mouth, somewhat amazed at her lack of inhibitions with him. This freedom in her sexuality was new. She trusted him in a profound way. He was right. Together they could fly.

He pushed her backward on the bed and took over the job of exploring. She told him exactly what she liked, how he made her feel, as he discovered all the secrets of her body. Eventually he settled his head between her thighs. She continued talking right up until she was on the brink, and then she stopped mid-word as she was rocked by another powerful orgasm.

Afterward, he said, "I thought you were going to be able to talk all the way through your orgasm."

She flushed and he captured her face between his hands. "I loved everything you said. You're so damn sexy, I nearly came while going down on you." He kissed her.

"Really?"

"I love the fact you aren't afraid to tell me what you want." He kissed her again. His voice was husky as he said, "Sexual peak, huh? You up for another round?"

She pushed him back on the bed and straddled him. "Where do you keep your condoms?"

"There's a box in the nightstand."

"I hope you have a big box."

"I think there are a dozen."

"That's not nearly enough."

He closed his eyes as he sank back into the pillow. She slipped a new condom on his erection. Slowly, she took him inside her again.

"I think you just may kill me," he muttered.

20

At ten the following morning, Mark hung up the phone. The DNA results were conclusive. There was a ninety-nine point nine percent likelihood that the bones were Angela Caruthers. He was scheduled to interview Jack at eleven thirty.

He looked back at the bed, where Libby lay sleeping. Sunlight spilled in from the east-facing window, giving her skin a golden glow. He hadn't wanted to rush this, their first morning together, but he didn't have a choice.

He slid back in bed next to her and gathered her in his arms. She opened her eyes. "'Bout time you woke up, lazybones," he said.

"Good morning," she said with a sleep-saturated smile. She ran a fingertip along the edge of his pectoral muscle. "You look delicious."

"That's 'cause I got laid last night." He nipped her neck and worked his way to her earlobe. "How 'bout you? Do you always look this good in the morning?"

"No. My skin has a four-orgasm glow today."

"Only four? I'm going to have to work harder." He reached into the nightstand and grabbed a condom.

He made love to her slowly, silently, her gasps of pleasure as he woke her body and mind the only sound in the room. He was ass over teakettle crazy for this woman. And it wasn't the sex—although that was nothing short of spectacular—it was Libby and her intelligent eyes, her forthright manner, her passion for her work, her courage in her convictions, and, of course, her sexy underwear.

He'd failed her last night. He'd left her in jeopardy and she could have paid for his mistake with her life. He didn't know if he would ever be able to forgive himself.

His mouth captured the sounds of her coming as her body shuddered in climax. His orgasm followed. An intense wave of pleasure, his relief was both physical and emotional.

Afterward, they lay in a spooning position while his hand stroked along her hip. "I have to leave for work soon."

"I should get some work done today, too. But frankly, I don't even care about the project at the moment." She rolled over and faced him. "I wish we could just pretend the rest of the world doesn't exist."

"You can. Stay here today. Get some rest," he grinned, "because when I get home, you're going to need your energy." He slid his fingers through her hair, and then tightened his grip and pulled her to him for a deep—but too-brief—kiss. "I'll try to be back by six. I'm taking tomorrow off. Sunday, too, if I can."

"If I'm going to take the weekend off, I'd better work today. I've got a report to write, interviews to transcribe. Can you drop me at Simone's so I can get the Suburban?"

"Sure. We've got twenty minutes to get ready."

She climbed out of bed. "Shower with me?"

"And another wish comes true." He followed her into the bathroom.

"You saw another shooting star last night?"

"No, I held one in my arms."

She stopped and faced him. "You better watch it. You say things like that and I'm going to fall in love with you."

His heartbeat sped up. "Maybe that's my plan." He knew it was early to talk about love but he wasn't interested in playing games.

She laced her fingers through his. "Then I don't stand a chance."

He pulled her against him and kissed her. He couldn't seem to get enough of kissing her.

After a moment, she pulled away and turned to the shower. "You only gave me twenty minutes."

"Will you go back to the Shelby house today?" he asked.

She paused. "I should. It'll be worse if I put it off, but I'm not going there alone." A small shudder passed through her and guilt jabbed at him. "Not today, anyway. I've got enough materials at the site to work on, plus I need to talk to Simone. She's going to kill me for not calling her last night and telling her what happened."

"Tell her you were in good hands."

She took his hands and pulled him into the shower with her. "I was in excellent hands."

He watched Libby follow the police chief down the front walkway and climb into the cop car. Before starting the engine, the chief kissed her. A long, lingering kiss that would have told him they were lovers if he hadn't known already.

His failed attack last night had pushed them together. Dammit. Another five minutes and Libby would have been locked in the tool shed. The Molotov cocktail would have taken care of the house, and he'd have been long gone before the fire was under control and anyone even found Libby.

The house would have been destroyed and with the evidence he'd left, Libby would have been blamed. If the fire ended up destroying the shed and killing Libby, then she would have been considered a victim of her own mental illness, her twisted desire for attention. She'd be dead and his worries would be over.

Now the police chief and the archaeologist were lovers. He needed to destroy the trust between them. He already had the pieces in place. The question was: would Colby follow the clues?

Simone was relieved to see the Suburban pull up to the site just before noon. Libby didn't come home last night. She assumed Libby stayed with the police chief. Worry hadn't set in until she wasn't able to reach her this morning. She finished her notes and then tucked her trowel in her pocket and climbed out of the unit. "Wrap up what you're working on, everyone," she called out. "Lunch starts in five."

She left the crew and joined Libby inside the RV. A grin spread across Libby's face as Simone pulled the door shut. "You got laid last night."

"Repeatedly."

"Hallelujah! So, is something going on between you two, or are you just a slut?"

Libby laughed. "There is definitely something going on. I'm crazy about him, and he seems to feel the same way."

"He'd better, or I'll have him neutered. Oh, God, Libby. I'm really happy for you." She walked to the coffeemaker and poured a cup of boiled down sludge, and then poured the thick burnt liquid down the drain and began brewing a fresh pot. "I've been worried."

"I'm sorry. I slept in." Libby's eyes turned serious. "I had a close call last night."

"Explain."

They ate their lunch together while Libby told her what had gone on the previous night. Simone rubbed her eyes as she took in all the details. She tried to make sense of the attack. "You were zapped by a 'laser. Was it your own?'"

"I have no idea," Libby said, surprise in her voice. "Mark didn't tell me if he found mine in my purse." She searched her bag. "It's not here. I wonder what that means?"

"Can they test to see if yours was fired?"

"I think so. And my blood would be on the barbs."

Simone stirred her yogurt, not really paying attention to the food in front of her. Libby could have burned to death. Aaron was a sick prick and she was going to make him pay.

"Something else you should know. The bones we found were Angela Caruthers. Mark told Jack and Jason last night."

Jason—the name alone hit her like a bee sting; said with Jack's name and she nearly suffered an anaphylaxis-type reaction. The fact EAC's excavation found Angela seemed like a cruel irony. "How did Jason take the news?" she asked.

"He's worried about Jack, worried that he'll be arrested for murdering Angela."

"Why would Jack hire us if he buried Angela in the site? That doesn't make sense. Jack's too smart to be that stupid."

"The spouse is always the starting point for a murder investigation. Makes marriage sound so appealing."

"There's no emotion stronger than love turned into hate," Simone said, wishing she didn't know that so well. "Have you got plans for the weekend?"

Libby nodded. "With Mark."

"Already you don't have time for me," Simone said with as much melodrama as she could muster. "Seriously, if you're busy—and being with Mark, I'm going to assume you will be both safe and busy—I think I'll head to Seattle." She couldn't do a damn thing about the mess she'd made of her life in Coho, but she could do something about Aaron.

"I thought you dumped your apartment?"

"I need to finish cleaning, and I have it until the end of the month. May as well have a last hurrah before I resign myself to small-town life." She tried to sound flippant.

"I like it here."

"Says the woman who is currently getting laid."

Libby laughed. "Okay, I concede your point. But Jason Caruthers is here."

"Jason's not my type," she said more sharply than she'd intended.

"Please. He's completely your type."

Simone looked down. "No. He's too pretty-boy for me."

"Simone, I know you. You want him. I just don't understand why you aren't going after him."

Simone had to put an end to this here and now. "He's the son of our client, and you know me. I'd just screw him and dump him. We don't need that." Ninety-five percent of the time, her words would be true, but in this one instance, she was lying. What happened between Jason and her was her secret, one she couldn't share with Libby.

21

On Saturday afternoon, Libby followed Mark through the woods on acreage he owned outside Coho. They wound their way to what Mark described as his favorite place on earth. Between the two of them, they carried a large picnic lunch, plenty of water, and fishing gear.

Libby's father had been an avid fisherman, but fishing was just one more thing he never shared with his children, and so she'd avoided it. The prospect of being with Mark for her first time fishing was remarkably appealing.

They scrambled down a steep slope and suddenly a narrow tributary was before them, lazily winding down from the mountains to the strait. A flat area adjacent to the glacier-fed river was grassy and shaded, and a small trail through shrubs provided access to the river. Even though it was a warm summer day, the air was crisp. She could practically smell the cold of the water, the scent mixing with the damp earth and leaves.

"What do you think?" Mark asked.

"It's amazing," she said, and meant it. She spread out the blanket on the flat above the bank and made herself comfortable while he organized his fishing gear.

Less than forty-eight hours before, she'd been bound, gagged, doused in gasoline, and tortured. Even falling in love with Mark—which she was certain was happening with every moment they spent together—wasn't quite enough to block out the horror of what

happened late Thursday night. Mark knew it; she knew it. They'd
talked about what happened late into the night last night, eventually
deciding this picnic would be a good escape from the fear and questions that hounded her. Right now she just needed a break, and Mark
was giving it to her.

"Time for your first casting lesson."

She quickly learned she had zero natural talent for casting. They
both laughed at her botched attempts, and he didn't even complain
when she snagged yet another of his hooks in the trees that lined
the river.

"Okay, so you know how to make a spearhead out of rock because
that's what Indians did a thousand years ago, but you can't catch a
fish?" Mark teased. "Wasn't fishing just as important as hunting?"

"Probably more important. Fish were abundant and easily harvested." She caught the humor in his eye and defended herself. "Well,
they were easily harvested when the rivers were full of them. This
tributary probably ran out of fish in the sixties."

He dropped his pole and slid his arms around her waist. "You can
tell yourself that if it makes you feel better."

"It does."

He picked her up and carried her down the path, stopping at the
edge of the bank. "Or you can go for a swim and see for yourself if
there are any fish in the river."

She clutched at his neck. "You wouldn't dare." But she could see
from his face that he would. "Mark Colby, if you drop me in the river,
then you're going swimming too."

"Deal," he said and jumped off the low bank into the frigid water.
They landed in a four-foot deep pool, just deep enough for Mark to
dunk her, which he did immediately. The water was so cold it burned.
She gasped for breath as she scrambled for purchase. Laughing, she
wrapped her arms around his neck and kissed him, his cold, wet body
plastered to hers in the middle of the river.

His hot lips warmed her to the core. She tightened her grip on him
and planted one foot on the silty river bottom. With her other foot she
swept his legs out from under him, and he went down.

She wrestled with him as long as she could stand the cold water—
about twenty seconds—and then scrambled up the bank, smearing
dirt on her wet clothes. She collapsed on the blanket. Mark dropped
down next to her. His eyes were a vivid blue, lit with laughter
and cold.

She knew why he'd dunked her in the river. Every moment of playfulness was a distraction, a step away from Tasers and duct tape. And now, lying on the blanket, a shivering muddy mess, she felt more alive, more in love, than ever in her life.

She pushed him onto his back and kissed him.

He smiled at her. "You look like you did on Monday at the site, all coated in dirt and beautiful. I knew then that I wanted to take you here. Make love to you outside." He unbuttoned her wet shirt. "You belong here, surrounded by trees, grass, water, dirt. An earthy place for an earthly woman."

"If I wasn't already hooked on you, that line would have done it."

"It wasn't a line."

The scary part was she believed him. He was too good to be true, which made her wonder if Mark had brought other women to this place or if this was as special for him as it was for her. But she didn't ask. She was better off not knowing and needed to stop looking for flaws and enjoy the moment. Sheltered as they were by the shrubs, she felt no inhibition and stripped his wet clothes from him while he did the same for her. Their lovemaking went from slow and languid to hot and urgent. She watched Mark's face as he came, reveling in the pleasure he took in her body, in her.

Afterward, Mark traced the lines of mud that had transferred from her clothes to her skin. "You have an impressive scar here," Mark said, running his fingers along the inside of her thigh.

"Barbed wire fence," she said. "I was working on a survey a few years ago. I tried to go over the fence at the same time a coworker tried to go under it—he lifted the wire at the wrong moment. I got caught on an extra sharp spur that cut through my pants, sliced open my thigh. I can say with authority that the inside upper thigh is an awkward place for stitches."

"Ouch." He slid down and kissed the scar. "Tell me about your work," he said. "Tell me about the layers of dirt, why they are so important, why you excavate them separately."

"Well, the different strata and their order tell us a lot." She pushed him onto his back and moved on top of him. "For example, this is a good demonstration of the Law of Superposition. If you took Geology 101—rocks for jocks—you've probably heard of that scientific law."

"Sounds familiar."

"The Law of Superposition means that the lower stratum, in this case, you, is the oldest; anything above, in this case, me, is younger.

Soils are deposited over time and the oldest stuff is on the bottom. If you can match up your strata across a site, you can get a good idea of what events were concurrent."

"How do you explain something like this?" he asked, slipping inside her, shocking her with his ready erection.

"Bioturbation." She was still sensitive from her recent orgasm and gasped at the end of the word.

He gave a bark of laughter. "Bio-*what?*"

Eyes closed, she answered, "Rodents, insects, roots. Natural processes for the different strata to become intermixed."

"And what about this?" He rolled her underneath him.

"Earthquake. Mudslide," she managed to gasp out.

"I don't have a condom on."

"Damn." She wrapped her legs around him, unwilling to let him leave her just yet, despite the risk of pregnancy. "I'm going to have to go on the pill."

"I'll buy," he offered, moving his hips in a way that made thinking impossible.

"Deal," she said with a groan. "Now let's discuss the Richter scale. I think this could be a 9.4—literally earth-shattering."

"Are all archaeologists like this during sex?"

"No. I'm much more fun. Are all cops as good in bed as you?"

He paused.

She knew she'd made a mistake. She relaxed her thighs and he slipped out of her.

"Perhaps you can tell me," he said.

He wanted to know if she slept with Aaron. She didn't know whether she felt annoyed or not. They hadn't known each other then and her previous relationship should have no bearing on this one. But Aaron and his lies had been between them from the beginning. She understood his curiosity. The same kind of curiosity made her wonder if she was the only woman he'd made love to next to this river. She pulled his face to hers and kissed him. "I didn't have sex with Aaron. You're the only cop I've ever been with."

"I was out of line. I shouldn't have said that."

She shrugged. "May as well get it out in the open."

"For what it's worth, I'm glad."

"Not nearly as glad as I am." She wanted so badly to believe that it was Aaron who attacked her. He was the villain she knew. The idea that it could be someone else terrified her. She asked him the one question she'd avoided so far. "Does he have an alibi for Thursday?"

"Bobby is having a hard time tracking him down. All I know is he wasn't on duty Thursday night."

So it still could be Aaron. She closed her eyes and allowed herself to remember the time when she knew him, the night she dumped him. Could that man have tried to kill her two nights ago?

Yes, definitely.

She looked at Mark. His eyes were guarded. Talk of Aaron had crushed their playful mood. She reached out and rubbed the stubble on his chin.

"I'll find out if it's Aaron, Libby. If he attacked you, he won't get away with it."

She rested her head on his chest. His hand slid over her back and then his fingers threaded through her hair. She closed her eyes in pleasure as his nails grazed her skin. "Why did you become a cop?"

"A cop is what I always wanted to be. I think when I was a kid, it was about the gun and the car. Then I got older and I wanted to help people. I wanted to chase down bad guys and save the day. I had a romanticized notion of what being a cop was like. By the time I found out how wrong I was, it didn't matter. I was hooked. The work suits me. I like reading people. I like following clues and working out the puzzle. I do less investigation now, but I like the community policing aspect of small-town police work. In Coho, my job is closer to my idealized vision of being a cop." He palmed the back of her head and massaged her scalp. "Sometimes I even get to save the girl." He grew serious again. "I'm going to find out who attacked you, and I'm going to protect you until your assailant is caught."

She stiffened. No man had ever offered to protect her before. Not her father. Especially not her father. She'd been taking care of herself and her little brother and sister since she was eleven years old. She didn't lift her head to face him. She didn't want him to see her reaction. Then he would know what an insecure basket case she was.

"What's going on?" he asked.

"Nothing."

With a finger under her chin, he urged her to meet his gaze. "Hey, didn't I just tell you I can read people? That includes you."

"Can we save this one for later?"

He stared at her for a long, silent moment. "Later, then." He kissed her gently. "I seem to remember we were discussing the Richter scale."

Grateful for the change in subject, she reached for a condom. "I will tell you your score after you've rocked my world. You should know the scale has no upper limit—so there's always room for improvement."

"You will definitely be the death of me."

Her lips settled into the crook of his neck as he slid within her. Words she'd never wanted to say to a man before formed in her throat. With silent lips, she pressed the words against his warm skin, not daring to speak them aloud.

"**G**od, this is good pizza," Libby said.

It was Sunday evening; their weekend respite was almost at an end. Mark had spoken on the phone with his officers several times in the last two days, but the time he'd taken off had been his longest break from the station since he moved to Coho. Libby sat at the table while he leaned against his kitchen counter and watched her, thoroughly enjoying the view as she licked the sauce from her fingers.

"I think I'll add the pizza place to my list of reasons to stay in Coho," she added.

He startled, shaking off the distracted fog that descended the second her index finger slipped inside her mouth. "I thought you moved here permanently."

"We're here for the duration of the project, with the plan to stay if I can grow the business from here. But I need more than one client to do that."

"So you're making a list of reasons to stay."

She grinned. "Yes, well, let's see, so far there's pizza and you."

Relief was accompanied with another emotion, and it wasn't just the pleasure he took in her willingness to admit this was more than a casual fling. He loved watching her laugh, watching her talk, watching her orgasm. She did all three with equal abandon. She unconsciously made eating pizza into an erotic event. She was fearless in sharing her body, and demanding in the sharing of his.

He'd never fallen this hard or this fast for someone. The timing wasn't great, not with her being involved with two open investigations, but he couldn't have waited, couldn't have put aside this attraction until one or both cases were resolved.

They'd spent the weekend making her feel safe, giving her a break from the stress of her project and the mystery of the attempt on her life. But tomorrow was Monday. Their return to the real world loomed.

"I want you to stay with me," he said, voicing the decision he'd made two days ago. "You'll be safer here than in the Shelby house or with Simone."

She sat up straighter. Her face became serious, an acknowledgement of the fact that however temporarily, he'd just asked her to move in with him.

"Are you sure?" she asked.

"More than I've ever been about anything. You're staying with me." He left out his hope that the living arrangement would continue after her assailant was caught.

"I still need to work at the Shelby house. It's where my office is."

"I'll have patrol pass the house regularly whenever you're there."

"Thank you."

"I'll need to know your schedule—just when you're going to be at the house," he added, realizing it sounded as though he'd be keeping tabs on her.

"I'll be there most of the day tomorrow. I have so much to do before I submit my draft on Friday. I'm meeting Jason for lunch, so I'll be away for an hour or two."

A rush of jealousy startled Mark from complacency. "You have a date with Jason?"

"It's a business meeting. You're the one who goaded him into calling our last lunch meeting a date."

"He's interested in you." He knew his words were a mistake. At least he didn't mention the embrace he'd witnessed on Thursday night. On a rational level, he understood why she hugged him. On an emotional level, he'd wanted to march across the yard and pull them apart. He wanted Jason to know she was *his*.

"I don't think so. I think he likes Simone—there is something strange going on between them. But more important, I'm not interested in him. In case you can't tell, I want you." She crossed the room and cupped his face in her hands. "But you're going to have to trust me. I'll probably continue to need Jason's help for the duration of this project. And, if not Jason, there will be some other male colleague. Being involved with an archaeologist is hard—I'm sometimes gone for months at a time, camping in the middle of nowhere, not reachable even by cell phone. This relationship won't survive without trust."

Time she knew the truth about what she could expect if their relationship continued, which he wanted more than anything. "Relationships with a cop are also hard. I've been in love before. But love isn't enough. She got tired of the odd hours and late nights, and wondering if I'd be injured in the line of duty."

"So she left?" His ego was mollified at Libby's shocked tone.

"She wanted me to go to law school. We compromised and I went to grad school, to get a degree in public administration. I thought she'd be satisfied if I became a police chief."

"You must have been pretty serious if you went back to school for her."

He nodded. "We were engaged." He was doing a lousy job explaining. "We lived together, but we never set a date for the wedding. I think we both knew it wasn't working." He paused. Now was as good a time as any to tell her the rest. "There's one thing you should know. Sheila—my ex-fiancée—had an affair with Jason."

She gasped. "You knew him when you worked in Seattle?"

"We worked the opposite side of a few cases. She met him the same way she met me—through her work as a court reporter."

"Now I understand your reaction to Jason."

"He didn't know she and I were together. She lied to him, to me. She had a shot at the rich lawyer of her dreams and went for it. When Jason discovered we were living together, he dumped her and told her to confess to me or he'd do it for her. She admitted to the affair, and I moved out of our apartment the same day. A few months after that, I finished my master's program, and Jason gave my name to the headhunter Coho had hired to find a police chief. What Sheila did has never been an issue between Jason and me."

"But Sheila's an issue now, or you wouldn't be telling me about her."

"I think he's interested in you. Apparently we have the same taste in women."

"The corollary being, am I the same type of woman, ready to jump from you to him? Don't hold me accountable for your ex-fiancée's actions, and I won't assume all cops are like Aaron."

He was making a mess of this. "I had that coming." He gathered her closer. "Listen, Libby. I'm crazy about you. I want this to work between us. I trust you. I don't care that you're working with Jason. I just want you to come home to me at the end of the day."

"That's what I want, too."

22

Libby paused by the rear door of the Shelby house, bracing herself to enter for the first time since the attack. Mark had wanted to be by her side this morning, but a traffic accident at the north end of town prevented him. Which was just as well. This was something she needed to face down on her own. She unlocked the door and stepped inside.

As promised, Jason had had a security system installed. She shut off the alarm, and then spent several minutes familiarizing herself with the system before resetting the security code. After that, she squared her shoulders and turned to face the kitchen.

A cleaning crew had visited over the weekend and the crisp scents of lemon and pine permeated the space, and yet she was certain she could still detect the faint odor of gasoline.

Reminded of the first sharp jolt from the Taser, her knees weakened. She stepped to the sink and braced her arms against the front, holding herself up. She ran the faucet and splashed cold water on her face and then closed her eyes. *Think of the frigid river water. Think of mud, laughter, fishing, and falling in love.*

She opened her eyes and looked around the kitchen again. *You can do this.*

She wanted to reclaim the room by preparing and eating something, but she had no appetite. She turned and went upstairs to her office.

She was engrossed in a transcript when her geomorphologist, Jerry

Santos, called. "Hey, Libby. What the hell are you doing sending me Mount St. Helens ash and claiming you found it a meter deep? You trying to mess with me or something?"

"Are you talking about the soil samples I sent over a week ago?"

"Yeah. I started processing them this morning."

"We didn't send you Mount St. Helens ash, Jerry. The samples we sent are from the site in Coho. Ash from the Mount St. Helens eruption didn't dump here on the peninsula."

"I know. But the bag you sent me is St. Helens."

"Wait a second—read me the provenience information written on the bag."

Jerry did while Libby opened the site master catalog on her computer.

"That sample came from just above Angela's remains—we sent it before we found the bones. I forgot to tell the police to contact you to get the samples back."

"Police? What the hell are you talking about?"

"That bag of St. Helens ash you have is police evidence."

"Evidence of what?"

"We found a murder victim in the site, a woman who has been missing for more than twenty years. It made the news here, but might not have made the headlines in Idaho. Stop processing all the samples that came from units 22, 23, and 24. I'll have the officer in charge of the investigation contact you," she said.

After the conversation ended, Libby leaned back in her chair. Angela had been buried under a large pocket of Mount St. Helens ash. The ash couldn't have fallen naturally on the Olympic Peninsula— Jerry had identified a clue to where she'd been buried before her remains were moved in 1984.

She picked up the phone to dial Mark, and then stopped. She would rather tell him in person and could use a break from the Shelby house. Traffic was light—as usual for Coho—when she crossed town, noting that the earlier accident had been cleared. Mark was probably at the station.

An officer she didn't know led her through the squad room to Mark's office. He smiled in surprise when he saw her. He looked gorgeous. His button-down shirt was open at the collar, bringing vivid memories of running her tongue over his exposed skin. She licked her lips.

His dimple deepened, and he gave her a sultry look before he said softly, "Cut that out, you're giving me a hard-on. I'm going to be stuck behind this desk all day."

She laughed. "I have news. I got a call from my geomorphologist this morning. We sent him some samples before we found the remains. Today he told me an ash sample we took a meter below the surface was from Mount St. Helens."

"As in the 1980 eruption?"

"Exactly. The sample was taken from just above the bones, where we uncovered a large ash stratum. The layer could only have been deposited on May 18, 1980, when St. Helens erupted. The ash cloud from St. Helens coated Eastern Washington within hours, but only trace amounts of ash ever made it to the Olympic Peninsula, and most of that traveled all the way around the world before getting here. Which means, the pocket of ash we sampled had to have been moved with her. There's no way a deposit of St. Helens' ash that thick is *in situ* on the peninsula."

"So you think she was in Eastern Washington before she was moved here in 1984."

"Yes. She must have been buried in a very shallow grave before May 18, 1980. You asked the ME if a body could decompose down to bones in less than five years—well, Eastern Washington's desert environment is perfect for rapid decomposition."

"And you assume she was buried in a shallow grave because the layer of dirt above the bones but beneath the ash deposit was thin."

"Yes. It's the Law of"—her face heated as she remembered exactly how she'd explained the principle to him on Saturday—"Superposition again."

His eyes flashed with amusement. "I don't think I'll ever forget that geologic law." He turned serious. "So it's likely her body was originally buried somewhere in Eastern Washington, then St. Helens exploded and the ash covered her grave."

"Yes. Whoever dug Angela up from her first resting place removed her bones with the soil and ash that was on top of her. I've already given you copies of the maps we drew of the ash layer with depth measurements. A snow shovel or something similarly wide and flat would make it possible to move the remains and dirt in solid pieces, which explains why her skeleton was still articulated and the ash layer intact."

"I need your geomorphologist's phone number."

She handed him Jerry's card.

He leaned back in his chair. "The person who killed her must not have worried about someone finding her accidentally, because even a dog could easily uncover a burial that shallow. I wonder what changed? Why was she moved?"

"I don't know. That's your job, Chief." She stood. "I've got to go." She paused and turned. "Maybe you should get an FBI profiler to review the case."

"You watch too many movies." He stood and followed her to the door.

"No. I read too many mysteries. I like Patricia Cornwell, don't you?"

"I don't have time for thriller fiction. I'm a cop. I live it."

She burst out laughing. "Uh, huh. And I'm Indiana Jones without the Fedora." She paused. "You know, I could buy a whip."

He closed the door, pressed her back against the solid panel, gave her a searing kiss, and then said, "And I've got the handcuffs."

Mark played phone tag with Jerry Santos for a while before finally connecting. Santos promised to send a full report of his analysis of the ash sample, along with all the remaining bags from the burial pit. Mark hung up. He couldn't believe his luck. He had a team of cops working overtime to ferret out every last bit of information from any small scrap of evidence they had, yet it was Libby who had just provided him with a major break.

The Mount St. Helens ash indicated Angela had originally been buried in Eastern Washington. Back in 1979, investigators had tried to place Angela in Eastern Washington. If they'd been able to prove Angela went east from Seattle instead of west, they'd have had a strong case against Jack, even without the body.

"Chief, you got a minute?"

Mark looked up to see Luke Roth in his office doorway. It was nearly noon and he'd planned to head out and get a bite to eat. "What do you need?"

"I've been following up on the Maitland investigation and have some questions."

"Fire away."

"You stated you'd argued with Ms. Maitland about the boxes she had, which contained Angela Caruthers' papers. Did Maitland know you planned to return with a warrant to seize the remaining boxes?"

"She did."

"Did she know how long it would take you to obtain the warrant?"

"I told her I would be back in an hour." His phone rang. Caller ID said Seattle PD. Could be Bobby. "Luke, I've got to take this call. We'll finish this when I'm done. Close the door," he instructed before picking up the phone.

"Listen, Colby." Surprise registered as he recognized the voice. Aaron Brady. "This has got to stop. You've got Internal Affairs crawling up my ass and all because I showed seriously bad judgment in getting involved with a whack job groupie."

Mark kept his voice level. "Brady, perfect timing. I have questions about your activities Thursday night."

"I was home reading my Bible. Look, I'm calling you cop to cop. You need to put a stop to this."

"Fine. Stop harassing Libby." Mark wanted to keep him on the phone, hoping he would slip up and say something that could be used against him.

"I didn't harass her before and I'm not harassing her now. *She* harassed *me* because I wouldn't help her with her financial troubles."

"That doesn't sound like a groupie. Decide on one story and stick to it."

"Oh, she definitely has a thing for cops. I bet she's already gunning for somebody in Coho, the poor bastard. I was just a bonus, because I had a connection to her client, which she wanted to use. The project she ran for my brother was in financial trouble."

"Sounds like a convenient excuse."

"Deny it all you want, Colby, but I've got the facts on my side. She took my brother to court. She lost. Hasn't she whined to you yet about the thirty thousand my brother supposedly owed her? He didn't owe her a dime. The judge agreed."

"I've read the court documents. That wasn't the issue, nor was that the finding."

"She claimed my brother agreed to the increased budget. She wanted me to back her statement. I wouldn't do it, no matter how good she fucked."

Anger gripped Mark. He wanted to rip Brady's throat out. "Libby lost because the signed copies of the contract addendum mysteriously disappeared. She had nothing else to back up her claim. There was a break-in at her office, and you were harassing her twenty-four/seven, so I have a personal favorite theory about what happened."

"I get it now," Brady said, his voice oozing satisfaction. "Smart woman, going straight for the top. Man, I should have called you sooner and saved you some trouble. I admit she's a fine piece of ass. Just remember, she'll fuck anything to get what she wants. She wanted me to get more money out of my brother. She's probably screwing you so you'll believe her bullshit stalking claims."

"You're full of shit if you think I believe a word you say."

"Does it bother you I had her first?" Brady asked in a whisper filled with taunting malice.

"It might, if it were true."

"She told you we didn't fuck?" He laughed. "I fucked her till my dick nearly fell off. I know what it feels like to be inside her. I know what she sounds like when she comes." He paused. "She has a scar from a barbed wire fence. Inside thigh. Two inches long."

"Don't call again. I don't have time for this." He slammed down the phone. Brady knew about her scar. He didn't believe Brady. He couldn't. But still, doubt crept in.

Or maybe it had never quite left.

He picked up his car keys and left the station.

23

L ibby sat across from Jason in her dining room. Because she was swamped with work, he'd brought lunch from a Chinese restaurant. She wondered what his purpose had been in arranging this meeting. She'd seen the rivalry mixed with respect between Mark and Jason, but now she understood why. Did he feel guilty about Sheila? Was he really blameless?

Their meal had reached the point of winding down, and Jason still hadn't broached whatever he wanted to talk about, which, she knew from experience, was unusual for him. This made her worry he was going to drop a bomb worse than last time.

Jason sat back, setting his chopsticks on his plate. "Jack and I have begun making arrangements to bury my mom. It'll be a while before the funeral but knowing we can bury her is a relief."

Reality slapped her into the present. She'd lost sight of what Jason and his father were dealing with. Guilt flooded her. "I'd like to attend when the time comes."

"Thank you. I want her killer found. I want a conviction. And I know that means waiting for the police to release her remains, but, after more than two decades, I'm ready to put her to rest."

"I've been going through her research, Jason. I can't help but feel as if some of it is missing. I wasn't able to go through all the boxes, but still, there doesn't seem to be enough data considering the number of years she put into it."

"The Coho PD should give you copies from the boxes you didn't get to go through. If you have trouble getting it from them, let me know. Also, Dan Parker called to let me know he found boxes in storage. I was going to pick them up over the weekend, but ended up staying in Coho. How is your report coming?"

"I'm behind." She didn't tell him the truth—that being assaulted had changed her priorities. Work was no longer first. Jason was Jack's son and Jack might not understand. "I hope what I have is what Rosalie wants. But, because I can't include conjecture or supposition, under threat of your lawsuit, she'll get the best I can manage."

Guilt flashed in Jason's eyes. "That brings us to what I wanted to talk to you about. I feel like I owe you an explanation."

"You don't owe me anything."

"I do, and the good news is that maybe in a few days your report won't matter. I've spent the last ten months negotiating a deal to sell Thorpe Log & Lumber. Now we're scheduled to sign and close on Thursday. If the deal goes through, I don't care what you write in that report."

Surprise rippled through her. "You managed to move up the closing date on this business deal so it would be complete before I send my draft to the Corps of Engineers."

He nodded. "It wasn't easy. You can't breathe a word of this to anyone. It still could fall through."

Stunned by the amount of trust he had in her, she asked, "Why are you telling me?"

"To take some of the pressure off you. You found my mom, and I know you had to work to convince the cops she wasn't Indian. If you hadn't pushed, then there never would have been a DNA test that verified her identity. Nothing I do can equal what you've done for Jack and me. For my mom. Giving you the freedom to write your report the way you need is small payment."

"Who is your buyer?"

"A consortium of investors. They want to make Coho into a living history museum. A tourist attraction. Like Williamsburg."

Libby set her glass down with a thud. "Coho is the perfect setting for that."

"They're buying everything with the guarantee that the historic district will remain intact. We've been trying to sell ever since the mill closed, and the historic district was always the sticking point. All company holdings are on the National Register of Historic Places. That scared off potential buyers. It was either break up the historic district or let some buildings fall into disrepair so they could be razed —not ethical, but still legal. Now we don't have to do anything that drastic. In fact, the buildings that need work will be returned to their late-nineteenth century state."

"Why did my report matter?"

"I couldn't take the chance that the investors would back off. There's another sawmill town on the Kitsap Peninsula—Port Gamble. They don't have as many structures or acres as TL&L, but they also don't have a racist bastard who ran things for nearly seventy years. The whole project is a celebration of history. Coho history. Like Williamsburg, they plan to do reenactments of actual events that happened in Coho, with the focus, fortunately, on the 1870s—before Lyle. But there will be displays and exhibits about TL&L in the twentieth century. If they know exactly what Lyle was, how he treated the tribe and the workers, I think they would choose to buy Port Gamble instead.

"So, Libby, if for any reason the deal doesn't close on Thursday, what you put in your report could cause the sale to fall apart."

"And there's the major problem. An accounting of Lyle's sins is exactly what Rosalie wants. If your buyers are likely to look elsewhere due to controversy, then anything I write could be a problem."

"I need to close on Thursday," Jason said. "If I don't, will you let me read your draft before you submit to the Corps?"

"I won't change anything, Jason."

"But you'll let me read it?"

"Yes."

He looked at his watch and stood abruptly. "It's later than I thought. I've got a meeting to get to."

Libby followed him through the living room to the front door. He opened the door, and then stopped. He turned and grabbed her waist, pulling her to him. "I almost forgot one thing. This." Then Jason kissed her.

She nearly lost her balance and placed her hands on his chest to steady herself. The kiss had caught her completely off-guard. Stunned, she barely managed to remember this man was her client's son—she couldn't blithely shove him away, to hell with the consequences. Instead, she gently pushed at his chest and stepped back. "Jason, I can't."

"You've told me about your client's brother. I'm not like him. This won't affect the project."

She could use her relationship with Mark as an excuse, but that would be tantamount to saying, *I'd be with you if I wasn't with Mark,* which wasn't true, and given their rivalry, was the kind of thing that could lead to more trouble between them.

"I'm sorry, Jason. This isn't what I want. I'm flattered, but I can't get involved with you."

His face was unreadable. She worried her words were too harsh.

"You don't sound likely to change your mind."

"I won't."

"I can still hope."

"Don't."

He nodded and disappeared through the door.

What the hell was that about? She'd still bet her business the man was really interested in Simone. Maybe he already knew of her involvement with Mark, and the rivalry between them went deeper than Mark was willing to admit.

Mark couldn't believe what he'd witnessed. Jason had kissed Libby. And she didn't shove him away. Shock and hurt didn't begin to describe how he felt as he drove aimlessly across town, away from the scene he couldn't get out of his mind. His knuckles on the steering wheel were white. He needed to get his emotions under control.

Aaron's words echoed in his head. They'd been the reason he'd gone to the Shelby house—to talk to Libby. Not to confront her. No. He'd managed to close the door on doubt, and just wanted to see her. He'd forgotten about her lunch meeting with Jason until he saw the gold Lexus parked out front, and then he'd been reluctant to interrupt, so he'd waited.

Jason. Again. The old wound opened, ten times more painful.

Back at the station, he escaped into his office. A message from Bobby waited on his desk. He called his ex-partner and close friend. He needed to talk to someone, and Bobby was the sharpest judge of character he knew. "What's going on, Bobby?"

"Brady's not our guy. Not for Thursday, anyway. He used his ATM card in Seattle at 11:30 that night. We've got video from both the machine and the convenience store."

"Brady called me today. He must've known he was in the clear.

He's pissed and wanted to rattle me." Mark didn't add he'd been successful.

"I don't like him, but we haven't got anything on him. I've talked to Internal Affairs. They're dropping their investigation. Brady may have stalked her before, but he didn't attack her Thursday. In fact, I've got a few questions about her myself."

A wave of unease washed over him. When Bobby followed his gut, he was the best investigator there was. "What?"

"Her friend Atherton. I caught her spying on Brady this weekend. I was doing a drive-by, to check up on him, when I saw her staked out by his apartment."

"She's worried about Libby."

"Maybe, but I'm not sure. She was sitting in her car, in front of his building. So I climbed in the passenger seat, uninvited. I scooped some papers off the seat before sitting down. One of those papers was Brady's work schedule."

"How did she get his schedule?"

"She claimed she got it from a contact in his precinct. But there's more. She had a camera. I asked her if she was the one who altered the photos used as evidence against Brady before. She admitted she was."

"Some people don't know what the right to remain silent means."

"Thank God, or we'd never have anything to work with. Anyway, she said she was just checking up on him and had purchased a new camera for the dig. She claimed she was trying the features on the new camera while she waited to see if Aaron was home. I don't buy it. Her story was too pat. Seems these women are too willing to cheat to get what they want."

"Could just be Atherton. Libby said she didn't know about the photos being altered until a few months ago."

Bobby paused. "Don't tell me you're screwing Libby Maitland."

He exercised his right to remain silent.

"What the fuck are you thinking? She's a victim and a potential suspect."

"I took her off the suspect list a week ago. My gut says she's on the level."

"That's your dick talking. Usually I'm the one who makes that mistake. You've got to end any relationship you have with her. Now. Jesus, do you want to lose your job?"

"I won't lose my job because of Libby."

"Didn't you tell me she tampered with evidence in your murder case?"

"She opened one box and copied some cassettes for her report. If she'd opened all the boxes before we identified Angela, it wouldn't have been an issue."

"You're in deep, buddy, if you're making excuses for her. Think about this. With Aaron Brady no longer a suspect, who else have you got? Libby has spent the last week trying to convince you he's our guy, but we know he's not the one. Her buddy Atherton has gone to some length to keep tabs on him. Why? Why was Maitland so eager to implicate Brady? She's the best suspect you've got."

If anyone else had asked those questions, Mark could ignore them. But he trusted Bobby's judgment implicitly. Cold dread ran through him. "I'll think about it," he said, and hung up.

He rested his forehead on his fingertips, shaken to the core. Had he made a huge judgment mistake? Hell, it wasn't nearly so simple.

He'd fallen in love with her.

But Bobby was right. He *had* to consider her as a suspect. Aaron's claim he'd slept with her had been convincing. If she lied about whether or not she had sex with him—when she could easily have told him the truth—what else had she lied about?

After seeing her in Jason's arms, her guilt seemed...possible. She could be playing Jason for financial reasons. Just like Brady claimed.

Luke knocked and then poked his head inside. "Chief, we need to finish going over the results in the Maitland investigation." He entered the room and shut the door. "You aren't going to like my findings. It's no secret you're involved with her."

"Don't make assumptions about my feelings or my ability to do the job, Officer Roth."

Luke's gaze dropped to the floor. "Sorry, Chief." He placed a stack of papers in front of Mark. "First of all, I obtained copies of all of her phone records for the last month. As Simone Atherton claimed, the phone call that was made to her at two a.m. Tuesday morning originated from the Shelby house. That could mean the stalker was there, in the house with her, but I'm inclined to think Maitland made that call herself. Atherton doesn't have a landline, so the call came on her cell phone, which is not an easy number to obtain."

Mark nodded, not liking the scenario, but aware he'd asked for trouble when he got involved with a woman connected to two active investigations.

"I've also followed up on the two gas jugs left at the Shelby house Thursday night. We found one empty jug inside the kitchen and a second full jug on the back porch. Libby Maitland bought two gas jugs and duct tape from Doug's Hardware two weeks ago. They have surveillance camera footage and a credit-card receipt."

In his role of devil's advocate, Mark said, "Those are both reasonable purchases. There are two gas-powered generators at the site."

"There's more."

Mark steeled himself.

"There was a price sticker on one of the cans. The sticker indicated the jug was purchased from Doug's, which means they are probably the same jugs purchased by her. Furthermore, we got partial prints off the cans, and we have a thumb and ring finger match with her prints, which she provided Thursday night for comparative purposes with the prints we lifted from the kitchen in her house."

"Go on."

"We'd talked to the neighbors Friday morning, asking if they'd seen the prowler the night before, but we hadn't asked about Maitland's activities. So yesterday I questioned the neighbors again. The next-door neighbor said she returned home from work Thursday sometime between noon and one o'clock. She was wearing dirty field clothes—including a blue T-shirt with some sort of white design or logo.

"The neighbor said she unloaded two large red plastic gasoline jugs from the back of her Suburban and left them on the porch. Our witness states that her movements indicated the jugs were heavy. The neighbor, Eli Banks, said he thought it was odd that she'd leave full gas containers on her porch. He's eighty-seven and doesn't get around very well. He spends much of his time on the upper balcony in the back of his house, or on his front porch."

He had to listen to Luke's evidence as a cop. As a cop, her activities bothered Mark. "It's reasonable to assume she filled the gas jugs on the way home, then placed them on the porch so the fumes wouldn't fill her vehicle. Her attacker could have made use of the jugs when he found them."

"Then why didn't she tell us she brought the jugs home herself?"

"That's the first question we need to ask her when you bring her in." Officially she was a suspect. If he didn't treat her like one, the repercussions would be enormous.

"I don't think she was hit with a Taser at all, Chief."

"She has wounds on her shoulder from the probes." He'd seen those small scabs repeatedly over the weekend.

"I think she pricked herself with the barbs then tossed the Taser in the backyard for us to find. We downloaded the firing history from the weapon. It had been fired once, for less than a second. Traceable tags discharge when a Taser is fired. She could have fired it once to scatter the tags we found throughout the kitchen. Those particular tags traced to Maitland's weapon. She purchased that Taser cartridge a week ago Saturday. Even if the firing log was inaccurate, the jolts she described should have depleted the alkaline batteries in the Taser. The batteries were full."

"Did you check the batteries for fingerprints?"

"Hers were the only ones on the batteries, and on the Taser. I think she's a superb actress."

A surreal emotional detachment descended upon him. *Yes, she is.*

"There's more," Luke said. "Her fingerprints were on the adhesive side of the duct tape that bound her, and her fingerprints were on the Molotov cocktail. We wondered why it didn't break, how the flame was extinguished before the room went up. The answer is simple. She staged it all."

"But how could she tape up her own wrists?"

"Her wrists were bound in front of her. So I tried it myself. Taping my wrists was easy. The hardest part would have been ripping off the roll, which is probably why the roll of tape was still attached at her wrists when you arrived."

"What about the gas? It would be dangerous for her to fill the kitchen with propane when she was coated in gasoline."

"I don't think it was such a big risk. You said in your report that the back door was open—letting fresh air in. All she had to do was wait for you to knock. Then she could have turned on the burners and rolled around in the gasoline on the floor."

He was bloodless. Adrift. The image of her in Jason's arms came rushing back and he could see the calculation in her stance. The perfection in her understated response.

Had she planned their argument Thursday night? He carefully went over the sequence of events in his mind. She confessed to opening the box unexpectedly, knowing he would be upset. The argument was the catalyst. He'd fallen for it.

There was only one thing missing from Luke's scenario. "She's not crazy, and she couldn't actually believe she'd be able to frame Brady.

Too many variables out of her control. She's smart enough to realize that. So what's her motive?"

"The project for Caruthers Commercial Development is in serious financial trouble."

He frowned at the young officer. "We don't have a warrant to look into her finances."

"I talked to the reporter who was at the library last week. He's working on a story about her and the possibility that she's created a stalker for herself because she seriously underbid the project. I believe she wants to make it look like someone is trying to stop the development by harassing her. Under those circumstances, she can claim to be too scared to finish the project and how out, Jack would have to release her if she has reason to fear for her and her crew's safety. This motive lines up with what she attempted with Brady three years ago, which the reporter also knew about. She was losing money on a project when she got involved with him, then tried to use his supposed stalking in the courts to help recoup her losses. She failed. I think she learned from that mistake and is being more proactive this time around."

Shit. Libby had given him her scope of work but refused to show him her cost proposal. Why all the secrecy if she didn't have something to hide?

Brady's words came back to him. *She'll fuck anything to get what she wants.*

"Where did the reporter get his information?"

"He didn't reveal his sources. I called around and learned the Corps of Engineers made several changes to the scope of work for the Caruthers project. Including a recent one that has apparently sent her costs spiraling out of control."

"Who did you talk to?"

"The Corps archaeologist, Dan Parker. He confirmed that the scope changed after the contract with Caruthers Commercial Development was signed. Each time more work was added, right up to the major addition that happened a week and a half ago. He claims he doesn't know anything about the project finances or if scoping changes will result in more money to Maitland's company. That's between her and the client.

"We've got her solid, Chief." He raised a hand and ticked off the evidence. "The phone call from her house, an eyewitness who places her with the gas cans, the duct tape was hers, her Taser with full batteries, her fingerprints on the tape and Molotov cocktail, and, she knew you were coming back—just in time to rescue her from her imaginary assailant." Luke paused. "You were her insurance policy."

Mark supposed that should bother him, but now an eerie detachment kept him from caring. He considered Luke's theory. In this instance, the evidence, all the facts available to him, pointed in one direction.

If Libby was the woman Aaron warned him against, then she was capable of what Luke described. She'd fabricated evidence when she doctored photos of Aaron. Just days ago she'd tampered with evidence when she opened the box and copied the tapes.

A woman who fabricated evidence would do anything to achieve her goal. Tampering with evidence proved she would do anything to save her business. By standing in Jason's arms, she showed she was a woman who would do anything to save herself.

Bobby was right. He'd followed his dick. He'd thought he was falling in love. But it had all been an act on her part. For her, it was all about money. Sex with him had been her insurance. She got involved with the police chief so no one would look too carefully at her actions. She could seduce him, and get out of a project she couldn't afford to complete.

How many times had she said her business would fail if she couldn't give Rosalie Warren the report she wanted? This was just another way to avoid that.

"Pick her up."

"Bring her in for questioning, or arrest her?"

"Arrest her."

"The charge?"

"Start with attempted arson."

24

Libby returned to the archaeological site mid-afternoon. She stood under the canopy with Simone, a site map rolled out on the table between them, arguing over where to place the next excavation block. Most of the crew was lying in the grass on a hillside, taking their afternoon break.

Alex paced near the screening station, talking on his cell phone. He looked agitated and Libby wondered what was wrong. He shut his phone and turned to her. "Can I talk to you for a sec?"

She followed him to the gravel lot.

"I was just on the phone with a friend of mine who works for Amy Seaver."

At the mention of the name, Libby stiffened. To say that she and Amy didn't get along was like calling the Grand Canyon a valley. Amy Seaver was a competitor with whom she shared a relationship of mutual animosity.

"Amy said you seriously messed up the bid on this project, and that you're going under."

"That's ridiculous." Seeing the look of concern on Alex's face, she continued, "Alex, you can't believe anything she says about me. Your job is secure."

"I'm not worried about my job. I know she's evil. I've worked for her."

Libby nodded; so had she, a decade ago.

"But it gets worse. Amy's telling people you've been faking having a stalker so you could get out of this contract."

"That's insane."

"The assault on Thursday was picked up by the Seattle papers when a reporter realized you were the same archaeologist who found Angela Caruthers. That reporter spoke with Amy."

"Oh crap," she said, feeling as though she'd been hit in the solar plexus. She remembered the reporter at the library Wednesday night. He wouldn't hesitate to print Amy's lies. "She wants this project." Just like last time. Amy had taken over the project after Aaron's brother fired her.

Alex nodded.

She sat abruptly, feeling as if a ghost of the Taser jolts ran through her system.

"Libby? Are you okay?"

"I've got to think."

How the hell do I handle this?

Call the reporter? No. Talking to a reporter could only make matters worse. But if the paper printed the story, what would she do with the shreds of her reputation?

Mark believed her, she reminded herself. The Coho Police Department would be on her side. No newspaper would publish a story if the police investigating the crime were behind her. Breathing became a tad easier. Amy Seaver had nothing to back up her crazy claims.

A police car, with Officer Roth at the wheel, pulled into the lot. This was a first, a visit from the police when she hadn't called them. She wondered if Mark had sent him to check up on her. She smiled, his protectiveness warming her. She stood and crossed to the lot. "Officer Roth, what brings you here today?"

"This isn't a social visit, Ms. Maitland," he said.

Assuming there had been some progress in their investigations, she responded, "Is this about Angela, or my stalker?"

"This is about you."

She'd always avoided Officer Roth's eyes, because she'd sensed he didn't like her, and she'd never wanted to feel his animosity full force. Now she received a blast of loathing. "What do you mean?" A chill went up her spine. "You heard the rumor Amy Seaver started, didn't you? You can't possibly think I'm making everything up after what happened on Thursday. You were there."

His eyes pierced her, an intense blue that reminded her of solid ice, cold hostility. "So you're denying you are in financial trouble?"

"Yes."

"And yet you know that's why I'm here. I find that a stretch, Ms. Maitland."

Goosebumps spread along her arms. She cleared her throat, which had gone dry. "Archaeology is a small field. Everyone knows everyone else. I know when someone sneezes on another excavation."

"How convenient for you."

"Amy Seaver is a competitor who dislikes me. She's jealous of this project."

"Why would anyone dislike you, Ms. Maitland?" he said with attitude.

"I'd like to talk to Mark." She reached for her cell phone.

"The chief sent me to get you. To bring you to the station. I don't think he'll take your call right now."

He spoke with chilling certainty. Her world shifted. "I'll go to the station later, after I've spoken with him."

"You need to come with me now."

She straightened her spine and reminded herself that she'd done nothing wrong and had nothing to be afraid of. "I won't go anywhere with you, officer. Not when you treat me with such hostility."

He reached for his handcuffs. She recoiled. "What are you doing?"

"I'm under orders from the chief, ma'am. You are under arrest."

She locked her knees when all she wanted to do was collapse. "Mark wouldn't—didn't—order that."

"Yes. He did."

"I'll drive myself to the station. You can't arrest me in front of my crew."

"Then you should have stayed at the Shelby house today. You can't drive yourself. You could just drive off."

"You'll just have to trust me," she snapped.

"I can't do that. Trust is not part of my job description."

"Yours and the police chief's," she muttered. She knew she was being obstinate, but she didn't care. Did Mark really order her arrest? She was about to find out.

Luke smiled with unholy pleasure. "Hold out your hands." He grabbed her arms and cuffed her behind her back.

Across the site, Simone surged to her feet and ran toward them.

"Call Jason," Libby said. "If he can't come, ask him to send someone—any lawyer he trusts. Tell him about Amy Seaver."

"Okay," she said. "But what the hell is going on?"

"Alex will explain."

Luke ushered her into the patrol car. Libby caught the shocked expressions on her employees' faces as the patrol car drove away.

"Why has she been arrested?" Jason asked as soon as Simone got a hold of him. "What is she being charged with?"

"All I know is Officer Roth cuffed her and put her in the back of a patrol car. I don't know why, but this could have something to do with a rumor started by one of our nastier competitors." She quickly gave him the details.

"Is the project in financial trouble?"

"No. We're still negotiating with Jack for the cost overruns due to the changes in scope."

"A rumor alone isn't enough for an arrest. There's got to be more."

She took a deep breath. She had to tell him. "I screwed up big time."

"What did you do, Simone?" His tone indicated he expected as much from her.

"I was in Seattle this weekend, checking up on Aaron, when a cop who's been helping Mark investigate Aaron caught me outside Aaron's place. He asked a lot of questions about the digital camera I'd just bought for the project and had with me in the car."

"And?"

"He asked if I'd doctored photos of Aaron three years ago, ones that Libby used to get the first restraining order." She paused. "I admitted I did."

His cursing blistered her ears. "I don't know which is worse, doctoring the photos, or admitting you did it. What were you thinking?"

"I was thinking about my friend," she answered angrily. "You have no idea what she went through when Aaron harassed her three years ago. And now he's tried to kill her!"

"You don't know it was him."

"Yes, I do. The guy is a total nutcase. I wasn't doing anything wrong when I sat in front of his apartment building. I was just checking up on him."

"With a brand new camera?" His tone said he didn't buy her story.

"Yes!"

"Did you invite the cop to search your vehicle?"

"No. He just opened the door and climbed inside."

"Good. Anything he saw could be inadmissible if it goes to court. Your confession however, is a different story. Fortunately, the doctored photos would have to be evidence in the current case to be a problem. Today, when he arrested Libby, did Officer Roth indicate he wanted to question you?"

"No."

"Good. Is there anything else I need to know?"

"I don't think so." She'd be damned if she volunteered anything else.

"There'd better not be." He hung up.

First, Libby was fingerprinted. The moment was hazy, unreal. This couldn't really be happening to her. Then an officer had her stand in front of a height chart and took her mug shot, and the full horror of what was happening hit her. Her legs wobbled until she locked her knees and straightened her spine. She stared into the camera lens with steely determination and went through all the motions required of her, not really seeing, not really hearing.

Officer Roth led her into an interrogation room, which was largely what she expected from television crime dramas. A table, chairs, and a two-way mirror. He recited the Miranda warning to her. She'd never in her life expected those words to be directed at her. A rational thought worked through the haze in her mind. "What am I being charged with?"

"Attempted arson."

"That's ridiculous."

"We could add attempted murder. Be happy we're starting with the lesser charge."

Attempted murder? That was insane. "I was the intended victim, so I don't see how attempted murder applies."

"The kitchen could have blown up with cops inside. For all we know, that's what you planned."

"That's crazy."

"Is that the defense you're going with?"

She wanted to respond to his bait, but didn't. She might be upset, but that didn't make her stupid. "I want my lawyer. In fact, the only person I'll talk to without my lawyer present is Mark Colby."

She had to see Mark. This must be some horrible mistake.

Luke left her locked in the interrogation room. She sat ramrod straight in her chair, staring toward the mirror and wondering whether Mark watched her from the other side.

At last, the door opened and he entered. He shut the door and then faced her, his expression stone cold. He didn't even remotely resemble the man she'd made love with. In that moment, she knew.

He believed the worst of her.

Part of her soul shattered, triggering a raw ache in her belly. Pain surged to the surface. She was going to cry. *No, dammit.* She crushed the urge down. *Not now.*

She stood and walked around the table to him. "Did you order my arrest?" she asked softly.

"Yes."

"Why?" Her voice broke on the single word.

"It's my job to arrest criminals."

He'd tried and convicted her already. She sucked in a deep breath and took refuge in anger. "You mentioned handcuffs earlier, but left out the part about an interrogation room with a two-way mirror."

His gaze raked her with chilling detachment that cut to the bone but said nothing.

She pointed to the mirror. "Who is listening?"

"This conversation is private. This isn't about us, Libby. This is about you. There is no *us.*"

"Oh, you've made that abundantly clear. Now let *me* make something clear," she spoke slowly, measuring out her words. "I will never, *ever*, forgive you for this."

He let out a peal of harsh, humorless laughter. "You break the law, you get treated like any other felon."

"I've done nothing wrong." She felt as if she bled from a thousand invisible cuts. "Nothing except screwing you, that is."

His gaze hardened. "At least you were a magnificent fuck."

Her hand connected with his cheek. The slap echoed in the small room.

He didn't flinch.

Slapping wasn't enough. He needed to hurt as much as she did. She curled her fingers into a fist.

He grabbed her hand. "Assaulting an officer is a felony."

She broke away from his touch as though it burned. "That's the only thing I'm guilty of." She held out her wrists. "If the big, bad, officer is afraid of me, you can put the cuffs back on."

At the knock at the door, Mark opened it without taking his eyes off her.

"Her lawyer's here," an officer said.

Before Mark could speak, Jason entered, a white knight if ever there was one. He calmly sat. "Sit here, Libby," he said, indicating the seat next to him. "Before I speak with my client in private, I'd like to know exactly what we're doing here."

"Ms. Maitland is suspected of filing several false police reports and taking the attack on Thursday night. For now, we're charging her with attempted arson."

Ms. Maitland. He hadn't called her that since he walked away from her on the night they first met. The coldness in his voice as he said her name opened yet another wound. *Don't let him see how much every tiny denial of their connection hurts. Be angry, not pathetic.* "Oh come on, *Mark,*" her voice dripped equal parts venom and honey. "No need to be so formal." She turned to Jason. "You should have heard what he called me when his dick was in my mouth."

Jason stood abruptly; his chair toppled over with a crash. "What the hell are you doing in this interview room?" he said to Mark. "Your relationship with my client is prejudicial."

"I had another officer ready to question her. Libby requested me." Mark's eyes glinted cold and metallic. "I'm not surprised she didn't tell you about us."

She'd worried about adding to the rivalry between them, but Mark saw her prudence as a sign of guilt. "Sorry, Jason. I guess you should know that I spent the weekend getting screwed by the police chief."

"Your anger is noted, Libby. Now shut up." He turned to Mark. "I need to speak with my client in private."

Mark's eyes swept over her. His look was dismissive. Insulting. "She's all yours," he said and left.

She slumped back in her chair, feeling her energy drain away. With Mark gone, she had no focal point for her anger, leaving her with nothing but debilitating pain. But now wasn't the time to wallow. She gathered her composure and faced Jason. "I should have told you about my relationship with Mark, but it was new and personal. What a joke…"

Her eyes welled with tears, and she pressed her fingertips against her nose to stop them.

Jason handed her a handkerchief. "Here. Now tell me what's going on."

Tears successfully suppressed, she told him everything she could about Amy Seaver, Aaron Brady, and her current stalker. She pointed out Amy had nabbed Aaron's brother as a client three years ago, and she still worked for the man, and she told him about the doctored photographs.

"I've heard about the photos. Simone admitted she doctored them."

"She told you? When?"

"Just before I came here. She's worried and she has reason to be. A Seattle cop—a friend of Mark's—caught her stalking Aaron this weekend."

"Oh, crap. Simone…" What would have happened if Aaron had caught her? When angry, Aaron turned violent. She'd never warned Simone, so she had no idea how dangerous Aaron could be. Libby had never told anyone, and now it was too late to tell the truth. Even to Jason.

"Her stupid need to play detective hasn't helped."

"She's only trying to protect me."

"And instead you get arrested. I want to post bond and get out of here."

"Wait. I want to know what evidence they have. I want to be questioned. Maybe I can convince them they've made a mistake."

"Once you've been charged, it's out of police hands. Now it's a matter for the prosecutor."

"Is it a problem if I let them question me?"

"Not as long as I'm here."

"Then I'd like to get this over with."

"Okay. I'll stop it if I don't like the way things are going."

To Libby's great relief, Officer Sara Eversall conducted the interview. If Luke Roth had been sent back in, she would have agreed with Jason about posting bond and leaving.

When questioned about her project finances, Libby let out a humorless laugh. "I underbid the project? Jack would be shocked. He accused me of taking him to the cleaners." She felt Mark's presence on the other side of the mirror with every breath she took. Watching. Judging. That thought revived her anger, which gave her the strength to continue. "Listen," she said to Sara. "You want proof I didn't underbid the project? You go to three archaeological consulting firms —any three with the exception of Seaver and Associates. Have them read my scope of work. You tell them to come up with a cost proposal. Not just money, but man-hours, broken down by each task outlined in the scope. Have them give you a low and a high range for every task. Then look at the hours I've allocated to each task. I nailed that bid. I risked nothing with my cost proposal. I knew what Jack could afford. If anything, I padded the hours." She turned to Jason, smiling wryly. "Could you please not tell him I said that?"

He winked at her. "Attorney-client privilege."

Sara said, "I understand that a week and a half ago, the Corps of Engineers increased the requirements for your background report. Significantly. Who's paying for the additions to the scope of work?"

Libby looked to Jason, not sure whether she should answer. She leaned over and told him she hadn't finished negotiating that task with Jack; he was using a loophole to try to get her to eat the costs.

"My client isn't going to answer that," he said.

Sara questioned Libby about the gas jugs used at the site.

"Two weeks ago, I purchased two red five-gallon gas jugs because the one we had leaked."

"A witness says he saw you place two gas jugs on your back porch on Thursday afternoon."

"That's a load of bull. The jugs are used at the site. They've never been near the Shelby house. You think I faked my own assault and attempted to burn down my home and office with my own gas jugs? Wouldn't that be stupid?"

"I'm not here to judge your IQ. I'm just asking questions."

"I'm obviously a little slow, so let me get this straight. I took my gas cans home from work on Thursday and put them on my back porch—in full view of some witness, because, as we've established, I'm not too bright—and later I poured the gas all over my own kitchen and myself. Then I shot myself with a Taser and taped up my own wrists."

"Yes," Sara said.

"Have you considered the possibility the witness is wrong?"

"I'm asking the questions, Ms. Maitland, not you. How many times were you zapped with the Taser?"

"I think he kept pressing the trigger. I know the pain stopped three times."

"How long do you think it went on, total?"

"It felt like forever. But if I had to guess, I'd say a few minutes."

"What did the pain feel like?"

Like I feel, right now, knowing the man I gave my body and heart to ordered my arrest. "Like I was being ripped apart from the inside by a thousand forks."

Sara paused and looked at her. Sympathy passed over her features but was quickly replaced by cool reserve. "There's one more thing I'd like you to explain. Can you explain how your fingerprints were on both the Molotov cocktail bottle and the adhesive side of the duct tape?"

She was speechless. Hostility, anger, and fight left her. Now she was scared.

Jason sat up straighter. "Which piece of tape had her fingerprints? The first piece from the roll, or all of them?"

Sara looked at him coolly. "I'm conducting this interview, Mr. Caruthers, not you."

"Then we're done." Jason stood and crossed the room to the sound switch and turned it off. "I'd like a moment alone with my client."

Sara left the room.

"You did well," Jason said. "Their motive is weak. The eyewitness could be a problem. I'll see what I can dig up."

"How could my fingerprints be on the adhesive side?" Horror washed through her at the answer: the whole thing had been meticulously planned. "I've been perfectly set up. My attacker Tasered me and put my fingerprints on the tape. But why would someone work so hard to frame me?"

"That's what I'd like to know. We'll get to the bottom of this. Tonight, spend some time writing down everything that's happened since your truck was stolen. Maybe a pattern will appear."

She nodded and tried to smile, but her life had taken on the surreal quality of a Warner Brothers cartoon. She was the hapless victim of a cunning trickster. This couldn't be happening to her. She was the type of person who put money in parking meters on Sunday, just to be sure.

The reality of her situation hit her with a clarity she'd missed up to now. She'd focused on Mark and her personal devastation, but this was so much worse than that. She'd been arrested. She could face trial. *For a felony.* "I don't know how I'm going to pay for your counsel, Jason," she said dully.

"Didn't you just say you're taking my dad to the cleaners?" he asked lightly.

She tried to give him a token laugh. All she could make was a dry choking sound.

He lifted her chin, forcing her to meet his warm brown eyes. "Listen, Libby, I'm certain the cops are building a case against Jack and he's going to be charged with my mother's murder. He didn't do it, and we're going to need you as a defense witness. You're no good without credibility. I will restore your credibility before he goes to trial. Pro bono."

"How can you be sure I'd be useful for his defense?"

His hand dropped from her chin while his eyes remained fixed on hers. "You would speak the truth. If he had buried my mom there, he would never have paid you to do the excavation. He knew your methods. He knew the scope. He'd have known she'd be found."

She nodded. "I said the same thing to Mark."

"A man who doesn't listen to reason. But a jury will."

That Jason believed her without hesitation when her lover was ready to toss her ass in jail caused her to crumble. She couldn't stop the tear that escaped. *Not now. Not here.* She breathed deeply and wiped her eyes. She hoped no one on the other side of the mirror watched.

Jason looked at her sympathetically. "Listen, I'm going to post bail and get you out of here."

Relief made her spine lose its starch. "Thank you."

He pulled her to him and supported her. His hand cupped the back of her head and stroked her hair while his body heat gave her the strength to stand.

"If I go home, and somebody attacks me again, will anyone come to my aid?" she asked against his chest.

"The alarm system is top of the line. The alarm monitoring company will notify emergency services. They have to respond. But even so, you shouldn't be alone. Have Simone stay with you. She can be useful. For a change."

Of course Jason had raced to Libby's side. Mark had known he would. Jason's surprise at learning they were lovers was as damning as all the evidence Luke had outlined, and only confirmed Mark's suspicion that Libby was using them both.

The interview was over and Sara waited for his feedback, but he was transfixed by the sight of Libby in Jason's arms. Again. He couldn't turn away. Jason slid his fingers through her silky hair as though he had the right. Mark's stone façade developed fractures.

"We need to see the cost proposal," Sara said.

"Get a warrant. And make sure it covers all her financial records. I want to know how she runs her projects. See if she's in trouble all around."

"Yes, sir."

That he was jealous of Jason was insane. She was playing Jason, too. Just like Shiella, she used the lawyer for her own ends. He ought to feel sorry for the man.

At this point, he should feel nothing but contempt for Libby. He remembered the soft panting sound she emitted just before orgasm. The way she looked at him as though his body was a masterpiece. He felt hollow. A shell.

She emerged from the interview room with her spine straight, head up, eyes cold. His gaze met hers, causing a break in her rigid demeanor. She looked victimized; her eyes revealed pure, raw pain. She took a deep breath, collected herself, and followed Jason down the hall. Mark's own façade slipped. A chink opened in the armor he'd built around his heart. What if she really was the victim?

Then he'd just savagely destroyed the woman he was hopelessly in love with.

He turned abruptly and crossed the station to his office, where he closed the door and leaned back against the panel. Only hours before he'd pinned her to this very same spot. He could almost smell her, taste her.

He slowly went over all the evidence Luke had outlined. He remembered Brady's words. Jason's kiss. Bobby's suspicion. He matched each of those things with the conversations he'd shared with Libby. Her reluctance to provide her budget information. Her panic over the change in the scope of her project. Her insistence Aaron was stalking her again—right down to her impossible claim he was at the library on Wednesday. She'd said she was wary of Jason's interest in her, and even stated the man wanted Simone, all while accepting date after date and then not pushing Jason away.

She was guilty as sin. Only after going over the evidence again and again could he breathe normally. That single moment, the idea she might be innocent, nearly destroyed him.

26

Simone waited in the lobby of the police station. With Jason's help, she'd paid Libby's bail. She was grateful Coho was a small town and the process was swift; any minute now Libby would be released and she would find out what in the hell was going on.

At last Libby and Jason stepped through the security door. One look at Libby's face and Simone knew her questions would have to wait. Libby had been…shattered. She hadn't looked this devastated, this afraid, even when Aaron was at his scary-worst. Libby was barely holding herself together.

"You're almost out of here," Simone said.

Libby nodded and made a beeline for the door.

Outside, Libby climbed into Simone's car. Simone faced Jason and then flinched at the look in his eye. Jason would never respect her, but at least she understood his scorn. "Thank you. For everything."

"Take care of her. But don't do anything stupid. Leave her legal defense to me."

Any other time, any other situation, she'd defend herself. But she couldn't, not with Libby trying so desperately not to break down into sobs in the car. Not with that damn knowing look in Jason's eyes. She gave him this round. If she had to, she'd give him every round—as long as he helped Libby.

At the Shelby house, Libby headed directly for her bedroom. Simone watched her climb the stairs, defeat in Libby's posture, in her slow shuffling steps.

She unloaded the groceries she'd purchased earlier, and then went upstairs to check on Libby. She found her standing in the hallway, staring into the guest bedroom at the wall that had been sprayed with blood a week ago. It had been a mistake to bring Libby here, but she had insisted because the security system was the best money could buy.

"Someone was here," Libby said. "Someone used a pickaxe to destroy Angela's mask. Someone sprayed blood on the wall." Her voice became more emphatic with each word. "It wasn't me."

"I know," Simone said.

"He came back on Thursday night and hurt me."

"Yes."

"He tied me up. He tried to kill me."

"I know. I believe you, Libby."

She kicked the wall. "Dammit. Why doesn't Mark?" Libby's razor-thin veneer of control broke as she bent down and cradled her foot. "Why is this happening?" She dropped to the floor as sobs shook her entire body.

This breakdown was exactly what Libby needed. Simone slid down the wall and settled on the floor next to her.

"I think I broke my toe," Libby complained.

"Really?"

"No. Not really. But it hurts. I suppose it's better than the pain the rest of me feels."

Simone patted her leg. "I'll be right back." She returned a moment later with the bag of groceries, a corkscrew, and two wine glasses. "Before going to the station, I ran to the store to get us dinner." She dug through the bag and handed Libby a box of chocolate-covered cream-filled cakes.

Libby laughed at the processed, hydrogenated treat, just as Simone had hoped she would. She'd have picked up a pint of Chunky Monkey but had a feeling that flavor of ice cream had been forever ruined for Libby.

"And, because I'm a classy woman, I got us wine to go with this gourmet meal." She opened the bottle and poured them each a glass.

They sat in the hall and sipped their wine in silence for a while, as early evening shadows shifted toward twilight. Finally Simone said, "So tell me what happened."

Libby sighed. "Well. Let's see. Last Thursday someone tried to kill me. Then I had the most incredible weekend of my life. We talked. We laughed. We made love. Then today he had me arrested."

"Hmm. You must be awful in bed."

Libby burst out laughing, even as she swiped at tears. "No. Well, not this time anyway. I'm pretty sure I wore him out." Her voice faded. "Damn, I can't believe I was arrested. How much was my bail?"

"Five thousand. I pulled it from the business account. We can get a cash advance from one of the credit cards if we need to cover it."

"Dating cops is seriously bad for my finances."

She smiled, relieved Libby could still make a joke. She was a strong woman; she'd get through this. "Did you talk to Mark?"

"Yes. He thinks I faked everything. I can't believe the man I spent the weekend with ordered my arrest without even talking to me first." She swirled the wine in her glass. Simone watched as she held her drink up to the light. The deep burgundy color gave a warm glow. "He tried and convicted me in his own mind." She looked Simone in the eye. "You know, he never even asked if I did it." She set the glass down and swiped at more tears. "Part of me wants to hit him, just to make him hurt as much as I do."

"I'm pretty sure he already does."

"You didn't see him—"

"I didn't need to. If he's been convinced you're guilty, he's as much a victim as you are."

That silenced Libby for a few minutes. Finally she said, "Last night I was this close"—she held up her hand, holding her thumb and fore-finger millimeters apart—"to blurting out that I love him. That seems ridiculous now. We've known each other for a little more than a week. What was I thinking?"

"Maybe that you love him. Do you?"

"I don't know. Maybe. Probably." She twirled the wine glass again, more interested in the light and color than in drinking it. "All I know is, I didn't hold anything back. I lived in the moment without reserva-tion. You would have been proud of me. I put all my old fears aside, all my stupid abandonment issues. I was totally open. I gave every-thing away." Her voice cracked. "Then he heard the rumor Amy Seaver started and believed that over me."

"How could a dumb rumor be this damaging? One look at the scope and budget would exonerate you."

"Not completely. We haven't finished negotiating the scoping changes with Jack, but that's not really the issue. They have evidence against me. To start with, my fingerprints were on the Molotov cocktail bottle and on the sticky side of the tape that was used to bind me."

"What?"

"I think the goal of the attack was to frame me."

"It worked."

Libby nodded. "They've also got a witness who says they saw me bring the gas cans home and put them on my back porch. It must be the old guy next door. He spends his days alternating between his back balcony and front porch. I wave every time I see him. He has yet to wave back."

"Why would he lie?"

"Who knows? Jason said he would have the witness investigated."

"Thank God Jason wasn't in Seattle today." Thank God he'd been willing to help Libby. Lord knew that if Simone had been the one arrested, he'd have let her rot in jail.

"Yeah. Convenient that we found his mother's dead body, so he had reason to stay in Coho this week," Libby said with rampant sarcasm.

"Don't bitch at me. I'm on your side," Simone said mildly.

Libby slouched against the wall. "I'm sorry. I want to fight with someone, I guess. I feel bad for Jason. I'm piling my crap on top of his already huge load. He tried to kiss me after our lunch meeting today."

So he really did want Libby. Disappointment jabbed her. "What did you do?"

"I turned him down. Then an hour later I had to ask him to be my defense lawyer. The whole situation is so damn humiliating." She gazed at the ceiling. "I don't know what to do."

Simone grabbed her hand and squeezed. "Life happens one day at a time. All you have to face is today. Truthfully, tomorrow will be worse—that reporter came by the site this afternoon, so you can expect at least one headline tomorrow—but we'll deal with it. We can fight this. You haven't done anything wrong and their motive is pure bullshit. So tomorrow, you hold your head up high and let them say what they want. The truth is on your side."

"But what if the truth isn't enough? My God, I just spent the weekend with Mark screwing his brains out, and even he doesn't believe me. Your opinion of my sexual talents aside, one would presume he'd be a sympathetic audience." She slipped her hand from Simone's and cradled her head. "He was my rescuer that night. If this goes to trial, the jury would see the chief of police—who found me bound and covered in gasoline, and who also happens to be my lover —testify for the prosecution that I faked the whole damn thing." She shook her head. "No one is going to believe me."

"Libby, there's no motive."

"They can claim I'm trying to frame Brady to get the Anti Harassment Order reinstated. I'm actually shocked that's not the motive they're going with.

"You can't frame someone who lives so far away. You'd have to track his every movement and only staqe incidents when he was without an alibi for several hours. It would be ridiculous to attempt such a thing."

"They seem to think I'm pretty stupid."

"And Mark knows you're not. They have no motive."

"What if they don't need one? What if they just claim I'm crazy? What if they say I've got some sort of weird variant of Munchausen's Syndrome, but instead of faking illness, I fake being a crime victim? No one believed me about Brady before, so I've got a history they can use against me. With everything that's been going on, *I'm* starting to wonder if I'm crazy!"

"But you're not. You've been set up. Now we've just got to figure out why."

That silenced her. Finally she shook her head. "I haven't a clue."

"What about Brady?" Simone said.

"I don't think he could pull off something this sophisticated. The only thing I can think of is that this relates to the Cultural Center."

"Someone wants to stop the project?"

Libby shrugged.

"Aren't there better contractors to go after? The architect and engineering firm is making ten times what we are."

"Yeah, but we're here now. The architects and engineers have been here and gone, and it'll be months before they're back. I'm the best target if someone is crazy mad about the Center."

"But you aren't even at the site every day. I'm running the excavation. Why not go after me, or the dig directly?"

"They must think that if I go down, so will the rest of you. It's more subtle to go after me. If they directly sabotaged the dig, then the police would track them down. This way the police come down on me and only me. The question is, are they going to ruin the contractor Jack hires to replace me?"

"There won't be another. Jack won't fire you. You're innocent."

"Simone, I could go to jail."

"With one lying eyewitness and no motive? Jason's a better lawyer than that."

"Lord, I hope so."

"He is. Your case is going to be tossed out so fast, and then Jason'll hit 'em with a wrongful arrest suit. Your chief'll be lucky to keep his badge after the lawsuit Coho will have to settle. He was involved with you and he used his position against you. He'll pay with his career."

"But he loves his job," Libby said softly.

There was no doubt in Simone's mind; in spite of everything, Libby loved Mark with every fragile piece of her shattered heart.

Mark immersed himself in the Caruthers investigation, staying at the station late into the night. He didn't want to think about what happened earlier in the day. He used every ounce of his will to focus on the evidence collected two decades ago. For brief periods, none lasting longer than a few minutes, his efforts were effective. He would have searched through Angela's boxes, but he couldn't look at them without thinking of Libby.

He reread the transcript of an interview with Jack conducted in early 1980. Did Jason know, then or now, that Angela had an affair with her grad school officemate? Jack had lied repeatedly before admitting the truth—that he'd known about the affair for months before her disappearance. Did Jason also know that at the time of his mother's disappearance Jack had been sleeping with a woman who worked for him? Would Jason be so eager to defend his father if he were aware of these details?

At one in the morning, the pages blurred before his eyes, and Mark accepted the inevitable. He needed to sleep. He left the station and headed home.

He braced himself before entering his bedroom for the first time since that morning. There he faced tangled sheets, the blankets half on the bed, half on the floor, and a pillow lodged between the bed and the headboard. In his mind, he saw Libby on the bed, tousled. Beautiful.

He lifted a pillow from the floor, held it for a moment, and then ripped off the pillowcase. He turned to the bed and yanked off the sheets. Downstairs, he tossed the bedding into the fireplace, went out back, and found an old can of lighter fluid. By the time he went to sleep in the guest bedroom, the sheets had been reduced to cinders.

27

Libby cried herself to sleep—something she hadn't done since she was a child and her father had once again left her brother, sister, and her alone with their increasingly cold mother. Now she'd been abandoned by another man, and for the first time she understood her mother and the bitterness she directed at her children because the real cause of her hurt was out of reach. She understood, but she didn't want to be like her. She didn't want to embrace the bitterness and block her ability to love even those who were closest to her.

She wanted to rise above the pain and the petty desire for revenge, but she remained human, and black anger surfaced every time she thought about the humiliation of being arrested in front of her employees, or considered Amy Seaver's calculating lies.

And she didn't know what to think of Mark.

Simone was right: Mark was a victim, too. He'd been manipulated. Whoever had framed her had toyed with Mark's sense of justice—and as a cop, she knew his sense of justice ran deeper than most.

Still, he'd made a choice when he found her guilty without even talking to her. He'd said repeatedly that he had to explore every option, couldn't rule anyone out as a suspect, yet she had a feeling he'd followed the evidence to her and...stopped.

She had a new day in front of her, and no idea how to face it. Simone left early for the site. Life—and the project—had to go on.

She deactivated the alarm long enough to grab the morning paper from the front porch and retreated back into the house. The *Seattle*

Times had nothing about her above the fold. A ship was being deployed to the Persian Gulf. The shellfish harvest would be down this year. Below the fold was a different story. A small blurb—"Archaeologist Digs Attention. Allegedly Fakes Attack After Finding Bones of Missing Woman"—was followed by instructions to read the full story on page A-8.

She groaned and threw the paper aside, not ready to read the article.

The phone rang. Caller ID said *Seattle Post-Intelligencer*. She unplugged the landline and turned on her cell phone. Anyone who really needed to reach her had the number.

She leaned on the small table and stared at the heavy, black, rotary-dial phone, a relic from the days when this was Angela Caruthers' house. She and Jack had a home in Seattle, but her dissertation topic meant spending several days at a time in Coho, and Libby had learned she'd claimed the Shelby house as her own. The house had remained in Jack and Jason's control after her disappearance. Libby was the first tenant since the early 1970s.

Angela had used this phone, this table. She'd sat in the bay window. For all Libby knew, Angela had argued with Jack in the kitchen much as Libby had with Mark. Libby couldn't do anything about her disastrous situation, but she could bury herself in someone else's problems. She made a pot of coffee and then headed upstairs with a full mug in hand. Angela's papers waited.

She took notes as she read, detailing Angela's areas of interest and jotting down avenues for further research. Angela's ethnographic study had been broad, but she'd focused in on a few key areas: the effect mill development had on tribal customs and practices, Millie Thorpe Montgomery's relationship with the tribe, and the change in mill/tribal relations after Lyle took over.

Libby's own focus was fractured. Several times she caught herself staring off into space, lost in the disturbing memory of having her mug shot taken or facing Mark inside the interrogation room. When she realized she'd read the same page of notes for the third time—and remembered nothing—she flopped back in her chair in frustration.

She surged to her feet and headed downstairs. She had to get her head in her work. She paced the living room and then stopped abruptly in front of the stereo. The cassette copy she'd made of Angela's interview with Frances Warren sat on a shelf next to the stereo. She put in the tape, hit play, and settled on the cushion in the bay window.

Frances Warren began by telling stories of the Kalahwamish, tribal tales passed down for generations. In Indian culture, an elder telling a story was considered a gift of the highest value. Libby took refuge in the elder's voice, receiving the gift as Angela had, with awe and reverence, thankful beyond measure for Frances' gift of distraction and escape.

Thirty minutes into the interview, the tape player shut off, returning Libby to the present. She flipped the tape over and sank back into her seat, ready to once again settle into a different culture and time. The focus of the interview shifted and Frances spoke of Millie Thorpe and Lyle Montgomery, eventually coming to the topic of Millie's death. A ripple of surprise ran through Libby. She'd read the story in the newspaper but no one in Coho had ever mentioned Millie's death in an interview. Strange that the story should come from an Indian, not the deceased's own children.

"Millie came to the reservation the day she died. She was wound up, afraid. She said Lyle was going to kill her. Soon. The sheriff, he wouldn't do anything about Lyle's beatings. He was in Lyle's pocket. Everyone was. It wasn't until later, after the union came in, that there was anyone to stand up to Lyle.

"The last time I saw Millie, she said she wanted to be sure Lyle never owned the mill. She knew if her children inherited TL&L, then Lyle would control them the same way he'd controlled her. She said she'd just been to her lawyer, and she'd made a new will. In it she left everything—the mill, the town, the hotel, the store, all of TL&L—to the Kalahwamish people. Her life was a nightmare, she said, but her death would mean something. She found justice in the idea he'd lose the mill to us, the Indians he hated so much.

"I was scared for Millie, scared for all of us. When Lyle found out what she'd done, he'd be dangerous. Of course, I never thought for a moment her will would hold up in court—even though the mill was legally Millie's—I was sure Lyle would have the will overturned.

"Millie told me she'd hidden the will with someone safe. She planned to tell everyone about leaving TL&L to the tribe, hoping that would protect her. Lyle wouldn't dare kill her if he knew the mill would go to us. She left here intending to go to the mill store. She said she'd make a big announcement right there in dry goods, telling everyone what she'd done. But she never made it to the store."

"What happened that night? How did my grandmother die?"

"She took a back road from my house—the old private road that runs by the ancestor's village. Her car went off the road near the old dry riverbed on George Warren's property and burst into flames. Of course, there was no reason for her car to go off the road or to burst into flames. The sheriff put out the story that she had probably swerved to avoid a deer. Too convenient, if you ask me. Lyle ran her off the road and torched the car. He probably assumed the will was with her."

"Lyle knew about the will?

I think the lawyer who wrote up the will tipped off Lyle, then Lyle chased her down and killed her. It's the lawyer's fault Millie was killed that night."

"What happened to the will?"

I don't know. It wasn't the one that was used after she died. Her lawyer, Mr Banks, used a will that had been signed five years before her death. That will left everything to her children."

"Did you tell anyone about the will? Did the sheriff investigate?"

"I tried. But I was an Indian speaking against Lyle Montgomery. That wouldn't work today, much less 1940. The sheriff accused me of being a money-grubbing Indian trying to steal a business I had no right to. Of course, that's why Millie couldn't leave the will with me in the first place. Nobody would believe or accept the will if it came from me or any other Kalahwamish. There was no one to turn to. We never found out who she gave the will to, or what happened to it, but I think it still exists."

"You don't think it was destroyed in the fire?"

"If she'd had the will with her, she would have shown it to me. She didn't. She said she hid it with someone safe. I think it's still hidden... and I think you can find it."

Goosebumps formed on Libby's arms. So simple and yet mind blowing. Angela and Frances spoke to her from the grave. This conversation explained both the focus of Angela's research and the paucity of results. Now Libby understood. Angela's ethnographic study was a cover for her real investigation—she was searching for her grandmother's will.

From Frances' description, it sounded as though Millie had died on or near the archaeological site. In 1976, Angela had sought out George Warren and purchased that property. Why? Were Angela's actions sentimental? Lyle was alive then; how did he react when Angela bought the land where Millie Thorpe Montgomery died?

Millie had been murdered—probably by her husband—because she made a will leaving TL&L to the Kalahwamish tribe. Did her granddaughter suffer the same fate, by the same man, for the same reason?

Libby shook her head at the wild speculation. Angela's murder was so far removed from Millie's. They couldn't be related.

In two days, Thorpe Log & Lumber would be sold to create a living history museum. Libby didn't know the selling price, but she did know the estimated value of all TL&L's holdings was well over one hundred million dollars.

If the will were found now, more than sixty years after Millie's death, what would happen? Would the will be honored?

If there was a connection between Millie and Angela's murder, was there also a connection to what was happening to Libby? Was someone trying to stop her from completing the search Angela had started?

28

S imone stood outside the police station, debating whether or not to confront Mark. She'd made a mess of things. Would speaking with him make the situation worse?

She entered the station and was told the chief wasn't available. She opted to wait and sat in the lobby for an hour and a half, alternating between fuming and being determined to outwait him. She called the site three times. Alex assured her the excavation was going smoothly.

Mark finally stepped into the lobby. He stood and stared at her for several seconds, before he said, "Come on," and led her to his office. He sat behind his desk and watched her. His chilling silence unnerved her.

"You've made a huge mistake," she finally said.

"I know. Yesterday I corrected it."

She had never seen anyone so cold. Gone was the charming man who'd pumped her for information on Libby a week ago. "Don't be obtuse. You know what I mean."

"Yes, I do. But I disagree about what my mistake was. It's inappropriate for me to speak to you at this time; this is an open investigation with pending charges."

"Why are you doing this? Why are you being this way?"

He merely stared at her.

"Fine, then speak to me as a witness. I was the one who received that call on Tuesday morning. There is no way in hell Libby would make a call like that to scare me."

He shrugged. "You're in on it with her. I'm still considering charging you as an accomplice."

"You can't scare me. Libby hasn't done anything wrong. I haven't done anything wrong. You know what does scare me? Libby was bound and gagged and doused in gasoline. Then the sonofabitch turned on the gas. One spark and she could have been killed. That's what scares me. It should scare you, too."

He flinched.

Hope flared. He had feelings for Libby. "And now that you've turned on her, she's in more danger than she was before. Aaron is crazy."

His eyes hardened. *Shit.* She shouldn't have mentioned Aaron. "I don't believe she has a stalker. And I don't believe she had one three years ago."

"Then let's talk about motive. No one knows Libby's finances better than I do. I helped write that proposal."

"Then you should work with Libby's lawyer to clear her name. That's not my job. Her case has been remanded to the courts."

"I don't care about her case. Jason will win it for her. I care about her heart, and what you're doing to it!"

"She doesn't have a heart."

"Because she gave it to you, and you crushed it."

"Look. If you're so eager to explain everything away, explain to me why Bobby found Aaron's work schedule in your possession?"

"Three years ago, Libby's complaints fell on deaf ears. When her truck was stolen last week, you didn't seem inclined to investigate. I wasn't going to wait and see if you decided her story had merit. I wasn't going to wait until *after* Aaron got violent to take action. So I decided to look into his activities myself, including tracking his work schedule."

"Strangely enough," Mark said, "every single stalking incident happened after six p.m. He switched to working days a few months ago. He's off by four. Just enough time to get to Coho. Did you and Libby intend to frame him completely, or were you just using him to convince me she really had a stalker?"

"She does have a stalker. If Aaron doesn't have an alibi, then it could be him."

"But he does have an alibi. He couldn't have attacked Libby on Thursday night."

Stunned, Simone sat back in her chair. "But, if Aaron didn't do it, who did?"

"Means, motive, and opportunity. That's what we look for. When I look at all three, I come up with two names: Libby Maitland and Simone Atherton."

"Me? That's ridiculous." She wouldn't let him scare her.

"Not from where I'm sitting."

"She's being framed. Someone wants you to blame her."

"If it looks like a duck, talks like a duck, and walks like a duck, it's a duck. It's not a Goddamn raccoon pretending to be a duck."

Simone stood and looked him straight in the eye. "You're wrong about Libby. I just hope you don't realize that too late to save her from whoever really is stalking her."

Libby entered Rosalie Warren's bedroom. The elder was sitting up in a hospital-type bed that was incongruous with the rest of her room, otherwise filled with a lifetime's worth of cultural treasures. Every inch of wall space was covered with a piece of Indian artwork of one sort or another. Faces, whales, salmon, even the Sasquatch motif decorated wood, hide, paper, canvas, and rock. Eyes stared at her from hundreds of angles.

"My collection," Rosalie said, seeing Libby's interest. "I'm leaving it to the tribal school. I want the kids to be able to touch these items and understand the proud culture they were born into. But until I take my last breath, I want to be in the center of it and know my place in the world." Another coughing spell consumed her. She caught her breath and continued, "I couldn't stay in the hospital. I had no sense of the ancestors there."

A lengthy and surprisingly comfortable silence ensued. Libby sensed the woman did not need awkward words of comfort. Rosalie Warren had accepted her fate. Libby wondered whether she'd ever find such grace.

Eventually Rosalie spoke. "I read about you in the paper."

"Was the story flattering?"

Rosalie's laugh was a deep, harsh bark. "Hardly." She coughed. "You said on the phone you have a tape of my mother talking to Angela. I'd like to hear it."

Libby played the tape. At the end of the interview, the elder stared at her, clearly stunned. "I didn't know about the will," she said softly.

"I think Angela and Frances were working together to find it."

"Yes. That has the ring of truth. The will would have been proof, of a sort, that Lyle killed Millie. I know my mother always wanted to prove Lyle killed her."

"And in 1979, Lyle was still alive. He'd have lost the mill and faced prosecution for Millie's murder. That was Angela's reason—you alluded she had a greater purpose when we first met—for documenting Lyle Montgomery's treatment of the Kalahwamish."

"I wonder if she disappeared because she found the will," Rosalie said.

"I'm beginning to think that's what happened. If the police listened to this tape in 1979, then they didn't make the connection between her work and her disappearance."

"What if the will wasn't destroyed when Angela disappeared?" Rosalie said. "It could still be out there somewhere. If she found it, then someone repeating her research could find it." She looked at Libby speculatively.

"You're making a lot of assumptions there."

"Let me think." She leaned back and closed her eyes. A minute later, she opened them and said, "The will is the key. It's your best bet to clear your name."

"You think what's happening to me is related?"

"Don't you?"

Libby nodded. "The stalking started the day we found the burial— the day we found Angela."

"Going back to that day, put yourself in the mind of the person who buried her in the site." She paused. "Even without my request for a detailed background report, Angela's research is relevant to your excavation. You were bound to find out about her ethnographic notes and use them for your report. If she was killed because she found the will, then her killer had to be very worried. Worried you would recognize she wasn't Indian, and worried she left information on her search for the will in her notes." Her brown eyes swept Libby from head to toe. "You found her and you were following up on her research. You must be her killer's worst nightmare."

"Which is why I'm facing jail time."

"You heard that tape and called me immediately. Why?"

"Because the more I looked at her research, the more I was sure she had an agenda. She may have started off doing a basic ethnography, but after this interview"—Libby tapped the tape—"she had a new mission. She bought the property where her grandmother was killed. Her research questions focused more and more on tribal interaction with mill management and Lyle's relations with the Kalahwamish. Millie's connection to the tribe. She was looking for the will, trying to figure out who Millie might have trusted. And your mother, Frances Warren, knew what Angela was doing. That's why Angela had unprecedented access to the tribe."

"How long did you take to come to that conclusion?"

"Fast. In reading her notes, I could sense her focus."

"Will the police draw the same conclusions when they go through her papers?"

"They didn't in 1979. They're not likely to now. They probably haven't read ethnographers' notes before. They wouldn't understand that her focus on recent history was unusual."

"Why did you call me and not the police?"

Libby gave Rosalie a tight smile. "I'm not exactly on the best of terms with them right now. They've got a witness who claims he saw me bring gasoline home so I could torch my house."

"And don't you find it interesting that you are at odds with the police, right when you have relevant information for them?"

"So my stalker's goal was to undermine my credibility with the police."

"At first, yes. Then, if you told the police you found a murder victim instead of an old Indian burial, they wouldn't take you seriously. But that didn't work. Think about this, when you were attacked, had Angela been identified?"

A chill spread through Libby as she remembered the sequence of events. "Not officially."

"I think your attacker was desperate to discredit you before she was identified. He or she staged an attack, leaving a trail of clues straight to you. Once it became clear you were crazy, your claim that you'd found a murder victim could have been determined to be another hoax. The bones would have been given to us for reburial without further investigation."

"But that didn't work. A DNA test confirmed we'd found Angela on Friday, the day after my attack but before my arrest."

"Things haven't gone according to plan for your attacker. So tell me, why is he or she still working so hard to frame you?"

Libby shrugged. "Too late to stop a plan in motion?"

"You mentioned a witness. Did you bring the gas cans home?"

"No. I didn't."

"When did the witness talk to the police?"

"I assume sometime over the weekend."

"After everyone in Coho knew Angela Caruthers had been found. So the witness lied after it was already too late to discredit you. Too late to stop the police from identifying Angela. The plan to frame you could have been dropped. But it wasn't. The witness lied anyway. What did they still have to gain?"

Libby gnawed on her thumbnail. "When you say *they* you mean the four people with something to lose. You mean Laura, Earl, and James Montgomery. You mean Jason Caruthers."

"Yes. What do they get out of framing you now?"

"At this point, there is only one reason to continue to frame me. To stop me from finishing Angela's research. To stop me from finding the will."

"Yes. This tells us they don't know what happened to the will either. *They didn't get it when they killed Angela.* The will is still out there."

29

A knock on the door of the RV startled Simone. The crew never knocked. Curious, she answered the door and came face to face with Jason. His gaze scanned her coolly from head to toe. Although she could see his frank appreciation of her snug tank top and shorts, she knew his thoughts weren't complimentary.

He stepped into the RV and closed the door. "I'm here to take a look at your financial information. For Libby's defense. I need a list of clients, projects, the works. Libby said you could give me everything I need."

Did she hear innuendo in that last sentence, or was that just wishful thinking? "Sure. Have a seat." She waved to the booth. "Would you like some coffee?"

"I just want the information."

"Everything is in the proposal package. I can print it out, but the computer here is slow. It'll take a few minutes."

He moved a box from the booth seat and sat. Simone began printing the documents he'd requested. Slowly, the ink jet printer came to life. The rhythmic clicking of the printer carriage was the only sound in the increasingly oppressive and tense silence.

The first section finished printing. She handed the pages to Jason. "I know you'll get the charges dropped," she said to break the tension.

"No thanks to you," he muttered.

"What's that supposed to mean?"

"Exactly what you think it means."

"You blame me for looking out for Libby."

"I think you've done her more damage than good."

"I don't care what you think. Three years ago, I was the only one who believed her. I was the only one who helped her. So I made a mistake. Libby has forgiven me. And my being caught with a camera and Aaron's work schedule isn't why Libby was arrested. If that were the case, I'd have been booked along with her."

"What do you mean *Aaron's work schedule*?"

She smiled tightly. "Did I forget to mention that part?"

"I don't think you forgot."

She was riled and defensive and didn't like being at a disadvantage with him. She stood to her full five-foot-two height. "Just say it, Jason. Let's deal with this here and now."

He moved to stand in front of her. A scant inch separated their bodies and Simone's pulse jumped. "You'd like that, wouldn't you? But I won't absolve you of your sins. You have to deal with your mistakes on your own."

"I don't need absolution."

"That's where we disagree."

"You don't want to be my confessor. You want to be my judge and jury. I need your judgment even less than I need your absolution." She cursed her short stature. He was nearly a foot taller than her, and she had to crane her neck to meet his eye, but she wouldn't look away. She wouldn't back down.

Their gazes remained locked. The moment stretched out long enough for her to forget the point she'd been trying to make. He smiled in a slow, sexy way. "You know what pisses me off about you the most, Simone?"

She laughed. "I have a wild guess."

"I don't like you, but still, I want you. I always have. I focused on Libby to convince myself to forget about you. It hasn't worked." He reached out and traced her collarbone. The gesture seemed like an impulse he couldn't control. He dropped his hand. "If you're interested in getting laid, give me a call." He tucked a business card into her cleavage and headed for the door. Before leaving, he stopped and turned back to her. "Have your client information delivered to the Dawes house. I need it today." Then he was gone.

She plucked his card from between her breasts and stared at his number. He was rude and insulting. She had a hundred and ten reasons to avoid him. But she knew it was only a matter of time before she gave in and dialed his number.

Before Libby left Rosalie's house, Rosalie gave her a small pistol. "The police will hardly race to your rescue if you call 9-1-1. Take the weapon. Lou will show you how to use it."

The last time she'd tried to arm herself, someone had used the weapon against her. She didn't want to take the gun, except she had no other way to protect herself. She spent the early part of the afternoon shooting at aluminum cans with Lou in an old gravel pit on the reservation. Lou was friendlier now that she wasn't desecrating a grave, and she found she enjoyed the target shooting.

From there, she went to the library to read every newspaper article she could find on Millie Thorpe Montgomery. According to Frances, Millie's lawyer was named Banks. Libby scanned the newspaper for references to him as well. A footnote to a 1946 article about union negotiations caught her eye. After the union formed, the union gained three percent ownership of the mill. A lawyer named Eli Banks brokered the deal. Banks received a cut that included two percent of the mill.

Two percent was a ridiculous payout for a negotiator. The agreement must have been a payoff from Lyle. Perhaps Banks had threatened to tell the sheriff about the will.

She left the library at seven p.m. At home, she read all her notes and interviews, searching for references to Millie. Simone called, wondering where she was, and Libby remembered she'd promised to move to the apartment. She was immersed in her research and didn't want to leave, nor did she want company. Her head was spinning and she wanted to read through Angela's notes without distraction. She wanted to see whether Angela left any veiled references to her search. She managed to convince Simone that she was fine and just needed to be alone.

By eleven p.m., she regretted her choice to stay in the Shelby house alone. When she'd spoken with Simone, it had still been light out. Now the darkness outside brought out a fear she hadn't experienced since she was a child. Every noise she heard sounded like a prowler invading her home. She checked the status of the alarm system for the fourth time, turned on the inside motion detectors and then retreated to her bedroom for the night.

She checked for a dial tone on her bedroom phone to be sure the landline hadn't been cut. Her imagination was getting away from her, but she knew she had reason to be afraid. She placed her cell phone and the loaded gun on her nightstand and then pulled a heavy dresser in front of her bedroom door. Finally, she crawled into bed, if only to pass the time until dawn when she could resume researching.

She lay in bed wide awake and mentally reviewed everything she knew. Angela Caruthers had been killed either by her grandfather, one of her uncles, her aunt, or possibly even Millie's lawyer. She kept no notes on her search for the will. The only evidence that she sought the document was the tape of an interview she had conducted at least three years before her death. As far as Libby knew, Angela hadn't transcribed the entire interview. She was careful. This explained the void in Jack's and Dan's knowledge of her research. She hadn't wanted anyone to know what she was doing.

Did Earl, James, and Laura know their father killed their mother? Millie was a battered woman. The suspicion must have crossed their minds. Did any of them condone Lyle's actions? Earl and Laura seemed to worship Lyle.

Then there was Jason. Handsome, sweet, kind, protective Jason. He knew about Libby's research. He'd located the boxes for her but then put limits on her report. He had scratches on his arms that could have come from blackberry vines. As far as she knew, he had been in town at the same time as every stalking event. He had a key to this house and he could lose upwards of twenty-five million dollars if the will was located and validated.

Libby would never believe he was involved in his mother's death, but he could be acting on behalf of his aunt and uncles now. He was smart enough, and this was a clever person's scheme.

She didn't dare go to the police. They already thought she was nuts. And if she did, the Montgomery family would find out she knew about the will. She'd be hanging a bull's-eye on her chest.

Libby had no clue how to proceed at this point. *If* Angela had located the will, and *if* the will had been left where she found it, and *if* all her sources were still available, then someone else doing the same research could *maybe* find the document again. A lot of ifs and she still ended in a maybe.

But still, Libby had only one option. She needed to find the will if she wanted to exonerate herself.

Angela had access to the ancestral home and in the 1970s she'd interviewed people who personally knew Millie. Many of those people were dead now. All Libby had were Angela's notes. They were incomplete and included absolutely nothing on the search for the will.

Who else stood to lose if the will was found? Was the lawyer still alive, ready to collect on his two percent? Did the now defunct union still have a three percent share? She decided to find out exactly who all the owners of TL&L were and the portion they retained. Time to know the enemy.

She slept fitfully and woke early, ready to begin a concentrated search. First, she developed a plan. Step one: set up a meeting with Jason to pick his brain about the structure and ownership of TL&L. He was the fastest route to the information, and she could cloak her snooping by making him believe it was for the report.

Step two: contact Dan Parker to find out who might know about Angela's research.

Step three: make appointments to interview the Montgomerys again. She would start with Earl, using the pretext that she needed to finish his interview.

Step Four: find the will and clear her name.

Piece of cake.

She called Jason and set up a dinner meeting with him. She had hoped to meet him earlier, but he explained that a dinner meeting would be better because she needed to be holding her head high among the townsfolk. They made plans to meet at a restaurant at seven.

Dan Parker was out of the office. She left a message asking him to call her ASAP. She left similar messages for a few professors at the University of Washington who taught there in the 1970s. Surely they would remember Angela—if nothing else, her disappearance would stand out in their minds. They could hopefully steer her to other grad students she'd known. Perhaps Angela had confided in someone.

Finally, she set up an appointment with Earl Montgomery for the following afternoon. She was surprised by his acquiescence, considering he hadn't exactly been forthcoming the first time around.

After each part of her plan had been implemented, she went through Angela's notes again and listed the names of people Angela had interviewed and then created a database of all the relevant information she had on each individual.

She had reached her research saturation point by the time she heard a knock on the front door in the early afternoon. At the sight of the Corps archaeologist through the door window, she quickly keyed off the alarm system. "Dan! What a surprise to see you! Please come in."

"I'm sorry, Libby, I don't really have time to stay. The police interviewed me today—about Angela. I gave them the box of Angela's research materials, but before giving the box over, I made copies for you. He dropped a carton onto the lounge and set it on the window seat.

Excitement over having fresh material jolted her. "Thank you. I hope you didn't get in trouble for making copies."

"I was questioned about that—the cop wanted to know if you'd asked me to make the copies for you."

Libby grimaced. Mark would hold her accountable for actions in which she had no knowledge or part.

"I told him you didn't know I'd located the box, let alone made copies. I didn't think I was doing anything wrong. Frankly, I still don't, but the way the cop acted you'd think I'd mugged an old lady."

"We had a little issue with Angela's boxes," Libby said.

"So I gathered. I explained to him that twenty years ago I packed everything of Angela's that remained in our office and stored it, hoping to give it all back to her someday. When I was making the copies for you, I found some of my own notes in there too, stuff I'd misfiled. That box was as much mine as anyone's and I had every right to go through it and make copies."

"I'm sorry he gave you a hard time. His behavior had more to do with me than with anything you did."

"Don't worry. He has other issues with me," Dan said.

His words confirmed her belief that Dan had been a suspect in Angela's disappearance. She realized that finding the will would clear him of suspicion, too.

"So, tell me, how is the report coming?" he asked. "Will I have a draft on Friday?"

"You'll have something. I met with Rosalie yesterday. She's satisfied with my progress. Even if I don't make the deadline, I think we can work something out." Rosalie was more than happy with what Libby had discovered. "Angela's research is quite…interesting."

"She worked hard. It'll be nice to see her research used at last."

You don't know the half of it. "I was wondering if you could tell me anything about Angela's research questions for her dissertation. I haven't been able to find them and she covered a broad range of tribal issues. What was her focus?"

"I don't know. Angela didn't talk about her research. Maybe that box will contain something."

"If you think of anything, will you let me know?"

"Sure." He cleared his throat. "There are some rumors flying around…about you."

At least he gave her an opportunity to address the issue. If she were tried and convicted with whispers and innuendo, her career was already over. "It's been one hell of a week," she said flippantly. Finding Angela would be significant enough. Being stalked, attacked, and framed was a special treat. But I didn't do anything wrong; my cost proposal will bear that out. I'm not worried." For a moment she almost believed herself.

"Glad to hear it. You do good work. We've got an on-call contract coming up and I'm hoping EAC will submit a proposal."

"I've already begun lining up my team."

"Good. For what it's worth, when you came up during my interview today, I told the cop that I believed the rumor about your finances began with Amy Seaver and it's well known in the archaeological community Amy resents your success."

That was a huge show of support coming from Dan Parker, and given Amy's basic psychotic behavior, she was sure to boil the Parker family bunny if she ever got wind of what he'd said. Gratefulness swept through her. Her peers might stand by her.

"I also told him I was aware of the financial trouble you had with a client three years ago," Dan continued. "But I didn't hesitate to accept you as the consultant on this project because I trust your integrity more than rumors."

She again felt the sting of tears, a sign of how fragile she really was. "Thank you, Dan. Your words mean more than I can say."

"Let me know if there's anything I can do to help."

"You already have."

He left. She studied the box he'd delivered. She had six hours until her dinner with Jason and a new set of notes.

M ark stared at the photos posted on the wall in the room they had set up for the Caruthers murder. All the information collected during the initial investigation and now was gathered here.

Color photos of a living, smiling Angela Caruthers hung next to photos of a hollow-eyed skull looking up from damp earth.

A timeline was posted along one wall. He read through the dates and events again.

August 19, 1979: Jack and Jason leave Seattle and drive to Spokane to visit Jack's parents. The departure is witnessed by a neighbor. Their arrival in Spokane is noted by several people, including business associates with whom Jack conducts meetings throughout the following week. Jack is not unobserved long enough to drive or fly to Seattle or Coho.

August 21, 1979, 12:00 p.m.: Angela leaves her office at UW. She tells Dan Parker she is going to collect research for her dissertation. Dan Parker is the last person on record to see her.

9:00 p.m.: Jack claims he received a phone call from Angela, during which she stated she was in Coho. The phone company is unable to provide any record that such a call occurred. The call was not collect and was not made from the Shelby house, the Montgomery house, or any of the other houses the Montgomery family had access to in Coho. A search of pay phone records for all of Coho was not conducted in 1979. Pay phone information is no longer available.

August 24, 1979, 10:00 p.m.: Jack reports Angela missing. After being unable to reach her for three days, Jack calls the Coho Police Department. A car is sent to the Shelby house. Officers report the house appears vacant. No evidence is found to indicate Angela ever arrived in Coho. Jack calls the Seattle PD, with the same results.

August 25, 1979: Jack and Jason return to Seattle. After a brief stop to check their Seattle home for Angela, Jack leaves Jason with a friend and drives to Coho. He files a formal missing person statement in Coho just before midnight.

September 3, 1979: Hikers camping over the holiday weekend find

Angela's vehicle on an old logging road in the North Cascades. No fingerprints or any physical evidence is recovered from the vehicle.

From there, the investigation was coordinated by the Seattle PD, because Seattle was where Angela was last seen, along with assistance from the Coho PD, where she was supposed to be when she was reported missing, and the National Park Service, who managed the land where her vehicle was found.

Mark's own officers had pathetic little to add to the investigation:

April 9-10, 1984: The Warren lot is covered with fill to level the area for paving

April 11, 1984: The Warren lot is paved.

This year:
July 12: Human remains are found during an archaeological excavation at the Warren lot.

July 15: The human remains are suspected of being a woman of Euro-American ancestry, buried just before the lot was paved in 1984.

July 16: The medical examiner finds the clavicles on the wrong sides of the skeleton, indicating the remains were moved post-mortem and post soft-tissue decomposition to the Warren site on April 9th or 10th 1984. A fake spearhead found with the remains indicates the person who buried her knew the Warren lot was an archaeological site and attempted to make the remains appear to be a prehistoric burial.

July 19: DNA tests confirm the remains found at the Warren site are those of Angela Caruthers.

July 22: Mount St. Helens ash found with Angela's remains indicates she was originally buried in Eastern Washington.

Mark looked at the pathetic list of dates and leads. Basically, they had nothing. No one knew whether Angela ever arrived in Coho on August 21, 1979. Jack had long been suspected of lying when he said he spoke with her that evening. Mark had spent several hours today interviewing Dan Parker. His story remained consistent with what he told police in 1979. He was forthcoming about the affair. His manner didn't trigger any investigative instincts. He was another dead end.

Mark looked at a snapshot that had been in the Seattle PD file. Angela and Jason stood on a ferry deck, a much smaller Seattle skyline behind them. A happy grin lit up Jason's face, revealing a gap where a tooth should have been. Angela had her arm around her son and laughed as the wind whipped her hair. Jason had his mother's eyes.

The photo was a painful photo to look at. Angela's laughing gaze begged the viewer to find her. She was young, beautiful, vibrant. A mother.

Mark had seen all this before when he worked for the Seattle Police Department. The only difference here was that he was less hardened. His time in Coho had softened the shell that had allowed him to investigate senseless death.

The son in the photograph grew into a man. People moved on. Tragedy faded. He knew all this, yet he looked at the picture and imagined Jason at nine. At nine, Mark's life had been simple. He'd spent his allowance on Legos and Micronauts. His sisters were aged four and two and his mother's attention stayed on them, leaving Mark free to ride his dirt bike and explore the Skagit Valley farm country where he grew up.

His world, his childhood, was vastly different from Jason's. Two months after this photo was taken, Angela disappeared. Mark didn't want to think about Jason's trauma of losing his mother. He didn't want to think about Jason, period. Every time he did, he saw Libby in Jason's arms, and another hairline crack appeared in the concrete shell he'd built to protect himself from his feelings.

30

Libby spent the afternoon going through the notes Dan gave her. The box was almost entirely filled with information on the union, which surprised Libby. The union, while important to the development of Coho, was off-topic for an ethnographic study. No Indians had been members of the Washington Logger's Union, Local 223, yet Angela interviewed several union members. She'd asked questions about union development and Lyle Montgomery, never once mentioning the tribe or tribal/union relations. The answers Angela received were guarded. After all, Lyle Montgomery's granddaughter was the interviewer.

From Angela's research, Libby learned that one man was pivotal in the unionization of TL&L, Nathan Simms. Nathan moved to Coho in 1938 and tried to organize a union. He left in 1942 for the war, was wounded, and returned in 1944. In 1946, the union formed in Coho. Nathan Simms was local president.

Libby knew more of the story. With both Lyle and Billy dead, the mill workers she'd interviewed had spoken freely about the unionization of TL&L. James Montgomery wasn't the only one eager to talk about Billy and how he facilitated the union in ways that would have made Lyle flip.

Angela conducted her research, however, while both her father and grandfather still lived. The mill workers she interviewed would have been guarded in their answers. And she would have been careful about what she put in writing. Everything Angela learned about

Billy's action to support the union would have endangered him. Prior to unionization, one organizer had been killed.

Had Angela interviewed Nathan Simms? There was no record of such a conversation but record keeping would have been unwise. Libby looked up Simms in the Coho phone book. No listing. How old would he be today? He could have children or grandchildren who knew the true story of how the union developed in Coho.

Libby searched the Internet and then made phone calls. She learned that Local 223 was part of a larger union that was now based in Portland, Oregon. She called union headquarters and maneuvered her way through the phone tree, eventually leaving a message for the union archivist who maintained all the old union records.

Two hours before her dinner meeting with Jason, she received a call from Jack, asking whether she was available for a quick meeting at the Dawes house. She agreed and headed right over.

Built in 1882, the Dawes house was second in size only to the Montgomery mansion. The house was heavily decorated with Queen Anne gingerbread, carved trim, and other Gothic embellishments. Inside, the house had all the detailed woodwork that proclaimed construction in a different age but the furnishings were thoroughly modern.

The ground floor served as the Coho office for Caruthers Commercial Development. A receptionist waved Libby into Jack's office, which at one time was a sitting room. She faced Jack with trepidation. Was he worried about her legal troubles? Was he going to fire her?

Jack circled his desk to greet her. Libby sat in the chair he indicated, and he leaned against the front of the desk just inches from where she sat. He crossed his ankles, his posture relaxed while he towered above her.

Libby's tension mounted at the power of his position versus the weakness of hers.

"A few years ago, the City of Coho contacted me and said they were planning to build a new facility for storing and repairing the school bus fleet. They no longer wanted nor needed the Warren lot. Without the tax-deduction that donation had provided, I decided it was time to sell the land."

This didn't sound like the introduction to being fired. She sat up straighter and wondered where he was leading.

"I kept the lot after Angela disappeared for sentimental reasons. She bought the land—she said it had something to do with her grand-

232 RACHEL GRANT

mother—but I never really knew what she meant by that. I looked through my files for the title to the land." He picked up a red spiral-bound notebook from the desk and handed it to Libby. "I found that in the file with the title."

Libby studied the cheap notebook. She flipped through the pages. Angela's now familiar scrawl filled the first half of the book. She looked up at Jack. "Is this a journal?"

"Of a sort. She kept a log detailing the purchase of the land—her dealings with George Warren, her plans for the property. There is much more in there than she ever told me."

Libby tightened her grip on the notebook. Did she include information on her search for the will in these pages? Did Jack understand what she was after? "Why did she want the land?"

"Her grandmother died there. Angela believed Lyle killed her. She wanted to prove Lyle was a murderer but couldn't. Short of that, she decided to buy the property and build a cultural center in Millie's honor. Angela felt that because Millie had a good relationship with the Kalahwamish, it would be fitting to honor her with a center that bridged the cultural divide between the tribe and the rest of the community."

"And after you found this notebook, you decided to go forward with Angela's plan?"

"Yes, except I planned to dedicate the Cultural Center to Angela, not Millie. Angela worked just as hard as her grandmother to improve relations between the Kalahwamish and the rest of Coho."

"Why haven't you told anyone you're building the Center in Angela's honor?"

"It's hard enough to raise investment capital. If I told everyone this was a sentimental project, they might believe I wasn't looking at this as a business deal and balk on the assumption that the Cultural Center isn't financially viable." He paused. "Plus, doing this for Angela was personal. Private."

"Why are you telling me?"

"I'd been debating whether or not I should share her journal with you since you first asked for her research notes. I wasn't sure if what she wrote in the notebook is relevant. There is a lot in there about Jason and me." He uncrossed his ankles and straightened his shoulders. "Now you've found Angela, and I can't tell you how much that means to me. I've decided you should have it. It might help with your research on Lyle. She mentions him often enough."

"Thank you, Jack."

He leaned back and she felt his scrutiny. She held his gaze. More than anyone else in Coho, Jack's opinion of her and her legal situation mattered. If he didn't have faith in her, he could use her legal troubles to break their contract. Libby would never recover, not financially, not professionally.

"I'm going to be honest," he said. "You weren't my first choice for the Coho project. I was leaning toward Seaver and Associates."

She did not let her dislike of Amy show on her face. "They are a reputable company. You would have done fine with them."

"You're being generous considering the things Amy said about you to the *Seattle Times*."

"I didn't read the article. Truth is, I don't like Amy, but she hires good people. I don't find fault with her work."

"Well, I think Amy Seaver has behaved abominably, and I think your work has been exceptional. I'm glad James pushed me to hire your company."

"James Montgomery selected us?"

"Yes. He's a major investor in the Center and has actively participated in the selection of the consultants. He's a huge asset to the project because I can't be in Coho full-time."

"I'll have to thank him the next time I see him."

"You can do that right now," James said from the doorway.

Jack pushed off his desk and greeted James with a handshake. Libby stood as well. She greeted James and studied him, looking for something, anything that would tell her how much he knew, whether he could possibly be the man who had attacked and framed her.

"I was just telling Libby how much of an asset she's been to the Cultural Center project. I was about to tell her I intend to keep her on no matter what happens with her legal situation," Jack said.

James smiled and looked like nothing more or less than the earnest man she'd interviewed over a week ago. "I knew you were the right choice. Amy Seaver was too eager to bad-mouth you. Very unprofessional."

So Amy's backstabbing had backfired. Interesting. Of course, given everything that had happened because she won the Cultural Center project, she couldn't help but wish it had been Amy who'd been the successful bidder.

Jack left James in his office and walked her to the door. "Have you given the police a copy of this notebook?" she asked.

Jack flinched. "No."

"Should I make them a copy?"

"Not yet. Before the Coho PD gets a copy, Jason should read it."

She wondered whether he wanted Jason to read it as Angela's son or as Jack's lawyer. "He hasn't read it yet?"

"No. He doesn't know this journal exists."

"I'm meeting Jason for dinner tonight. Can I show it to him then?"

He hesitated. "Fine," he said at last.

She stepped outside and stared at the notebook in her hands. A surge of excitement coursed through her. She practically ran all the way to the Shelby house, where she settled down on the window seat in the living room with a fresh cup of tea and Angela's journal and began to read.

April 17, 1976

Today George Warren agreed to sell me the property where Lyle killed my grandmother. I've been making offers for months now and he finally caved. It was the cultural center proposal that cinched the deal. I still have to figure out how I'm going to tell Jack about my plans for the cultural center. He's going to kill me when he finds out about the promises I made.

But I don't care. I want that land. Ever since Frances told me about Millie, I've wanted to own that property. I want to build the center and put Millie's name on it and tell Lyle that I know what he did. I even know why.

If I can just find the proof I need, I can go after Lyle. I can't fix the past but I can do something now.

Libby read on. Angela never once stated explicitly she was looking for Millie's will, but it was there, in the words in between. As Jack said, she mentioned Lyle frequently. She appeared obsessed with taking him down.

She chronicled her reluctance to tell Jack about her plans for the cultural center. In early 1978, she made the decision to tell Jack "everything." Libby suspected she meant both the cultural center and her search for the will. Then Angela came face to face with evidence Jack was having another affair. She feared she would lose him if she told him what she'd done. She feared he would be angry if he knew her search would result in giving Jason's inheritance away.

That was as close as Angela came to outright mentioning the will.

Over time, the book became less an account of her plans for the cultural center and rant against Lyle and became more of a journal.

She described a Jack Libby knew well: a handsome man with charisma that could be overpowering when focused intently on a person.

Angela expressed pride and anxiety over the fact that she thought Jason had the same gift. She didn't want to watch her son follow in his father's footsteps and use his charm to get what he wanted all while remaining emotionally reserved from his prey. And that was how Angela felt. Not Jack's partner, not his friend, but his prey.

She believed he had chosen her because she fit his needs. Pretty and wealthy, she had polish and education. She was the perfect wife for all his business functions.

Angela felt out of place at Jack's business functions and saw the way his secretary had stepped into the wife's role. Devastated, she'd thrown herself into her studies, desperate to have her own life and her own feeling of importance, separate from her husband, separate from her son. Her search for the will was an extension of that need.

She said she loved Jack intensely but he wasn't and couldn't be there for her. Eventually she turned to her ever-present and ever-available officemate, Dan Parker. Libby set the book down, shaken to the core. It was obvious why Jack hadn't given the notebook to the police. Even Libby had trouble holding on to the idea he was innocent of his wife's murder.

She forced herself to read the rest. Angela's last entry was dated August 19, 1979, two days before her disappearance. She said she'd ended her affair with Dan. In spite of his affairs, she loved Jack and wouldn't leave him.

Was it possible Angela's search for the will had nothing to do with her death? Had Dan killed her after she dumped him? Dan could easily have gotten the Clovis point found in Angela's hands. He would have quickly recognized the signs that he was digging through an archaeological site. He would know exactly how to make bones look like a prehistoric burial.

But Dan had approved the scope of work. He'd outlined the methodology and leaned on Jack to pay for the ground penetrating radar. It wouldn't make sense for him to do that if he'd killed her. She returned to the only logical conclusion. Jack and Dan were innocent. Angela was killed because she was looking for Millie's will.

She closed the journal and wondered how Jack had reacted after reading about Angela's affair and then finding out he needed a permit from Dan Parker or he wouldn't be able to build the Cultural Center in her honor. What an ugly tangled mess. Even messier than Libby's life.

The more she thought about it, the more she understood one fundamental truth: for all his faults, Jack had loved Angela. The Cultural Center was his private way of showing his love. But it came far, far too late.

31

L ibby was apprehensive about returning to the restaurant she'd dined at the night her troubles started, but in Coho there weren't many choices. She suspected the Thorpe Hotel restaurant with its walled booths would be too private for the showy evening Jason wanted.

He was already seated when she arrived. He greeted her warmly, clasping her hands and kissing her cheek, smiling his most polished smile. The show was on. She hoped she was up to her part.

"Relax," he whispered in her ear.

She was grateful for his help. Hopefully he wouldn't guess her true reason for being nervous. She had to pick his brain for information about his mother and the mill without letting him know about the will.

They ordered drinks and chatted of inconsequential things. She was surprised by his even manner. His murdered mother had just been found and his father could face prosecution for the crime, but he sat there exuding calmness, serenity, and a frank sexuality that women inherently responded to. Libby included.

She found herself wondering whether he would have been a wiser choice over Mark. He, at least, seemed to trust her. Then she reminded herself she didn't trust him.

There was also the fact that she had been drawn to Mark with an intensity she'd never felt before. Pursuing Jason instead of Mark would have been like ignoring the laws of gravity in an attempt to fly.

Her first true test of the evening came when Mark entered the restaurant. With a date. Libby recognized Heather, the waitress from the tavern, who beamed from ear to ear as she followed the hostess to their table.

Libby understood for the first time how stiflingly small Coho was. Her salad turned to sawdust. Jason must've seen the cracks in her composure. He glanced up and exchanged nods with Mark. Mark stared at her for a moment and then followed the hostess to his table.

Jason grabbed her hand and gave her fingers a squeeze without missing a beat in the conversation. "The division of the mill isn't complicated. My great-grandmother left each of her four children a quarter share of TL&L. When the mill unionized, concessions were granted. A few changes made. Five percent of the profit was supposed to go to the union, with the understanding that the employees would work harder if they could reap the rewards. Each of Millie's four children gave up one point two five percent of the company to equal five percent. In the end, three percent went to the union and two percent ended up going to the lawyer who brokered the deal." He held up a hand. "Please. No lawyer jokes. I've heard them all."

She smiled and tried to look amused, as though she wasn't aware that Mark was on a date in another part of the restaurant.

Jason leaned forward and said softly, "You're doing great." Then he leaned back and continued. "The lawyer, Eli Banks, will get his two percent of the proceeds when we sell TL&L. The union will still get three percent, even though there's no longer a local chapter. I inherited from my grandfather Billy twenty-three point seven five percent. Laura, Earl, and James each have the same amount."

The lawyer was still alive. Of all her suspects, he was the only one she was certain had knowledge of the will. "Does the lawyer still live in Coho?"

"You don't know," he said, surprised. "Eli Banks is your next-door neighbor, the one who claims to have seen you with gas cans on your back porch."

Mark's evening didn't start well. He'd entered the restaurant with Heather and immediately saw Libby and Jason together, while Heather chatted happily with the hostess, making it clear they were friends. He glanced at the reservation sheet as the hostess grabbed the menus. Caruthers/Maitland was written next to seven o'clock.

Heather had pushed for this evening out and now he knew he'd been set up—she'd wanted him to see Libby and Jason together. The hostess led them to a two-seat table, and Heather grabbed the one with the back to Libby. Mark would be forced to stare at her and Jason throughout the meal.

After the hostess left, Mark frowned at his companion. "You knew they'd be here."

Heather's eyes widened and she flushed. "No! I—I—"

Everyone lied to cops. Suspects, victims, witnesses: they all had reasons to lie and they all thought they could get away with it. His instinct for lies and truth had been fine-tuned by people far savvier than Heather. "Don't. I get lied to enough on the job. I'm not in the mood for it on my night off. Tell me who put you up to this." He spoke quietly so his voice wouldn't carry beyond their small table.

"No one!" She flushed again when her sharp response caught other diners' attention, and then continued in a softer voice, "I'm sorry, Mark. Okay, I knew they'd be here, but that's all there is to it. There's been talk at the bar. I knew that you and she…I just thought it might be easier for you if you knew she'd already moved on."

This was the truth. Heather's face had gone through every shade of red and it was obvious she was a novice at scheming. His anger evaporated as he began to feel sorry for her. "He's her lawyer, Heather. Just because they're having dinner together doesn't mean she's moved on." Strange he could say that to Heather when he didn't believe it himself.

"Oh," she said, sounding like a deflating balloon. "Do you want to leave?" He guessed she'd passed embarrassment on the way to mortification.

"No." The weight in his chest lifted. "You need a night out, and so, frankly, do I."

Her smile blossomed from timid relief to real happiness. At least at the end of the evening there would be no awkward goodnight with Heather waiting for a kiss. Mortification was an effective antidote to infatuation.

L ibby's jaw dropped. Her mind raced. Now she understood why her next-door neighbor had lied. He'd ruined Libby so he could finally receive his payout sixty-two years after he betrayed Millie Thorpe in exchange for two percent of the mill. The man stood to gain two million dollars. But he must be in his nineties and couldn't be agile enough to be behind the physical attacks. So who else was involved? She looked across the table. Jason was certainly strong enough. "Why would he lie?" she finally asked, feigning ignorance.

"By all accounts, he's a few bricks short of a stack. I interviewed him today, and I can tell you with complete confidence his testimony won't ever hold up in court. Which brings me to some good news. The case against you is pretty much dead." He paused. When she didn't say anything, he added, "This is the part where you throw your arms around me and shower me with kisses." He winked at her.

"I'm tempted," she said, afraid to believe his words could be true.

"Banks' story changed three times during the interview. He was disoriented. Confused. Tomorrow I've got a meeting with the DA. I'm going to ask her not to file based on this and other new evidence. Just before coming here, I dropped off a copy of my findings at the Coho PD. Your case is in the hands of the prosecutor now, but I want Mark to attend the meeting with the DA because I want him to re-open the investigation of your attack."

"Good luck with that."

"There is no doubt in my mind that he'll do what I want after he reviews the evidence. There were more problems with the finger-print evidence than they would have you believe. Your prints were only on the first piece of tape ripped from the roll that night—the strip that covered your mouth. I did my own test with a roll of the same brand of duct tape. I was surprised at how easily I could get the tape around my wrists two times. But the tape was wrapped around your wrists five times. That was nearly impossible to do and have it remain smooth—like the tape was on you. You would've needed to use your mouth, chin, shoulder, neck, or knees. You would have been bound to get some of your own hair or clothing fibers stuck in the tape. Or there would be teeth marks, possibly saliva. None of which was found on the duct tape around your wrists. Plus, because the attacker used your own roll of duct tape, the fingerprints are only circumstantial. You could have used the roll yourself, unwinding a piece longer than necessary, getting your fingerprints on it, then winding the tape back on the unused part of the roll."

"That makes sense," she said. Inside she was reeling, thrilled that the evidence against her could be easily countered, but afraid to hope that the threat of standing trial was really gone.

"There's more. There were several other unmatched sets of fingerprints on the wine bottle used for the Molotov cocktail. The investigator matched your prints but never matched the others. I want those prints run. Your attacker could have taken the bottle from your recycle bin. Whose fingerprints could be on the bottle?"

Libby clearly remembered Mark's arms surrounding her as he helped her open the bottle of wine the night he'd kissed her the first time. "Mark," she said.

"I was really hoping you'd say that. If one of those sets of prints are his, then he's just become a defense witness. This is important because the Molotov cocktail is the strongest evidence they have for attempted arson, and right now that's the only thing you've been charged with."

She smiled at the idea of Mark being forced to testify on her behalf. "And the other prints? Could they belong to my attacker?"

"It's more likely they were already there. Any number of people could have touched that bottle before you purchased it. But if we can prove that both yours and Mark's fingerprints got on the bottle under normal circumstances, then their evidence supporting the arson charge is weak."

Jason explained how her attacker might have used her Taser and a second one to make it seem she wasn't Tasered at all. "We're looking at a carefully premeditated attack. The police don't have the proof they need to show you weren't attacked Thursday night. I believe reasonable doubt is on your side."

The waiter came and laid out their main course. The theories Jason outlined weren't the solid proof of innocence she wanted. But she knew what she went through that night and Jason's scenario made sense. Would the prosecutor accept it as such? And what about Mark?

After she finished eating, Libby pulled out Angela's journal and set it on the table in front of Jason. She explained what it was. "Your mom's writing is very personal. In the end, she is painfully frank about her marriage, mistakes she made, mistakes Jack made. There may be more in there than you want to know."

He looked at the book as though he were afraid to touch it. "As her son, I'm bothered that Jack didn't give this to the police sooner. There may be information that would help their investigation. As a lawyer, I'm glad I'll have a chance to read it before we tell the cops she kept a journal."

She wanted to give Jason a moment alone and excused herself to use the restroom. She passed by Mark's table and a fresh jolt of pain hit her. She'd been better off when she was angry. Before leaving the restroom, she paused to collect herself, and then squared her shoulders and stepped into the narrow corridor and came face to face with Mark.

The cold mask had dropped from his features. In his eyes she saw pain that mirrored her own. "Did you plan to use Jason from the start, or did you choose him because you knew how much it would bother me?"

She blinked against the sting his accusation triggered. Pain or not, he continued to believe the worst of her. "I'm not using Jason. He's helping me because you had me arrested, and I needed a lawyer." *He's a victim, too. Don't let the anger win.*

She started to brush past him, but he caught her arm and stopped her. She met his gaze. Probing. Intense. Just like when he'd questioned her after searching the blackberries. They'd shared so much, and yet they'd gotten nowhere. She shrugged out of his grip and straightened her spine. "Go back to your date, Mark, and leave me alone."

"It's not—"

"Is everything okay, Libby?" Jason asked as he entered the corridor.

She frowned. Was Mark about to deny being on a date? Did it matter at this point?

Mark's gaze narrowed with Jason's protective intrusion. "Libby's always fine," he said, then he turned and left.

"Well, that was…awkward," she said.

"He shouldn't talk to you without a lawyer present, and he knows it. You can talk to him tomorrow, after I meet with the prosecutor."

Was that really why Jason had intruded? She didn't know what to think—of Jason or Mark.

They returned to their table, paid their bill, and left the restaurant. Standing next to her truck, Jason pulled her into his arms for a comforting hug. She leaned into him and wished she could trust him, but he was too high on her list of suspects.

"I know you're in love with Mark," he said.

She wanted to protest, but couldn't.

"And he's trying not to care," he added. He met her gaze and stroked her cheek, and then his gaze lifted over her head, toward the restaurant, and he smiled. "I'm not above helping you get some petty revenge." He cupped her face in both hands and leaned down and kissed her full on the lips. "Goodnight, Libby."

She looked over her shoulder and saw Mark and the waitress exiting the restaurant. A mean satinfaction slid through her. She'd suffered alone the last two days. The flash of pain in Mark's eyes was at least a sign he felt something other than contempt for her.

She climbed into her Suburban, blew Jason a kiss, and drove off. She made it all the way home before her tears began to flow again.

Dinner hadn't been what Mark would call fun, and now, thank God it was over. Heather, at least, had enjoyed herself.

After confronting Libby, Mark returned to the table in a bleak mood. Heather's intention had backfired. He hadn't taken one look at Libby with Jason and known he needed to move on. No, instead he had to face the knowledge he still wanted her. Or at least wanted what he'd thought they could have together. Heather took one look at him and winced. "I'm sorry," she said. "I shouldn't have asked you here tonight." Her voice dropped to a whisper. "You're in love with her, aren't you?"

Mark tried to speak, but couldn't.

"Maybe she's innocent," she offered hopefully.

"That's for the court to decide."

"But what do you think?"

"What I think and what I want are two different things."

"For your sake, I'm going to hope she's innocent."

Mark smiled, surprised by the change in Heather's attitude toward Libby. Heather was a kind woman—foolish, but kind.

They left the restaurant just in time to see Jason's less-than-brotherly kiss on Libby's lips, and Mark stopped dead in his tracks. This was the image that had tormented him since Monday. He got hold of himself and resumed walking.

Libby drove off as Heather climbed into her vehicle. He could go home. He unlocked his car and then heard footsteps behind him and turned to see Jason.

"Tomorrow I'm meeting with the DA," Jason said. "I'm certain she's going to choose not to file charges against Libby after she reviews my findings."

"Good for you." Mark opened his car door.

"I want you to re-open the investigation of Libby's assault."

"I won't waste more taxpayer money investigating her claims."

"I sent a copy of my findings to your office. Read my brief and then tell me you think she's guilty."

"I'm sure you are very persuasive." In spite of the coldness of his tone, part of him acknowledged he really did hope Jason could convince him.

Jason shook his head as though he pitied Mark. "You had her, yet you fucked it up."

"Did it ever occur to you that *she* fucked up? That she played me like she's playing you?"

"No. Because I reviewed the evidence."

"So did I."

"No. You didn't. Listen, I'm willing to cut you some slack because I know police procedure. Given the pile of evidence against her, you had to bring her in. I'll even grant that given your relationship, you had to tread very carefully, and talking to her first—interviewing her privately—could have gotten your ass in deep trouble. But where you fucked up was believing the bullshit instead of trusting your instincts about Libby. You could have stepped back, told her you had to recuse yourself, and let Officer Eversall handle it. But you were stupid and sent in Roth, whose lack of experience in investigation and bias against Libby were obvious from the start. Face it. You fucked up, big time."

He glared at Jason. Libby had damned herself before Luke ever started investigating. "The evidence against Libby is solid and supported by her actions. She falsified evidence in the past. She tampered with evidence in your mother's homicide. She lied about her relationship with Brady."

Jason held up a hand and ticked off his responses. "*Simone*—not Libby—falsified evidence. The 'tampering' argument is weak, considering she was given those boxes for the express purpose of going through them and making copies. And Aaron? I don't know what you're talking about, but only a fool would take that prick's word over Libby's."

Mark stared at Jason, his heart beating at a slow but resounding tempo. Jason was the last person he should discuss lying women with.

Jason shook his head. "This is really about Sheila, isn't it?"

Mark's hand clenched into a fist. "Hell no."

"It is. Sheila got your head so fucking twisted that—because of me —you can't see Libby for who she is."

"I see Libby just fine."

"No. You don't." Jason paused. "You followed one trail of evidence, then let your emotions take over. You stopped asking questions and instead decided guilt. That's not the type of cop I expected you to be." He turned and strode to his Lexus, his footsteps echoing in the quiet night.

Mark stood frozen, staring after Jason and hating the hope the lawyer had stirred. Could Mark really be that wrong about Libby? Had he fucked up on an unbelievable scale?

All he knew was he'd never wanted to be wrong so badly. Wound up with anger, self-loathing, and treacherous hope, he decided to go to the station and read Jason's report. While there, he'd review the fingerprint evidence and the notes on the interview with Eli Banks. Jason was probably half in love with Libby himself. He could be wrong.

Guilty or innocent, Mark didn't doubt that Jason could get her off. Libby would do well with a man like Jason at her side. *Shit.* He'd never felt so raw and exposed.

The station was quiet. He strode to his office. An inch-thick manila envelope from Jason sat front and center on his desk. Mark reached for it with a combination of apprehension and hope, knowing it was Jason's opening salvo in his quest to clear Libby. In the cover letter, Jason requested Mark's attendance at tomorrow's meeting with the prosecutor and said he included copies of his findings so Mark could familiarize himself with the case. As if Mark didn't have the details memorized.

He looked through the attached documents. Jason was thorough and fast. In addition to copies of Libby's cost proposal and scope of work, he'd included man-hour estimates from other archaeological consulting firms, just as Libby had suggested. Based on man-hour estimates alone, her cost proposal was in the middle range, higher than three, lower than two. Mark wondered briefly how Jason had gotten such a quick response from the other consulting firms. If they had a connection to Libby, they might've skewed their estimates to help her.

The cost estimate included additions to the scope of work. Jack had signed off on all the additions with the exception of the last one, which was in negotiation. Libby's estimate for the new task wasn't an alarming sum. Compared to the overall budget, it was hardly significant.

She didn't have a motive.

Mark rocked back in his chair and stared at the ceiling. His stomach clenched as if he'd been punched in the gut. Without motive, he had a hard time believing Libby was guilty of anything.

Jason had a plausible theory for how her fingerprints could be found on the adhesive side of the duct tape that covered her mouth, plausible enough for reasonable doubt and therefore limiting the fingerprint evidence's impact in court. Like Jason told him her prints were only found on the first piece ripped from the roll.

Shit. Mark was the worst cop in history. In any other situation, he would have thoroughly reviewed the evidence before ordering her arrest.

There were problems with the wine bottle used for the Molotov cocktail. Other fingerprints found on the bottle hadn't been matched. Jason wanted them run to prove the attacker used a wine bottle found in Libby's recycle bin.

Mark hadn't looked closely at the bottle that night, nor had he seen it since. He left his office and went to the evidence room. He found the bin that stored the Maitland evidence. One look at the bottle confirmed what he'd both hoped and dreaded. It was the bottle he'd opened for Libby five nights before her attack. Some of the unmatched prints were his.

Jason would make Mark the star defense witness. Her fingerprints on the bottle weren't evidence of her guilt any more than his meant he was the attacker. Except for the eyewitness, they had nothing solid to support attempted arson.

He returned to his office and continued reading Jason's brief. Next Jason dealt with the Taser. He acknowledged the three important pieces of evidence against her: the Anti-Felon Identification tags which were found in Libby's kitchen were traced back to one of the air cartridges she had purchased, the batteries in her Taser had not been depleted, and the downloadable weapon log showed the weapon had been fired only once and for less than a second. Jason theorized that Libby's attacker had brought a Taser to the house that night. He or she affixed Libby's own air cartridge to the weapon before shooting her.

After Libby had been bound and subdued, the assailant then attached the dispelled cartridge to Libby's Taser and fired one short blast to make it look like hers had been used only long enough to release the tags.

Jason's argument was convincing. It fit well with the increasing possibility that Libby was framed. Even if they managed to keep the Taser as evidence, the weapon only supported a hoax charge, not attempted arson. Mark doubted the prosecutor would want to pursue a hoax case if they couldn't prove attempted arson.

Mark moved on from the Taser data to Jason's transcript of his interview with Eli Banks. Jason had hired a court reporter to record the session and the document was signed and notarized. Banks changed the timing of Libby's return home twice during the interview. He changed his description of what she wore and described the gas cans as metal, not plastic. He adamantly insisted that whatever he told the police when they interviewed him was correct, and he couldn't be expected to remember everything. Just forty-eight hours after Luke interviewed Banks, his story had changed completely.

Without the witness, without fingerprints, without motive, they had no case. He should, in fact, look to see whether anyone else bought a Taser in the week prior to Libby's attack.

But if she was innocent, then his words, his treatment of her, was awful.

She would never forgive him.

Mark pulled Luke's file on the investigation. The notes were incomplete. Luke had interviewed Banks alone; there would be no testimony to corroborate his account of how lucid the elderly man had been. Luke's information on motive was based on hearsay. He didn't seek out any sources to counterpoint the hearsay argument. In contrast, Jason provided letters from no less than ten of Libby's previous clients, all lauding her work and professionalism. Every one of them said they would be pleased to work with her again. Jason had gathered this in just two days. It seemed Libby was well-liked enough that many people dropped what they were doing to draft a letter on her behalf.

That the letters were necessary was his fault. He hadn't trusted Libby. He didn't talk to her before ordering her arrest. To avoid impropriety, he had to treat her like any other suspect, and so he did. Along the way, he accepted the evidence as fact, her guilt as given.

Again he sat back in his chair and gazed at the ceiling. Just an hour ago he'd accused her of using Jason. He rubbed his temples with his fingertips, trying to ease the headache that rapidly formed. Jason was right. He'd fucked up, big time.

He wanted to speak with her, but speaking to her without counsel present was a serious breach of ethics. He didn't care.

He grabbed his car keys and headed out the door.

32

Libby felt antsy. She tried to watch television, but nothing engaged her attention. She prowled around the house looking for something to do. She went over Angela's notes again, but she'd practically memorized them at this point. She dropped the papers in disgust and paced the living room, wondering where the hell Millie could have hidden the will. She had died within a few hours of signing the will. Where had she gone before going to see Frances Warren?

Her mind raced. She wouldn't be able to sleep anytime soon. Realizing what she needed more than anything was a walk, she opened the front door and stood on the porch. The bright full moon was on the rise. The night was mild and the sky clear, perfect for an invigorating walk.

She went back inside and changed into her most comfortable yoga pants, a sweatshirt, and running shoes. She wished she still had her Taser. She wouldn't bring a loaded gun on her walk but might have felt comfortable carrying the non-lethal weapon for protection. Ironically, Coho was the safest town she'd ever lived in, and yet here she was the most at risk.

Outside, she took a deep breath. She crossed the street and walked along the shore of the bay until she came to the decommissioned sawmill. She studied the pier where she and Mark had eaten Chunky Monkey, and then turned her back on the memory and headed toward the apartment building where Simone and the crew lived.

She stood in front of the building. Simone's light was on. She should go up and see her, tell her everything she'd learned in the last two days but didn't want to talk right then.

The soft sound of music reached her, and she realized Simone was playing her violin. Libby sat on a bench in front of the building and listened. She recognized the piece, a Bach violin sonata, one Simone turned to when she was upset. Presumably, Simone's unease came from what was happening to Libby, but Libby knew Simone wouldn't tell her if anything else was wrong.

The melancholic notes brought Jason to mind. Libby wondered if she thought of him because of the intensity of Simone's playing, and if Jason was part of what disturbed her. Libby listened for several minutes before deciding to let Simone battle her demons with music while Libby fought hers with exercise.

Mark sat in his parked car at the end of the alley that serviced Libby's house. He debated his options. He could go home, get some sleep, review everything in the morning, and question Libby one more time with Jason present. The interview would be professional, impersonal, and all aboveboard.

Or he could go to her house right now and talk to her, alone, no lawyer. The conversation would be very personal and very unethical. The second option held more appeal.

She was awake. Nearly every window of her house glowed brightly.

He made his decision and walked to the door of the Shelby house and knocked. He began to worry when she didn't answer, reminded too much of what he'd found the last time he knocked on her door late at night. But tonight the house didn't have the same feel. He circled the structure. Everything seemed normal.

He called the alarm company. When the system was first installed, she'd told him the code word that would authorize the alarm company to speak with him. Luckily, she hadn't changed the word. He was told that the alarm system was working fine and that the interior motion detectors had been activated seventeen minutes before.

Mark hung up and stared at the house. The motion detectors meant she had gone to bed with every light blazing or she wasn't home. He figured she wasn't home.

Had she gone to Jason's? He cursed himself for the thought. More likely she'd gone to Simone's. He got in his car and drove to the apartment building and caught sight of a figure in dark clothing walking up the hill toward the Montgomery mansion. He recognized the subtle sway of her hips and her proud posture.

He parked his car and followed her on foot. He breathed a sigh of relief as she passed the Dawes house where Jack and Jason stayed. She wasn't seeking a clandestine tryst. For a brief moment, he wished she were headed to his house for that purpose. Where was a shooting star when you needed one?

He followed her easily. She had dressed in traditional nighttime reconnaissance black, but the milky light of the moon made her skin shine. His belief in her innocence wavered when she crossed the lawn in front of the Montgomery mansion, but then, the yard was vast and the boundary between it and the adjacent park undefined. People cut across the lawn all the time.

What was she up to? Whatever it was, he should probably stop her before she committed a crime more serious than trespassing. He'd do it to protect her, but knew she'd never see it that way.

L ibby found herself headed to the Montgomery mansion as if by magnetic force. She stood in front of the Gothic monstrosity, a structure both beautiful and garish at the same time. This house was the embodiment of Lyle Montgomery: it loomed over the town, dominating the landscape, demanding attention. The focal point of the town should be the waterfront, but all eyes were drawn inescapably to the beauty and menace of this house.

Someone who lived in that house had attacked her. Someone had framed her. Mesmerized by the moonlit silhouette, she stared up at the rounded tower where Millie had retreated in the last years of her life. The poor woman had suffered so much.

The house offered no answers or solace, so Libby headed for the large, beautiful historic oak tree in the center of the front lawn, a living connection to a happier time that predated Angela, Millie, and Lyle.

She rounded the shadowy trunk, and a man materialized in front of her. She shrieked and stumbled backward as terror-laced adrenaline flooded her system.

Strong arms seized her and kept her from falling. She sucked in a deep breath to release a full scream, but a hand covered her mouth. She struggled against the man's strong grip.

"Libby, calm down. It's me," Mark whispered. He stepped back, pulling her with him into a ray of moonlight filtered through a tree branch, so she could see his handsome face. She caught her breath as her body came down from the adrenaline jolt, but then she remembered exactly who had her in a firm hold. This man wasn't her ally. He could very well cart her off to jail for trespassing.

She attempted to break free, but he shook his head and said, "Calm down." They were chest to chest. He removed his hand from her mouth. "What the hell are you doing?"

"None of your damn business!" she hissed.

He patted her down, making her grateful she didn't have a Taser. "Why are you here?"

"I was just checking out the house. Call it background research." True, if one really stretched things.

"At nearly midnight?"

She nodded.

"In the dark?"

"Full moon," she said sheepishly.

His mouth curved in the slightest hint of a smile. "Without permission?"

She nodded, guiltily this time.

His dimple made a brief appearance. He shifted her in his arms so he held her in more of an embrace than a prison. Against her will, she found herself settling against him.

"Care to explain?" he asked, his voice changing from harsh to husky.

"No way."

He laughed softly and held her gaze as though he wanted to read her soul. Then he lowered his head and she realized he was going to kiss her. Worse yet, in spite of everything, she wanted it. Him. The attraction that burned between them was a force of nature she could not ignore. It didn't matter how hurt she was, how much he distrusted her.

She rose up on her toes and met him halfway—an uncontrollable, instinctive response—but it was her shattered ego that made her open her mouth and initiate a deeper kiss. Her arms slipped around his neck as her tongue stroked his in a hot exploration. She didn't think;

she just reveled in the feel of his hard body against hers. She'd never expected to feel this intense heat again.

He pressed her back against the tree and lifted her. She wrapped her legs around his waist and gasped at the need that shot through her as his hard length pressed against her center.

This. Her whole body burned with need. She'd craved this passion, this fiery oblivion, from the moment her heart had shattered in the interrogation room.

The thought pulled her from the brink of surrender and brought to mind her arrest. His low opinion of her. His most recent accusation in the restaurant. The memories piled up, bringing with them sharp, painful, Taser like jolts. Sense returned. Hurt returned. The anger—the nasty bitterness that reminded her of her mother in the most awful way—was there too.

He groaned softly as his mouth left hers and explored the column of her throat, unaware that her world had just shifted. She released her legs from his waist and returned to earth, both literally and figuratively. With her feet planted, she shoved at his chest.

He lifted his head and she saw shock in his lust-filled eyes. It only took him a moment to catch up, and his arms locked around her. Once again, she was his prisoner.

"Let me go," she said, pushing harder on his wide and—she knew from experience—perfect pecs.

He breathed heavily as sanity returned to his features. His eyes dimmed. "Not until you tell me what you're doing here."

"Nothing," she said.

"Just this once, tell me the truth."

His words, his complete lack of faith in her, opened a new wound. Still, she had to tell him. "I've learned some things about Angela. I think her murder is related to what's happening to me. I was out for a walk, to clear my head. Then something about seeing this house in the moonlight made me reckless; I wanted to see it up close. That's all."

She watched him struggle, knew he wanted to believe her. She waited to see which side of him would win, her lover or the pragmatic cop who didn't trust anyone—not even, apparently, himself.

His internal battle was over in the blink of an eye—the cop won.

Crestfallen, she pulled out of his arms, surprised the cop would release her, and wondered what the lover, if he had been the victor, would have done. Of course, if the lover had won, they probably would have raced to the damp grass to see who could pull off their underwear the fastest, forgetting condoms, moonlight, and all other considerations. But that was useless speculation and heartbreaking fantasy. With Mark, the lover would never win. He was a cop first, last, and, with her, always.

"Jason isn't here," he said. "He's staying at the Dawes house."

Perhaps it was progress of sorts that this was not the cop but the jealous lover talking. "I know very well where Jason is staying."

"I saw him kiss you."

"I think that was his plan."

"No. On Monday."

Monday. Hours before she'd been arrested. A rush of anger took her breath away. She struggled out of his arms. Finally, she gathered enough air to speak. "Does that mean being kissed by Jason is an arrestable offense?"

"You didn't exactly shove him away. You pushed me away the first time I kissed you."

"*You* aren't my client's son. I had to be careful with Jason."

"How very pragmatic of you."

"I've learned to be pragmatic the hard way. See you around, officer." She started for the sidewalk.

"Libby—" He caught her arm, stopping her. "Tell me what's going on. Who do you think is after you?"

Her bitterness ran deep, perhaps even deeper than before. How could she let him slip past her defenses and hurt her again? She was worse than her mother. "Listen to Angela's tapes. Figure it out for yourself. We both know you won't believe anything I say anyway."

Mark turned her to face him. "I want to believe you, Libby. But I can't let our relationship get in the way of the investigation."

She yanked out of his grasp. Another hard-earned lesson from childhood came back to her. She would never again beg a man to stay. She would never be like her mother and beg a man to love her. She was done begging him to believe her. She glared at him. "If you want to believe me, Mark, then just do it—you don't get to kiss me like you did a moment ago then hide behind your damn badge."

"I'm not hiding. Damn it, Libby! I'm not even supposed to be talking to you without your lawyer present."

"No problem. I'll leave."

"Wait. Did you sleep with Aaron?"

His words stunned her to the core. Never in a million years had she seen that question coming. She narrowed her gaze. "Who wants to know? The cop or the lover?"

"Aaron called me on Monday. He described your scar."

Her mouth dropped open. Monday. Again. Before she'd been arrested. "You sonofabitch!" She stepped closer and tapped his chest. "You believed Aaron. Over me. You don't even know him. But you know me."

His arms encircled her, trapping her again. "You lied to me."

"No, Mark. I didn't."

"Then how does he know about your scar? Make me understand."

The fight left her even though the ache hadn't. Her gaze held his. She loved him. Not even the pain of his distrust could destroy her feelings—no matter how much she wished otherwise. Yet he demanded she explain herself, her past, something she should be allowed to keep locked away in her own box of painful memories.

"I didn't lie to you. I didn't have sex with Aaron." Her voice shook. She cleared her throat. "If you really want to know the story, you have to let me walk away from here after I tell you. You have to leave me alone. Forever." She refused to be like her mother. She would rather be alone than spend her life pining for a man incapable of loving her back.

"I'll let you walk away, but I don't agree to the last part."

"You won't have a choice." She breathed deeply. "Aaron and I were on our third date. I wanted to like him, but somehow, didn't. I have good instincts, but I didn't trust them. Aaron was in my house, in my bedroom." She paused. "My mistake, I know." A shudder ran through her. She lived with this memory and the aftermath on a daily basis.

"We kissed. I was trying to convince myself he was okay. Things went further than I wanted. He removed my clothing until I wore only my bra and underwear. I was stupid, passive, trying to figure out how I was going to stop him, because I wasn't interested—I certainly wasn't aroused. He asked about the scar. It was fresh then—I'd gotten the stitches only a month before.

"He reached for my underwear and a wave of revulsion I couldn't control came over me. My skin started to crawl. I couldn't have sex with him. I couldn't touch him. I couldn't kiss him, and I certainly couldn't let him do any of those things to me. I just…shut down. I said no.

"He called me a cock tease and said I owed him. I told him to get out." She closed her eyes. "He lunged at me, but I shoved him away, so he slammed me into the wall. That dazed me. I had a goose egg on the back of my head that lasted several days." Of their own accord, her fingers gingerly probed the back of her head, even though the lump was long gone.

"He twisted my arm behind my back and shoved me face first into the wall then ripped at my underwear and said crap about how he knew from the first moment we'd met that I'd like it rough. He tried to kiss me, even then. I jabbed him in the eye with my free hand. He let go of me, and I ran out of the room. He tackled me from behind and slammed me onto the floor.

"I was pinned in the hallway. He slapped me across the face then wrapped a hand around my throat while his other hand worked to unhook his belt." She opened her eyes again and met Mark's shocked gaze. "I couldn't breathe. He lifted his weight off me to loosen his tight belt, giving me enough leverage to knee him in the balls. I was able to shove him off and run.

"In the kitchen, I grabbed a knife and told him to get the hell out, that I'd cut him open if he took one step closer. He laughed and said, 'Have fun trying to blame this on me,' then waltzed to the door like nothing happened. He had the gall to say he'd call me as he walked out."

"I'll kill him." Mark pulled her closer and stroked her hair.

Warmth invaded her. He didn't blame her. He didn't say she'd asked for it by letting Aaron into her bedroom in the first place.

"Why didn't you report the assault?"

"I was nearly naked with him in my own home. I let things go too far. Be honest. How well would the system have treated my assault case in those circumstances? Keep in mind the accused was a cop."

"It would have been difficult. But you had bruises to back up your claim."

"I told the crew I had the flu and stayed home for a week."

"No one saw your bruises."

"No one." She touched her neck, remembering the pain of Aaron's fingers. She'd told Mark more than she'd ever told anyone. "I didn't want to fight a public battle. The guy was my client's brother. I had a crew to pay, a project to run. I wanted to forget what happened and move on."

"And after you healed and no longer had physical evidence, Brady started stalking you."

"Yes. I had a lunch meeting with my client. Aaron showed up and acted as though nothing happened. I was in a fix. I hadn't reported the assault. I certainly couldn't accuse him of attempted rape in front of my client. I was forced to pretend everything was fine. Then the stalking started."

She leaned back and studied him. She'd learned to read him and knew he believed her. Her heart broke that he was willing to listen now. Her voice hardened. "Don't think for a minute that every time Jason called a business meeting a date I didn't want to run away screaming. You want to know why I didn't shove Jason away when he kissed me? Look at what happened when I shoved Aaron away, and ask yourself, do you really think I could have handled my client's son any other way? I *had* to be pragmatic."

His arms tensed. "I've been a complete ass."

"True. Now we made a deal. I told you about Aaron. You have to let me go."

His hands dropped from her waist and she was free. Before he could change his mind, she bolted and ran all the way home.

33

M ark watched Libby leave, stunned to the core. Why hadn't he guessed Aaron had beaten her? All the signs were there. He remembered her reaction to hearing the sound of someone being choked in the blackberries. No wonder she'd been terrified. No wonder she'd been convinced Aaron was stalking her again.

He leaned against the tree. He was the fool Jason had called him and worse. If she hadn't stopped him, he would have made love to her right there up against the historic oak planted by James Thorpe in honor of the birth of his first child in 1855. He grimaced, remembering he'd learned that fun fact from Libby when they drove around Coho last Thursday.

She had him in knots. He wanted to go after her. He wanted to beat Brady to a bloody pulp for assaulting her. He wanted to undo the hurt he'd caused her and beg her forgiveness.

But he could do none of those things.

He went home and managed a few hours of fitful sleep, but by six a.m., he was wide awake and thinking about Libby's answer when he asked who she suspected was after her: *"Listen to Angela's tapes. Figure it out for yourself."*

As soon as he arrived at the station, he put Sara back on the task of going through Angela's research notes, starting with the cassettes. Nothing of interest had turned up in the initial inspection done by other officers over the weekend. Mark himself had only done a cursory examination. If Sara failed to find anything of interest, he would take a turn. For now, he had a huge backlog of paperwork to complete. Unfortunately, said paperwork was what threatened to put his exhausted body into a state of slumber he hadn't been able to achieve the night before.

After an hour at his desk, the page before him blurred, and he stood to refill his coffee mug.

"Chief, this just arrived for you." His receptionist crossed his office and handed him a spiral-bound notebook. "It's from Jason Caruthers."

Mark quickly read Jason's cover letter and found he was suddenly wide awake. Thirty minutes later, he put down the notebook and paced his office. Angela's journal was important. He just had to figure out which details were relevant to her death.

Sara knocked on his office door. She held a cassette in her hand. "Chief, I think I've found what we're looking for."

Mark, Luke, and Sara gathered in the investigation room. Sara put the tape in the cassette deck and they all listened to Angela's interview with Frances Warren, in which Frances described a will Millie Montgomery supposedly made just hours before she died.

"Why wasn't this brought to my attention on Monday?" Mark asked.

Luke answered. "I didn't listen to the tape. I spent hours listening to some of the other tapes then found the transcripts and realized I could have saved time. I planned to match each tape with a transcript, then listen to the ones that hadn't been transcribed."

"But you didn't do that."

"No."

Instead, he'd spent his weekend hours investigating Libby. Mark swallowed his anger and addressed the issue at hand. "Next time I give you an investigative task, I expect you to follow it. All the tapes need to be listened to, whether they were transcribed or not."

Luke looked down. "Yes, sir."

Mark flipped through the notebook Angela had used as a journal. After listening to the tape, he understood Angela's obsessive search for proof Lyle had killed his wife. "Angela believed Frances Warren's story about the will."

"So?" Luke said. "What does Millie have to do with Angela's murder?"

Jason was right. Luke was too green to have been trusted with investigating Libby's assault. Mark's fault again. "Frances said she believed Angela could find the will. I think Angela was looking for it."

"Why do you think that?" Sara asked. At least she was asking the right questions. Plus, she'd immediately recognized this interview was important, proving she had good instincts.

He held up the notebook. "I just read her journal. She never mentions the will explicitly. But it's there. She was looking for something to prove Lyle killed Millie. At one point, she worries that if Jack finds out what she's doing, he'll be upset that she's trying to give Jason's inheritance away. She was looking for Millie's will.

"Luke, I want you to go to the library and get copies of all newspaper articles about the crash that killed Millie. Contact the sheriff's office and request the investigation file from their archives."

He nodded but said, "What's the point? We're investigating Angela's death, not Millie's."

Luke had no idea his job was hanging by a thread. "It's likely Angela was killed because she was looking for the will. Losing TL&L is a pretty strong motive to kill someone. Especially if she found it."

Mark remembered an important point from his argument with Libby a week ago, when she justified going through Angela's boxes. She had wondered why the Kalahwamish would grant Angela—Lyle Montgomery's granddaughter—access to study them. Now he understood. Frances Warren set Angela on a path to find the will and then aided her research as much as possible.

Cold dread ran through him. Rosalie Warren had done essentially the same thing for Libby when she told her to follow Angela's research. Could one of the Montgomerys be Libby's stalker? Were they trying to get her thrown off the project before she followed Angela's research all the way to the will?

"This opens up the suspect list considerably," he resumed. "We need to look at the activities of the Montgomerys—all of them—during the time Angela disappeared. Did they provide statements to the police in 1979, detailing their whereabouts?"

"They weren't considered suspects at the time, sir," Sara said. "I'll check the file and keep my fingers crossed." She reached for the older investigation files.

Out in the hallway there was a commotion. The dispatcher called out, "Where is the chief?"

Mark jogged to the end of the corridor to the dispatcher's desk. "What's going on?"

"We've got a homicide at 24 Bay View Way."

His chest froze. Libby lived at 22 Bay View Way.

"The victim?" he asked.

"Eli Banks. He was stabbed. His housekeeper just found him."

34

S omeone pounded on the door of the Shelby house, startling Libby from a deep, dreamless sleep. A moment later, her cell phone began to ring and vibrate on the nightstand. Caller ID said Simone.

"What?" she growled into the phone.

"Thank God you're okay! Open the front door! We need to talk! I have coffee. Have you heard about your neighbor?"

Groggy, Libby couldn't respond to the rapid-fire sentences. She shook her head to clear it. "I'll be right down. Keep your panties on." Her clothes were in a pile next to the bed. She pulled on a pair of yoga pants and headed downstairs. After shutting off the alarm, she opened the door.

"You look like hell." Simone breezed by and walked straight to the dining room. She pulled up the blinds. The window faced the house next door—Eli Banks' home.

"I love you, too," Libby said. "Why aren't you at the site?"

"Everything's fine at the site. I'm here because your neighbor was found murdered this morning. The police are there now."

Fear cleared the bleariness from Libby's mind. *Eli Banks. Murdered.* She stepped up to the window and looked across the small side yard that ran between the two houses. Sara Eversall crossed Eli's dining room. The officer caught Libby's gaze, made a beeline for the window, and with a tight smile closed the blinds.

With nothing to see next door, Libby faced Simone. "How did you hear about Eli Banks?"

Simone handed Libby one of the two lattes she held. "Mark called the site. It was an off-the-record sort of call. I gather he believes you now."

"Doesn't make any difference. He's a cop first. Lover last. Jerk in between."

Simone ignored her. "He said he wanted me to check on you. He'd tried to call you, but you didn't answer—he figured you saw his name on caller ID and were ignoring him, but he wants to know if you're okay." She took a large gulp of her latte before she continued. "Basically, I told him to check on you himself if he was that concerned."

"Don't do me any favors."

"He said he couldn't, that your next-door neighbor had been stabbed to death and he was needed at the scene. He told me to page him, adding 10-34 to my phone number if you didn't respond, and 10-99 if you were okay. I paged him while waiting for you to unlock the door."

"10-99?"

"Police code for duty completed, everything's fine—or secure, or something—that's what he told me, anyway."

"And 10-34?"

"Trouble, help needed. I think." Simone gazed out the window. "I'm sure someone will be coming over to question you. Being next door, and all."

"You mean being their prime suspect, and all."

Simone did a double take. "What?"

"That neighbor is the guy who said I planted the gas cans. With him dead, they have no witness. No witness, no case. They could say I had a strong motive."

"To turn a weak attempted arson charge into Murder One? I don't think so."

Simone had a point. Libby paced the room. It *did* sound ridiculous. But the Montgomerys had framed her once. If they killed their accomplice, they would certainly want to pin that on her as well. How could they frame her this time?

The answer came to her in a rush. She sucked in a breath. "My hairbrush has been missing since the night I was attacked."

"So?" Simone said, clearly confused.

"I've looked for it everywhere. What if my attacker took it so he'd have strands of my hair to leave on Eli Banks' body?"

"Whoa. What the hell are you talking about?"

"I was framed once. They could be doing it again. He was stabbed?"

"That's what Mark said."

Libby entered the kitchen and stared at the knife block. One slot was empty. Cold dread ran through her. "One of the knives is missing." She found it difficult to breathe and tried to remember when she'd last used the knife. But she'd barely entered the kitchen this week. She'd chosen to skip meals rather than spend time in this room that still—in her mind—smelled of gasoline and pain.

"Libby, tell me what's happening."

A cold calm descended on her. She wasn't a clueless victim anymore. She knew what was going on and could use what she knew to clear herself. "C'mon upstairs. I'll tell you while I shower and get dressed. I want to be ready when the police get here."

Simone leaned against the sink while Libby showered, all the while relaying the details of her investigation into Angela's research, her suspicions about why she was harassed, and why she was attacked.

"So who do you think is behind this? Surely not Jason?"

Libby added conditioner to her hair and massaged her scalp. "I'm not ready to trust him. I'm not ready to trust anyone who stands to lose twenty-five million dollars if that will is found."

"He was nine. He couldn't have killed his mother."

"I know that. But he has a lot to lose now. He could be involved. I want to trust him, but I can't."

Simone was quiet.

"What are you thinking?"

"I'm thinking that he's worked awfully hard to clear you when he has a lot of other stuff on his plate. I'm thinking your suspicions are pretty shitty."

"Thanks. That makes me feel great." She rinsed her hair and shut off the shower. She stood in the tub, glad to be behind an opaque curtain, so Simone couldn't see how much her comment bothered her. "People can be foolish when money and family are at stake."

"Jason is interested in you."

"No, he's not. Not really. His actions toward me have been… forced. Feigned interest could be a front to get more information and catch me off-guard." She reached around the curtain and grabbed a towel and began to dry off. "Please don't tell Jason what I've told you. You can't tell anyone. If the Montgomerys know I'm looking for the will, then I won't be able to interview them." She stepped out of the shower and headed for her bedroom. Simone followed.

"Being alone with one of them should be the last thing you do right now."

"I have an interview scheduled with Earl at four this afternoon." She collected underwear and clothing for the day. "Maybe I'll find out something important. It must be one of them. My money is on Laura."

"You shouldn't go to the interview alone."

"I have a gun."

Simone startled. "You're serious."

"Very."

She flopped down on the bed. "What do we do now?"

"Find the will."

At one in the afternoon, Mark took a break from the Banks murder investigation and went to Libby's. She didn't answer his knock. He walked toward the street and looked up at her office. He could see her looking through the open window. "Libby, answer the damn door," he shouted.

She would make the coming conversation as difficult as possible. He knew he had it coming, but she also needed to look at the situation from his point of view. He might have been wrong about her, but his actions as a cop were not only justified, they were necessary.

When she finally answered the door, the rush he experienced shocked him. Smart, funny, earthy, and beautiful. Libby was everything he wanted. But her expression was cold. Scary cold. "Chief Colby. What a surprise to see you."

In a perfect world, this would be the time when he melted her icy reserve. But this world was so far from perfect, and he had an investigation that took priority over his miserable, screwed-up love life. "Cut the crap, Libby." He entered the house and closed the door. "You know why I'm here."

"If you're here to search the house, then you've entered without permission or a warrant. Anything you find won't be admissible in court."

Damn, she really wanted to push his buttons. He had a lot to make up for, but when it came to his job, he wouldn't hesitate to push back.

"Do you want to do this at the police station, with your lawyer present?"

"Not particularly."

"As a material witness, I have every right to detain you."

Her eyes were as green and cold as the bay outside her front window. "You wouldn't dare."

"Try me," he said and meant it. Hell, if she were at the station, at least he'd know she was safe, protected.

Her bravado left her and she looked afraid. Of him. Dammit. He was fucking this up, again. He pulled her to him. "You'll never know how relieved I was to receive Simone's page today."

She pulled away. "Don't touch me."

"You can be angry with me all you want. I'm still glad you're okay."

"What do you want?"

"Did you see or hear anything next door between three and four this morning?"

She shook her head. "I was asleep. Besides, these walls are thick—built when lumber was cheap and milled just a block away. An explosion could go off next door and I wouldn't hear it."

The requisite question about the Banks murder out of the way, he could zero in on why he'd really come to talk to her. "Tell me what you know about the will."

"Will?" she asked.

"You flinched, Libby. I've finally realized something that I should have guessed before—it would have saved us a lot of trouble. You're a terrible liar."

Her eyes narrowed. "But you had me arrested because I'm such a fantastic liar."

"No. You were arrested because we had overwhelming evidence against you. Now tell me about the will."

"I don't know what you're talking about."

"Yes, you do." He strode to the kitchen. He paused a moment on the threshold, caught for a moment with the image of Libby bound on the floor. He shook the memory off and entered the room. Even though his subsequent actions had been justified, in remembering what she'd gone through, he recognized it wouldn't be easy to bridge the gap between them. But he wouldn't give up even if it took every damn day of his sorry life.

He picked up the empty coffee pot and began filling the reservoir with water. Time to focus on the job. He had an assault and two murders to solve. "Don't make this difficult. This is important. We'll deal with our relationship later." He reached for the coffee canister and noticed the empty slot in the knife block next to it.

"We don't have a—" She stopped talking when he pulled out a blade.

He studied the manufacturer's mark. The knives were expensive and German made but not uncommon. They'd found only a set of cheap Chinese knives in Eli's house. He glanced at the sink. It was spotless, no dishes or knives waiting to be washed. "You're missing a knife.

"I noticed that this morning, after Simone told me Eli had been stabbed."

"Which knife is missing?"

She walked up to the block and pulled out a large chef's knife. "This is the ten-inch. The missing one must be the eight-inch."

Exactly the knife that had been found in Eli's chest.

He hated this. She should be his prime suspect. As a cop, he lived by the rule that there is no such thing as coincidence. Investigation is usually absolutely straightforward. Follow the evidence and find the suspect. But that wasn't the case here. She'd been set up.

Now he knew with certainty they would find Libby's fingerprints on the murder weapon. But he couldn't—*wouldn't*—arrest her again, meaning he had to find the real murderer, fast. "Any guess when the knife disappeared?"

"I don't know. I haven't been in here much since last Thursday. I haven't cooked at all." She paused. "Was Eli killed with my knife?"

Yes. "Maybe."

"My hairbrush is also missing. You might find my hairs on Eli's body."

Crap. Could the situation get any worse? "When did you first notice your brush was missing?"

"When I showered last Thursday. After I was attacked." She met his gaze and he knew they were both thinking about the same thing. Her voice turned husky. "Before we went to your house."

"Your brush has been missing for a week. That's serious premeditation."

"I didn't kill Eli." Fear had entered her voice.

He held her steady gaze. Trusting her went against years of

training and experience, but none of that mattered. Not with her, not in this situation. "I believe you."

Her shoulders dropped as she let out a breath. He wanted to reach out and hold her but didn't think she'd allow it. "So, tell me about the will."

"What do you want to know?" Some of her chilly reserve was gone.

"Do you think Angela found it?" he asked.

She bit her lip and nodded, slowly. "I think so."

"And you think Earl, Laura, or James killed her?"

"One, all three, I don't know. Lyle is my chief suspect."

"But Lyle didn't kill Eli Banks last night, and I believe the two crimes are related."

She didn't ask why. She must have come to the same conclusion. "You might want to find out who Eli's heirs are," she said. "He owns two percent of the mill."

That was news to him. "Two percent. How'd he manage that?"

"The usual way. Blackmail."

Mark started. "What?"

She smiled, clearly pleased with herself. "Maybe I should become a cop."

"Maybe not."

"Yeah," she said, "I'm not nearly annoying enough."

He gave her a pointed look. "But you're getting there."

She laughed. She reached for the coffee and scooped grounds into the filter. She had accepted their unspoken truce. "Eli Banks was the lawyer who wrote out the will. He probably told Lyle about the will the minute Millie left his office. Years after she died, Eli pretended to broker a deal between the union and the mill. Part of that deal gave him two percent of TL&L and the union three percent. I can't think of any reason for the Montgomerys to give Eli two percent of the mill except blackmail."

"Did Eli have the will?"

"He might have had a copy. Or he just threatened to talk. Either way they had to pay him off. I bet when the union negotiations were going down, Eli saw his chance for a big payoff that was nice and legal, no money laundering required."

"The union got three percent. How does that fit into the puzzle?"

"I don't know."

"Was Eli involved with the union in any other capacity?"

"Not that I've heard. I think the union is important, though. By all accounts, Millie wanted TL&L unionized. And I think Angela focused on the union in the last months of her research."

"Was she looking for someone Millie trusted?" he asked.

"I think so. You should know that the union had no Kalahwamish Indian members. The union shouldn't have been a part of her study."

A small thrill of excitement spread through him. Libby was on the right track, he was sure of it. He reached for a mug and waited for the coffee maker to finish brewing. "I want to know everything you know about the union. I don't care if it seems insignificant."

"Billy—Millie's oldest child and Angela's father—came back from the war in 1945. The union started in 1946. That wasn't a coincidence. Everyone thinks Billy got the union going."

"But no one knows?"

"No. He had to work in secret. It was too dangerous. Lyle had organizers beaten. One was killed. Then someone—probably Billy— set up a system for controlling the flow of information. Everyone worked in cells—similar to the triangular structure of terrorist cells. Traitors were rooted out with false information. The workers managed to hold a secure meeting.

"Lyle didn't know about the union until he showed up at work one day to find all the employees on strike. They stood solidly together. No scabs. The mill shut down for a month, until Lyle—his children really—Lyle only ran TL&L in their name—gave in and signed the agreement supposedly brokered by Eli Banks. The union got better pay, better hours, vacation time, and three percent of the mill's annual profits to divide among the membership."

"And Eli Banks got another two percent," he said.

"Yes. Doesn't seem fair, does it?"

"How many people were on strike for a month to get three percent?"

"Two-hundred and thirty-seven loggers and mill workers," she said.

"Why would the union agree to Banks receiving such a large share?"

"Fear, probably. After a month, they were anxious and needed to get back to work. They were all—absolutely everyone—living on company land. They faced eviction and starvation. They were saved because TL&L had a huge post-war contract with the US government to provide lumber for housing. The company had a deadline to meet or they'd lose the contract and no more federal contracts would be forthcoming. Without that contract, Lyle might've evicted everyone and started over. He had cash reserves from the war—he could've outwaited the union. Guess who bid the contract with the government?"

"Billy."

"Exactly. He timed everything. He set up the contract. He knew the supply dates would make Lyle cave. He personally selected the strike date. I'm sure of it."

Mark poured himself a cup of coffee and sat at the table. Libby hesitated, and then joined him.

"Seems to me this information is as off-topic for you as it was for Angela," he said

"I've interviewed a lot of people in the last two weeks. Many of them wanted to talk about Billy Montgomery whether I asked about him or not. When Lyle was alive, no one could openly talk about what he did. Billy's a folk hero in Coho. He earned several medals for bravery while fighting in the Pacific Theater, but people here think that's nothing compared to taking on his father. He was on his own, and in his own way, he won."

"But his dad never knew."

"No. Billy didn't want credit, and he didn't want to destroy Lyle. He just wanted to make things better for Coho. He couldn't take on Lyle in the open—he would have lost. His brothers and sister sided with their father every time. If he wanted to stay and make things better in Coho, he had to work in secret."

"And Billy was Angela's father."

"Yes. She hated Lyle. I don't think I realized quite how much until I read her journal." Libby stopped suddenly, clearly worried about her slip.

"I've read the journal. Jason sent it to me this morning."

"Good. I thought you should have it."

"Angela wasn't like Billy," Mark resumed. "She wanted to openly confront Lyle."

"Yes. But she was careful. She knew she would be in danger if Lyle found out she was looking for Millie's will. So she kept it to herself. She was so cautious she never even wrote exactly what she was looking for in her journal."

"But at some point, Lyle learned what she was looking for, and she disappeared."

Libby nodded. "Yesterday I left a message for the union archivist; I'm trying to track down a union organizer Millie might have trusted."

"Good. I want to know everything you find out."

"I'm going to interview Earl Montgomery today at four."

"Be careful. Bring Simone or someone from your crew with you." He looked at his watch and cursed. "I should run." He touched her hand. "I mean it about being careful. If I could do it without any of the Montgomerys finding out, I would officially re-open the investigation into your attack. But I don't want to give them any hint that you're cooperating with me. They've worked so hard to keep us at odds; it would be nice if they believe their plan is working."

She looked startled, and then wary. "So you understand that one of them is my stalker? One of them attacked and framed me?"

"Yes. I've listened to the tape and read Angela's journal. I went over the timeline of your stalking and I think the Montgomerys wanted to destroy your credibility. I intend to figure out who attacked you and make them pay. "

"You're a little late," she said.

"You have to understand, based on the evidence, my actions were correct. They did a damn good job of framing you."

"I don't have to understand anything."

He'd expected her to hold on to her anger, but he was still disappointed. They would never be able to move forward if she couldn't view the situation from his perspective. "I had to treat you like any other suspect. I had to make the call to arrest you."

"But you didn't have to believe it."

"Libby, I've been a cop for eighteen years. Do you want to know how many times I've seen that much evidence against a suspect and then found out they were innocent?" He didn't wait for her to answer. "Exactly none."

"But you *know* me. I'm not just some other suspect."

"That only made the situation worse. I *wanted* to believe you were innocent because I'm in love with you. But I'm a cop and trusting cops end up dead cops. We follow evidence, not feelings."

He hadn't meant to tell her he loved her. He waited for her reaction.

"It's too late," she said.

His pager beeped. He looked at the number, recognizing it as the medical examiner's. "Listen, I've gotta run—there's this minor little investigation going on—we can talk later." He sprinted toward the front door.

She followed. "There is no *later* for us."

He couldn't leave this way. He stopped short and turned. She walked right into him and he trapped her in his arms, cupped her face, and kissed her. He smiled when her hands gripped his shirt and pulled him closer, and she made a soft sound that said she wanted more. He kissed her as though he had all the time in the world and nothing else on his mind.

She looked dazed when he reluctantly let her go. "I intend to change your mind," he said. He'd already told her how he felt; there was no point in holding back now. "I'm completely, totally, crazy in love with you, Libby. I'll do whatever it takes to win you back."

35

With recorder and notebook in hand, Libby set out for her interview with Earl. She'd taken Mark's advice and asked Alex to accompany her for the interview, but he'd called and told her he was running late and would meet her at the Montgomery mansion, so she walked alone across the historic district to a Gothic mansion that featured prominently in her own personal horror movie.

En route, she passed white picket fences surrounding lush green lawns, which fronted immaculate old houses complete with gingerbread siding, cupolas, and mullioned windows. Had Jason's deal had gone through? Had the town been sold? In the coming months, the streets could be filled with people in period costume, reenacting the lives of those who lived here one hundred twenty-five years ago.

What would happen to the town and the deal if she found the will? Legally everything in the historic district could belong to the tribe.

Her cell phone rang, bringing her back to the present. She answered the phone and kept walking.

"Hi, Ms. Maitland. I'm the archivist for the Millworker's Union. I understand you're interested in locating someone who was in the union in the 1940s. You're in luck. I was able to pull the Coho chapter boxes quickly, and even found the name you were looking for—Nathan Simms, right?"

"Yes, that's right."

"There's a notation in the file. In the seventies, another researcher wanted to get in touch with Mr. Simms. We managed to track down an address for her. It's old, but the address is a starting point."

"Was the researcher named Angela Caruthers?"

"How on earth did you know that?"

"Actually, it's her research I'm following up on. I would love the address."

She stopped long enough to jot down the Richland, Washington address. After disconnecting, she dialed Eastern Washington information for the number. A Simms still lived at that address. She called the number and an answering machine picked up. An elderly female voice spoke very carefully, "You have reached the Simms residence."

Her heart beat loudly as adrenaline flooded her system. She was on the right track. She could feel it. She left a message.

She'd promised Mark she'd keep him updated and dialed his work number, and then hesitated. Throughout the day, her feelings for him had bounced between gut-wrenching pain and euphoric hope. Maybe they could work things out. But could she trust him to stand by her, or was he like her father?

She both regretted responding to his kiss and savored the memory. She screwed up her courage and hit the call button. She was relieved when her call went straight to voicemail. She left a message and continued walking to the Montgomery house.

James greeted her warmly when he answered the door. He led her to the sitting room and went to find Earl. She walked to the shelf where Earl displayed his artifact collection. An empty space where the Elko-Eared point had been made her wonder what Laura had done with the tool. Had the artifact found its way to Eli's crime scene in hopes of implicating her further?

Her excitement at having located Nathan Simms and her mixed feelings for Mark had distracted her, and for a moment she'd forgotten the danger she was in. She couldn't let that happen again while she was in this house, with these people. Especially because Alex hadn't arrived yet.

"Looking for another artifact to add to your collection?" Earl said as he entered the room.

"Archaeologists don't collect artifacts. We aren't thieves—like pothunters." She instantly regretted her words. This had to be the worst start to an interview, ever. Regardless, she didn't want to miss a word of their conversation and held up her tape recorder and hit the record button. "Can I tape this?"

"Go ahead. Then you can have it on record that I didn't steal any of those artifacts. Those were all collected from my own land or with the landowner's permission."

"Most of these points are from Eastern Washington. You have property there?"

"We have a fishing cabin on a large property in Pasco. After rainstorms, I like to hike around to see what artifacts have washed to the surface."

She studied several diagnostic points. "These points are datable. You could use them to estimate the age of the site on your land. This point base in particular," she said. She lifted a caramel-colored CCS point base from the tray. "The ears are a distinctive style popular about two thousand years ago. Too bad you don't have the rest of the point."

"That one was broken when I found it. Cattle probably."

Grazing cattle often stepped on artifacts and broke them. Of course, cattle graze on federal land—it wasn't likely they were grazing on his property—and the federal government didn't give permission to artifact collectors. She smiled at his gaffe. "That point isn't a style you find very often east of the Cascades. You should fill out a site form for your property. Finding a point like this out there is exciting—you could have an example of trade goods."

He looked distraught for a moment. "I think I found it on land we sold nearly twenty years ago. Besides, I don't want any site form filled out. Then there would be all sorts of restrictions on the property."

She flipped the point in her hand. Something about it seemed familiar. "Whether a form is on file or not, knowingly destroying an archaeological site is illegal."

Earl glared at her. "I know that. I just don't want the state getting involved with my property."

She set the point base back on the shelf. She still hadn't found out anything useful but she'd managed to thoroughly antagonize him. Was she a good interviewer or what?

"Alex, one of my employees, will be joining us, but he's running late so we may as well get started." She sat on the couch and placed the tape recorder on the coffee table. She wasn't going to get anything useful about Coho anyway. She decided to bring up the subject that really interested her. "It must be quite a shock, to have your niece found after all these years."

He nodded, but didn't say anything.

She needed to get him to talk. "Do you think finding Angela will help Jason with closure?"

"Jason will only get closure if his no-good father ends up in jail."

"Why do you say that?" she asked.

"Are you a moron? The man killed my niece. Yet you ask why I want him punished?"

"You think Jack killed Angela?"

"*Everybody* thinks Jack killed Angela."

"Everybody isn't always right."

"You'd better hope everybody can be wrong with the trouble you've gotten yourself into." His grin was pure malice.

Libby shivered, Earl moved to the top of her suspect list.

Her cell phone rang. She looked at the caller ID. Eastern Washington area code. During a normal interview, she'd never answer her cell phone, but she already needed a break from Earl, and this was the call she'd been waiting for. "I'm sorry, Mr. Montgomery. I really need to take this call." She stood.

"Stay here," he said and left the room.

She sat and answered the phone, craning her neck to make certain he wouldn't hear the conversation. She watched him climb the stairs on the other side of the vestibule.

"Hello, Ms. Maitland. This is Enid Simms. I just got your message." The elderly voice sounded kind. One thing Libby had discovered over the years, people loved to talk about their past. They liked feeling as if their experience was important.

"Thank you for returning my call."

"My pleasure, dear. I understand you're interested in finding out about my late husband, and the union in Coho?"

"Yes, I am. I wasn't aware your husband had passed away." Disappointment filled Libby; he was her only viable lead.

"Oh yes, my Nathan died in 1972."

"I'm sorry for your loss." Simms had died before Angela found the will; maybe Enid was the key. "Were you married to him when he lived in Coho?"

"Oh no, I was in my teens then. I didn't marry Nathan until 1952, when I was twenty-one."

"That must've been quite an age difference between you and your husband; wasn't he about thirty when the union formed?"

"Yes, he was fifteen years older than me. He worried about that—

that I'd be all alone in my old age. Turned out he was right, but I was widowed much earlier than I should have been. I'm only seventy-one and I've already been a widow for thirty years!"

"I'm so sorry to hear that."

"I had twenty good years with my Nathan. For that I'm grateful."

Libby smiled. Definitely a glass half-full sort of woman. After dealing with the harshness of Earl Montgomery, Enid Simms was a relief.

Remembering where she was, Libby said, "I hate to say this, but unfortunately, I can't take the time to interview you right now. Can I call you back later, say, in an hour or so?"

"Certainly, dear, I'll be home the rest of the day. I love having a chance to talk about my Nathan. I just hope you'll call me back—not like the last person who interviewed me about Nathan and the union."

Libby jolted. "Was this recent?"

"No, no dear. It was a long time ago. Sometime in the seventies."

She caught her breath. Enid was referring to Angela. *And Angela hadn't contacted her again.* "Pardon me, Ms. Simms, but was the person who interviewed you named Angela Caruthers?"

"That's it! Such a lovely girl, do you know her?"

"I'm following up on her research." Libby glanced again at the doorway through which Earl disappeared. She kept her voice low.

"She came to my house," Enid said. "We had tea and went through Nathan's papers. She was very excited by something she found and wanted to take the papers with her, but I couldn't let her. So we agreed she would come back in a few days and we'd go make copies together."

Surprised that she could speak at all, Libby attempted to maintain an even voice. "Ms. Simms, this is very important. Do you remember *when* Angela came to your house?"

Enid was silent for a moment. "Let's see." Libby could hear her tapping the phone. "It was sunny. We sat out on the veranda after she carried the boxes down from the attic. No, I'm afraid I can't pinpoint the date."

"How about the year?" Her knuckles gripped the phone until her fingers ached.

"I'm pretty sure Carter was president. Oh yes, I remember. The summer of the second gas shortage. I remember asking her how she could afford to drive all the way to Richland, with gas prices so high.

She said she didn't mind the cost. She was just glad the gas lines had disappeared and she didn't have to wait for hours to fill up. What year would that be, dear?"

Libby closed her eyes, remembering the headlines on the random newspapers she'd found in Angela's boxes. "Seventy-nine," she answered, her throat dry. "Do you remember why you didn't make copies that day?"

"Hmmm. There was something—she wanted another witness when she opened the envelope—I think it was something like that."

"Why didn't she come back the next day?"

"Oh! I remember! She wanted to surprise her son. He just had a birthday, and was with his father in Moscow or Spokane someplace near the state line. She decided because she was already in Richland, she'd surprise them. She said she would stop in again on her way back a few days later. But she never returned."

That didn't sound good for Jack's alibi. It was possible Angela had gone to see him and he'd killed her. But somehow she still didn't believe Jack killed his wife. "Ms. Simms, I need you to do me a really, really important favor. I want you to call this number." She pulled out Mark's business card with his personal cell phone number written on the back. "Do you have a pen?"

"Yes, dear."

She gave the number and added, "Tell Mark Colby—he's the police chief of Coho—everything you've just told me. I have bad news about Angela. She was murdered in 1979. It's possible you were the last person to see her alive. Will you please call him?"

"Oh my, yes."

"One more thing, Ms. Simms. Do you know where Angela was headed that night after she left your house? Was she going straight to Spokane or staying somewhere else?"

After a lengthy silence, Enid Simms finally spoke. "It was so long ago. I can't be sure, but I seem to remember something about a family cabin in Pasco."

Enid's words fit with what Libby believed. Jack was in the clear. Earl was the most likely suspect. "You had a lot of Mount St. Helens ash out there in the Tri-Cities, didn't you?" she asked.

"The ash was a few inches deep in some places. It looked like we had a big snowstorm."

Libby heard a noise and looked up. Earl stood in the doorway.

"When you call Mark Colby, tell him I'm 10-34." She disconnected and then dialed 9-1-1.

Earl raised a gun and aimed it at her head. "Drop the phone."

36

Mark paced the investigation room. "Okay," he said to Sara and Luke. "According to the 1979 investigation, Earl was at the family cabin in Pasco when Angela disappeared. Laura was in Seattle. James and Lyle were here in Coho. Let's suppose Earl is our killer because he was in Eastern Washington, which was covered in St. Helens ash."

"So now we need to place Angela in Pasco," Sara said.

"Placing Angela in Pasco doesn't clear Jack," Luke said. "He still claims she called him and said she was in Coho. She could have called him from the Pasco cabin, then he could have driven down and killed her."

"But Earl was in Pasco," Sara said. "Jack couldn't have killed her if she was with Earl."

"We follow all leads, but will start with Earl," Mark said. "I want phone records for the cabin for that night."

Mark's cell phone vibrated in his pocket. He didn't recognize the number but answered anyway.

"Mr. Colby? My name is Enid Simms. I was just speaking with Libby Maitland, and she asked me to call you and tell you about a conversation we just had. She said that Angela Caruthers, that lovely young woman, was murdered. Such a shame. And that I might be the last person to have seen her alive."

The woman had his full attention. "I am very interested in what you have to say, Ms. Simms. Please, tell me, when did you see Ms. Caruthers?"

"So you found the will," Earl stated. "Is it in Pasco? I tore the cabin apart looking for it. She couldn't have hidden it there."

Libby didn't take her eyes off Earl or his gun. "It's not in Pasco." She could feel her purse with her foot. The pistol was there. If only she could get it. She didn't dare look down.

"I heard everything. Sound travels well through the vent." He pointed to a grill in the wall above her head. "I know you were talking to a Ms. Simms. I remember the name Simms. A union leader. She must be his wife. So my mother gave the will to the union leader."

Libby didn't respond. Her feet were hidden from his view behind the coffee table and a large vase of flowers. With her foot, she slowly inched her purse closer.

"Now all I have to do is find Simms to find the will." He picked up her cell phone. "Caller ID is so useful."

Libby leaned toward her purse.

"Stay exactly where you are."

"You won't get away with killing me." Libby could feel adrenaline pulsing through her. Every sound, every sensation, every moment was magnified. "Ms. Simms is calling Mark right now."

"Ms. Simms is a crazy old woman who's gonna break her hip and die very soon. She called the chief at your request. Everyone knows you're crazy. You're going to fake another attempt on your life, but something's going to go tragically wrong. This time, you'll die."

"Mark knows everything—about the will, about the stalking. He's on to you."

"Oh, sure. Even if you were stupid enough to go running to the chief when you learned about the will, he would never believe you. No one in this town would believe you if you said the sky was blue."

"He believes me," she said, fear, anger, and adrenaline mixing together.

"I'm sure you were a nice piece of ass. But he's not going to risk his career over you. Soon you'll be indicted for the Banks murder."

She couldn't get to her gun. She had to stall for time to give Enid a chance to relay her message to Mark or for Alex to arrive. And maybe, just maybe, James was innocent. Maybe he'd come to her rescue. "Exactly how did you set me up for that?" she said.

"You haven't noticed? We took your hairbrush and your knife the night you were attacked."

"We?" she asked, losing hope.

"James and I."

Disappointment hit her with a sharp jab. *Stay focused*. Her purse was open and she could see the handle of the gun. *Keep him talking*. "Who killed your mother? Was it Lyle?"

"Of course," he answered, as if it were of no consequence. "Who cares? The bitch deserved to die. She was giving my mill away."

"But the mill was never yours. You only rubber-stamped your daddy's decisions."

Her cell phone rang. He ignored it. She had to get a reaction out of him, to distract him. "When did you first realize your father killed your mother?"

"The day she died," he said. "He came home smelling like gasoline. He'd run her off the road, then doused her car with fuel and lit a match. He delighted in telling me that. I washed his clothes for him."

She felt sickened a twelve-year-old could so blithely cover up his mother's murder. "Why did you kill Eli?"

"He couldn't keep his story straight and he wanted more money."

Libby glanced down to the tape recorder. The wheels were turning. Mark would come. He'd be too late to save her, but he'd have his evidence against Earl.

"You've been very clever. Your plan to frame me was flawless. How did you know about Aaron Brady?"

"James offered to check your references for Jack. We'd hoped to find an incompetent archaeologist for the dig, but you were even better. You had past financial troubles and a cop who supposedly stalked you. That was when James got the idea to stalk you and make you look crazy."

"Did you and James plan to attack and frame me from the beginning?"

"No. With your credibility problems the first few 'stalking' incidents should have been enough to discredit you. Who'd have guessed Mark Colby would fall for you?"

"So you escalated the stalking. You know, Aaron called me. He also called Mark. How did you get him involved?"

Earl laughed. "You got Colby to investigate him again. I bet that pissed him off. Guess he came gunning for you. Couldn't have planned that better myself."

"How did you manage to start the rumor I was in financial trouble?"

"James did that. Based on your past trouble with Brady, he knew you'd be vulnerable. We floated the idea that you wanted to get out of the project. The reporter ran with it."

"Was Laura involved? Is that why she said I stole the artifact?"

"Laura knew about the will and about Angela. She had to help me get rid of Angela's car. But we didn't think we could trust her to keep her story straight with you. She said you stole the artifact only because you pissed her off."

"What about Jason? Was he part of this?"

"Jason doesn't know shit. He'd probably try to give the mill away, just like his bitch of a mother."

"Then how did his arms get scratched?"

"James took Laura's precious dog and trapped him in the blackberries behind the house. Laura cried and cried and hero Jason dug the damn dog out."

Before she could ask another question, her cell phone rang again.

"**A**n officer from the Richland PD will come by your house this afternoon to collect the papers you and Angela went through," Mark said to Enid Simms.

"Oh, I almost forgot. Miss Maitland wanted me to tell you something. Although I didn't really understand...she said she's ten-something. Ten-thirty? Does that sound right?"

Mark's heart stopped. "Ten-thirty-four?"

"That's it!"

"Did she tell you where she was when you spoke?"

"No, she didn't."

"How long ago did you talk?"

"Just before I called you."

They'd been on the phone a few minutes. "Thank you. I have to find Libby now." He hung up and then dialed Libby's cell phone. No answer. He glanced at his watch. Four twenty. *Shit. She was scheduled to interview Earl Montgomery at four.*

The beat of his pounding heart could be felt all the way to the fingers that gripped the phone. He dialed the site. A crew member answered. Without preamble, he demanded to know whether Libby had gone to see Earl alone.

"Alex was supposed to go with her, but he's still here, we had a problem—"

"She's alone? At the Montgomery mansion?"

"Is something wrong?" the young woman asked.

"Yes." He hung up and tried her cell again as he ran down the corridor. He called for backup to the officers in the squad room. Outside, in his police car, he hit the sirens and tore out of the station.

With Earl distracted by her ringing cell phone, Libby seized her chance. She braced her back against the couch and then kicked the wooden coffee table into Earl's knees. He let out a yell as he dropped to the floor.

She grabbed her gun.

He scrambled to his back and pointed the barrel of his weapon at her. She kicked it away and stepped on his hand. His scream was loud and full of pain.

She pulled back the hammer on her gun and aimed at his face as she placed all the weight of her body on his hand. "Move and you're dead. I'd love an excuse to shoot you."

Hard angry eyes stared up at her, but he said nothing.

"You fucked up again, didn't you, Earl?" James asked in a cold voice. He stood in the doorway, the gun in his hand aimed at Libby's chest. "I'm not as stupid as my brother, Libby. So now you have to decide which one of us you want to shoot. Your gun is aimed at him. And I'll shoot you in the time it takes for you to shift your aim to me."

"You were the brains, weren't you, James? Earl was just your tool. Were you the one who Tasered me?"

"Yes."

"Were you going to kill me?"

"The plan was to frame you, not kill you. That dumb fuck on the ground there wanted to just kill you. But then there would have been another homicide investigation. With you alive and framed, the investigation would have ended with you. Colby messed with my plans when he showed up that night. But I'd planned carefully, so it still worked. He believed you set it up."

"You started this the day we found the burial. How did you know we'd found Angela?"

"Jack kept me informed on all developments for the Cultural Center because I was the biggest investor."

"Our find could have been a real burial."

"Earl is the moron who buried her; he knew where she was. If you'd handed her over to the tribe like you were supposed to, I would've left you alone after that."

"How did you steal my truck?"

"Easy. I took your spare key from the Shelby house."

"You have keys to every TL&L house, don't you?"

"Of course."

"How did you cool the engine?"

"I drove your truck a block away and hid it in one of our garages. The engine hadn't heated much but to speed things along I set a fan on it. Then I waited for you to notice the truck was missing."

"And you returned it after I entered the police station."

"You are stalling, Ms. Maitland."

"If I shoot your brother, even if you shoot me, you'll have a hell of a time explaining the mess."

"I don't particularly care. Earl's the fuckup who got us in this situation. He killed Angela without finding out where the damn will was. Then I gave him a simple job—move Angela's body before the land she was buried on was sold. So he moved her to Jack's property. Do me a favor. Kill him. The papers were signed an hour ago. I'll get his share, you'll both be dead, and I'll be a hero for shooting the psycho woman who killed my brother."

Earl's eyes hardened. He was now angrier with James than at her. In a swift motion, she switched her aim to James.

James pulled the trigger. His gun clicked, but there was no bang.

Libby fired.

James collapsed.

In that split second, Earl hit her across the back of her legs with the vase, knocking her to her knees.

She pushed his gun out of reach. Earl swung at her. The vase hit her in the back. She fell forward, trapping her own gun between her body and the floor.

Before she could move, the vase hit her head. Nausea rose. She heard sirens. Enid Simms must have talked to Mark.

Libby rolled to her side and rammed her elbow into Earl's face. He shoved her forward. With his weight on her back, he buried her face in the rug, keeping her arm and gun trapped. Hands wrapped around her throat. Earl squeezed.

She struggled for breath and bucked beneath him. His hold didn't loosen. She needed air.

A crashing sound came from the front hall.

His grip tightened.

She released the gun and clawed at the fingers on her neck. She screamed without sound as pain burned her throat. Her lungs ached and her head throbbed with the need to breathe.

Earl's weight lifted from her back. The fingers that gripped her neck released. She took a shuddering breath and twisted to see Mark with Earl in a chokehold.

Libby coughed. Pain shot down her windpipe.

The room filled with officers. Luke Roth handcuffed Earl.

She needed to speak. Mark pulled her to her feet and whispered her name. She took a slow breath and found her voice. She looked at Mark and rasped, "I told Earl you believed me."

37

M ark stood on Libby's doorstep, holding a dozen roses and an envelope. His heart pounded in time with his knock. He hadn't seen her for three days.

Simone answered, swinging the door wide. "Libby will be down in a second."

He stepped into the living room. "How is she doing?"

"I don't really know. I'm just trying to give her space."

He frowned. "Should I leave?"

"Stay," said the voice he'd longed to hear for days. Libby stood on the stairs, wearing a wool sweater over flannel shirt and sweatpants. The heat was on in the house, even though it was over seventy degrees outside—a perfect Pacific Northwest summer day.

His heart slowed, but the beat became more pronounced when her lips curved in a slow, warm smile as she descended the last of the steps. He dropped the roses, crossed the room, and took her in his arms. He had to touch her, hold her, warm her.

He'd spent the last days wrapping up the Caruthers and Banks murders, and the investigation of James Montgomery's death. Libby had been interviewed several times by the assistant district attorney. Mark had informed the ADA of their relationship and removed himself from the interview process beyond what was strictly necessary.

She rested her forehead on his shoulder and relaxed against him.

Mark closed his eyes and breathed in her sweet scent. The soft click of the front door told him Simone had left.

He had no idea how long he held her before he finally said, "I brought you something."

She chuckled against his chest. "I saw. They're all over the floor."

"Not the roses. This." He loosened his hold and handed her the envelope.

She stepped back and studied the envelope warily. "Is this a copy?"

"Yes."

She dropped to the couch, and he sat beside her to read over her shoulder.

November 16, 1946

Enclosed within the attached envelope is the will entrusted to me by Millicent Thorpe Montgomery on October 28, 1940. I am writing this letter to explain why I have it and to confirm that to the best of my knowledge it is indeed a legal and binding document. It is my understanding that Eli Banks, the lawyer who drafted it, witnessed the will signing. I have not read the will, as Mrs. Montgomery presented it to me in a sealed notarized envelope and I wanted to be sure that the contents remained intact. The date of the notary seal is the same date mentioned above, October 28, 1940.

Millicent Montgomery came to my home and gave me this envelope. She told me inside was a new will in which she'd named the Kalahwamish tribe as her heirs. Upon her death, the tribe would gain everything she owned, all of Thorpe Log & Lumber and its properties and assets. If anything happened to her, I was to present this will to a judge or other legal authority outside the jurisdiction of the sheriff's office, who was on Lyle's payroll.

Millie trusted me because she knew I was trying to organize a union for the sawmill workers. I was not loyal to her husband, Lyle Montgomery. I was the only person in Coho she could trust.

I never saw or spoke with her again. She died a few hours later in a car accident.

I wanted to abide by Millie's wishes but I couldn't let the mill go to the Indians. I know Millie meant well in leaving the mill to them, but it would be just plain wrong to entrust good white folks' jobs to heathens.

I figured Millie would be just as pleased to know I used the will to leverage Lyle into accepting the union. Lyle hates the idea of a union as much as he hates Indians. Millie will have her revenge against him, and the mill workers will get better wages and better working conditions.

This letter contains a fair and accurate accounting of events.
Sincerely,
Nathan Simms

When Libby finished reading she said, "His wife might be the sweetest thing since cotton candy, but I'm glad I never met him. If he'd done what Millie trusted him to do back in 1940, Angela would never have been murdered."

"It seems Millie had a knack for trusting the wrong man."

Libby studied the page again. "The date of the letter—that's the day before the union's first strike."

"Yes. It looks like he planned to go public with the will if the union didn't go through. He had his envelope notarized and it said 'Millie Thorpe Montgomery' on the front. Angela must have known she found Millie's will when she saw that and the notary seal date. But she couldn't open it. She needed to wait, like we did, and open the envelope in the presence of an authority from a court. We're looking up the notary records now, for both Simms's seal and Millie's. If we can find them, then there's no doubt the will is authentic."

"Is it still valid, sixty-two years later?"

"That's for a court to decide."

"The corporation that bought TL&L last week will fight this."

"It's a tangled mess. It looks like Laura plans to fight the will, but her case is weak. We're tracking down evidence to confirm Earl's statement she helped him move Angela's car to the North Cascades in 1979."

"But Earl won't get anything, even if the will is declared invalid?"

"He can't profit from a crime. He may have been only twelve in 1940, but he was an accessory after the fact to his own mother's murder. We have your tape for evidence of that." He reached for her hand. "And I love the fact that the tape is completely admissible. He gave you verbal permission to record your conversation at the beginning of the tape."

"Standard operating procedure," she responded.

"Archaeological methods and police methods blend very well." He brought her hand to his lips.

She didn't pull away, but she said, "I need time, Mark."

"I'll wait." He stood. He could give her space. He could give her time. He'd give her whatever the hell she wanted. "I love you, Libby.

You can have as much time as you need. I'll do whatever I can to help you get through this."

She smiled. She'd lost her anger around the time she squared off with James with a loaded gun. Now he saw only remorse in her haunted eyes.

The tape had provided the exact number of seconds between the gunshots and his arrival. If he'd arrived seventy-eight seconds sooner, he could have prevented Libby from having to kill.

"We have more evidence linking Earl to Angela's murder. He's talking, trying to get a deal. Earl said you recognized a point base he forgot to remove from his collection. He thought he was busted when you started questioning him about it."

"The caramel colored point base. I did think it looked familiar, but I didn't realize why until this morning when I was looking at artifacts from the site and came across the other half. We'd found it in the burial pit."

"He found the artifact when he dug the pit. He broke the stone with his shovel and couldn't find the tip. The artifact gave him the idea of including an arrowhead in Angela's hands, to make her look like an Indian burial if she were ever found. But he couldn't use the broken one—not without both pieces. He'd bought the Helenite one at a tourist shop on one of his trips to Pasco and still had the fake point in the car. He knew it was a replica, but didn't know the Helenite was manufactured and easily identifiable.

"Earl is doing his best to lay the blame on James. He said James found your Taser in your purse the night he smashed the mask. He purchased his own the next day. James was an opportunist. He spent his time looking for ways to exploit what you could provide—from gas cans, to car keys, to Tasers."

"Tell me something. Why didn't James' gun fire?"

"His revolver was old. Older revolvers are carried and stored with the firing chamber in the cylinder empty—this prevents people from shooting themselves if they drop the gun—James must have forgotten the firing chamber was empty."

"And if he'd had a chance to fire again?"

"He'd have shot you." The click of the hammer hitting the empty chamber had been audible on the tape. The sound would fill Mark's nightmares for years to come. Just as he'd never forget how she looked now, sitting before him, her neck bruised from Earl's attack. "Shooting him was one hundred percent justified." He didn't say he had convinced the DA to ignore the fact she was carrying concealed without a permit.

"I wish I could forget the look on his face when I shot him."

"He doesn't deserve your remorse, Libby. If he'd loaded that first chamber, I could have arrived at the scene to find you dead on the floor. Then I would have killed him, but my actions might not have been justified."

That empty chamber had saved him as much as Libby.

He pulled her to her feet. She didn't resist the embrace but stood stiff for a moment before her body melted into his again. Relief spread through him as he accepted her surrender. He would give her all the time she needed.

Libby stood alone by Millie's grave, clutching a bouquet of flowers she'd picked from the Shelby house garden. She stared at the weathered headstone and wondered what she was doing here. Millie's grave couldn't answer her questions, couldn't take away the cold that had seeped into her bones the moment she pulled the trigger and killed Millie's youngest child.

Was she here seeking forgiveness? She didn't know.

She heard a car door slam and turned to see Jason's gold Lexus parked next to her Suburban.

Crap. Jason was the last person she wanted to see right now. He was also the one person she most needed to talk to. He approached slowly. The smile he usually greeted her with was absent. He stopped in front of her and stood silent. Waiting.

The chill she'd felt for days intensified. She shivered. Did the frigid feeling come from Jason, or from herself?

"Hell," he said at last, and he reached out and hugged her, crushing the flowers she held between them. Finally, he stepped back and looked her in the eye. "You're avoiding me."

"I'm avoiding everyone."

"Except Simone."

"Truth is, I'm not even talking to her."

"I owe you an apology," he said.

Libby looked away. The last thing she wanted or expected from Jason was an apology. One of the reasons she hadn't wanted to see him was because she felt guilty for having been suspicious of him, and for not telling him about his mother's quest to find Millie's will.

"You don't owe me an apology," she said. "I owe you one. I'm sorry I didn't tell you about the will."

He shrugged. "I understand. A hundred million is a lot of money. You didn't know if I could walk away from that. And I *do* owe you an apology. When I kissed you at lunch that day, I spotted Mark in his parked car. I knew he saw us."

"You saw Mark. That's why you kissed me."

"Remember, I didn't know you were seeing him," Jason said in a rush. "But I knew he was interested in you. So was I. I figured if I had any hope of getting you to go out with me, I had to act."

"Admit you suspected. I'm not stupid, Jason, and neither are you."

"Okay. I admit I suspected there was something between you, which is why I'm sorry." He paused. "It would have been easier if there'd been any real chemistry between us. Then you'd have known you could trust me. You could have told me about the will. I would have known James was your stalker. He asked me a lot of questions about you, under the guise of interest in your dig." Jason's laugh was sharp, bitter. "I realize now he was pumping me for information he could use against you."

"I'm sorry, Jason."

"James was not the man I thought he was." He was quiet for a moment and then said, "I heard you finished your report."

"Yes. I finished it yesterday." Libby set the flowers next to the headstone and brushed dirt from the etched lettering. "Rosalie told me that after your mother's mom died, Billy started bringing her to the reservation. He was close to Frances and Rosalie and wanted the two most important women still in his life to be substitute mother figures. Your mother grew up learning about Millie from the tribe's perspective.

"The mill workers believed she fell in love with the wrong man and the entire population of Coho had to pay for it. The tribe was different. They hated Lyle, too, but they didn't blame Millie. They knew she was trapped. They understood what it felt like to be trapped by a white man and admired her courage every time she stood up to him. They accepted both her strengths and her weaknesses. Your mother grew up in that kind of atmosphere. She had perhaps the most honest and complete picture of Millie. And, somewhere along the line, she decided to avenge her, stand up for her, as no one had from the moment Lyle threw the first punch at his twenty-year-old bride."

"This became personal for you, didn't it?" Jason asked.

"Yes. I got sucked in to Millie's story just as much as your mother did. When I talked to Enid on the phone and realized that the will was still intact, that it could still be valid, I think I felt the same satisfaction your mother must have felt. I understood her need to bring Lyle down." Libby also knew what it was like to be beaten and terrorized by a man, though on a far smaller scale.

"But you wanted to bring Earl and James down."

"It was more than that. I had to listen to several loggers and mill workers complain about how Millie betrayed them. But not one of them ever once tried to help her. They were complicit with Lyle every time they went to work and accepted him as their boss.

"I'm glad I found the will so the world will know that Millie fought Lyle right to the end. She was brave in a way none of them could imagine. She woke up every day with a man who beat the crap out of her. She protected her children and did what she could to protect the town. None of those big burly loggers stood up to Lyle."

"I've never thought of Millie and the loggers that way before," he said.

Libby softened her voice. "That's because you're a man."

He laughed, and then said, "But I would have helped Millie."

"I know you would have. Because you helped me." She paused. "Are you going to fight the will?"

"No. That will was signed with the blood of my mother and great-grandmother. If a court decides the will is invalid and the agreement to sell TL&L was legal, then I'll give the tribe the money." Jason bent down and smoothed the flower petals that were crushed when he hugged her. "We'll bury my mom here, next to Millie," he said. "Earl's talking. Mark came by today and told Jack and me what happened, how Earl ended up killing my mother."

"I assume Earl was at the Pasco cabin the night Angela found the will."

"Yes. She was already there when he arrived. He saw her car parked out front and was curious. She rarely went to Pasco, and she never got along with Earl—she hated his pothunting, but he refused to stop. Earl snuck inside the cabin to find out what she was up to. She was on the phone with Jack. Earl heard her say she was in Coho—she probably said that because she planned to surprise us in Spokane the next day—and he said he was curious about why she lied, so he stayed hidden and kept listening. Next she called Lyle. She told Lyle she'd found the will. She said she would use the will to give TL&L to the tribe and demand the Coho PD open an investigation of Millie's death. Thirty-nine years after killing his wife, Lyle was finally going to face prosecution."

"But Earl heard everything."

"Yes. She thought no one knew where she was. Dad and I were safe in Spokane. She must have been looking for the will for years at that point. If Earl hadn't been there, she would have driven to Spokane the next day and surprised Jack and me." Jason looked up at the twilight sky. "According to her journal, she'd just ended her affair with Dan. She probably wanted to surprise us because she planned to confront Jack about his own affairs. I think she was hoping for a new start between them."

"I think you're right. But Earl killed her and hid her body on the Pasco property. Five years later, Lyle sold off the part of the land where she was buried. Earl retrieved her, moved her bones to the lot that was about to be paved. He must have really freaked out when he heard we were going to dig there."

"He'd never told anyone where he hid her. He didn't know what to do. So he told James what he'd done. James thought Earl was stupid, so he took over from there."

Each time Jason said the name James she flinched. She'd killed him. It had been justified, but that wasn't complete solace. She'd taken a man's life.

Every time she allowed herself to think about what happened in the Montgomery mansion on Thursday afternoon, she felt a deep regret. She had brought her own gun to the house with the intention of defending herself. Had she wanted the fight?

She held her guilt close to her as always. She was the reason her father stayed away. It was her fault Aaron had beaten her. Her fault he had stalked her. If she'd done things differently, the stalking would never have happened. Then when she'd met Mark, she would've had a clean slate. But she'd screwed up in the past, and she paid for it in the present.

Jason took her hands and squeezed her fingers. "I'll leave you alone now. I just wanted to thank you for what you did for my mom and for me. And I wanted to say I'm sorry I made it harder for Mark to trust you. That wasn't my intention."

"Thank you, Jason."

He took several steps and then stopped. "How is Simone?"

She smiled. "You should ask her that question."

"She's not taking my calls."

"Keep trying."

"I will," he said, and walked away.

Alone again, she sat next to Millie's grave in the gathering darkness. She and Jason had talked longer than she'd realized. The sun had gone down and the summer twilight offered only gray light and shadow. The perfect ambiance for her melancholy mood.

She stared at the lichen growing on Millie's stone. "You can't choose who you love, can you, Millie? I suppose you learned that hard lesson more than anyone. Funny, but given all that I know about you, the one thing I don't know is if you loved Lyle or not. You must have loved him in the beginning. You were so young and foolish, or fooled. I know you were a woman of your time, trapped by circumstance. Strong enough to fight even at the end, but never strong enough to leave. But how could you leave your children?" She rearranged the crushed flowers. "I suppose you could have still loved him even after you learned to hate him. But did Lyle ever love you?"

Did her own father ever love her mother? Had he loved his daughter?

She closed her eyes and asked herself what she wanted. The answer came to her in an instant. She wanted to forgive herself for being unlovable.

She didn't know how long she sat there but she wasn't cold anymore. Something had left her. Perhaps because she brought closure to Millie, Angela, and even Rosalie, she could give herself closure.

She'd done nothing wrong when she refused to have sex with Aaron. She didn't deserve to be beaten and nearly raped any more than Millie deserved to be beaten and Angela deserved death. It had never occurred to Libby to blame Millie, so why had she blamed herself?

She stood and walked away, knowing exactly where she had to go. Ten minutes later, she pulled into Mark's driveway. His house was dark, and his car wasn't parked in front. She rang the bell anyway. There was no answer.

She sat on the front steps and waited. Full darkness descended and the minutes became hours. Stars lit the night sky and she watched the pinpoints of light in their slow rotation around the North Star. She had made three different wishes on shooting stars, when Mark finally pulled into his driveway, fulfilling her first wish.

Mark made a call on his cell phone as he walked toward her. "Simone," he said when he came to a stop in front of Libby. "You can stop worrying. Libby's at my place." He listened for a moment. "I'll take good care of her." He hung up. "I think Simone's a little peeved with you for not checking in."

Libby smiled. "Simone is never 'a little' anything. I'm sorry she was worried."

"And what about me?" Mark pulled her to her feet.

"Were you worried?"

"I've been waiting for you at the Shelby house since eight."

"So I was here and you were there."

He kissed her lightly and then pulled back and studied her. "Something's changed."

"It took me a while, but I've come to my senses."

"I was ready to give you all the time you need."

Her hands cupped his cheeks, her thumb pressed lightly into his dimple. "I don't need any more time." An enormous rush of joy infused her. They really had a future together. "What do we do now?"

"There are five colors in your flannel shirt. I'm betting your bra matches the blue, but hoping for red."

She laughed and let him pull her inside his house. In the vestibule, he hooked a finger through a belt loop on her jeans and pulled her closer. He kissed her throat and undid the top button of her shirt, and then stopped suddenly.

"Why are you stopping?"

"I almost lost you." He touched her neck, gently tracing a bruise. "I wish I'd gotten there sooner."

"I've learned to stop wishing to change the past. Now I only make wishes for the future." Libby undid another button on her shirt. "Think about this." She flashed a red bra strap.

"God, I love you," he said, making her second wish come true.

"I love you, too. Now, I'm two for three in wishes on stars. Take me upstairs and make my last wish come true."

AUTHOR'S NOTE

Port Gamble, Washington, a small, historic, company-owned sawmill town not far from where I live, was the inspiration for the setting of this story. Years after the first draft of this book was written, my husband was at a meeting with members of the Port Gamble S'Klallam Tribe to discuss protection of cultural resources during environmental clean up of the mill site.

At the meeting, while discussing the tribe's relationship with the company that owns the town, one of the tribal members told my husband that when the mill was founded in the 1850s an agreement was made with the tribe in which the mill founders promised to return the land to the tribe upon closure of the mill.

The mill closed in 1997.

The woman went on to tell my husband that a tribal elder had been keeper of this promissory note, but the document had been lost.

My husband was stunned to hear a tale so similar to a major plot point in my fictional story. To the best of my knowledge, no such document has been located. If such a document existed, it may have been destroyed long ago. But of course, I can't help but wonder, what if…

It is worth noting that claims to the territory that is now the town of Port Gamble remains a point of contention between several Northwest tribes.

ACKNOWLEDGMENTS

Thank you to my dear friends, Teresa Tennant, Paula Burke, Holly VanSchaick, and Tara Morgan, who all read early drafts of this book, when it was so far from polished, it had to be painful. I owe you all, big time. Thanks also to Marcia Montgomery, Dana Thompson, and Heather Staples for your friendship, support, and proofreading.

Thank you to Chris Karlsen, for critiquing this book and for helping with the police procedural details. Chris's information was detailed and accurate, any errors are my own.

Thank you to the authors who have critiqued this manuscript over the years, including Adrianne Lee, Gwen Hernandez, and Sharon Wray, you women are the best!

This book was my 2008 Golden Heart® finalist, the one that made me a Pixie Chick. Even though none of the Pixies critiqued this book, it still feels like "our" book. Thank you, ladies, for being beside me on this journey.

Thank you to my agent, Elizabeth Winick Rubinstein, for your support and encouragement.

Jill Barnett, I owe you so much. You were able to tell me what was wrong with a scene and why, but you always left it to me to figure out how to fix it. I learned so much from you about craft, which has shaped who I am as a writer. I am grateful for your willingness to share your knowledge and treasure your friendship.

To my sisters, Becky Stevens and Naomi Raine, for listening to me blather on about writing over the years and for reading. Naomi, my cover and website designer, thank you for the endless hours of work and for your patience. I'm so lucky to have you!

To my children, who don't remember a time when I wasn't writing, thank you for learning how to cook so you can make dinner when I need to work. I love you both more than I can say.

Dave, thank you for your encouragement and support all those years ago when I first told you I wanted to write a book. Thanks for the plotting help and for making sure my archaeological details are accurate. I love you.

ABOUT THE AUTHOR

Four-time Golden Heart(R) finalist Rachel Grant worked for over a decade as a professional archaeologist and mines her experiences for storylines and settings, which are as diverse as excavating a cemetery underneath an historic art museum in San Francisco, survey and excavation of many prehistoric Native American sites in the Pacific Northwest, researching an historic concrete house in Virginia, and mapping a seventeenth century Spanish and Dutch fort on the island of Sint Maarten in the Netherlands Antilles.

She lives in the Pacific Northwest with her husband and children.

For more information:
www.Rachel-Grant.net
contact@rachel-grant.net

Made in the USA
San Bernardino, CA
26 May 2020